ALL TITLES BY SICHAN SIV

GOLDEN BONES
Memoir

GOLDEN WORDS
Poetry

GOLDEN THREE
Personal Memories

GOLDEN TOWER
Photography

GOLDEN NINER
In Honor of President George Bush

GOLDEN STATE
Fiction

PRAISE FOR *GOLDEN BONES*

"Required reading."

—*New York Post*

"A great American story, told by a great American."

—*American Spectator*

"Spine-tingling cliffhanger of a tale. Powerful narrative."

—*Philadelphia Bulletin*

"Gripping firsthand account of pain, perseverance, and survival. Always compelling."

—*Publishers Weekly*

GOLDEN STATE

Love and Conflict in Hostile Lands

SICHAN SIV

iUniverse LLC
Bloomington

GOLDEN STATE
LOVE AND CONFLICT IN HOSTILE LANDS

iUniverse books may be ordered through booksellers or by contacting:

iUniverse
1663 Liberty Drive
Bloomington, IN 47403
www.iuniverse.com
1-800-Authors (1-800-288-4677)

ISBN: 978-1-4917-2656-3 (sc)
ISBN: 978-1-4917-2658-7 (hc)
ISBN: 978-1-4917-2657-0 (e)

Library of Congress Control Number: 2014903362

Printed in the United States of America.

iUniverse rev. date: 04/02/2014

Author's Note

I T IS INDEED a thrill to see you here. Some of us have met before through my other works and in various interactions and presentations. I am grateful for your friendship and support.

Golden State is my first work of fiction. There is no resemblance whatsoever to any real-life people or situations. It was crafted out of my imagination, after having watched hundreds of sunrises, sunsets, full moons and stars that populate our marvelous universe.

In my research, I am thankful to have met exceptional people in extraordinary places all around the world.

My deepest appreciation goes to everyone for their kind assistance. First among equals is my beloved Martha, the best editor.

There is nothing better than doing nothing. We came with nothing. We will leave with nothing.

Life is ours when we have faith, family, and friends. I've got you. To me, that is everything.

Thanks for the golden memories!

Sichan Siv
New York
April 2014

Contents

Cast of Principal Characters

THE AMERICANS:

Goldin "Goldie" Baume, "The Cowboy"
Sandi Bryce, national security adviser
Henry Goldman, "The Golden Man"
Laura and Charles Hawkins, Goldie's closest friends
David Cardey, chairman of Senate foreign relations committee
Bill Kartona, president of the United States
Rosalee Ann Whiney Kartona, First Lady of the United States
Bob Kaufman, Senate majority leader
Alain Lamenace, US Marine Corps colonel
Georgia Ragan, US Air Force pilot
Carmelita Ramirez, Texas state trooper

THE BHUTANESE:

Jigme Wangdi
Kunzang Wangdi

THE BRITISH:

Sir Geoffrey Boyd, prime minister

The Chinese:

Hu Ba Long, chief of staff, People's Liberation Army
Li Lewis, financial adviser
Liu Shao Xi, governor of Jiangsu
Shi Won Yu, prime minister
The president of China (unnamed)

The Colombian (French):

María de Bourbon, president of Colombia

The French:

Camille Isabelle Antonietta de Bourbon, France's first daughter
Marie de Bourbon, president of France
Billie Samas, "The Architect"
Sylvie Vartan, personal assistant to the president

The Indians:

Srichandra Shivaram, prime minister of India
The intelligence chief (unnamed)

The Letadorians:

Jean-Lionel Kadak, CIA graduate, Goldie's classmate at Choate-Rosemary (Assistant: Alice)
Jean-Bedel Lemel, pianist, Goldie's classmate at Columbia (Assistant: Rose)
Marie-Catherine Samas, dean of the diplomatic corps in Washington, DC

The Russians:

Boris "Beebee" Brandrokochev, Russian tycoon
Vladimir Chevsin, prime minister of Russia
Marina Shakarova, president of Russia

ONE

The Inauguration

FOUR TOWN HOUSES connect to give birth to the seventy-thousand-square-foot presidential guest mansion. It stands across Pennsylvania Avenue from the White House Eisenhower Executive Office Building, and next to the Renwick Gallery.

The future First Lady, known to family and friends as simply Rosalee, is already sound asleep in the master bedroom, on the second floor of Blair House, after spending a busy day serving breakfast to the homeless, visiting an orphanage and a VA hospital, having lunch with female journalists, drinking tea with congressional wives, and attending a public concert at the Lincoln Memorial.

It has been a busy day for the president-elect as well: painting a house for a black single mother of three, lunching with religious leaders, playing a volleyball game with neglected youths, and attending a public concert at the Lincoln Memorial. The last event was a joint appearance with his wife.

Light snow is falling outside. It should clear up by morning, according to weather forecasts.

News networks have been covering their activities from the crack of dawn.

On the eve of his inauguration, President-Elect Bill Kartona is looking forward to the next twelve hours. He has a very important and historic event ahead of him. Tomorrow at noon, he will become, at thirty-six, the youngest person ever to be sworn in as president of the United States—the undisputed leader of the world.

Sitting in front of the fireplace and sipping his favorite brandy, he finishes reading the draft of his forty-eight-minute inaugural speech.

Earlier, he'd thought it might be too long. Yet although he is an admirer of Ronald Reagan, who once said that no human attention span could be more than twenty minutes, he's broken his own rule. He's decided that the American people and the rest of the world want to hear his vision for the next eight years. He has successfully defeated a war hero, and a most popular president, and has brought the winds of change to Washington.

He puts the glass and the draft speech down on the coffee table and stands up. He is ready to turn in. Then he hears knocks on the door.

Only one person can gain access to him by signaling with two knocks followed by one: his choice for national security adviser. He throws his silk robe on the blue armchair near the fireplace of the sitting room, and, wearing only his cotton pajamas, hurries to open the door. There stands his most trusted friend since their college years. He pulls her in by the hip, closes the door, and kisses her on the lips.

"What is it, shuhgah?"

"There was a coup in … and the king was … major interests are in great … an NSC meeting …"

The adviser cannot complete any of her sentences, her mouth being kissed fervently by the next occupant of the Oval Office. He takes a quick break to whisper into her left ear.

"This is our last chance to be together before a new chapter begins," he says with extraordinary confidence. "In twelve hours, I will be the most powerful person on earth. And you will be with me twenty-four seven for the next eight years. Isn't it great?" He gently leads her into the bathroom across the hall and closes the door behind them.

TWO

The Other Leaders

PARIS, FRANCE, 1313 HOURS

I T IS LUNCHTIME in the City of Light. Marie de Bourbon, the French president, spreads the *pâté de foie gras* on the toast while listening to the *conseiller diplomatique* giving an update on France's former colony of Letador in Africa. The ministers of foreign affairs and interior also sit at the table.

The president has already ordered the evacuation of some fifty thousand French citizens, mostly women and children. Many, however, have decided to go to Senegal and Madagascar. Life is much better at either place than in the mother country.

"Madame," the *conseiller* says, "the new American president is not fully briefed on the situation yet. But I understand that the *George H. W. Bush* is on her way to the coast of Africa. She left Cam Ranh Bay two days ago."

"In my congratulatory call this morning, I invited him to Paris. He invited me to Washington and to New Orleans. He said that he would let his predecessor handle this situation for his last twelve hours, but added that he would follow our lead on Africa afterward."

"I have a Francophonie meeting in Bamako next week and could also fly to Washington to meet my new counterpart," says Foreign Minster Descartes.

"If you could, you should go there before Bamako," says the president. "And you may want to add Brasilia to your itinerary. I'll talk to my Portuguese colleague as well. The Angolans have already mobilized their forces. We don't want them to cross the borders. All pressure should be applied."

The president turns quickly to the television screen and sees a motorcade leaving Washington National Cathedral. The commentator reports that the future First Lady has just finished a church service and is on her way to Blair House to pick up her husband, who could not get up, as a result of a severe cold, and stayed in bed to nurture his voice for the swearing-in and inaugural address. They will drive across the street to have tea with the soon-to-be former president and First Lady.

"*Étrange!*" the French president says, murmuring. "His voice sounded perfectly clear when I talked to him this morning, which is around midnight over there."

"Maybe he has been so excited about this historic event, partying all night," says Interior Minister de Villegrasse, with a disgusted look at the television.

"What else do we know about him?" asks the president.

"He came to France once when he was a high school student …"

Moscow, Russia, 2010 Hours

The Russian prime minister has just finished a second bottle of vodka and two dishes of red and black caviar with some of his closest political allies at his dacha about twenty minutes from the Kremlin by helicopter. They are sitting around rectangular tables with tall silver candelabras across from an enormous fireplace. Munching on some of his favorite snacks, he walks back and forth, his eyes fixed on the television screen.

The anchors stop commenting when the president-elect raises his right hand. Closed captions in Russian appear right away.

Jaipur, India, 2113 Hours

The prime minister of India is about to make a toast to his guest of honor when his chief of staff whispers into his right ear that the new president of the United States is about to be sworn in. He nods his head and tells the heir to the British throne, a Sandhurst classmate, that what they talked about during their afternoon elephant polo game is about to happen. They turn their heads to the north side of the banquet hall. The gold-and-red curtains are drawn to show an enormous screen with a beautiful shot of the western side of the US Capitol.

"I, William Alexander Kartona …"

Guangzhou, China, 2315 Hours

Eighty-eight kilometers west of Guangzhou, the Chinese president has just finished his thirty-six-course dinner with twenty-three of his political cronies, including the administrator of Hong Kong, the first secretary of the Communist party of Guangdong province, and the mayor of Shanghai.

They have been following the inaugural celebrations for the past twenty-four hours on eight enormous television screens positioned around the cavernous octagonal dining room of the president's winter home, which is perched at an elevation of 888 meters.

They are eagerly awaiting the climax: the inaugural address. They have bet on the length of the speech, the number of times the word *economy* is used, and any applause lasting more than sixty seconds. Finance Minister Lu is put in charge of record keeping. Each deposits $600,000. The winner will take all: $14.4 million.

The CCTV network camera scans the audience on the west side of the Capitol and stops. The Chinese president walks to the HD television screen on the south side of the ballroom. He points to a woman in red dress and shouts: "Hu!"

General Hu stands up, glances at the screen, and salutes the president: "Yes, sir!"

" ...the office of the president of the United States ..." The giant television screens carry Chinese captions at the bottom.

Atsugi, Japan, 0117 Hours

It is already January 21 in the Pacific. The prime minister's ancestral mansion was built during the last samurai period on a hill overlooking the river, about five kilometers north of Atsugi. Her parents are celebrating their sixtieth wedding anniversary. Some one hundred of her closest relatives have gathered during the day in front of television sets all around the spacious property, including the library annex and the guesthouse.

She arrives from Haneda, where she saw the Russian president off, shortly before the swearing in of the American president. She joins her parents in the living room after a series of bows.

As other television stations around the world are doing, NHK is reporting live from the Capitol.

" ...to the best of my ability ..."

The Japanese captions run on the top of the screen.

Vladivostok, Russia, 0315 Hours

It is early morning in Vladivostok. The president has just returned from a very successful visit to Japan, where she hit it off with the prime minister.

They are the first women to run their countries, and they have much in common. Both are former engineers. Both are judo black belts. Both play electric guitar and have been to the United States on a Thelonious Monk program. And both speak the other's native language.

The president is lying naked on her stomach, having a massage, while gulping vodka nonstop. Her eyes have been glued to the television set since she was in the Jacuzzi and the steam room. She finds the new

American president very attractive, intellectually and physically. She has followed him closely since he announced his candidacy for governor of Mississippi. She voted for him in the primary and the general election. She is delighted that her candidate is being sworn in as the youngest president in history. She wants to meet him as soon as possible. She thinks she has found her match.

She is a single mother of two teenage children. She kicked her ex-husband out after she found him in the arms of a television anchorwoman in Kiev. She has been at the Kremlin for two years. Although power and politics keep her busy, she yearns for some affection.

"So help me God!" she repeats in Russian without reading the captions.

Nukualofa, Tonga, 0420 Hours

This is probably one of the farthest places away to watch the inaugural ceremony of the new president.

The sky is slowly turning orange, awaiting the first sunray.

Beebee is flanked by two gorgeous women. They are tall and blond and look like sixteen-year-old versions of Brigitte Bardot. They are in flowery red-and-blue bikinis; he wears a Hawaiian shirt and a colorful swimsuit with fish motifs.

One of the richest men in Russia, perhaps *the* richest, Boris Brandrokochev has stayed up all night to watch the inauguration festivities with intense interest. He is in his South Pacific dacha, where he takes refuge from the stress and pressure of his continuous fight to be first in everything. He has told his business and political buddies in Moscow, including the prime minister, that he will not be with them at their annual orgy of vodka and caviar.

"So help me God." The new president of the United States repeats the last words of his oath after the chief justice. His wife is holding the family Bible. He tries to kiss her on the lips, but she gives him her right cheek, blocking his face from camera range.

"*Sbojei pomoshyu,*" Beebee says. "So help me God." He gets up and puts his hands in the underwear of his two companions. He takes them by their buttocks to the balcony of his winter home on his private island. He likes to take a swim with them in the ocean naked when the sun rises.

London, England

It is still January 20 but late in the evening. It is still question time at the British Parliament. The weekly session has been scheduled later than usual to allow members of the House of Commons to watch the inaugural event in Washington. It is running even later than usual; the speaker has misplaced his official dress and taken a long time to find his robe and wig.

The opposition leader is called upon immediately after the prime minister finishes his opening remarks. After thanking the speaker, he gives a long monologue rebutting everything that was said by the prime minister.

"The prime minister claimed that he was the first foreign leader to congratulate the new American president, but it seems that he was actually stepping on the French president's high heels."

The assembly erupts in laughter.

"He told us that he had been assured by the president that America would follow our lead on Africa, while the president actually said that he would follow the French *jupon.*"

Again the assembly laughs, this time applauding as well.

"Quiet! Quiet!" shouts the speaker. "The prime minister!"

"Mr. Speaker, my right honorable friend is totally mistaken on all points. I said a moment ago that I was the first to talk to President Kartona after he was sworn in. Not before he took the oath of office. As for Africa, we will have to work together with America, France, Portugal, and others to maintain security and stability. I have known the American president since we were at Oxford together."

Sounds of booing echo throughout the chamber.

"He is a man of high integrity, leadership, and vision. I am very confident that we will continue to have a strong, special relationship with the United States."

Back in Washington, DC, television cameras follow the new president and First Lady back inside the Capitol building. He sits down at a small table covered with a green felt tablecloth. He is to sign a new executive order. Like Bill Clinton in 1993, Bill Kartona looks puzzled to viewers when he sees six pens in front of him. His personal aide rushes to whisper that he should use all of them to sign the order and then give the pens to the congressional leaders.

THREE

The Friends

HUNTSVILLE, ALABAMA

CHARLES AND LAURA Hawkins are having a late start as always. He no longer complains. He's stopped paying attention to her repetitions of "Okay, I am almost done." He knows that she says this each time they leave the house just to keep him posted. He once counted how many times she repeated she was almost ready: thirty-six.

He sits down and plays the piano. She actually encouraged him to learn to play piano and bought a baby grand for him. She knew he hated nothing more than waiting around and doing nothing.

He once took some piano lessons at a music school when his schoolmates were under twelve years of age and they were accompanied by their parents of his age. They were practicing Mozart and Schubert. And he was tapping "Hey Jude." After six months, he left. He got a few songs under his belt, and he is still tapping. His former classmates have participated in all kinds of contests, including the Chopin Competition.

They have been home to visit her parents for the Christmas holidays. They usually go the beach on their last weekend. The beach is Point Clear on the Alabama gulf.

"Charlie. I am really done. Let's go. We are running late."

"Why don't you get into the car? And I'll load the last bag."

"Thanks."

"You're welcome."

About thirty minutes later, they are on Interstate 65 South. Charles turns the radio on, trying to listen to some music.

"Can we not have any noise, please? I am trying to organize my purse."

"You can't organize your purse with music in the background?"

"No, I can't."

"How about some classical music?"

"No. No noise, please."

"How about listening to the radio reporting on the inauguration? He must be delivering his inaugural speech at this very moment."

"No. I've said no noise, please."

"Okay."

Charles turns the radio off and puts the car on cruise control. Fifteen minutes later, he starts to whistle.

"No noise, please. I am almost done."

Charles stops whistling.

"I'm done, Charles."

"Great. Let me find a classical station—"

"No, not yet. I am organizing my lists."

"Okay."

Twenty minutes later, Charles starts to hum.

"No noise, please. I am almost done."

Charles stops humming.

"I'm done, Charles."

"Great. Let me—"

"No noise, please. I have to make some phone calls."

One hour later, Laura finishes her calls and turns to her husband. "I'm done, Charles. You want something to eat or drink?"

"No, I'm not hungry. Maybe just some water."

She hands him a bottle of water. "Here you are."

"Can you please open it for me?"

"Sorry. Here it is. I'm going to have some snacks."

"Laura?"

"Yes? Please wait till I finish eating my snacks. You know I hate speaking with my mouth full."

Charles turns briefly to his lovely brunette wife. He admires her strong character but still gently presses on.

"Okay. I was going to ask if we could listen to the radio. Kartona must be still speaking."

"Okay."

On the radio is a live broadcast of the new president's inaugural address: "It is very important for us to work together to maintain peace and stability around the world. America cannot and will not …"

There are some chiseling sounds in the background. The commentator says, over the president, "I am chiseling his words on a number of stone tablets so that we will never forget what we can and cannot do."

The radio suddenly breaks into a commercial: "This is very important, very special. Redneck Sushi is having a very special deal for you and your family. Only nineteen ninety-nine. Yes, you hear me! Nineteen ninety-nine for all you can eat. So what are you waiting for? Get out and get in. All you can eat for nineteen ninety-nine! Redneck Sushi."

"Ha ha ha, Redneck Sushi in the middle of the inaugural speech of the president of the United States of America," Charles exclaims in disbelief. As do many Americans and the rest of the world, he wants to hear what the leader of the free world has to say every four years.

"I've told you," says Laura. "They don't care about what's going on in Washington. This is a different world."

Fifteen minutes later, Charles has gathered enough evidence to make a strong case to establish his position in the Hawkins household—he thinks.

"I am all done, Charles. What is it that you want to tell me?"

"Well, Laura, do you love your husband?"

"Yes, I do. What is it, honey? Is something bothering you?"

"Since we got married, I have been the only one who drives us all the time. Am I right?"

"Well, most of the time."

"Okay, most of the time. Normally, he who—"

"He or she who," Laura says.

"Okay, he or she who works, who drives, who is in the driver's seat should enjoy some privileges. Right?"

"Right," Laura says.

"If that is the case, why can't I hum, whistle, or listen to music while driving?"

Laura laughs and pinches his right cheek and asks, "Where are we?"

"We've just passed Birmingham."

"Here's what we are going to do: we stop briefly in Montgomery. I'll buy you a CD player, a nice headset, an iPod, or whatever. You can listen to your heart's content without making any noise."

"That sounds like a good idea."

"I am surprised you didn't bring yours with you."

"I was going to, but you said I was using too much space."

"Sorry, I didn't think of it. By the way, let's stop at a post office. I need to mail something."

"No problem."

"Also, I'd like to stop at a thrift shop if we see one."

"I will stop at every post office and at every thrift store all the way to Mobile if I can stay in the car and listen to my music."

"Good boy!"

FOUR

The Ally

NORFOLK, VIRGINIA

I T TOOK THE Newport News Shipbuilding company five years, from
conception to construction to completion, to get the latest of the Nimitz-
class aircraft carriers ready for commissioning by the new president of the
United States. She cost $6 billion.

The *USS Margaret Thatcher* is the first carrier to be named after an
allied leader. She measures 1,200 feet long, and her flight deck is 260
feet wide. She is powered by two nuclear reactors with four shafts and
displaces some 120,000 tons at a cruising speed of forty miles per hour.
She carries one hundred fixed-wing aircraft and helicopters. Her crew
consists of a ship's company of 3,400 and an air wing of 2,600.

Most of the people invited to the commissioning of the carrier
are those who have worked in the recently concluded presidential
campaign and those who have provided it with strong financial
support.

It has been raining, and weather forecasters predict that it will turn to freezing rain the day of the ceremony.

Many of the president's supporters and invitees decide to stay in the Washington area after the inaugural festivities. They move to the nearby towns the day before, fearing that the weather may hamper their road travel. All motels and hotels in Hampton, Newport News, Norfolk, Portsmouth, and Williamsburg have been reserved by the organizing committee for the participants.

The British embassy throws a black-tie dinner in Williamsburg in honor of British Prime Minister Geoffrey Boyd, who barely survived a no-confidence vote the day before in the parliament. His wife, Cherie, who is five months pregnant, accompanies him. A large contingent of the Thatcher family, including her grandchildren and great-grandchildren, make up an impressive British delegation.

This is the first time a US warship is named after a woman and that a US aircraft carrier is named after a foreign leader. It is only the second time a US warship is named after a British prime minister.

Sir Winston Churchill, an honorary American citizen, had his name placed on a guided missile destroyer that is the thirty-first of a group of sixty-two Arleigh Burke–class destroyers. President Bill Clinton announced the news when he addressed both houses of the British Parliament in 1995.

Other US warships named after British citizens includes *Alfred*, an armed merchantman named after King Alfred the Great; *Raleigh*, a continental frigate named after Sir Walter Raleigh; and *Effingham*, named after Thomas Howard, the third Earl of Effingham, who resigned his commission rather than fight the Americans during the American Revolutionary War.

Friday morning the sky opens up with another heavy rain. Fortunately, as though on cue, it stops at 10:00 a.m. and the sun comes out. The ceremony is pushed back only forty-five minutes.

The program begins one hour late with the Star-Spangled Banner. After that come the benediction, and speeches by the shipbuilder, the chief of naval operations, and the president. The grand finale is a flyover by F-45 joint fighters. Many participants buy souvenirs with the new carrier logo: baseball caps, shirts (polo, T-), pens, pencils, jackets, golf towels, bags, computer cases, etc.

The president and First Lady say goodbye to their British guests—the prime minister and his wife and the Thatcher family—and board *Marine One* for Camp David.

FIVE

The Opposition

T HE GOVERNORS ARE descending on Washington the weekend after the inauguration for their annual conference organized by the National Governors Association. They have a lot of issues to take up with the new president and the new Congress. The Republicans control most state houses, including those of the three most populous states: New York, Texas, and California. One out of four Americans lives in a state that has a Republican as governor.

The current class of governors is the most diverse group in history. They are thirty Republicans and twenty Democrats. Regarding their previous occupations, ten were politicians, five were doctors, five were lawyers, five were business leaders, five were generals and admirals, five were sports personalities, three were ambassadors, two were movie stars, two were university professors, one was a high school teacher, one was a rock musician, one was a chef, and one was a preacher. The five sports celebrities include an Olympic swimmer, an Indy 500 three-timer, a

French open and Wimbledon winner, a professional bull rider, and a wrestler. There are twenty-four men and twenty-four women, one gay and one lesbian. Forty-five of them are married with children. Only five are single or single parents. They and their spouses or partners will be guests at the White House the following week for a state dinner on Wednesday.

Immediately after the inauguration, the leadership of each party meets to prepare for the upcoming legislative battles. The Democrats now control the House, but the Senate is still in the hands of the Republicans. They control the confirmation process of all presidential nominees, starting with cabinet and subcabinet secretaries, agency heads, and ambassadors.

Of all the fifteen executive departments, only five secretaries have been confirmed: agriculture, commerce, defense, homeland security, and state.

Senate committees have packed their schedules with confirmation hearings. The Republican Senate is trying hard to show a lot of goodwill for the new president. Its leadership is meeting every day at 6:30 p.m. with the majority leader to go over the day's activities and discuss what is coming up the following day. He usually goes around the table, counterclockwise.

"Dave?" he says, calling on the chairman of the foreign relations committee.

"We got the secretary out of the committee and voted on by the full Senate on the same day. This week we are going to look at the deputy secretaries, the UN ambassador, and the undersecretaries. Next week we will handle the assistant secretaries, et cetera."

"Who has Treasury?" the leader asks.

"I do." The chairman of the finance committee raises her hand.

"What's the latest, Bobbie?"

"We are still reviewing his background. He seemed to forget to pay taxes twice when he worked at the World Bank and the IMF."

"I don't want to prejudge this, but it may not fly well if we end up having a Treasury secretary who did not pay taxes. Justice?"

"We may have more problems with this one than with the one for Treasury," says the chairman of the judiciary committee.

"Let's hear it."

"She was stopped for speeding six times: once in Wyoming, where she was going eighty-three miles per hour in a sixty-five-miles-per-hour zone, once in South Dakota, twice in Texas, and twice in New Jersey in just over a one-year period. The ones in Texas happened on the same day within one hour in two adjacent counties. The ones in Wyoming and South Dakota took place on the same day, first west of Cody, and then between Spearfish and Sturgis, where she almost ran over a group of bikers on the way to their annual rally. In New Jersey, she was going ninety-six miles an hour on Interstate 295, the same road that New Jersey governor Jon Corzine was traveling in April 2007 when he crashed, breaking a leg, a collarbone, and six or seven ribs. And she was going five miles per hour faster than Corzine."

"Was she a race car driver?"

"No. The sheriff was reported to have said that if she was going that fast, she would go very far in her life."

"That's why she is the nominee for attorney general of the United States at such a young age. How old is she?"

"Thirty-seven."

"What else did she do in her innocent years?"

"She hired two illegal immigrants while she was attorney general of Florida. She slapped her teaching assistant while she was teaching constitutional law at Yale."

"While didn't they check all of these?"

"Well, she is one of the foks."

"What?"

"FOKs: Friends of Kartona."

"So?"

"FOKs are a level closer or higher than FOBs, or Friends of Bill. I don't know how close she is to him. She may be closer than we thought."

"Okay. Let's try to be as accommodating as possible at least for these two departments. They are two of the big four. However, I don't want you all to overlook anything. We want to move as expeditiously as possible within the ethical and legal framework. Values are the rules of the kingdom, as long as I am the leader. It's seven o'clock. I am thirsty. Let's have a drink!"

This is Majority Leader Bob Kaufman's favorite time of day. He has thirty minutes to unwind with his closest colleagues. They swap jokes, laugh out loud, and call it a day. He then heads home to have dinner with his wife, one of the most famous faces in America. Both have been married once before. Each has one child from the previous marriage, but they have none together.

They are smart, beautiful, and powerful. They are on the A-list in the nation's capital, but they rarely go out in the evenings. He is an early-to-bed kind of guy, which works well for both of them. So is she. She has to get up at four in the morning to get ready for her morning shows. Still, they are the golden couple of Washington, DC.

The Democrats also have their own powwow on the House side. The Speaker, the majority leader, and other leadership members meet in the morning in the Speaker's dining room at 8:30 a.m. for coffee. Having one of their people at the other end of Pennsylvania Avenue has energized them. Their order of the day, the month, and the year is to get the president's budget passed at any cost and to implement all the president's promises during the campaign—or at least make every attempt to do so.

SIX

The Riders

ESPERANZA, TEXAS

GOLDIE BAUME IS holding his first Children Summit of the year at his ranch. There are a dozen children of his staff and friends. He invites them to spend a Saturday afternoon with him. He tries to teach them some etiquette rules before they are stuck in some bad habits.

Here are some of his "no" rules:

»   no chewing gum, no running, no screaming, no shouting, no yelling, no using bad words

»   no talking with food in the mouth

And his "yes" rules:

»   Maintain straight posture whether sitting or standing up.

»   Keep eye contact.

»   Always say "yes" as opposed to "yeah," and always say "please" and "thank you."

If the children pass the first test, they will be invited to breakfast, lunch, and, finally, dinner—all of which are scheduled later throughout the year. Almost all of them make it all the way to Goldie's dinner, which usually does not take place until around Halloween or at the end of the year because of his heavy schedule.

Goldie has to speak with his financial adviser in Dallas to go over his portfolio. They try to have a conversation at the beginning of every quarter to review the one that has just ended. This one is more important than usual because they have to look at the whole year.

It is unusual for a person who has spent over a decade of his professional experience in banking and finance to have a financial adviser. But he is not usual, not common, and not ordinary. At least, that's what he thinks. He seems to spend more time taking care of other people's lives than his own.

"Good morning, Goldie. Happy New Year!"

"Morning, Randy. Happy New Year to you too!"

"You've got all the papers handy?"

"Yes, I have them all right here." Goldie brings a green folder to the camera so that his financial adviser can see it on his office screen in Dallas.

"Let me go over it quickly. The picture is not pretty, but it isn't ugly either. Your portfolio decreased by three point eight percent for the whole year. You were down by ten point six seven percent in the third quarter alone. If it were all equity, you would have been down by around thirteen percent during that quarter. Considering the fact that the market has been down, it's not too bad." The adviser pauses to drink some water and continues. "We are not day traders or market timers. You are a long-term investor. We have kept the balance about fifteen percent fixed income and eighty-five percent equity, a moderate risk. I recommend we maintain the same asset allocation."

"Let's hear it," Goldie says.

"All right. Here they are: three percent of cash and cash equivalents, five percent of commodities, thirty percent of fixed income, sixteen percent of international developed markets, five percent of international emerging markets, five percent of real estate, twenty-six percent of US large cap equity, and ten percent of US small cap equity. What do you say?"

"It sounds good to me." Goldie nods.

"Great. How were your holidays?"

"Fantastic!"

"Where were you?"

"In Europe."

"Where in Europe?"

"France."

"Anything exciting?"

"Everything I do is exciting."

"Great. By the way, thanks so much for sending me a copy of *Golden Bones*. I read it on Christmas Day in one sitting. I've never done that. It's amazing, beyond belief. I've ordered enough copies for the rest of my extended family for their New Year's presents."

"You're welcome. I'm glad you liked it. Thank you for helping spread the golden word. I'll see you in April."

"Be safe wherever you go. See you in April!"

Goldie can't go to El Paso soon enough. He decides to get himself a little present for the New Year. He parks at the back of the Harley-Davidson dealership and walks to the showroom through a side door. This is one of the largest Harley-Davidson dealerships in the United States, if not in the world.

He has his mind set on an Ultra Classic. *Black and gold, solid yellow, solid green, or solid red?* he thinks. He is unable to decide. Each of them looks good.

He comes back to the black and gold. A woman is sitting on it.

"How is it?" he asks.

"It is a great feeling. Do you want to try?"

"Yes, please."

"What do you think?" she asks him after he straightens the bike from its inclined position.

He sits up straight and looks straight ahead. "Wow. It is indeed a great feeling."

"Are you going to get one today?"

"Not sure yet. How about you?"

"No. Not today. I do not live here. I just came to visit my parents."

Noticing she is wearing a leather jacket with a C-5M patch on her shoulder, Goldie becomes curious.

"Are you a pilot or a biker?"

"Actually, I am both."

Goldie raises his eyebrows. "Really? What are you flying?"

"A cargo plane."

"Wow. And what do you ride?"

"A Road King."

"Wow."

She asks him the same question. "Are you a pilot or a biker or both?"

"Actually, I am also both."

"Really? What do you fly and what do you ride?"

"I fly a Cessna, and I ride a Honda and a Yamaha."

"That's great."

"I am very intrigued by all of this. May I invite you for a drink?"

"Sorry, I do not drink."

"I don't mean an alcoholic drink. How about a soda, tea, or coffee?"

"All right, but only if you tell me where I can get some swimming pool supplies first."

"I need those myself. Why don't you follow me? We'll get our supplies and then we can have our drinks. I mean our beverages."

"Roger."

Goldie leads his new acquaintance to get swimming pool supplies and then to the nearest coffee shop. The minute they sit down and order their drinks, Goldie asks, "If you already have a bike, do you plan to get another one?"

"No. I am thinking about trading for a new one."

"What do you have in mind?"

"I am thinking about an Ultra Classic."

"Really? What colors?"

"Gold and black."

"I'll be damned!" Goldie seems pleased to have heard two of his favorite colors.

"Sorry?"

"Nothing. So what kind of cargo plane do you fly? MDs or Boeings for FedEx, UPS?"

"No. Nothing that fancy. I fly a Galaxy."

"A Galaxy? My goodness! So you are an air force pilot?"

"Yes, I am."

"Thank you for your service."

"You are welcome."

"How long have you been flying the Galaxy?"

"I graduated from the Air Force Academy in the top tier. So I could choose anything I wanted. Most of my peers chose bombers and fighters."

"And you?"

"I always wanted to fly big planes. After initial flight training, I have been with the Air Mobility Command, flying all the big planes. I am now an instructor pilot for the Galaxy."

"An instructor pilot for the Galaxy? What did you major in?"

"I got my BS in aeronautical engineering from the Air Force Academy—"

"Sorry to interrupt, but I was waiting to get into the Academy …"

"What happened?"

"It's a long story. So where did you go after the Academy?"

"I trained at test pilot school at Edwards Air Force Base in California, and at the squadron officer school at Maxwell, in Montgomery, Alabama."

"What else?"

"Then I got my master's in mechanical engineering from California State–Long Beach, then military arts and sciences at the Air Command and Staff College and strategic studies at the Air War College, both at Maxwell."

Goldie leans forward in his seat. "My goodness. Where else did you train and serve?"

"Reese Air Force Base, Texas; Charleston, South Carolina; McConnell, Kansas; Scott, Illinois; and Randolph and Kelly, Texas."

"You were in San Antonio?"

"Yes, I was commander of the Twelfth Flying Training Wing at Randolph before I went to Andrews."

"You were at Andrews too?"

"Yes, I was commander of the Eighty-Ninth Airlift Wing at Joint Base Andrews."

"*Air Force One?*"

"Yes, it was one of the birds in my wing."

"Oh my God! You must be at least a colonel."

"Yes, I am."

"Are you still with the air force?"

Her phone rings and she excuses herself. "Yes, Mom? I got all of them. I will be home shortly. Yes, see you soon. I love you too."

Goldie has observed that his guest does not use contractions. Maybe she has been brought up that way. Maybe her parents were teachers.

The colonel turns to Goldie. "Sorry. It was my mother. She worried that I might get lost. So where was I?"

"Are you still with the air force?"

"No. I retired from active duty after Andrews. I am in a reserve unit in San Antonio at Kelly/Lackland."

"You are in San Antonio now?" Goldie is surprised at her answer.

"Yes, I have been teaching."

"I can't believe this. What are you teaching in San Antonio?"

"Remember, I am a C-5M instructor."

"You are teaching pilots to fly the C-5M Galaxy?"

"Yes, I am."

"Oh my God!" Goldie offers his guest some more tea.

"How about you?" she asks.

"Well, I work on a ranch near Esperanza, about ninety minutes from here, off I-10. If you have time, I'd like to invite you over for a ride."

"A plane or a horse?"

"Both. Do you ride? I mean, do you ride horses?"

"Yes, I do. Thanks for the invitation. I will take a rain check. But when you come to San Antonio, please call me. I will introduce you to my family and my students. Here is my card."

"Thanks. Here is mine."

"Thanks again for helping me find all those supplies and load them in my truck."

"You are welcome."

Goldie stands there for a few minutes, totally mesmerized, and then walks to his Hummer. Six women roll in on their shining bikes. They are well dressed in their leather gear. The backs of their jackets read "G♥lden R!ders."

VIRGINIA

After the commissioning of the USS *Margaret Thatcher*, the British prime minister and his entourage take a White House helicopter and fly to George Washington's home at Mt. Vernon. He and his wife are guests of honor at a luncheon hosted by the British American Society.

Following the function, they receive a guided tour of the house. Then they fly to Andrews Air Force Base in Maryland to board a Royal Air Force plane for Toronto. A Commonwealth meeting is awaiting them.

MARYLAND

The weekend after the inauguration, the new president assembles his national security team at the presidential retreat of Camp David. He meets his national security adviser first, in front of the fireplace of Laurel Lodge. He wears a pair of blue jeans, brown boots, and a flannel shirt under a blazer. His belt buckle carries the seal of the president of the United States. He sits down in the leather armchair, puts both feet on the stool, and receives a folder labeled "Eyes Only."

"We all agree that he is the man who can do it," says Sandi Bryce, the national security adviser. "If something goes wrong, he is the perfect clause of deniability. I want you to meet him whenever you feel like it. The sooner the better."

She wears a smart-looking knee-length red skirt, showing a shiny pair of black leather boots. She has a blue turtleneck under a wool blouse. As soon as the president opens the folder, she lowers herself into the armchair in front of him and crosses her legs slowly the minute he glances at her.

MEMORANDUM FOR THE PRESIDENT

FROM: DR. SANDI BRYCE, NATIONAL SECURITY ADVISER

SUBJECT: OUR MAN IN AFRICA

He was born on the continent, adopted by his parents' relatives in Texas and Oklahoma, went to Choate-Rosemary, traveled to Cambodia at 14, and Letador at 16. Those were his first two overseas trips before he finished ranch management at Texas A&M and international business and law at Columbia. He lived in Tokyo for a few years, where he worked for an investment bank. He traveled all over Asia and the Pacific.

He retired at 36 and currently lives on a 13,000-acre ranch near the Eagle Mountains, in southwest Texas. His EE Ranch (for Eagle and Elephant) spreads over four counties between central and mountain time ...

The president looks at Dr. Bryce above his reading glasses. "Why would we choose a cowboy for such an important mission? Does he know anything about Africa? Why would I meet him in the first place?"

"Please read on," says the adviser.

The president begins to read aloud. "He has developed many contacts and maintained good relationships with all the key players ... He is the ideal candidate to undertake the Golden Gate mission and the perfect person to help us defuse the upcoming tension and the potential confrontation between us, China, Russia, and France ..." The president closes the folder without reading the rest of the memo. "All right, I'll see him."

"It's already on your schedule. You'll see him on February thirteenth!"

He smiles at his national security adviser. She never ceases to amaze him. He reaches out to her hips and brings her toward him.

Snow falls very heavily as the National Security Council members await the new president of the United States in a secure room next door. Topic du jour: the next world war.

ALABAMA

Charles and Laura Hawkins have spent a wonderful time relaxing, refreshing, and rejuvenating in Point Clear. It is now the moment to go home. The minute they leave Mobile on Interstate 65 North, Charles notices that Laura is working on her postcards. He estimates that with the postcards, the purse, the lists, and the phone calls, they will be north of Birmingham by the time she is done, or maybe Tennessee if they don't get off Interstate 65.

He discreetly puts his headset on.

"What are you doing, Charles?"

"I am listening to music."

"Charles, honey, why are you doing this?"

"Doing what?"

"Why are you listening to music? This is our last day in Alabama, in America, and you put your headset on. When you have your headset on, it's like you've closed the doors and left me outside in the cold. Why can't we spend some quiet quality time *together*?"

Charles takes his headset off. He smiles, chuckles, and bursts into roaring laughter.

His best friend once told him that there is a Cambodian saying that goes, "You should never go to court with a Chinese or argue with a woman, because you will lose on both counts."

SEVEN

The Players

GOLDIE BAUME WALKS into the Fifth Avenue Presbyterian Church at Fifty-Fifth Street and Fifth Avenue in Manhattan. At that moment, he feels a vibration and reaches for his phone. "Merritt28 rl.1 r.5 13.13" flashes on the screen and disappears in six seconds.

Merritt Parkway to exit 28, turn right, stay on the road for 1.1 miles, make another right, stay on that street for another half a mile, arrive at 1:13 p.m.—that is how he interprets the message.

His father was a Presbyterian minister who, according to his mother, was once a guest preacher at the Fifth Avenue Presbyterian Church (FAPC). It was quite an honor for a small-town clergyman to be invited to give a sermon at such a prestigious house of worship. Whenever he is in Manhattan on Sunday, he always goes there for the 9:30 a.m. service. It is his way to pay respect to his parents' memories.

Another place he always goes on Sunday when he is in town is the National Presbyterian Church in Washington, DC, on Nebraska Avenue.

His father was a guest preacher there once when Dr. Craig Barnes, the very eloquent minister, was away on vacation in Canada. Goldie attended it quite often when he was an intern at the White House during the last year of President Jeb Bush's tenure.

He walks to the eighth pew from the back on the left aisle. He is about to sit down when his eye catches something. Something is missing. As far as he can remember, there has always been a mother with her daughter in a wheelchair two pews in front of him. This Sunday they are not there.

The announcement at the beginning of the service informs the congregation that the church is switching to the summer schedule the following week, with only one service at 10:00 a.m.

His aunt always reminded him to visit FAPC whenever he was in New York City. But she did not have to. He chose Columbia over Harvard for this very reason.

During the liturgy of praise and confession, the congregation stands up and begins to sing hymn number five: "O Lord, Thou Art My God and King." He reaches for the hymnal, turns a few pages, and sees hymn number six instead: "Heaven and Earth, and Sea and Land." His attention is always attracted to anything related to the skies. He mouths number five while reading number six. "... made this earth so rich and fair ... moon and stars with silvery light ... hill and valley and fruitful land ..."

After the service, he walks down Fifth Avenue and notices the choir is singing at St. Thomas Episcopal Church at Fifty-Third Street. An usher in a morning coat gives him a program. Upon entering the church, he moves to the right and finds an empty space on pew 113 next to the first column. He sits down and listens.

He glances at his watch and realizes that he still has some time to make a quick dash to the Museum of Modern Art to get some gift items at the shop.

PALAIS DE L'ÉLYSÉE, PARIS

As Marie de Bourbon, the French president, continues to read the background of the person she would love to have one day at her country home for the weekend, her eyes begin to tear up.

His mother was a librarian. She showered him with all kinds of books. His favorite was *Golden Bones*, the story of a Cambodian refugee who survived communist atrocities, escaped through the jungle, went to America, picked apples, drove a taxi, and became a presidential aide at the White House under George H. W. Bush, the 41st president of the United States. When he knew how to read, it was the first book he finished in one sitting.

His mother died in Sudan. She was traveling on a church mission and the bus was attacked by the Jinjaweed. He was four years old at the time, and his uncle immediately adopted him. His oldest cousin was driving him to get an ice cream when they were hit by a drunk driver. The cousin died instantly, but he was unscathed, still trapped in the baby seat.

His uncle died when his crop duster caught fire and crashed. He was eight.

The president reaches out to a Kleenex box and pulls a tissue out to blot her tears. She sips some Colombian coffee, puts the cup down very slowly, and returns to the top-secret file prepared by her advisers.

His aunt died a few years later, shortly after she returned from Africa. He was eleven when he was sent to live with another uncle in Texoma, Oklahoma. When he was twelve, he was sent to spend summer vacations learning the ropes at another aunt's ranch in the Texas Panhandle.

His uncle and aunt, who did not have any children, spent all their savings to send him to the best schools and fund all his travels around the world. He went to Asia when he was 14 and to Africa when he was 16.

President de Bourbon can no longer continue to read. She suddenly slams closed the folder, puts her head between her hands, and begins to cry. She is afraid to read the rest of the briefing. After a few minutes, she turns in the leather chair and looks through the window to search for her soul. Tears continue to tumble down her beautiful cheeks, leaving behind streaks in her attractive makeup.

CONNECTICUT

Goldie arrives at 1:10 p.m. at the Round Hill Country Club in Greenwich, Connecticut, one of the nation's most exclusive clubs. He is never late for an appointment. He hates keeping people waiting. It is also his practice to scout the locale.

He stops briefly to look at the portraits of former club presidents in the corridor. He notices that there are four people of the same last name, a generation apart, on the wood panels.

He loves history and can easily associate with the occupants of the White House or 10 Downing Street.

He crosses the wood floor of the main dining room and walks to the patio. At the far right corner, a short and slightly balding man wearing a pair of denim pants and a green polo shirt with a club logo on it and a pair of sunglasses pushes his chair back to get up. With a smile, Goldie firmly grabs his right hand.

"Goldie, how nice of you to come!"

"My pleasure. Great to see you, Henry."

His host, Henry Goldman, points to the chair across the metal table covered with a green cotton cloth.

"Please have a seat. What would you like to drink?"

"What are you drinking?"

"Iced tea. But you're welcome to have anything you want."

"I'll also have iced tea."

"Would you like something to eat?"

"What do they have here?" Goldie asks.

"Everything is simpler in the summer. Most people are either in Maine, Wyoming, or the Caribbean. They relax the dress code, which is normally coat and tie, and the menu is simpler and shorter. All kinds of sandwiches."

"What are you going to have?"

"Probably a tuna sandwich."

He goes with the host, as he usually tends to do, perhaps trying simply to please. "A tuna sandwich is fine with me."

"You are a cheap date for a person named Gold!" replies Goldman. They both laugh.

"I see that your forebears have been leading this club," Goldie says.

"For four generations my last name was on the top of the board. The members have been pressuring me to take over the presidency. To pay tribute to my ancestors, so they say."

"Are you going to do it?"

"No. Not now. I don't have time."

Goldie surveys the well-tended grounds—green lawns and beautiful flowers—as a nice, cool summer breeze caresses his face. Henry follows his moving head.

"This is the only golf course in the country where you can play an eighteen-hole round without seeing a single building. You should play here sometime."

"I am not in New York enough to come here and play golf."

"Not to worry. Here's your lifetime membership. Your golf set is in the clubhouse. And this is the key to your locker. Number thirteen. In fact, nobody ever locks their locker."

"Thanks, Henry. But I can't imagine you asked me to come here to give me a country club membership." Goldie offers a teasing smile to his host, who returns the favor.

After the waiter brings the iced tea and sandwiches, Henry leans over the table to bring his face closer to Goldie's.

"If your schedule permits, I would very much appreciate it if you could take a quick trip to Letador and look at the situation on the ground. The Chinese and Russians are trying to take control of the country by buying off people. Our partners are very concerned that the situation will get worse and be out of control by the end of the year. You know all the key players, including many members of the royal family."

Goldie finishes chewing. He brings the napkin to his lips and folds it on his lap. "What about Washington?" he asks.

"They are all busy with their conventions and the nominations next month. I think we may lose the White House and end up having a kid from Mississippi. Our contacts in Langley and elsewhere predicted we could have a major confrontation with Moscow and Beijing if we do not try to defuse the tension fast enough."

"When do you think I should leave?"

"The sooner the better. In fact, you can leave today if you want to. Please take my helicopter to Teterboro and my plane to Paridor. Our people are waiting for you there and will take you wherever you want to go. You will be briefed along the way."

"You think of everything. But I usually work alone."

"I understand. You have carte blanche to do whatever you see fit. Our people are at your disposal twenty-four seven if you need anything."

"Thanks. I will let you know."

"By the way, you did not see the girl in the wheelchair at FAPC this morning because her aunt, who is like a mother to her and who was always with her, was killed this week by a drunk driver. I have established an anonymous scholarship fund for her and arranged for someone to take care of her until she finishes college, and especially to bring her to FAPC on Sundays. So you will see her again when you go there next."

"You do think of everything, Henry. I am impressed."

They get up at the same time and give each other a firm handshake.

"Thanks again, Goldie. Safe travels. See you when you get back."

"My pleasure. See you then."

Henry catches the eye of two elderly ladies on the left side of the terrace. Both are very well dressed in colorful cotton outfits, with sunglasses and straw hats. He walks over and kisses their hands.

EIGHT

The Competitor

WUXI, CHINA

THE PRESIDENT SIPS tea and eats candies, cookies, and sweets with his seven closest allies at the stone garden. The walled compound belongs to the head of the communist party of Jiangsu Province. It is composed of many wooden pavilions built on stilts over an artificial pond full of goldfish. They are connected to each other by covered breezeways.

The governor and party head of Jiangsu is the host of the exclusive gathering. He and his family have been there for generations. They helped build the eighty-eight-meter-high Buddha at Lingshan, reputedly the tallest copper Buddha statue in the world. It was a contradiction in terms for a Communist Party chief to build a religious monument.

"Henry Goldman thinks in billions, is a lothario, and has a Peter Pan mentality," says the adviser.

"So you found your equal," says the president.

"Well, sort of. But I make money for our party, for our country. He, for himself."

A strikingly beautiful, tall and slender attendant wearing a short red skirt flapping in the wind, and bearing eye-catching cleavage brings a new pot of tea to the round, lacquered wooden table.

They stop talking. As she pours tea for the president, her breast touches his shoulder and her naked leg presses against his right hip. He tries to control his breath.

"How many goldfish do you have, Liu?" the president asks the host.

"Eight hundred eighty-eight, sir."

"All the time?"

"Yes, sir. When one dies, we replace it with a new one."

"*Xie xie*, Xue," Governor Liu says, thanking Xue for the tea after she finishes filling all the empty teacups.

They all look at her as she walks away, leaving behind her incredible scent.

The financial adviser clears his throat and slowly resumes the briefing.

"He decided to stop aging at thirty-six, when he made his first billion-dollar profit in one year. He has never met a woman under sixty that he does not want to have sex with."

The president, the councilor, the chairman, the governor, the mayor, the chief, the general, and the money man laugh together. It is a topic that they all enjoy. They get together every month at different locations to get updates on their wealth and their power.

"We now also own every single five-star hotel along the western coast of Africa: Nouakchott, Dakar, Banjul, Bissau, Conakry, Freetown, Monrovia, Abidjan, Accra, Lome, and Porto Novo."

"Li-Ta-Do?"

"Yes, sir. We were the first to build one at Paridor, the financial center of West Africa. Our restaurant—Emperors' Golden Dragon—is the place to see and to be seen. Everybody who is somebody is there. We know who has arrived, who is leaving, who is going to the jungle, who is on the beach … who is sleeping with whom."

"How about the gold?" the president asks.

"The mines (gold, silver, copper), the oil, the gas, the forest—about eighty-seven percent of the country's riches are under the control of the rebels. The Russians are making tons of money by supplying arms through Angola, their former Cold War ally."

"The French?"

"The French have the elite in their pockets."

The president is the only one to ask questions. And Lewis "Lou" Liu—the financial adviser and the youngest of the group, who looks even younger than his age—is the only one to answer. The other six people, all men, sit, drink tea, eat sweets, and listen silently.

They move to the peacock pavilion to continue their meeting with a lavish dinner of some forty courses. They call it the emperor's meal. They toast each other nonstop. They talk about their global influence, wealth, and power.

About nine in the evening an attendant who has been invisible rushes to pull out the chair for the president to stand up. Everyone gets up at the same time, and he makes the final toast.

"To the emperor!"

"To the emperor!" all the diners repeat after him.

The president turns to the governor and provincial party chief. "Eight hundred eighty-eight goldfish, Liu?"

"Yes, sir, eight hundred eighty-eight"

He then turns to Lou, the financial adviser. "The plane?"

"I am working on it, sir."

"I don't want to hear that kind of answer ever again," the president says to his financial man.

"It will be done, sir."

"That's better."

Governor Liu accompanies his guest of honor to the dragon pavilion, and says good night to his boss by bowing his head almost to the ground. The president and eternal emperor pats Liu's head and enters his golden chamber. There waits his company for the night, in a long red silk robe with her long black hair down.

"Xue?"

"No, sir, I am her twin sister, Xie."

CONNECTICUT

From the Round Hill Country Club, Goldie decides to go south to Long Island Sound. He gets out, walks a few minutes for some fresh ocean air, and returns to his car. He gets on Interstate 95 South. He usually varies his route for different scenery, even though there is hardly anything eye-catching between Greenwich and Manhattan. To the contrary, the traffic is much heavier on I-95 than the Merritt Parkway. There are commercial vehicles, including buses and heavy trucks. It does not bother him. Actually, he loves trucks. At one point in his life, he was a truck driver.

Goldie once drove from Portland, Oregon to Portland, Maine. It now seems like a lifetime ago to him.

He tunes in to a radio talk show. He began to listen to them regularly during his days as a truck driver, when he developed a habit of tuning in to one of his favorite stations before moving and hitting the road.

Now one of his dreams is to drive on I-95 from Maine to Florida or vice versa. Or better yet, to ride one of his beloved motorcycles on that route—perhaps at the next bike rally in Daytona in March.

He has been to a number of rallies around the country. His favorite one is the Memorial Day weekend rally in Washington. The bikers assemble in the Pentagon parking lot and take a short ride across the Potomac River on Arlington Memorial Bridge at the Lincoln Monument. They go east on Independence Avenue to the Capitol and west on Constitution Avenue to end up at the Washington Monument. This rally is organized to honor those who are still considered prisoners of war or missing in action. He feels a strong affinity with the military. One thing that he regrets most in his life is that he never served in the armed forces.

Another dream of his is to travel by train on the Texas Eagle from Los Angeles to Chicago, stopping in Tucson, El Paso, San Antonio, Dallas, Little Rock, and St. Louis. Or the other way around, westward. He still has many things to do on his list. The list seems to get longer, and the time shorter. He knows that he has to prioritize; otherwise, he will end up unable to fulfill his dreams.

Back in New York after his lunch at the Round Hill Country Club in Greenwich, Goldie returns his rental car at Forty-Eighth Street and

Second Avenue and walks to the Trump World Tower to have an early dinner at Megu, one of his favorite Japanese restaurants in the Big Apple. He tells the hostess that he is joining the Tanihara party of five.

"Please follow me."

From the corner table overlooking the United Nations, two smiling couples wave at him. They get up at the same time and start bowing as he approaches the table.

He greets his dining companions. "*Konnichiwa, mina san. Ogenkidesuka.*" (Good evening everyone. How are you doing?)

They respond almost in unison. "*Hai, genkidesu. Arigato gosaimasu. Gorudi san wa, ogenkidesuka.*" (Fine. Thank you very much. How are you, Goldie?)

"*Genkidesu. Arigato gosaimasu.*"

Goldie is always happy to see his Columbia classmates and former colleagues. Two of them met in New York and married at the Columbia University chapel.

The other two met in Tokyo through him while he was living and working there. They get together on a regular basis at every opportunity. They are some of his closest Japanese friends, in addition to the one that is not there.

Goldie takes the only seat left, at the head of the table between the two women. He offers his apologies by bowing gently. "I am so sorry to be late."

"No, you are not late. We are early. We had barely warmed the seats when you arrived."

They all agree to order Japanese beer and a platter of sashimi and sushi to start. And they begin to catch up.

Goldie speaks first. "So how did I get so lucky as to have your company for dinner tonight?"

The two women giggle and look at each other and at their husbands, and all of them turn to Tanihara-san.

"As you may remember, Yuko and I were married here ten years ago this week, and we thought it would be fun to celebrate our tenth anniversary in New York. We called Taka-san and let him know about our plan. He happened to have a meeting here. So he and Akiko-san came. And here we are."

"Congratulations," Goldie replies. "I cannot thank you enough for letting me know that you were going to be in New York. I think of you often, and I am grateful that you've included me in this celebration."

"Gorudi-san, we are the ones who should thank you for being here," Yuko says with a smile. "You introduced all of us, and you were so kind and helpful to us when we started our careers. In fact, we were discussing going to Texas and surprising you if you couldn't be here with us tonight."

"That would be so wonderful. I'd be happy to show you around, including my little corner of Japan. Let it be known tonight that the four of you have a standing invitation to visit me in the great state of Texas." He picks up a roll of tuna sushi, dips it in the soy sauce with wasabi, and puts it in his mouth.

Akiko-san says, "Gorudi-san, I don't remember you being left-handed."

"Oh! You've noticed that I use chopsticks with my left hand?"

"Yes," his Japanese friends say in unison.

"When I was living in Tokyo and working with you, I was taken quite a bit by two things: sumo and *Kusajishi*. I was too skinny to learn sumo wrestling, but I became a fervent fan. On the other hand, I managed to get some training in *Kusajishi* in Kamakura. And I never missed an archery festival there. When I built my little dream paradise in Texas, I designed an arena similar to *Kumakura-gū*. And I practiced the sport on a regular basis. One day, I lost my balance while galloping and shooting an arrow and fell off my horse. I broke a few ribs and a collarbone. I couldn't use my right hand for a while, so I learned to use my left hand."

"So sorry about the accident."

"Now I am ambidextrous."

"You always make the most out of everything."

"*Domo arigato gosaimasu.*" (Thank you very much.)

When it comes time to order the main course, Goldie chooses to be the last to place his order. He asks for *unagi* (eel). They all switch to sake—a mixture of hot and cold. The waitress pours the cold one for the ladies and the hot one for the gentlemen.

Goldie proposes a series of toasts.

"First, happy anniversary to the Taniharas. Then to all of us. And, finally, to Ogono-san, who is not with us." They sip the sake three times and bow three times.

"What else do you have at your dream paradise ranch, besides the Kumakura-gū?"

"Two places in Japan that really capture my imagination are the Hakone *onsen ryokan* and the Kinkaku-ji in Kyoto. I stayed at the *ryokan* with Ogono sensei a few times. We had the tatami suites on the south side. And mine had the most breathtaking view of Fuji-san. I just sat there looking at the lake and mountain for hours, speechless, drinking tea and eating sweets.

"Ogono sensei and I arrived one day at Kinkaku-ji in late afternoon. I couldn't believe the reflections of the Golden Pavilion on the surrounding area, especially on the water. In my landscape at the ranch, I had a smaller scaled golden pavilion built in the middle of a little pond. It looks magnificent at both sunrise and sunset."

"It sounds like a little paradise indeed," says Akiko-san.

"Thanks. Enough said about me. Thank you for your interest. Now, please fill me in from your sides. But let us toast one more time!"

St. Petersburg, Russia

In the ornate hall with walls completely covered by paintings, the Russian Prime Minister Vladimir Chevsin empties his vodka while reading the latest report from the field.

> The French definitely control the western part of the country and the majority of the population, the elite, the banks, the trading houses, all international transactions, and the gateway to the outside world.

> There are six nonstop Air France flights a day between Paris and Paridor, as the French call Lisbonouro. They are the only major airline that connects Letador to the

outside world. The other regional flights are all to former French colonies: Abidjan, Antananarivo, Bamako, Cotonou, Dakar, Kinshasa, Nouakchott, Ouagadougou, etc. They are run by TAI and UTA, subsidiaries of Air France.

The French are having a hard time influencing the mineral-rich eastern part of the country, which they refer to as the Golden Jungle.

We have reason to believe that the Chinese have been making headway into the country, even though there is hardly any presence of Chinese citizens. Besides an Olympic stadium which they have just completed in Paridor, they plan to build a hydroelectric dam on the Enies River about 150 kilometers from the capital. The project has been put on hold after long, sustained protests from European environmental NGOs.

We believe that they use a Senegalese front company to take over the telecommunications sector, including microwave towers all around the country, spreading from the seaside in the west all the way to the border with Angola on the east and southeast.

The Chinese have placed their people in hotels, restaurants, and most of the service industry sectors.

Most of the French-run companies in the western part of the country, especially those in the capital and the seaport, are secretly on China's payroll.

He picks up the red phone after it rings twice, emitting the tune of the title cut from the *Love Story* soundtrack. "Hello, my love!"

NINE

The Land

G OLDIE HAS DECIDED to take a commercial flight instead of a private jet. He does not usually take private planes unless he flies them. He has multiple ratings, including airline transport pilot. He has flown many kinds of aircraft, from a single-engine propeller and open-cockpit plane to a multi-engine jet, not to mention helicopters, seaplanes, and gliders.

He normally does not pilot the aircraft if the flight lasts eight hours or more. During his many years of volunteering for the Civil Air Patrol, an auxiliary of the US Air Force, he's established a routine similar to the organization's standards: a maximum fourteen-hour work day, with eight hours of flight duty and an eight-hour-minimum rest period between assignments.

Besides, he does not feel it beneficial to fly an $8,000-an-hour jet when he could instead spend time thinking about his next steps and getting some rest in order to hit the ground running.

He tries to be both a strategist and a tactician.

Normally he can fall asleep anywhere. But during the eight-hour flight from Newark to Paridor, he cannot close his eyes. He shuts the door of his first-class suite, turns on the "do not disturb" light, and goes into deep thought.

This is his first trip to Africa in three decades. For a long time, he has considered it to be a death continent. All the people he loves died in Africa. And the one person he loves the most almost destroyed him there. Although he never wants to set foot in Africa again, he has stayed in touch with friends there, especially Charles and Laura Hawkins.

But things changed recently after he met with GPS. He had just spent a week in Dili visiting his old friend, the president of Timor-Leste. He always stops in Cambodia whenever he is in Asia. He has a lot of fond memories since he went there for the first time when he was fourteen.

They had been paying him a retainer fee of $3,650,000 a year, or $10,000 a day, for an assignment that they said only he could do. That's what they told him when he agreed to the handshake deal two years ago in Sihanoukville. They found him relaxing on the beach and told him about the proposed arrangement from their boss.

GPS, the most successful private equity firm, had just completed raising a new fund of $75 billion to invest in emerging markets. They could use his skills to help close their deals around the world. The amount of work? "Maximum: ten days," they said. "A modest retainer fee plus *all* expenses for your generous time, and five percent of all profits!"

"I suppose it's all legal and moral," he said teasingly.

They smiled and nodded their heads. "Yes. This is a matter of mutual trust. Our chairman has complete trust and confidence in you. You may not have to do anything, but he wants you to have this arrangement in appreciation of your friendship. We'll have the paperwork sent to your ranch in Texas."

In the meantime, he was free to do anything, or nothing, as he pleased. That was it.

Goldie is the first to clear customs at Roberts International Airport, an ultra-modern complex similar to any airport in the Western world. He scans the welcoming crowd of smiling faces and signs with names, both handwritten and printed. He quickly notices a Troy University baseball cap on the top of a broadly smiling face. He and the other man walk toward each other with their arms wide open.

"Charles Hawkins!"

"Goldie Baume!"

"So good to see you, man."

The two former classmates give each other a long bear hug.

"Welcome back to Africa," says Charles.

"Thank you."

"Is that all you travel with? A small backpack?" Charles asks with great surprise.

"Yes, I never check any luggage. I can always get what I need at my destination. And I can also help the local economy."

"What if you have a royal audience at the palace?"

"I get there at two o'clock in the morning on Saturday. I doubt anybody is awake at that time. They will all be asleep with their mistresses. Anyway, a twenty-four seven Paris-trained tailor at my hotel can get a suit made in a few hours with just one fitting."

"I am always amazed with the ingenuity of those people. Are you hungry?"

"I could use a bite."

"All right. The two best restaurants here are Cajun and Chinese food," Charles says while leading his friend through the parking lot. "What are you hungry for?"

"You choose. I eat anything that is edible."

"The Cajun restaurant, SONO, or Stars of New Orleans, is owned by a former LSU quarterback. He came home to Monrovia when he turned thirty. eighty percent of football players screw up their lives. They get rich fast, and their bodies are a total mess. This guy left before he screwed up his life. His restaurant is one of the most popular in the city. It is always crowded. I didn't make a reservation. I doubt we can get a table. The other choice is the Emperors of China."

"A Chinese restaurant is on the top of the culinary list in Monrovia?"

"It's probably owned by the Chinese Communist government. But the food is out of this world."

"Is Laura going to meet us there?" Goldie asks after they get inside a Ford F-150 truck.

"No, Laura is in Maputo. Mozambique is the head of the African Union, and she has a presentation to make on human trafficking at the NGO conference that is part of the AU annual meeting."

"So I won't get to see her at all on this trip."

"Yes, you will. She overlaps with you for one day in Paridor before she goes to Freetown. She travels all the time. After we lost John, she totally immersed herself in humanitarian work. The people love her. Some governments don't. They think she is stirring up a lot of trouble. By the way, are you still collecting airsick bags?"

"Only the most exotic ones. I didn't take one from the American United flight."

"You will get some exotic ones flying in and out of Paridor."

"Why?"

"Letador is the most important French outpost of their *mission civilisatrice*. They own the air and sea access to Paridor."

"Golden Paris, as opposed to Golden Lisbon?"

"That's correct."

Twenty minutes after leaving the airport, Charles pulls into the brightly lit parking lot in front of the restaurant. There are cars and SUVs everywhere. He continues the conversation after he and Goldie are seated at a corner table.

"They built and maintain the seaport, which is a four-hour drive from the capital on a divided highway."

"It was a gift of the United States to the Letadorian people when the country became independent?"

"Right. Let's get some food and drinks."

"You order," Goldie replies.

"Some Tsingtao beer!" Charles says to the server.

"And the international airport?" Goldie asks.

"The French built it in the fifties. They have continued to expand it and maintain it till now."

"I believe Air France flew one of its first Boeing 707s from Paris to Paridor in 1958, the same year that Pan Am flew its first B707 from New York to Paris."

"The French went so far as to bring back some of their global reach. The two Air France regional subsidiaries that connect Paridor to all capitals of French Africa are TAI and UTA." *Transport Africain International* and *Union des Transports Africains*, thinks Goldie. "They say you can go anywhere in Africa and the rest of the world if you go through Paris and Paridor," he adds.

"You are correct again," replies Charles. "Here's to you and your return to Africa."

"Here's to you and Laura."

They clink the necks of the beer bottles as the Liberian waitresses in cheongsams slit on the sides all the way to their waists bring the first eight appetizers of the thirty-six-course emperor's dinner.

"By the way, when are you coming to the US again?" Goldie asks.

"Probably during the holidays. We plan to stay on till the end of January. It will be the first time we are in the country during the inauguration. It will be interesting to watch it in real time."

"If you have time, please come see me in Texas."

"Of course, we will. I'll check with Laura. She is the CSO, in addition to being the CFO of the family."

"CSO?"

"Chief scheduling officer, or chief shopping officer."

"I see. And what do you get for doing everything she wants you to do?"

"She gives me fifty dollars each time she wants me to get a haircut."

"Speaking of haircuts, do you still collect haircuts?"

"Yes, I still do."

"Tell me more about it."

"Unlike many people, I do not have a regular barber. My hair is very easy to cut. If I schedule well, chances are that I can have my hair cut at a different place around the world each time I need one."

"How often do you travel?"

"Often enough."

"What are some of the most exotic haircuts you have gotten?"

"In Malé, the Maldives, I had a Buddhist barber in a Muslim country. I had my first haircut by a woman in Mongolia, in Ulaanbaatar, and the first by a pregnant woman in Choybalsan. I once sat under a tree, holding my own mirror, in Cambodia."

"Wow. What are some of the best and some of the worst?"

"The worst was probably in Bamako. And it was also the most expensive at the time, the equivalent of almost thirty dollars."

"The best?"

"They would have to be Malé, Siem Reap, Ft. Riley, and Randolph Air Force Base."

"What do you get out of this collection?"

"A collection of life stories. I've learned a great deal about their families, their cultures, their faiths, their livelihoods, et cetera. The one at Randolph had been on his feet for forty-six years."

"I can't imagine being on the same job for four decades, much less standing up the whole time."

"I can't either. When he retired, I lost a friend."

"You should write a book."

"Maybe I should."

"What's the working title?"

"Perhaps something like *Learn about the World's Culture with Your Head!*"

"Not bad. I like that. Okay. Here's to your new book."

"Hear, hear!"

Moscow, Russia

The prime minister of Russia, Vladimir Chevsin, is pondering if it is time to move now. The Americans are having their political conventions only three weeks apart, the republicans first.

With an incumbent president, the Republicans did not have to get bogged down in a bloody primary battle. The Democrats had to go through a lengthy process. It now looks as if the governor of Mississippi has gathered enough delegate votes to win the nomination at the Las Vegas convention.

The prime minister was chosen to catch up with the Chinese, primarily on economic issues, and the Americans, on military power. The president—Marina Sharakova—however, made it clear to him that she does not want any unnecessary confrontation with the United States, especially if the Democrats get the White House back.

Although he speaks Chinese fluently, he has not visited China since he became prime minister. He has been deferential to the president to have her state visit first. But he has taken the Chinese premier hunting and ice fishing on a weekend trip far from Moscow.

He admires her marksmanship and finds her quite attractive both intellectually and physically. He wonders if she even knows how beautiful she is. Each of them is given enough latitude to deal with each other's country, but not enough to make decisions on the spot. "I will get back to you on that one soon enough," has become their catch phrase whenever they are unable to answer right away.

He wants to get to know her better, and his biggest question is how a woman so smart and so pretty could remain a virgin. Their relationship has been cordial and cautious, and he is prepared to go beyond that. He picks up the phone and orders the flowers.

LETADOR, WEST AFRICA

Goldie feels a little apprehensive as the view of the terrain of the west coast of Africa is becoming more visible under the full moon; dense jungle and mountains stretch all the way to the sea. For him it is a trip to a past that is full of bittersweet memories. The UTA flight purser tells him to be the first to disembark.

The plane makes a long final approach from the northeast for runway 23. He looks for the Enies River and sees the full moon reflecting briefly on the water before the bright lights of Paridor appear on the left side of the aircraft.

"Paridor vous souhaite la bienvenue!" (Welcome to Paridor!) announces the flight attendant.

At the end of the Jetway, an attractive, fair-skinned woman smiles at him and introduces herself. "I am the personal assistant to Prince Jean-Bedel. His royal highness requests the pleasure of your company at the palace. Please follow me."

"I'll be happy to. But I am in jeans and a polo shirt and it is two o'clock in the morning. Will you allow me to go to the hotel first and—"

"It's quite all right. His royal highness is in a swimsuit, and he does not wear a shirt. He walks around barefoot. So you are actually overdressed."

The prince is half naked at two o'clock in the morning. Some things do not change. I wonder if he surrounds himself with beautiful women like this one.

"Excuse me, what are you thinking about?" asks the prince's assistant.

"Excuse me?"

"You were quiet for a brief moment. I am just curious if you were thinking about something. Something bad about me."

"I was wondering what the prince is doing wearing a swimsuit so late."

"He has been swimming. You did not answer the second part of my question."

A security officer leads them through various doors of the airport terminal to a small motorcade of three cars: a lead police car, a Mercedes, and a Renault. She motions for him to enter the Mercedes and walks to the other side to sit behind the driver.

"I am sorry," says Goldie. "You were asking me something?"

"The second part of my question! You did not answer. You were thinking about something. Something bad about me."

"No, absolutely not."

"Shall I believe you?"

"Are you a psychic?" Goldie is curious.

"As a matter of fact, no. If anything, I am a good guesser."

"Really?"

"Maybe. I can read some people's minds—men's minds. You did not expect to see a woman, an attractive woman, an attractive Caucasian woman, waiting for you at an airport at two o'clock in the morning. No, I am not the prince's girlfriend. I told you I am his personal assistant."

"I am sorry I got your title wrong, but I did not get your name."

"Rose."

"Rose! That's it?"

"We all go by first names here."

Some things do not change.

"That's right," says Rose with a gentle smile, "some things do not change. Is that what you were thinking about?" Goldie is speechless. "That's what the French say: *Plus ça change, plus ça reste la même chose.*" She looks at him, still smiling. "Okay. I will ask them not to use the blasting sirens and the rotating flashing lights." She picks up the radio and calls the lead police car.

"Thank you, Rose."

"You're welcome. And now you want to know about my background too."

"My lips are sealed." Goldie returns a gentle smile.

"My father was from Montreal. He came here as a young engineer to build roads in remote villages. He met my mother while his crew was working near her village. They fell in love and got married, and had me.

"How did I meet the prince? He came to Montreal once, and the Canada Letador Association gave him a reception. My parents took me there. That's how we met. How long have I been here? Just two years.

"How do I get to be so close to him? My mother was a nurse. She once worked at the royal palace. She took care of the prince from the time he was a baby until he went to grade school. At that time my parents returned to Canada.

"How old was I when I met the prince? I was thirteen. I remember he told me he came from a little vacation with a friend in Wyoming. I think it was you.

"How long before we get to the palace? Another ten minutes. Don't worry! I am done answering the questions that you never asked."

Goldie breathes a sigh of relief. He would hate to be her husband.

Rose turns to him, smiles, and wags her index finger.

The motorcade arrives at the palace and goes through the west gate, which is reserved only for close family friends. It passes in front of a number of

French colonial villas surrounded by very well-tended gardens of colorful flowers, beautiful plants, and tall trees.

Jean-Bedel—the prince—wears a wide grin and opens his arms wide as he walks toward his guest.

"My brother, Goldie! Welcome back to where you belong."

"Great to be back, Bedel. Why are you up so late?"

"It's not for me. I wanted to be the first to welcome you to Letador."

"The second!" Goldie says, correcting his old friend from high school.

"The first!" Jean-Bedel says. "Rose is an extension of me!"

They both laugh and embrace each other.

TEN

The Past Is Present

SOUTH TEXAS, THREE MONTHS BEFORE THE INAUGURATION

GOLDIE LOADS TWO shells into his Remington 700, puts the butt of the hunting rifle gently on the wooden floor, and leans it against the right corner of the blind. He and Daniel have been there for nearly one hour in the pitch black of early morning. They look intently through the narrow opening as the upcoming sunlight begins to chase away the darkness. They try to maintain complete silence, and only whisper to each other when they need to.

Daniel, Goldie's hunting guide, taps his left shoulder and signals with his right hand for him to peep through the left opening. Goldie notices the shapes of some deer about one hundred yards away. He is not interested in deer this morning and turns his eyes to the front opening. He sees a family of javelinas munching on corn spread around by the game feeder.

Daniel taps on Goldie's left shoulder again and hands him a pair of binoculars.

"I know you want a nilgai this morning, but look at the eight-pointer."

He brings the binoculars to his eyes and looks again through the left opening.

"He is about seven years old, a hundred fifty pounds," whispers Daniel. "He should appear straight ahead of you in three minutes. Get your gun ready."

"How about the javelinas?"

"They will move on shortly when the deer arrive."

He hands the binoculars back to Daniel, who has been sitting to his left. He rests the gun on the window frame, making sure that the barrel does not touch it.

"Aim at the heart, take a deep breath, and squeeze the trigger gently all the way," Daniel whispers in his left ear.

Through the sight mounted on top of his gun, he sees his prey looking toward him for a few long seconds before bending its head to the ground.

Bang!

"Good shot, Goldie. He was dead before he hit the ground," Daniel says, congratulating his guest. They give each other a high five.

Bonn, Germany

Beebee, the Russian tycoon, sits at the back of the black Mercedes as his driver speeds on the autobahn from Cologne to the former capital of West Germany. He listens to the recording describing his opponent, whom he has yet to meet.

"He is an Europeanist, knowing everything about Europe and hardly anything else. He has been to London, Paris, Rome, Frankfurt, and Zurich more often than you and I have been to a polo game. And we play it every week. Outside of Europe, he has been only to Japan and Cuba. In fact, he owns an enormous complex on the western side of the island.

"This is quite unusual for somebody who has a global financial reach. The simple reason is that he does not want to be in a plane for more than eight hours.

"There was an exception. Some years ago, he decided to travel incognito with a group of people on a three-week trip around the world on a private jet. It was an expedition organized by the New York–based

American Museum of Natural History, to which he was an anonymous benefactor."

Beebee stops the tape to light a cigar, and he then continues listening to the information about his business nemesis.

"Participants flew in a modified Boeing 777 with only forty-eight seats. The trip took them to Cusco/Machu Picchu, Easter Island, Samoa, the Great Barrier Reef, Angkor, Lhasa, the Taj Mahal, a safari in Tanzania, Luxor, and Fez.

"He met a young French scholar who was trained in both anthropology and architecture at Angkor. She was one of the speakers on the expedition.

"There are some eighty cathedrals in France. Notre-Dame and Chartres are his two favorite. He tends to favor the latter one. He has been a supporter of the international stained-glass society, which is headquartered in Chartres. The annual meeting focuses on Christianity in general, and various topics ranging from styles—Romanesque, Gothic— to emphasis on architecture, facade, sculpture, light, windows, et cetera.

"That is why he is now in Chartres with his—"

Beebee stops the tape and leans back to stretch his long legs. He dismisses the intelligence report on Henry Goldman but ponders his next steps.

PARIS, FRANCE

Goldie goes straight to the Hotel Crillon after leaving Charles de Gaulle airport. He checks in to a nice suite overlooking the Place de la Concorde. After five days in the Golden Jungle, he is ready to be pampered. He soaks himself in a warm bubble bath in a Jacuzzi. He puts on a navy blue pinstripe suit.

He walks to the reception. He is about to identify himself to the gendarme when a young Sylvie Vartan rushes toward him. Her attractive scent almost kills him.

"Monsieur Baume?"

"Oui?"

"Monsieur le Conseiller vous demande pardon d'être en retard. Je me permets de vous tenir compagnie jusqu'il arrive. Suivez moi, s'il vous plaît."

(The counselor apologizes for being late. Allow me to keep your company till he arrives. Please follow me.)

"With pleasure. I'll follow you anywhere."

"*Vous etes tres gentil.*" (You are so kind.)

"I am sorry; I didn't get your name."

"Sylvie. Sylvie Vartan."

"*Comme la chanteuse?*" (Like the singer?)

"*Oui, monsieur.*"

"I'll be damned," whispers Goldie to himself.

Sylvie is approached by a colleague who hands her a message. She turns to Goldie and asks him to follow her across the street to the Palais. She leads him into a palatial salon d'attente full of Louis XIV furniture and excuses herself. As he admires the paintings and chandeliers, a voice from the distant past jolts his mind, body, and soul.

"*Mike papa charlie!*"

He turns around and is completely stunned. The person behind the voice is a woman he once loved. And still does. A most attractive woman, a young Catherine Deneuve.

And she is the president of France.

"*Mon Petit Chou!*" she exclaims. She opens her arms to hug him and kisses him on his cheeks and lightly on the lips.

"I don't have time to explain everything. It would be wonderful if you could come to Marseille and spend this weekend with me. Sylvie will give you all details. By the way, if you are free tomorrow, be my guest at the state dinner I am hosting for the king of England. *A bientot!*"

She kisses him again lightly on the lips and turns around, leaving him open-mouthed and still feeling stunned.

Santa Fe, New Mexico

For the first time in his life, Henry Goldman has to fight two increasingly powerful enemies—a Chinese and a Russian. He always considers any business deal a battle. Now it looks like he has two wars on his hands. Any step he makes, he has to watch out for attacks from every angle.

As much as he wants to stay on the top of the world, he does not want to be bothered while he is on the first of his winter vacations. His key advisers, however, insist that he give them thirty minutes every day before he hits the ski slopes. They are flying to Santa Fe from Asia and Europe. They want him to hear their findings, and they need instructions from him to act quickly. Time is of the essence.

He listens impatiently while sipping café au lait, with a panoramic view of the Sangre de Cristo Mountains behind him.

"Lewis Li is a Stanford business school graduate. After spending a dozen years in New York, Frankfurt, and Tokyo, he returned to Shanghai, where his father is mayor and a close political ally of the president. He was brought into the inner circle by his father and has been put in charge of all investments for the party. He is the financial engineer behind the enormous growth in profit for the Council for the Development of China (or CDC) during the past decade. The Chinese leaders have given him carte blanche in managing their monies. The Russian version of Lewis Li is Boris Brandrokochev."

"Beebee," Henry says, interrupting.

"Yes, Beebee. He is equally ruthless in his—"

"All right. Let's continue tomorrow. Goldie?" Henry stands up to leave the verandah.

"He is in Paris, meeting with the diplomatic adviser of the president."

FRANCE

On the TGV express train to Marseille, Goldie looks at the French countryside parading in the distance: small villages, church spires, rolling hills, dairy farms.

"*C'est une chanson qui nous ressemble.*"

The French version of the Nat King Cole song "Autumn Leaves," "Les feuilles mortes," plays softly in his head. He begins to tear up. The memory seems still very fresh.

That Sunday, while rereading *Golden Bones* in Portuguese and Spanish in a hammock, he heard an explosion, a screeching sound, and a bang. He rushed outside and saw a car with a flat tire and an unconscious driver.

Her head was on the steering wheels. He opened the door and carried the driver, who was still breathing, into his house. She had a cut over her left eyebrow. It bled.

He put her down on his bed and immediately tended to her wound.

Toi tu m'aimais et je t'aimais …

He boiled some water and frantically looked for something in the kitchen.

He came out with some dried roots and put them in the kettle.

Nous vivions tous les deux ensemble …

A moment later, the driver opened her eyes and touched her head with her right arm.

"Where am I? What happened?"

"You are at my house. You had an accident. Please drink this."

Goldie gave her the glass of his hot drink.

"What is it?"

"It's a medicine. Don't worry. Just take it and have a rest."

He helped her get up and brought the drink to her beautiful red lips. He put her down gently after she drank his special tea, and covered her with a blanket. A few minutes after she closed her blue eyes, he left to inspect the car.

He presumed that the left front tire had blown out. She lost control of the car, which swerved toward the river. It hit a tamarind tree, which stopped it before it plunged into the river.

Toi qui m'aimais moi qui t'aimais …

There was a spare tire in the trunk, and he set out to change the tire.

Mais la vie sépare ceux qui s'aiment …

They saw each other every weekend for six months. It was the best six months of his life. She would bring a bottle of red wine, ham, saucisson, and baguettes.

One day, she asked him to meet her in the capital. She had an invitation to a performance in the royal palace. She wanted him to be her escort to the function.

"But I don't have a tuxedo."

"Don't worry. I had one made for you."

"You know my size?"

"Of course. I have been holding you in my arms for six months."

They laughed and kissed passionately.

The night of the event, Goldie arrived early. The palace grounds looked quiet. He was escorted by the protocol officer to the grand ballroom and shown a seat front and center.

"Madame Marie?" he said, asking for his companion. (People are addressed by their first names there.)

"*Elle n'est pas encore la. Je vais voir tout de suite.*" (She is not here yet. I'll find out right away.)

He became very antsy and looked toward the doors every few minutes.

The protocol officer returned when it was time to begin the program.

"*Madame Marie est indisposée. On va commencer le programme maintenant.*" (She is indisposed. We will begin the program momentarily.)

"*Et les autres invités?*" (And the other guests?)

"*Vous êtes le seul invité.*" (You are the only guest.)

Goldie had been in the African country for only six months doing some good deeds in a remote village: building schools, digging wells. He learned a little bit about the customs of the kingdom. There was a big gap between life in the village and life in the capital. And an even bigger one between life in those places and life in the royal palace.

In their tradition, the principal dancer would spend the night with the guest of honor. He was very confused. Why would someone he loved dearly invite him to the palace so that he would sleep with somebody else?

Goldie's thoughts and view of the French countryside are abruptly interrupted by another TGV train going in the opposite direction.

He is hoping to find an answer in a few hours. A lot of answers. But most importantly, he is now facing a bittersweet situation in which happy memories, laughter, and love are juxtaposed with sadness, tears, and a broken heart.

He will find out soon enough. He was only sixteen then. Completely young and innocent indeed. Or was he? Does he still love her after all these years?

The French say, "*Une de perdue, dix de retrouvée.*" (One lost, ten recovered.) But he has not found anyone since he lost her. Is he loyal to a fault? Or is he just being himself? Selfishly himself? Was he hurt so much that he began to hate women? *Hate* may be a strong word. How about *scared*? He was scared so badly that he has never been interested in love again. Ever?

Suddenly the train public address system announces that they have arrived in Marseille. He grabs his bag and gets on the platform. Two men in suits with dark glasses and earpieces welcome him and lead him to a Peugeot limousine. They leave the train station following a police car with flashing lights and a blasting siren.

He leans over to the agent in the front seat with the driver.

"Could you please tell them not to use the lights and the siren?"

"Oui, monsieur!"

Within minutes they are in the countryside. Shortly after, they are at the gate of "La Forêt d'Or."

"Welcome to the Golden Forest, the weekend home of the French president," says the security officer.

Goldie has been frowning very often, showing his apprehension since leaving Paris. He does not know what to expect. For the first time in his life, he is totally clueless. He knows for sure that it is going to be emotional. And he is at the mercy of his heart more than his head.

He is prepared to take the bull by the horns.

Marie de Bourbon, president of the French Republic, waits for him in the gold-and-green room next to the dining hall. She walks toward him, throws her arms around him, and kisses him on the lips. Then she holds his head between her hands, and asks pointedly, "*Tu es toujours en colère avec moi?*" (Are you still angry with me?)

"No. I am not. I am—"

She puts her beautiful fingers on his lips. "I am so sorry to hurt you. I have my reasons. That's why we are here. Thank you so much for coming. We have a lot to catch up on."

She takes him by the left hand and leads him to the back porch, which offers a spectacular view of the countryside and the blue Mediterranean in the distance. They sit down to have a light lunch. Ham, saucisson, baguettes, and red wine. There is no waiter. She serves him everything, just like she did every weekend for six months in the remote African village.

"*Mon Petit Chou! A toi!*" She toasts him.

"*A toi! A nous.*" He returns the toast and adds, "*J'écoute.*" (I am listening.)

She does not want to start right away. She wants them to enjoy their traditional lunch first. Goldie is on pins and needles.

"You saved my life," she says. "And I will never forget that. You did not ask, and I did not volunteer any information. During those six wonderful months, I realized that you became madly in love with me, and I fell truly in love with you. I was married when I met you. My husband was in Paris for a business meeting. Our marriage was in trouble. So I went to France to try to save it."

She pauses for a minute, reaches out for some tissues, and continues.

"You were so young, almost half my age. I thought that if I truly loved you, I should leave you. You had a life in front of you, and it was not fair for me to take it away from you. It was perfect timing when my royal friends at the palace wanted to give me a performance. The principal dancer was a daughter of the king, and I thought that you would be tempted to sleep with her and forget me.

"Father Lamartine told me that you had six more months before you finished your fellowship with him.

"The people in the palace reported to me that you looked very restless that evening; that at the end you presented the bouquet of flowers to the princess, kissed her hand, and left with tears in your eyes."

Goldie parts his lips as if to interject something, but he can't, and he decides to let his hostess and former lover speak.

"I ended up getting a divorce. I was later sent to Bhutan, then Mongolia. After Mongolia, I served in Cambodia for four years and left the foreign service." She stops to drink some water. "All these years, I've tried to forget you. When Father Lamartine got very sick in Montpelier, I went to see him. He gave me all of your letters to him. He told me not to read them until he was gone." She pours some tea for him and for herself. "Even without reading your letters, I knew you still loved me very much. I thank you for that. And I am sure you know that I have always loved you very much as well. But as fate would have it, we were not destined to live together. The Cambodians have this concept of the rabbit and the moon. They can live together in the same universe, but not as a couple."

"I hope you understand that *l'amour pur n'attend rien. Il donne, et ne demande pas.* [Pure love waits for nothing. It gives and does not ask.]"

The president stands up after her long, emotional monologue. Goldie is still so stunned that he cannot get up fast enough to pull the chair out for her. She takes his right hand this time. "Let's go riding. We'll continue after dinner."

At the barn, Goldie sees two beautiful horses with Western saddles.

They look like quarter horses, he thinks.

"They are quarter horses," says the president after seemingly reading his mind. "You'll have the brown one. Her name is María. I'll ride the black one."

"And his name is Oro, I presume?"

"You're right."

For a long moment, they ride horses side by side in complete silence: Goldie and María on the right, the president and Oro on the left. They take deep breaths of fresh air and listen to the soothing sounds of whispering wind, birdsong, and the rushing waters of a nearby creek. They are followed at a distance by four security officers on horses, and one in a four-wheel-drive vehicle.

Goldie cannot hold it until after dinner. "So what did you do in Bhutan besides opening a new embassy?"

"I traveled all over the country. I was inspired by the description of the Kingdom of the Thunder Dragon in *Golden Bones*. I read it again in your Portuguese and Spanish editions in Notneh."

"You told me you were one of the French girls mentioned on page two hundred ninety-nine."

"Yes, you have a good memory. I still have a picture with the author. Four years later, he came to speak and sign his memoir at the American Library in Paris."

"Did you see him again?"

"No, I was away that summer in Colombia. I was so disappointed. But I asked my twin sister to go. She got a copy of his personally autographed memoir and a photo with him also."

"Did she tell him about you?"

"She did. And he recounted with uncanny precision the questions he asked us after his presentation at the US mission in New York."

"What were some of the questions? Did you speak in English or French?"

"We spoke in both. He had impeccable French. It was his second language before English. And our English was very good too. He asked who the first American ambassadors to France were. We all knew Franklin, Jefferson. But when he asked who the first French ambassadors to America were, none of us knew the answer. Quite embarrassing."

"I can't remember how many times I've read *Golden Bones*."

"Me neither," de Bourbon says.

"Back to Bhutan?"

"I traveled all over the country, visited all the *dzongs*. Then I wrote a book: *Un amour incomplet!*"

"'An Incomplete Love!' And you used a pseudonym."

"You are right. And you are right," she says in confirmation.

"You did not go to Cannes when the film version received a Palme d'Or."

"I did not want anybody to conclude that I was the principal character in the book."

"Nobody could, except Father Lamartine and me. Even though you reversed the roles and moved the setting to South America, we still did."

"I read one of your letters to Father Lamartine in which you said your love for me 'is forever! And forever is not even long enough!' Those were some of the most beautiful words I've ever heard in my life. I remain very touched. But something is not clear to me."

"What is it?" Goldie squeezes her hand, pressing for answer.

"Rosalee."

"You are talking about the wife of the presidential candidate?"

"I am talking about your former girlfriend."

"It's the same person. And here's the story."

"I am all ears." De Bourbon looks at her former boyfriend and squeezes his hand to signal his turn to recount the past.

Goldie takes a deep breath and begins.

"Two years before you and I met in Notneh, she and I went to Cambodia on a church mission. We were fourteen. She fell off the verandah of a village chief in Ratanakiri while trying to feed a baby elephant."

"I know that story. Please fast forward." De Bourbon is anxious for the story to get to where she wants to hear.

"Her family moved to New York while I was in Letador with you. We met again at Choate-Rosemary Hall. We became closer, and even closer when we were at Columbia. We were close enough to be intimate, but we never made love, if that's what you really want to clarify. You know why?"

"I do. You were trying to forget me, and you couldn't. I have been with you all the time since you lost your virginity to me."

"Then she met Kartona. She invited me to her wedding."

"Did you go?"

"No, I did not. I was in Brazil in a remote village in the Amazon, near the Colombian border. It would have taken me a few days just to get to the nearest airport. I sent her a silver elephant box from Cambodia."

"Does she still have it?"

"She does. She sent me a picture of her and the box the other day. She said that she would take it with her to the White House if her husband were elected president."

"Thank you for sharing this with me. How about the Cambodian teacher?"

"Vanna? How do you know?"

"Remember, I lived in Cambodia for four years. I met her in Siem Reap. She told me about you. She sang your praises. She is one of your biggest admirers. She named one son after you. Is he yours?"

"No, he is not. He is my godson. Rosalee and I met Vanna while we were watching the sunset at the Elephant Terrace. She was a few years younger than us. She looked even younger. She asked us in good English where we came from. When we said 'America,' she asked, 'Which state?' We told her we were from Texas. 'The capital is Austin, and the three largest cities are Houston, San Antonio, and Dallas,' Vanna responded. We were stunned." Goldie turns his horse closer to de Bourbon's. "And one of her friends started reciting the states and their capitals: 'California: Sacramento, New York: Albany, Connecticut: Hartford, Massachusetts: Boston, Florida: Tallahassee, Wisconsin: Madison,' et cetera. We were speechless."

De Bourbon smiles, breathes more fresh air deeply and slowly, and signals for Goldie to carry on.

"Vanna and I stayed in touch. She later became a teacher. I saw her each time I went to Angkor. She took me to the Bayon one day to see a nun who was also an astrologer. The nun wore all white, and her head was shaven. She burned three incense sticks, said some prayers, looked at my palms, and asked for my birth date, which Vanna gave her in the Khmer lunar calendar. She did some calculations on a small portable chalkboard and closed her eyes while holding both of my hands. A moment later, she opened her eyes and gave me her finding."

"What was it?" de Bourbon asks.

"She said that I was somehow cursed at a younger age. In fact, she said that in my first twelve years, everybody who was dear to me died. I thought she must be talking about my mother, one of my aunts, my uncle, my older cousin, et cetera. She also said that I should have stayed far away from the water, the ocean. We had lived near the Gulf of Mexico until I was sent to live with another aunt in Texoma. Then, for the next six years, I would be hurt by the people whom I loved the most. It would not be until the later cycles of my life that I would be able to find true happiness."

The twelve-year cycles of twelve, twenty-four, thirty-six, forty-eight, sixty, seventy-two, eighty-four, ninety-six ... de Bourbon thinks.

"I had a lot of affection for Vanna. I think she was in love with me at one point. But I did not want to go beyond pure friendship. I was afraid I might hurt her. I seemed to be afraid of women after Notneh."

"You did the right thing. You sent all her children to school. You went to her wedding."

"Yes, she married a nurse. I was living in Tokyo at the time and flew to Siem Reap for the weekend. It was a beautiful ceremony. I remember she had to change clothes ten times. Ironically enough, it took only fifteen minutes for her to change each time, because she had three people helping her get dressed."

"How about the Bhutanese princess and the state trooper?" de Bourbon asks, showing her attractive smile.

"You know everything."

"I do."

"I bet you know all the answers too."

"I do. But I want to hear them directly from you." She looks at him and rewards him with another big smile, showing all her bright teeth.

"I met the princess's father in Delhi. He was ambassador to India and asked me if I could keep an eye on his daughter, Kunzang Wangdi. She is now a student at UTEP."

"The University of Texas in El Paso, which is the only complex of buildings in the world outside of Bhutan with Bhutanese architecture," the French president adds.

"Right. I try to check in with her every month. Or whenever I go to El Paso, I take her to lunch or dinner. She is so young, only twenty-two."

"Very beautiful. One of the most beautiful women in Bhutan. I was at her parents' wedding."

"Really?" Goldie seems surprised.

"Her father is the half-brother of the king. I had just arrived in Thimphu to be the first resident ambassador. I went from Paro, which is still listed the number-one most terrifying airport, directly to the palace in Thimphu to present my credentials. I returned the following day for the wedding. It was my first introduction to Bhutanese culture. And they had quite an elaborate ceremony at the palace."

"As for the state trooper, Carmelita Ramirez," Goldie says, "we met when she was in high school. I had a regular pool guy who came to clean and maintain the pool each week. One day, I looked out the window and there was this stunning girl vacuuming my pool under a ninety-degree sun. I went out to greet her. She said that Frank, her father, had to be out of town for family business for a few weeks. I ended up cleaning the pool with her, and she taught me how to maintain it." Goldie stops briefly. "I went to her graduation, saw her through college. She got a degree in criminal justice and was recruited on campus by the FBI. Her father became a good friend of mine even after he stopped working on my pool. In fact, he recommended a contractor to me when I wanted to build a new swimming pool. I lost touch with her for a few years, and suddenly she resurfaced with a child after her father passed away."

"And your pool is in the shape of France." The president reaches for his left hand and holds it for a while.

"Carmelita did not want to go back to Nicaragua, where she was stationed at the time. She needed to stay with her mother. I introduced her to the Texas department of public safety, and they hired her right away. They needed an officer with international experience, and she was the perfect candidate."

"Are you seeing her now?"

"Not romantically. She asked me in front of her mother after her father's funeral to be the godfather of her son."

"And you said yes on the spot."

"I did. If anything, we are very close friends. Again, I don't want to hurt her. I don't want to hurt anybody."

"Especially Rosalee?"

"Especially Rosalee. I met her before I met you. My feelings toward her are very different from the ones I have for you."

"Thank you. I presume you will vote for her husband."

"I cannot confirm or deny."

"I admire your strength, loyalty, and determination."

"I always think that if I am hurt, that is my bad karma."

"Let's go back to watch the sunset from the cupola. You have one too, I believe."

"I do," says Goldie. "I built one after you told me about it in Notneh. And I watch the sunrise and sunset at every opportunity."

"And the full moon. There is a lunar perigee tonight. It will bring the super moon the closest to earth it has been in two decades. It appears fourteen percent closer and forty percent brighter. It is a special night for us."

"It is indeed. I have looked at every full moon for the past thirty years since I met you."

"I look at it too. That's why we are still connected."

The president squeezes his hand. They hold hands for a long while before letting go. She starts to canter, and he follows. A few minutes later, they are back at the stable.

Goldie and Marie arrive at the cupola at the time the sun is at the horizon. She pours the wine for both of them, and they toast each other, the sun, and the moon. She puts her arm around his waist, and he responds kindly. They stay in complete silence until the sun is below the horizon.

They turn to face each other. They both have tears in their eyes. They bring their faces closer. When their lips are about to touch, they shut their eyes.

At dinner, Marie de Bourbon surprises Goldie by having her chef prepare one of his favorite dishes: rognon de veau. After they have been served the cheese plate, it is her turn to tell the story.

"The night you watched the royal dance, I was on my way to Paris. I felt half empty. I cried almost nonstop. I did not know if I was doing the right thing. I knew I would hurt you, and that hurt me, too. I was hoping that the hurt would be temporary for both of us. I was determined to give you your life. And I should go on with mine."

She pours some red wine, first for him and then for herself, and she takes a sip of it. "Jean and I were fellow énarques. We fell in love while we were at ENA. Maybe I just *thought* we were in love. He was in the finance section and was hired away from the Ministry of Finance and Economy by Airbus to represent them in Asia. They told him he could live anywhere. He chose Shanghai. I was in diplomacy and graduated at the top of my class. I joined the Quai d'Orsay. After a few short rotations in the ministry, they told me to choose any embassy in the world, starting with Washington, London, Berlin, Moscow, and Tokyo. They were shocked when I said Paridor. I was halfway through my assignment in Letador when I had that fateful flat tire in Notneh and met you."

"I did not know you were a diplomat." Goldie says. "Your car did not have a diplomatic license plate. I did not even know that you were French. I thought you were Canadian."

"I like to travel incognito. That's the best way to mix with the ordinary people."

"You didn't tell me anything beyond working in Paridor."

"You never asked, and I saw no need to volunteer information."

Marie takes a sip of champagne after they toast each other. Goldie listens intently.

"Jean got involved with a Chinese girl in Hangzhou while on holiday. She became pregnant and asked him to marry her. She was nineteen years old and the daughter of the governor of Jiangsu Province, quite connected to the top Chinese leadership. So he asked me for a divorce. And I agreed. It took us a long time to settle it. I had a lot of family properties, including this one, which I wanted to keep."

"Where is he now?"

"Still in China. He left Airbus a few years later and opened a French restaurant in Suzhou, where his wife is from. It became so successful that he now owns two dozen restaurants in China, Mongolia, and Korea, and one in Vladivostok."

"What is it called?"

"Le Poulet d'Or."

"I ate there all the time when I went to Ulaanbaatar and Seoul. And Vladivostok."

"Apparently it's one of the favorites of the Russian president, Marina Shakarova."

"Back to Letador. What happened to the princess?"

"She got pregnant without being married. It was a very bad omen for the royal family. The Queen Mother called me for help. I asked my cousin in Montreal to take her in. She delivered twins and later went to school in Vancouver and got a degree in international studies."

"Who's the father? And where is she?"

"You wouldn't believe it." She signals for Goldie to lean toward her, and she whispers slowly in his ear.

"Oh my God!" says Goldie. "And nobody knows?"

"Except the Queen Mother, my cousin, and me, and the princess of course, and now you."

The super moon is now above the treetops as the former lovers raise their champagne glasses. They get up at the same time from the dining table on the south veranda. After admiring the full moon with him for a magic moment while holding his hands, the president moves to stand in front of him. He wraps his arms around her and squeezes her tightly. She turns her face toward him and closes her eyes. He brings his face closer to her. When his lips gently touch her, she turns her face away and breaks his embrace.

"Come with me. I have something to show you." She takes him by his waist to the master bedroom. At the bedside table, there is a stone in the shape of a heart.

"Do you remember this?" she asks while putting it in his hand.

"Amazing. You still have it with you after all these years. I am deeply touched. I don't know what to say."

"I have it with me all the time—here in France, in Bhutan, Mongolia, and Cambodia. I had it with me during my campaigns for mayor of Marseille, for the presidency—"

"I found it in the Enies River. And I gave it to you on a full moon."

"And now we are all together on a full moon."

Goldie overhears the voice of his new old lover, which wakes him up slowly. *"Merci beaucoup pour le rapport."* (Thank you very much for the briefing.) The door of the master bedroom swings open, and in walks the French president herself, carrying a silver tray of orange juice, café au lait, and croissants with a small bottle of jam and a yellow tulip.

"I am sorry to let you get up alone. I had an emergency meeting with my national security team from Paris. But here is your favorite breakfast."

"Thanks. Is it Letador?"

"It is."

"I just came from there. I wanted to pass the information on to you, which is why I went to see your diplomatic counselor. But Sylvie took me to see you."

"I know. When I heard you were going to see Jean-David, I concluded that the stars and moon were aligning for us to be reconnected. And we must put an end to our misery."

"I was told to be the first to get off the plane in Paridor. I was greeted by a protocol officer who asked me to go with her to the royal palace. I was in jeans, and it was two o'clock in the morning. Jean-Bedel, the number-two prince, was having a party that was still going full force at the Golden Moon Pavilion on the palace grounds. He and I were classmates at Columbia. He got word from another classmate that I was going to be in Letador and asked his people to bring me to the palace."

"You are close to him and to another half-brother?"

"You're right. Bedel is one of the ABC princes, the other two being Jean-Albert and Jean-Charles. I met them and the other siblings at our graduation. I saw them regularly in New York, Tokyo, et cetera. J. B. and I once went to Mongolia together to hunt."

"And the KLM brothers?"

"Jean-Kit, Jean-Lionel, and Jean-Marc? I met Lionel at Choate. I volunteered to show him around the campus when I learned that he was from Letador. He was a new freshman; I became his tutor and mentor. We did a lot of things together. I taught him how to ice skate and rescued him after he fell through the ice at a frozen pond in New Hampshire."

"They all have different personalities."

"Some are totally opposite."

"Like Bedel and Lionel. Did you ever meet the sisters?"

"Only the two oldest ones."

"Marie-Anne and Marie-Brigitte?"

"Yes. The sisters do not seem to get involved in politics and policy."

"They are like the Queen Mother. They focus only on social programs."

"Both Bedel and Lionel told me separately that the Russians and Chinese are making serious inroads into Letador, especially for oil and gas, and that recently diamonds and gold have been discovered in the east. They are buying off all the corrupt officials from the prime minister all the way down to the provincial governors and village chiefs. They are currently engaged in a bidding war. For example, the minister of mines and minerals asks $100,000 for a meeting with him, so they try to outbid each other—not just to have exclusive dealings but also to prevent the others from getting even a tiny share of the spoils."

"I am very concerned that the situation may explode within the next few months."

"And there could be a major confrontation between the Chinese, the Russians, and you."

"Thanks so much for your concern. My people predicted this morning that the situation will be full of coup attempts and that there might be one within the next six months."

"I quite agree with that assessment."

"When are you going back to Texas?"

"Whenever you want me to go."

"I have to fly to Madrid tomorrow. You're welcome to stay here as long as you want."

"I don't want to be alone by myself."

"I knew you would say that. Take this number down. Only three people have it: my twin sister, my daughter, and now you. Call me anytime. Take good care of yourself, and be careful. By the way, do you want to spend Christmas with me?"

"I will be delighted."

"Wonderful. I'll introduce you to my sister and daughter."

"It will be my privilege."

"Do you want to stay in bed, or do you want to go out?"

"Whatever you want to do."

"Let's go riding some more. I'll have the staff bring some food for us to have a picnic by the creek. When we come back, we can spend the rest of this weekend reliving the magic of Notneh."

"The pleasure will be all mine."

"Ours!"

"Ours, of course!"

Monday morning after breakfast, Marie de Bourbon surprises Goldie. "Why don't you fly with me to Madrid? We go from Marseille/Provence to Cuatro Vientos. You can leave me there and fly back to America."

"Of course; I will be so thrilled."

"You can handle the radio. I'll fly the plane. It's a Falcon 1200."

"What's our call sign?"

"Golden Rooster!"

"I should have guessed."

Marseille Airport

"The preflight has been completed, madame," a French air force colonel says the minute the French president arrives with her copilot.

"Merci." Marie de Bourbon slides into the left seat in the cockpit, followed by Goldie, who sits on the right. They both go through the checklist, and she starts the engines.

After verifying all systems are working properly, the pilot-in-chief turns to Goldie. "Why don't you start with Ground and carry on."

"Yes, Ma'am." He keys the microphone. "Provence Ground, Golden Rooster IFR to Cuatro Vientos airport, ready to copy."

Ground replies: "Golden Rooster cleared to Cuatro Vientos airport as filed. Fly runway heading, climb and maintain six thousand. Departure frequency one three one point two two five, squawk one three three one."

"Golden Rooster, cleared to Cuatro Vientos airport as filed. Fly runway heading, climb and maintain six thousand. Departure frequency one three one point two two five, squawk one three three one."

"Golden Rooster, read back is correct. Contact ground on one one niner point zero seven five when ready to taxi."

"Provence Ground, Golden Rooster with Echo, ready to taxi, IFR."

"Golden Rooster, line up and wait runway three two right using taxiway runway one four left. Contact tower on one one niner point five when ready.

"Line up and wait runway three two right, using taxiway runway one four left, Golden Rooster."

Goldie calls the tower after they arrive at the designated runway: "Provence Tower, Golden Rooster at three two right ready for takeoff, IFR to Cuatro Vientos."

"Golden Rooster cleared for takeoff runway three two right."

"Cleared for takeoff runway three two right, Golden Rooster."

The minute after they are airborne, the tower calls on the radio: "Golden Rooster, contact Provence Departure on one three one point two two five."

Goldie keys the mike. "Provence Departure, Golden Rooster climbing through three thousand for six thousand."

"Golden Rooster, Provence Departure, roger. Altimeter two niner eight four." Even before Goldie can acknowledge the instruction, he receives another one: "Golden Rooster, turn left heading two five zero. Resume own navigation, climb and maintain six thousand."

"Turning left, heading two five zero. Resume own navigation, climb and maintain six thousand. Golden Rooster."

Soon enough, they are flying at a cruising altitude of some thirty thousand feet toward Madrid's Cuatro Vientos airport. They get through air route control centers at Montpelier, Toulouse, Toulon, Bordeaux, and Madrid.

After they land, Marie de Bourbon kisses Goldie good-bye in the cockpit and boards a helicopter for the royal palace. She is scheduled to have lunch with the king and queen of Spain.

She feels quite pleased with herself. The weekend turns out to be one of the best since she returned from her first diplomatic assignment in Letador. She will cherish it forever.

ELEVEN

The Elephant

THE TRADITIONAL ONE-HUNDRED-DAY honeymoon heads for a separation if not a divorce immediately after President Kartona presents his budget to Congress in his State of the Union Address. The euphoria dies very quickly after the inauguration.

Mother Nature has not been kind either during the first quarter. There have been a lot of fires in Arkansas, Texas, and New Mexico. The Midwest has been hit very hard by a series of deadly tornadoes. Tuscaloosa, Alabama; Joplin, Missouri; and Jackson, Mississippi—the president's birthplace—have been almost obliterated by the storms.

Except for the cabinet secretaries, none of the subcabinet positions has been filled. The House is still controlled by his party, although with the thinnest margin in history—twenty-four seats. But the Senate, which is responsible for all confirmations, is in opposition hands and is filibuster proof.

In comes the Cowboy. To the White House. At the Oval Office.

"Goldie, how nice of you to come!" The president looks toward his guest above his reading glasses, closes his global briefing book, and extends his right hand.

Goldie grabs the president's hand firmly and replies politely, "It is my honor, sir."

"Don't be too formal. Call me Bill. Please come over here, and let's sit down by the fireplace with Abe."

National Security Adviser Sandi Bryce waits for the photographer to finish taking pictures; President Kartona smiles and says, "Thank you, Sandi," signaling that he does not want her to be in the Oval Office meeting, as originally planned.

As she is leaving, the president turns to his guest. "I understand you had a good lunch with Dr. Bryce."

"She is an impressive person. She has very high regard for you"

"One of the smartest people I've ever met. I can't imagine life without her … I mean as president," he says, immediately clarifying his paraphrasing of Ronald Reagan's words about his wife, Nancy.

"Rosalee told me you have known each other for a long time."

"Yes, we have. She is one of the smartest people I've ever met."

"I agree. I'm lucky to have her."

"You certainly are. And we are proud to have her as First Lady."

"I've read Dr. Bryce's report. It seems you know all the key players very well, and that you've known them for a long time. I want to nominate you as my special envoy with ambassadorial rank."

Goldie looks at the coffee table for a moment. This is a surprise. There was no clue during lunch with the national security adviser that he would be offered a job.

"What do you say? You want to take some time to think about it? Or you can tell me now?" The president turns his head toward a portrait of Abraham Lincoln when he realizes that his guest is looking at him. He presses on. "In the best interest of the United States and the American people, Goldie—"

"I can tell you now, Mr. President." He takes a deep breath before he continues. "I am delighted to respond positively to your request. I am honored that you ask me to serve. But I don't want any power, position, prestige, or privilege. I prefer to carry out the Golden Gate mission on my own, discreetly. I operate best alone and independently. If you agree to that, I am ready."

"Perfect. Thanks very much, Goldie. You report to me directly, through Dr. Bryce. Let her know when you need something. We stand by to support you twenty-four seven. Keep State and everybody else out of this." The president walks to his desk and takes a blue box with the presidential seal from a drawer. "Do you wear cufflinks, Goldie?"

"Occasionally, sir."

"These are not the cheap ones produced by the DNC. These are pure gold, handcrafted by a master jeweler in San Antonio. I give these out only to heads of state and government." Kartona hands Goldie the box.

"Thank you, Mr. President. I am very grateful."

"Don't mention it. How's Henry?"

"Goldman?" Goldie asks to clarify the Kartona's question.

"Yes, Henry Goldman."

"Fine, sir. He sends you warm greetings."

"Please return mine and tell him, 'No hard feelings.' Thanks for coming, Goldie. Good luck. Look forward to hearing from you."

"Thanks again, Mr. President. My pleasure."

Outside the Oval Office, Goldie is greeted by a twentysomething blonde wearing a tight navy blue suit, a beautiful smile, and no jewelry.

She addresses him with a strong southern accent. "Sir, if you have a moment, the First Lady would like to see you."

"Yes, of course. Here?" he asks, presuming that the First Lady is using her office in the West Wing.

"No, in the private quarters. Please follow me."

He puts his new presidential cufflinks in the left pocket of his pin-striped suit and follows behind the young aide. They pass the Cabinet Room on the right and walk along the colonnade. The rose garden is blanketed with a few inches of snow from the previous evening. Goldie tries to remember when he was last at the White House. He takes some deep breaths of cold, fresh air, trying to get ready for another big challenge of his life.

"It is so wonderful to see you, Goldie!" says the First Lady as she opens wide her arms to hug him very warmly. After the doors have been closed, she gives him a kiss on his lips and wipes the red lipstick imprints off right away. She takes him by the right hand and pushes him into a leather armchair and lowers herself into another one on the right. "Do you think of me?" she asks.

"What do you think?"

"I know you do. Thank you. Are you still angry at me?"

"No, I am not. I am—"

"I am so sorry to hurt you. I did not mean it. But, as you said when we were younger, 'Everything happens for a reason,' and I always remember our trip to Cambodia."

"It is also one of my most memorable trips. Recently you had another good trip to Cambodia."

"Yes, as you know, I went by myself. Bill could not make it because of the budget negotiations. We wanted to show that we are a Pacific nation, and so the first trip by the First Lady was to that area—one of the fastest-growing economic regions in the world. They wanted me to do the usual Japan, Korea, China thing. I said I would do all of that, but I wanted to include Cambodia, and you know why?"

"I am grateful that you were thinking of me."

"Of course, all the time. You heard about the elephant incident?"

"Yes, but not every detail. What happened? The elephant almost got killed."

"You remember the baby elephant we met in the province called Mountain of Diamonds when we were on the church mission trip?"

"Ratanakiri!"

"That's right. Some years ago I read a story about a girl lost in the jungle there. She survived by herself for nearly two decades. Later, after being caught stealing food, she was reunited with her parents because they recognized the birthmarks on her left thigh. They called her the 'jungle woman.'"

"Yes, she is from that province."

"At the Elephant Terrace at Angkor, where you and I sat watching the sunset, the king organized a sacred plowing ceremony, with a reenactment of a royal coronation from the Angkor period. Very colorful: officials on palanquins, parasols, dancers, soldiers, and a lot of elephants."

"I saw the beautiful pictures."

"The last elephant was a huge female. She turned to look at me a few times, then broke away from the parade and walked slowly toward the king and me. The secret service agents were ready to ferry me away, thinking I could be in danger. But the palace attendants brought bananas and cane sugar for us to offer to the elephant." The First Lady offers Goldie some pastries. "The king gave me the honor to do it first. The elephant would not take them from me. She stood there, looked at me, and tried to smell me and touch me. Suddenly she walked back a few steps, made a loud sound, and raised her trunk very high. That was the moment the agents were ready to pull the trigger."

"Were you scared?"

"No. Not at all. The king was smiling; the Cambodians were smiling."

"And you kept on smiling."

"I did."

"Then?" Goldie pours some tea for the First Lady.

"Thanks. Then she lowered her trunk and used it to gently push me away from the edge of the terrace. I noticed she had tears in her eyes."

"You must have met the elephant before," Goldie says.

"You would not believe it."

"Was it the baby we met in Ratanakiri?"

"It was she."

"Amazing! Unbelievable! I remember you lost your balance trying to put a banana in her mouth and fell off the balcony of the village chief's house. And you cut your knees." Goldie recounts the incident with details.

"I remember you cleaned my wounds with your tongue and took very good care of me during the entire trip."

"We were so young and so innocent," the First Lady says softly.

"I remember we were lying on our backs on the haystacks, looking at the full moon. And you told me to look at every full moon. And we would be always connected."

"Such a wonderful memory!"

"We were fourteen. And so much in love."

TWELVE

The Nominee

A T THE OTHER end of Pennsylvania Avenue, the chairman of the Senate Foreign Relations Committee calls the meeting to order. They are considering the nomination of Michelle Alexander as the next US ambassador to Japan. If confirmed, she will be only the second woman to lead the US embassy in Japan.

Senator David Cardey from Idaho is chairing the hearing. He is known to be always kind and courteous, and to always ask very substantive questions. After all, he knows the subject better than many members of the committee from bottom up: Peace Corps volunteer, refugee worker in Africa, relief worker in the South Pacific, foreign affairs columnist, international relations professor, national security council staffer, etc.

He invites the nominee—Michelle Alexander—to make a brief statement by first introducing her family who are sitting behind her.

"Thank you very much, Madam Ambassador, for the statement

and for your service to our nation. You have indeed a very impressive background, having served on all continents and dealt with all kinds of issues from human rights to nuclear problems. You were the youngest person to become a career ambassador. Japanese is one of the thirteen languages you speak fluently, and I understand you know the prime minister of Japan very well. You are indeed very qualified to represent the United States and the American people in Japan." He offers a friendly smile. The nominee returns the courtesy.

Chairman Cardey continues to speak without reading the notes prepared by his staff. "Your statement touches on all important issues concerning our bilateral relations with Japan: cultural, economic, military, strategic …"

The soon-to-be ambassador feels even more confident that she will sail through the hearing. She may be voted out of the committee after this meeting, and the full Senate will approve her nomination so that she can be in place in time for the state visit of the emperor.

"Have you ever stood in line outside an American embassy?"

"No, sir." The nominee knots her eyebrows, having not expected this kind of question.

"How do you get additional pages if your regular passport runs out of space?"

"I usually ask my colleague at the consulate to get them for me."

"Without leaving your desk?"

"No, sir. We work at the same embassy, so we help each other out."

"I am glad to know that our embassy staff maintains a good teamwork spirit."

The nominee remains silent.

"Have you ever seen the line outside our embassy in Tokyo?"

"No, sir. We are not allowed to visit the capital to which we are going to be posted."

"I bet you have seen the line outside our embassy in Mexico City."

"Yes, I have."

"What would you do if you had to stand in the American citizen line for one hour under the scorching sun? And when you got to the door, the embassy staff spoke a non-English language to you?" Chairman Cardey ends the question with a dry smile.

Alexander is completely caught off guard. She struggles to find an answer.

She recalls what the administration's top legislative relations officer has been telling all the nominees who are not lucky enough to get their jobs without going through senate confirmation hearings: "Remember, if you don't know the answer, take a sip of water. There is a glass in front of you. Do it slowly. It will give you one minute to think about an answer and help keep your mouth less dry. The senator may move on to the next question. The rule is that you must let them speak. They like to talk. It's eighty–twenty. They talk eighty percent of the time and even more. They can ask you any questions. They don't have to relate to your areas of expertise. No matter what happens, never give up. Be always deferential. Be prepared for the worst. And hope for the best."

As if on cue, the chairman moves on to the next question.

"What would you do if you lost your passport in a foreign country, it is a local holiday, and the embassy is closed? You call, and you get a ten-minute recording in the local language, which you do not speak."

This question is even tougher than the previous one.

Is this guy trying to derail my nomination?

"And when you get to the English recording, all it says is that the embassy is closed for some Mother Crocodile Festival or the Monkey God Holiday, or Triple Happiness Week."

The nominee touches the glass of water one more time. Her mouth has gotten dry very quickly.

Chairman Cardey does not relent and keeps on talking without notes.

"This is what happened to some of my constituents in Iran last summer. They are potato farmers, truck drivers, volunteer firemen, real people, real Americans. They were hiking near the border of Azerbaijan. Their passports were stolen from their backpacks. They called the US embassy in Tehran, and guess what they heard? A recording in Farsi. How do you expect a fireman from Caldwell, Idaho, to speak Farsi? Besides, he can never understand that *his* embassy, the embassy of the United States of America, speaks a language that is not his. He wanted to get back to America quickly because he was urgently needed at home. He is one of the few people in Idaho who is qualified as an area incident commander. They needed him to help put out that fire in Yellowstone, the fire that was destroying our forests fast and furiously. It was getting as big as the one in 1988. And he could not get through to a human being at our embassy for four days." The chairman pauses, looks around the horseshoe-shaped table, and says, "My time is up. I give the floor to the ranking member, the distinguished senator from Oregon."

"Thank you Mr. Chairman. Since I joined the committee, we all have been talking about the importance of US foreign policy, our strategy, and our global leadership, but not once have we talked about human interactions."

The senator from Oregon looks at Senator Cardey briefly and says, "Mr. Chairman, you and I do not agree on every issue, but I wholeheartedly support you on this one. We need to start paying attention to what the American people send us to Washington to do: to be the good stewards of their tax dollars, of course, in addition to keeping our values unchallenged and our leadership in the world unquestioned. But if a firefighter had to wait for four days to get to talk to an American embassy official about getting a new passport while his home state was burning to the ground because our embassy does not speak English and is closed for some Annual Camel Spitting Competition, I think we have screwed up our priorities. I rest my case. I have no question, Mr. Chairman. Thank you."

"Thank you for your support, Senator. Now I'd like to call on the distinguished senator from North Dakota."

"Thank you, Mr. Chairman," the senator says while bringing the microphone to his mouth. "Madam Ambassador, in your opening statement, you made a reference to one of your predecessors as having said that the relationship between the United States and Japan is the most important, bar none. My great-grandfather served with Senator Mike Mansfield in the Senate. He went to visit him in Tokyo twice. They were from different parties, but they had developed a great friendship. They respected each other. If you were the nominee for ambassador to Brazil,

China, India, or France, Germany, or the UK, would you make a similar statement or find one that is similar to the one you referred to?"

"Senator, you made a good point about the importance of all our bilateral relations. I think we have paid equal attention to everyone we deal with. If I were sent to a different country, I would find the relationship between the United States and that country equally important. I am sure there is some statement somewhere that would support that fact."

"Thank you for that candid response, Madam Ambassador. I notice that you speak thirteen languages fluently." The senator of North Dakota reads through his notes. "Besides French, German, Italian, Russian, Portuguese, and Spanish, you also speak some other languages of which I've never heard. I have no idea where Achuar-Shiwiar, Chachi, Cofán, or Epena are spoken. Thank you, Mr. Chairman."

"I give the floor to the distinguished senator from Connecticut." The committee chairman continues to call on his colleagues who are sitting at the elevated table, alternating between Republicans and Democrats.

"Thank you, Mr. Chairman. President George H. W. Bush once threw up on the Japanese prime minister. I believe it was in 1992. Am I right?"

"Yes, senator. It was in January 1992."

"My memory is failing. Can you help me out? Who was the prime minister?"

"I believe it was Mr. Miyazawa?"

"Thank you. Is it true that after he left the White House, President Bush—I mean George H.W. Bush—invited the prime minister to visit him in Houston? And he told the prime minister that *this time the dinner is on me?*"

The hearing room bursts into laughter. The nominee offers no reaction except for a polite smile. She is still concerned about the fate of her nomination. If anything, hers will be the first time that the nomination is not acted upon positively on the same day by the committee and the full Senate.

"I don't know all the details, Senator. But I will happily get back to you on that question."

"Thank you, Madam Ambassador. I'd appreciate that very much."

The chairman immediately brings the hearing to conclusion. There is no statement on when they are going to vote on the nomination.

His parting words are simple: "Thank you very much for coming. You can be assured that my colleagues and I will act upon your nomination as expeditiously as feasible. The committee is adjourned." He bangs the gavel.

ORANGE, VIRGINIA

Michelle Alexander is trying to recover from her confirmation hearing at her weekend home. Sounds of propeller planes can be heard from the nearby airport, where a skydiving contest is being held. She is watching the Sunday morning show reporting on her nomination.

"The NONO (National Occupy Now Organization), which was born during the third year of the Obama administration, sees the way the Republican Senate treats the nominee for ambassador to Japan as a wholesale abomination. The NONO president, a single mother, whose grandmother made her family name famous during the Occupy Wall Street years, sees it as an opportunity to call to arms the almost dormant National Organization of Women, the National Alliance of Women Professionals, Women Rule the World, the American Council of Foreign Service Officers, and a few lesser-known and even more dormant communities of permanent protesters, to mount a joint strategy to attack what they call the 'do nothing, obstructionist Senate.'

"Our sources told us that they have a video conference call this weekend to mobilize their membership to descend on Capitol Hill next weekend. They plan to have one hundred thousand protesters at their Occupy the Senate Now event. Alexis Barbara Canales, CBS News, Washington."

The minute the report is over, the host asks, "What do we know about NONO? I ask you, Monica."

"What was not mentioned in the opening segment is that the NONO leadership is a group of trust funders who are getting bored with having been trusted with more money than they can spend on parties, and they are looking for something to challenge a society that worked hard to send them to Ivy League schools and provide them with millions of dollars to start their lives when they turned eighteen. The president, vice president, secretary, and treasurer of NONO are not employed."

"What do you say to Monica? I ask you, Andrea."

"What Monica did not say is that the NONO people have as their ultimate objective the means to say no to everything they see, hear, and smell without ever offering any alternative solutions."

"What do you say to what Monica and Andrea said? I ask you, Caroline."

"What is so disturbing about this stupid movement is that they are so well funded that they don't have to worry about raising money to fight for their non-cause."

"What would you say to the NONO people? I ask you, Victoria."

"What would I say to the NONO people? *Noooooooooooooo!*"

Tokyo, Japan

Ambassador Sono Motomura, the retired veteran diplomat, and two colleagues have been summoned to brief the head of the Japanese government on the latest development. Prime Minister Yuko Akahana herself has a regularly scheduled audience with the emperor in the afternoon and would like to be updated on the confirmation of her good friend Michelle Alexander.

"Madam Prime Minister, I was in Washington for six years and got to know the members of the Senate Committee on Foreign Relations quite well, especially those in the subcommittee on Asia and the Pacific, which oversees our relations with the United States,"

Ambassador Motomura pauses to hand a list of the subcommittee membership to the prime minister. "We had our staff at every hearing of the subcommittee and the full committee, and we still do. We monitored very closely the hearings of three nominees as ambassadors to Japan while I was ambassador there. Each was on substantive issues and went through very fast. Each nominee was voted out of the committee unanimously and was acted upon by the full senate on the same day."

Motomura starts coughing. The prime minister offers him some green tea in a little cup, which he receives with both hands, his head bowed. After sipping the tea, he puts the cup down gently and continues. "We have asked our embassy in Washington to research all confirmation hearings of all nominees as ambassadors to every country in the world for the past two hundred years. There was not one instance when there was anything asked on the nominees in the hearing or in writing, outside of issues involving bilateral relations.

"The committee, especially the present one under the chairmanship of Senator David Cardey of Idaho, has been always very fair. We met when he was still a junior senator from Idaho. He and his wife live in the same neighborhood I live in, just a few houses away. He and I used to play tennis regularly at St. Albans."

"I went to school there when my father was posted in Washington," the prime minister says.

"Yes. They now have your picture on their distinguished alumni wall."

"What is the composition of the committee membership?" the prime minister asks.

"There are seventeen members: nine Republicans and eight Democrats. Almost all are conservatives, including the Democrats. Only two are known as liberals: a moderate Republican and one Democrat." Motomura continues with more details on the memberships.

"In the Asia and Pacific subcommittee, five have been to Japan and two speak Japanese, including the Senator from Utah who was born in Sapporo, where his father was a Mormon missionary. He is married to a Japanese classmate from Waseda. They have two children: a girl who is a banker in Frankfurt and a son who is a missionary in Sudan. The Utah senator is the leading voice of our Friends of Japan group on the Hill. For some reason, he did not ask to speak at the hearing, although he was with the senator from California; they were the two who presented the nominee to the committee."

"Do you know why?" Akahana asks.

"I can only guess that he did not want to cast any shadow on his colleagues for being the undisputed expert on Japan in the US Senate and

Congress as a whole. And maybe he was afraid to offend his colleagues in the mountains."

"Colleagues in the mountains?" Akahana frowns and sips some of her green tea.

"Yes, Ma'am. There are almost equal numbers of senators from the mountain states, which I call the mountain people, and those from the coastal states, which I call the beach people. It is quite uncanny. This is the first time this has happened in the history of the US Senate."

"Who are they?"

"The mountain people are the senators from Idaho (the committee chairman), Colorado, Montana, New Mexico, North Dakota, South Dakota, Utah, and Wyoming." Motomura moves some papers around and picks up one sheet. "The beach people are the senators from Mississippi (the president's home state), Florida, South Carolina, Virginia, Connecticut, Maine, Washington, Oregon, and California, who is the subcommittee chair. And then we have Texas, a cowboy state, which is a country by itself."

"*So desuka,*" (Really?) asks Prime Minister Akahana.

"*Hai so desu.*" (Yes.)

"Please continue."

"The senator from Utah was the only one who went to shake hands with the ambassador nominee at the end. He whispered to her: '何がおきてもきぼうをすてない.'" *(naniga okitemo kibo o sutenai)*

"*So desuka.*"

"*Hai so desu.*"

"Is it from the book *Golden Bones?*"

"*Hai so desu.*"

"What is next?"

"There is a movement mobilized by NONO, which stands for National Occupy Now Organization. They are mounting a major offensive on Capitol Hill. It is called Occupy the Senate Now."

"What do they plan to accomplish?"

"They attack the Foreign Relations Committee for ganging up on a woman. They think they are helping the nominee. But I believe that by doing what they are doing, they are antagonizing the Senate, and they are going to hurt her nomination."

"Why do you think so?"

"Because the Senate, like the House, listens to its constituency. Outside the Beltway, people have been getting angrier and angrier by what is now known as the "Idaho Fireman's Fire." It started on the front page of the *Caldwell Sentinel*, a small weekly paper in the fireman's hometown, and in all the Idaho dailies the day after the chairman mentioned his saga in the hearing. The wire services and the national newspapers picked up the story immediately. And then the networks, the cable news channels, the weeklies. Almost all of them sided with the chairman and the fireman."

"*So desuka.*"

"Some call for the secretary of state to resign. Others ask the ambassador to Iran to be fired. The *New York Post* had a front-page picture of the raging fire with the caption 'FIRE THEM!' Ironically enough, the nominee has nothing to do with all of this. And she is the one to suffer the consequences if the committee puts a hold on her nomination."

"Is there anything we can do to help her, Michelle Alexander?"

"I am afraid there is nothing we can do, either from here in Tokyo or from there in Washington. Our embassy is working hard to gather information and lets us know. And we react quite rapidly."

"Please keep me posted."

"Yes, Madam Prime Minister." Motomura stands up and bows to Prime Minister Akahana, who returns the courtesy.

THIRTEEN

The Ugly Barbarian

GOLDIE IS PLEASED that he was able to watch his favorite Sunday news program, *Say What*. Having been through a few hearings himself, he feels sorry for the nominee who has nothing at all to do with all the raging fight.

He turns to what lies ahead on his schedule. Each time he is in San Antonio, he has a number of things that he wants to do only in the Alamo City.

First he needs to renew his concealed handgun license. He doesn't have to, but he wants to go through the training again to refresh his memory.

He travels for about a half hour through light traffic to get to the Bull Lets Hold Firing Range. He and his classmates—twenty of them, thirteen men and seven women—sit through an indoor morning class. They take a written test and afterward head outside to the range. The instructor asks them to line up and loudly barks instructions. "Rule number one. This is my rule. Anybody seen pointing a gun, loaded or unloaded, at another person is fired from this class immediately. Do you hear me?"

Half of the class responds. "Yes."

"*I can't hear you!*" he shouts.

"*Yes sir!*"

"All right. The guns must be pointed downrange at all time. Now we are going to load five rounds."

He walks back and forth from one end of the line to the other. He inspects everyone, stops, helps some slow students, and moves on.

"Keep your guns pointed downrange. After you've loaded them, wait for my order. Is everybody loaded?"

"Yes."

"*I can't hear you!*"

"*Yes sir!*"

"Now we are going to fire five rounds."

Bang, bang, bang, bang, bang!

"Cease fire! Cease fire!" the instructor shouts. "Who fired? Did I say 'fire'? I said, 'We are going to fire five rounds.' Wait until I say 'fire' before you fire. Do you understand?"

"*Yes sir!*"

"Now we are going to fire five rounds."

Silence.

"Fire!"

Bang, bang, bang, bang. bang, bang, bang, bang, bang, bang, bang, bang, bang!

Back at home, Goldie immediately drafts an e-mail to his flight crew—Marty Goodson, the mission observer, and José Nochebuena, the mission scanner. He always makes sure that all details are in writing.

Marty and José,

I tried to reach you by phone all afternoon without any luck. I presume you must be still shooting away at the ranch and you are eating something that you killed for dinner tonight. I thought I would shoot you this initial game plan for our fire watch mission tomorrow.

Per Erin's e-mail, the following counties have been assigned to us: McMullen, Live Oak, Jim Wells, Duval, Webb, Zapata, Jim Hogg, Brooks, Hidalgo, and Starr. We should plan to meet tomorrow at 1013 and brief immediately. The weather looks fantastic. I'll take care of all CAP- and FAA-related issues, flight plan, NOTAMS, etc. I'd like you to come up with some coordinates of these beautiful counties.

This is a 4-hour mission, and we have 4 hr gas plus reserve. I think it's best that we do the whole thing at once instead of landing halfway for a pee or to refuel. I suggest you don't intake too much liquid a few hours b4 launch, and we all should remember to drain the main vein b4 preflight. Please put in coordinates so that we can fly tirelessly. José can certainly help Marty with the map book in the backseat in addition to taking aerial photos. I think it might be good for him to do some radio work as well, especially on the way back. I'd like you to take a mental picture of these 10 lucky counties. Please have 2 waypoints in the flight plan b4 departure.

I've excerpted some key points for the ops instructions to refresh our memories:

Sortie objective: locate and record lat and long of any fires in search area; identify and record any lake, river or water source that is at least 10 feet deep (useful for helicopter tanker) that can be potential source of water to fight the fire. Monitor 122.025 for an air attack aircraft working the fire. Stay clear of the fire if AA is present. If no AA, but firefighters are present, contact them and offer assistance.

Fire intelligence:

> » type of vegetation/fuel ahead of fire: grass, brush, timber structure, vehicle, etc.
>
> » fire size in acres
>
> » potential threats: qty and type of houses, facilities, ag commodities
>
> » lat/lon: degrees/minutes.decimals
>
> » useful info: water supplies, hazards, etc.

We plan to fly sortie about 4,000 AGL or higher to get better coverage. All flights must be 1,000 AGL or above except for takeoff and landing

Am up for another 90 minutes, if you want to talk. Otherwise, I'll see you tomorrow.

Goldie

He reads it one more time and presses the Send button. In one second, the word *sent* appears on the screen.

Goldie plays an old segment of the Jay Leno show on the television screen. He usually tries to lighten up a little before he turns in. He goes to the refrigerator and grabs a can of Coors Light. He looks at it and puts it back. He doesn't feel like drinking before any flight, even though the rule is "eight hours from bottle to throttle." He pours some watermelon juice into a tall blue glass and goes back to his favorite rocking chair.

His laptop beeps. He checks for the new e-mail.

Thanks for the e-mail, Goldie, and the refresher.

I did get to eat what I killed. I'll make some sausage and give you some next week.

No question. I'll see you manana, amigo.

Can't wait to rock and roll with you again, man.

Marty (& José)

The three of them meet in the briefing room at 10:13 a.m., review the flight plan together, and head for the men's room.

"Let's drain the main vein, guys!" Marty says to the air crew.

They stand side by side, spread their legs, unzip their pants, and urinate.

"Wow, it feels good to get rid of it," Marty, the skinniest of the three, says with a great sense of satisfaction.

He closes his fly and turns on his heels.

"Hey, Marty, wait a minute!" Goldie shouts.

"Yo, what's up, chief?"

"You didn't wash your hands after you peed."

"You noticed that?"

"Yes, and I didn't even have to turn my head."

"You are so smart, Goldie. No, I never wash my hands after I pee."

"I am just curious."

"I always wash my hands *before* I touch my dick, *before* I pee."

"Why?"

"Because my dick is the cleanest part of my body. I take good care of him so that he can always take good care of me."

José, the shortest of the trio, who has a shaven head, chimes in. "Goldie, Marty thinks that his dick is more awake than some FAA guys."

"José is right. My dick is always in an alpha, alpha, alpha, alpha mode." Marty replies.

"What's the hell is alpha, alpha, alpha, alpha mode?" Goldie asks.

"He is always awake, alert, and alive."

"Is that what the navy taught you? To be always awake, alert, and alive?"

"Actually, I believe it was George Patton who said 'Be alert and be alive.' Yours truly added 'always awake.'" Marty says.

"I did not know you were such a person of wisdom. You think of everything."

"My dick never lets me down whenever I want to land," Marty replies.

"You treat him like he is your best buddy. Do you have a name for him, Marty?" Goldie asks.

"Tango Uniform Bravo! Both of you can make three guesses. He who gets it right will receive a steak dinner at the new Brazilian restaurant."

"Tango Uniform Bravo?" José says.

"You heard me right."

Goldie starts first. "The Ultimate Boss!"

"Nope."

José. makes a guess. "The Unpredictable Banana."

"Nope."

"The Unbelievable Bomber." Goldie says, taking another stab at it.

"Nope."

"We give up," says José.

"The Ugly Barbarian!"

"Pardon me?" says Goldie.

"The U-gly Bar-ba-rian!" Marty says very slowly. "His nickname is Tub or Tubby, for close friends."

"I can't believe this!" Goldie replies.

SHANGHAI, CHINA

Charles and Laura Hawkins get off the flight from Los Angeles, which arrives on time in Shanghai. They are on the way to Cambodia to give a speech on development challenges in Africa. Goldie has helped arrange the trip to give his closest friends a close look at one of the places that has been close to his heart.

Outside the gate, the Hawkinses see "Domestic Transfer" to the left and "International Transfer" to the right. They figure that the connection is probably in the same terminal and may be only on a different floor. They turn right and follow the sign. About one hundred yards farther, they find multiple doors with the sign "International Transfer" above. All doors are locked. They turn around and ask a cleaning lady who obviously does not speak English. She points her finger somewhere.

"Can you please tell us how we get to International Transfer?"

"No inglis. Go, go." She keeps on pointing.

The second person they ask is a collector of luggage pushcarts. He does the same thing, pointing his finger somewhere.

"No inglis. Go, go."

Charles and Laura arrive at the Domestic Transfer area and find a counter for passengers to Hong Kong, Macau, and Taiwan.

The first agent tells them to go through Immigration and go upstairs to check in again.

"But we don't have Chinese visas."

"It's okay. No problem."

The China Immigration line seems longer. Charles and Laura get antsy. They only have forty-five minutes left to make the connection. They are sent to a supervisor's counter to get new stamps. They are told to get out through Customs and check in again at the departure level.

Charlie knows for sure that they are going to miss the flight to Sihanoukville.

Finally, they find the Shanghai Airlines counter on aisle J and the answer they dread to hear: "The check-in is closed for the flight."

Laura tries to reason with the agent, begs him to let them board the flight, to call the gate and say that they are still coming through.

The answer is still no.

Charles cannot stand seeing his wife being said no to numerous times. He finally jumps in.

"What do you suggest we should do? All you can do is say 'No, no, no.' Is that what you are trained to do? To just say no to your customers? Is there someone in your company who can tell us what to do since we missed a flight through no fault of our own? You are the only airline that flies to Sihanoukville from here, and the next flight is tomorrow. What do you think we should do for the next twenty-four hours? Pace this terminal from one end to another, from aisles A to M? Or visit the three empty information counters with a big question mark? Can you please give us one yes answer? And we are not leaving this counter until we get a yes answer."

DOUBLE E RANCH

Back at home, Goldie picks up the phone on the first ring. His riding buddy is on the other end of the line. He knows it must be the news that he has been waiting for.

"I found the only one you're looking for, Cowboy. Check your e-mail now. I've just sent you his pictures."

Goldie obliges very quickly. He has always wanted to own a bull, or at least invest in one.

"Oh my God. He is awesome."

"One thousand eight hundred ninety pounds of sheer terror."

"Has anybody ridden him?"

"None. Not one survived two seconds. Not even the BBC."

"BBC?" Goldie asks, wanting to make sure they are not talking about the news network.

"The bloody Brazilian chick! The attractive and new champ of the PBR."

"Ah, that one. My mind is a little slow this morning."

"You know what she said about your potential new pet?"

"What?"

"'I'll ride anyone. They will give everything to be ridden by me. This one threw me off before even my ass touched his.'"

"Wow. What else can you tell me about him?" Goldie is impressed with the information.

"He is truly the champ's champ. The king of the arena. He is the combination of Bodacious, I Am Gangster, Take Your Dumb Ass Off My Back, and Are You Crazy, Stupid, or Both?"

"I can't wait to meet him."

"You are in luck, buddy. He is coming to your neck of the woods. He'll be at the San Antonio Stock Show and Rodeo."

"Wow. When can I see him?"

"I already scheduled an appointment for you to say hello to him on Tuesday at two thirty p.m."

"Thanks so much, buddy."

"Anything for the golden cowboy. I'll see you there."

"See you there. Hey, wait a minute. What is his name?"

"The Ugly Barbarian!"

"I can't believe this," Goldie says to himself.

FOURTEEN

The Father

THE WHITE HOUSE

T HE PRESIDENT USUALLY receives the dean of the diplomatic corps shortly after the inauguration. It is a courtesy call from the foreign envoy who has served the longest as ambassador to the United States.

The previous president had the whole family of the ambassador in and spent at least thirty minutes on the reception. Bill Kartona, the current president, wants none of that. He plans to have a photo taken standing up in front of the Oval Office desk. In, photo, chitchat, out.

This morning he is in a bad mood. He does not read the briefing book and pays little attention to what is said by his chief of staff and national security adviser at their daily 8:00 a.m. meeting. He is still angry at the Senate leadership, which is blocking all his nominations, the latest one the nominee for ambassador to Japan, one of his former lovers.

The Oval Office door swings open, and in walks a beauty. He did not know that the dean of the diplomatic corps was a woman—a rather stunning woman.

"I am Marie-Catherine Samas," says the visitor as she extends her right hand to take the president's. "I am so thrilled to see you"— she pauses a moment, pulls him close to her, and whispers the last word—"again!"

The president is baffled and smitten. He did not expect his guest to be so attractive and charming. He should have read the briefing book.

"I am so thrilled to see you too," he politely answers, and he relieves his hand from her grip.

After the photographer leaves, he invites the dean to sit down by the fireplace, violating his own rule of a courtesy handshake. She does not move but rather whispers that she wants to share something very personal with him. She tells him she is not comfortable doing so in a room with windows and peepholes.

The president obliges by leading her into the so-called Clinton room, a windowless office next to the Oval Office where the forty-second president had an affair with his twenty-two-year-old intern.

As she follows him, her breast touches the president's right shoulder. He tries to figure out where he has smelled that perfume before.

After they sit down comfortably facing each other, the visitor begins to lift her skirt slowly. The president tries to stop her and turns his head away. But he can't.

Samas takes Kartona's hand and leads it along, following the skirt. His face is getting red and his heart is beating faster.

Soon enough, he notices the tattoo of a roaring lion on her right thigh. Something flashes in his mind's eyes. He is sure that he has seen this before—but where and when?

The guest moves so close to him that he can see the tattoo very clearly, and their legs are squeezed between one another. The president does not attempt to move back.

"Do you remember meeting a young girl in Paris when you were a Rhodes scholar?"

"Is it you?" asks the president, even more baffled.

The dean nods.

"After I fell off the bicycle at Bois de Boulogne, you picked me up, took me to your hotel room, and tended to my knee wounds. You noticed the lion tattoo."

"Now I remember," Kartona says.

"You went back to England the following day." Samas begins to choke. Suddenly, tears start to roll down her cheeks. "I returned home afterward."

"Where?"

"Letador!" Samas brings Kartona's other hand to rest on her other thigh.

"I did not know you were African."

"My mother was French. My brother and I have very fair skin."

"Where is your mother?" Kartona asks while his hands are firmly on her thighs.

"She passed away after the complicated birth of my brother. My grandmother brought us up."

"And your father?"

"He died a few months ago. He was killed in the coup."

"I am so sorry. Was he somebody important?"

"He was the king!"

"He was the king? So you are a princess?"

She nods her head again. After wiping tears from her cheeks with a tissue that the president hands her, she continues.

"I was pregnant and later delivered twins: a boy and a girl. My grandmother smuggled me and my children out to Canada. The court astrologers believe that any woman who has twins of opposite sexes will bring calamity to the family. And the fact that I lost my virginity without being married would bring shame to the palace."

"And who is the father? Is he here with you?"

She continues to sob, now more violently. "Yes. He is here with me. It is you!"

FIFTEEN

The Plane

WEST TEXAS

THE SPEED LIMIT is eighty miles per hour on this stretch of Interstate 10 almost all the way to El Paso. Goldie is passed by everyone: the eighteen wheelers, the campers, the truckers, the regular cars, and the motorcycles.

He normally cruises at 113 kilometers per hour, or 83 miles per hour, thinking that with everybody going at 85 miles per hour he will be okay if he gets stopped, as he is just following the flow.

Goldie has a lot of errands to do each time he goes to El Paso. He needs a new supply of pool chemicals. His pool is not very big, but with thirty thousand gallons of water, he has to use at least two one-pound bags of fast-dissolving shock treatment and super chlorinator. He will get the whole box, and another box of muriatic acid, which usually comes in two one-gallon containers. He is also out of stabilized chlorinating tablets to control bacteria and algae. He needs all of these to try to turn his pool water from green to clear blue.

He needs to get some Mexican beach pebbles about two to three inches in diameter, cement, and concrete bonding adhesive and acrylic fortifier. He always wanted to build by himself what he calls a PP, or pleasure path, a little patch in the yard where you can self-massage your feet when you walk barefoot on it.

Juanita, his residence manager also gave him a long grocery list. Normally she can get most of the produce and cooking items in Sierra Blanca, but he offers to get them in El Paso while in town to see the person for whom he is beginning to develop some affection.

While thinking of her, he notices a state trooper blasting a siren with flashers on the other side of the divided highway. He feels sorry for the people who are speeding.

As his mind wanders back to his new love, a voice suddenly comes from out of nowhere, ordering him to stop.

"Green truck! Pull over!"

Goldie looks through the rearview mirror and sees a police car with flashing lights rotating between red, white, and blue. The voice orders him to turn the engine off and get out of the truck with both hands on his head. Then he is told to get back into the truck and keep his hands there, and not to turn his head or look into the rearview mirror until he is told to do so.

What's going on? He thinks to himself. *Everybody is speeding faster than me; why did they single me out?*

He sees from the corner of his eye that the officer gets out of the patrol car with one hand on her gun. He begins to worry. He has never been in trouble with the law before. In fact, he has been one of the biggest benefactors of charitable law enforcement organizations in the state.

The officer walks slowly to the right of his truck, opens the door on the passenger's side, gets in, and sits down.

"Where do you think you are going, Genghis Khan? And why so fast?"

Goldie immediately recognizes the voice and the perfume. They belong to someone whom he once loved.

"Jesus Christ! You scared me to death."

"Why don't you ever call me? I know you've been away," the state trooper says. "Juanita told me that you have been all over the world."

"I told her not to tell anybody."

"Not even me? I am not just anybody."

"Well, except you, of course. So why did you stop me? To tell me that you miss me too?"

He leans over to kiss her on the left cheek. She turns her face to position her lips toward his; they touch briefly before she leans back.

"The secret service is looking for you. What did you do, Goldie?"

"The secret service?" Goldie says with surprise evident in his voice.

"They called us when they could not get a hold of you. The chief instructed me to find you within one hour or lose my job. So I called Juanita, and she said you were on your way to do some errands and to see a princess."

"She is not supposed to tell anyone about my whereabouts."

"Not even me? I am not just anyone."

"Well, except you, of course. What does the secret service want?"

"I don't know. They wouldn't tell us. Here they are."

Two black Suburbans with darkened windows speed in the opposite direction.

"They are going to turn around at the next crossover. Stay in there," says the officer as she exits the truck.

One secret service van stops in front, and the other behind it. A man in dark suit and dark sunglasses jumps out of the one in front and rushes toward him.

"Good morning, sir. The First Lady would like to visit your ranch tomorrow, and we need to take a look at it first before we can let her go. Will you allow us a quick tour?"

"Yes, of course. Do you know how to get there?"

"Yes, we do. We were there this morning, but your staff would not let us in."

"All right, I will give them a call. What time is she planning to go?"

"Late afternoon, most likely. She has a full schedule during the day."

Goldie calls his ranch manager, Guillermo, on the phone. "Willy?"

"Sí, señor."

"The Secret Service is coming with a few agents. Please let them in and show them the usual places."

"Sí, señor. Todo está bien, señor?"

"Todo está bien. No hay problema!" (Everything is okay. There is no problem.)

"Sí, señor."

The secret service vans kick up dust when they leave Goldie. The state trooper turns on her heels and walks toward her patrol car. She gives him a hurt look when he grabs her arm. "The First Lady!"

"She is an old friend," he says to her in a reassuring tone, sensing a feeling of jealousy on her part.

"I am sure she is. Well, have fun with your old friend tomorrow," says she before getting into her car.

Goldie closes the door for her and kisses her left cheek. She turns her head to look into the rearview mirror, and their lips touch.

"I'll call you soon."

"Thanks. I'll try not to hold my breath." She leaves him in another cloud of dust.

Goldie gets into his truck and drives home. He is delighted that the timing could not be better. He has a lot to catch up on with his former girlfriend. And a lot to show off about his ranch.

He is pleased with himself that he has just planted a dozen crape myrtles—some of the First Lady's favorite plants—near the swimming pool.

Goldie put them in full sun, which will allow them to grow to fifteen feet tall. He spaced them thirteen feet apart. He watered them at least three times a week until they were well established, and more frequently during times of drought. He plans to fertilize them only in the spring, as they are fast growing. He prunes the dormant branches lightly to encourage heavier flowering. They are now blooming with their red flowers—the First Lady's favorite color.

Goldie lets his memories wander as he drives. He was fresh out of high school and was waiting to hear about admission to the US Air Force Academy. He needed a job and went to the Lords of the Roads driving school in San Antonio. He went through a weeklong training and later earned his commercial driver's license.

He learned that most truck drivers drive an average of five hundred miles a day. He was offered a job with a San Antonio-based national freight company. He hauled his first cargo in an eighteen-wheeler from the Alamo City to Amarillo, some five hundred miles in eight hours. He made short rest and refueling stops. And he established a practice of stopping only every three or four hours. He took Interstate 10 West to Ozona and went almost straight north toward Big Lake, Big Spring, Post, Floydada, and Plainview.

There he came upon half a dozen motorcyclists on the way to their annual rendezvous in Sturgis, South Dakota. Everyone had tattoos. All wore battered jeans. Most had T-shirts or sleeveless shirts. A few had helmets; the rest had skullcaps. The group was led by a big guy on a Victory motorcycle pulling a trailer.

It was early August, and Texas had gone through one of the longest droughts in history. It had been triple-digit heat for months. In Amarillo, the city dictated the following watering schedule: odd-numbered houses could water on Sundays, Tuesdays, and Thursdays; and even-numbered houses could water only on Mondays, Wednesdays, and Saturdays. Goldie followed the bikers to Amarillo, where they parted company. He marveled at the bikers who rode in 105 degrees with little body protection from the sun.

He dreamed about having his own bike and joining the annual rally in South Dakota.

He dreamed about having his own truck and hauling freight all over the United States.

He dreamed about having a small ranch, raising some cattle and working on the land.

And he never stopped dreaming.

The following day, he picked up another load and departed for

Breckenridge, Colorado. He took Interstate 40 west and passed the Cadillac Ranch on the left. At Bushland he went north and northwest toward Dalhart and Texline, where he crossed into New Mexico to Clayton, already at 5,050 feet elevation and in the Mountain Time zone. The scenery suddenly became green.

He picked up Interstate 25 north at Raton, where he met another group of thirteen motorcycles. This group was properly dressed with complete leather gear, including chaps, riding boots, full-fingered gloves, and full-faced helmets. Their jackets had the words "G♥lden R!ders" emblazoned at the back. They were led by a female biker on a big, loud Harley-Davidson. The rest were a mixture of BMW, Harley-Davidson, Honda, Kawasaki, Suzuki, Triumph, and Yamaha. They were followed by a chase truck towing a motorcycle trailer. They rode staggered in perfect formation and changed lanes only occasionally.

Goldie got high on seeing the beautiful bikes and handsome riders. He promised himself that he would get his first bike soon enough. Near Denver, instead of continuing north, they got off Interstate 25 and turned left on Route 6 to meet Interstate 70 near Golden. This was the exact road that Goldie planned to take to go to Breckenridge. He wondered if the bikers were taking a more scenic route before heading for Sturgis a few days later.

The traffic went up and down various peaks and slowed down quite a bit. It allowed him to keep up with the bikers. Goldie tried not to get too distracted by the breathtaking views of valleys and mountains, some of them still capped with snow. The descents could be quite steep, especially for heavy trucks and trailers. There were a lot of emergency ramps for runaway trucks to help them stop in case of brake failures. He wondered if he could save money fast enough to get a Road King or whether he should start with a less expensive bike.

Near the Eisenhower Tunnel, the left lane came to a stall, and he began to pass the bikers on the right. He noticed that all the bikers were women—not just their leader, whose blond hair was sticking out from the bottom of her helmet. Most of them appeared to be in their fifties or younger. And they were all very attractive.

Goldie had heard of the Motor Maids, the all-female motorcycle club, but not the G♥lden R!ders. He wondered who they were. He lost them after the tunnel, and then he had to get off Interstate 70 at Frisco in order to go south for Breckenridge.

It was also about 550 miles on his second haul from Amarillo, but it took him nearly ten hours because he had to slow down a lot while going up and down the peaks all the way from Trinidad, Colorado.

It was still bright when he got to his delivery station. He checked in to a motel and jumped naked into a Jacuzzi. It didn't get dark until nine thirty at night.

Goldie normally does not answer a call when he is in his study. The ringtone of his cell phone, "Strangers in the Night," interrupts his wandering memories. Guillermo, his ranch manager, is on the other end, asking him to speak to the lead secret service agent.

"I am sorry to bother you again, sir. But your ranch manager told us that we cannot drive any motor vehicle on the ranch. We can go in only on horses or in horse-drawn wagons. And the main house is six miles from the gate. We need to bring a lot of equipment with us. Much of it cannot be removed from our vehicles. I beg you to reconsider your ranch rules, please."

Goldie tells the lead agent that they can bring the vehicles to the main house if they keep their speed below fifteen miles an hour. They can go anywhere except the master bedroom. He asks to speak to Guillermo and repeats his orders. He chuckles and relishes his "no motor vehicles on the ranch" rule. He had gotten the idea after spending a week with some friends at the Silver Tip Ranch in Montana. Located between Yellowstone National Park and Absaroka Beartooth National Forest, the seven-hundred-acre ranch is accessible only by horses and horse-drawn carriages, which take about three hours to reach. There, the only sounds heard are whispering winds and rushing water.

The White House

President Bill Kartona wants to know everything about his key opposition leaders, which he puts on a mental blacklist. His legislative staff, with information provided by the FBI, has compiled a thick three-ring binder briefing book marked "SECRET."

1. He is currently the second longest serving majority leader of the senate, after Mike Mansfield, who occupied the position from 1961 to 1977. They are from the same state, Montana, but different parties. He always reaches out to the Democrats on a number of issues.

The president skips the boring description of the senator from Montana and goes to the number two on his blacklist.

2. The chairman of the foreign relations committee was born in Gardiner, Montana, and went to the University of Montana–Missoula. He dreamed of becoming a game warden but changed his mind after serving as a Peace Corps volunteer in Guatemala.

We have reason to believe that he fathered a child with a Russian exchange student from Vladivostok. She interned in Boise, Idaho, which is at the same latitude as her hometown. It was there that she met the chairman, who was at the time (and still remains) the youngest speaker of any state house in history. He asked her to have an abortion, but she refused, thinking that he would marry her. He did not offer, and she did not ask. She returned to Vladivostok, three months pregnant. He supported her until the baby girl was born. When he got married, she asked him to stop the financial support. They remain on friendly terms until now. We are not sure if he has ever seen his daughter.

Kartona is very intrigued with this information, which he was not previously aware of. He can't wait to discover the identity of the woman. He thinks his enemy has an Achilles' heel.

Her name is Marina Shakarova, president of the Russian Federation.

"I'll be damned," exclaims the president.

Double E Ranch

Goldie is holding on to his cowboy hat as the second White House helicopter lands about fifty yards away on the green lawn, not far from the swimming pool. He runs toward the white-topped US Marine helicopter the minute the propellers stop moving. A marine opens the door, and the First Lady exits.

She looks so beautiful in her black-and-white dress, wearing a large straw hat and a pair of oversize sunglasses. She gives him her right hand. He removes his hat, grabs her hand gently, and brings it to his lips to kiss.

"You are so charming," whispers the First Lady.

"It is always my pleasure. You arrived in time to watch one of the most beautiful sunsets in the country. Let's have some tea. I have some lemongrass tea if you want it."

"You decide for me."

"You are so kind. I notice that you came by yourself."

"I want to be alone with you."

"We can never be alone together. We know that."

"We were alone together at the White House, when you came to see me a few months ago."

"I see your point."

Goldie takes his guest to the balcony overlooking the pool, where a silver tea set has been placed. The First Lady walks to the rail and admires the pool and the surrounding area.

"Do you still love her that much?"

He is startled by her question and spills the tea.

"Your pool is in the shape of France, and there is a half-moon tile where Marseille is."

Totally speechless, he brings her the tea. He is torn between two persons he has loved more than anything else in his life—two women who have also hurt him. But he holds no grudges.

"I admire your loyalty, strength, and determination," says the First Lady.

Goldie tries to defuse the tension. "If you married me, you would not be the First Lady."

"If you married me, you would not be a cowboy. You would be the president of the United States."

He goes back to get his tea and raises the cup to her.

"To you! Here we are, alone together."

"To us! Alone together again."

He takes the First Lady to the cupola, where there is an unobstructed 360-degree view of the Double E Ranch.

"How do you keep it so green?"

"I developed an irrigation system similar to what the Khmer people used in the twelfth century, except I have a rigorous maintenance schedule."

"Tell me about the ranch, cattle, fence, wells, et cetera."

"The fence consists of three strands of barbed wire on top of hog wire. They divide the ranch into three four-thousand-acre pastures."

"Do you have names for the pastures?"

"Northeast of the ranch house is María, and to—"

"Named after Marie?"

"Yes," says Goldie sheepishly.

"And what and who is the next lucky one?"

"Eugenia," he says, "after my aunt Jeannie."

"And next?" the First Lady asks anxiously.

Goldie smiles and said slowly, "Rosalia."

She rewards him with an affectionate smile. "And what else? Who else?"

"The last one is named after my mother, Marjorie: Margarita!"

"How many acres do you have?"

"Only thirteen thousand. Rather small by Texas standards."

"And cattle?"

"Six hundred. In the north—Kansas, Montana, Wyoming—you need only two acres per head. In the Texas Panhandle, you need about thirty. Down here you need even more. But I turned everything green with the irrigation after I bought this country over a decade ago."

"I understand you also have a bull."

Goldie chuckles at the mention of his new pet.

"Yes, I do. I actually owned half of it at the beginning. The other investor sold the other half to me after he moved to Azerbaijan to oversee a pipeline project. He is about nineteen hundred pounds and has never been ridden by anyone past four seconds. Not yet."

"Where does he live?"

"He has his own little kingdom over there." Goldie points to the north side of the ranch. "Between the Japanese archery range and the Mongolian ger."

"What is his name?"

"TUB." Goldie smiles.

"TUB?" the First Lady asks with great surprise. "That does not sound like the name of a great bull."

Goldie can no longer control his laughter.

"TUB is short for The Ugly Barbarian."

"The Ugly Barbarian? How did you come up with a name like that?"

"Well, he came to me with that name."

"When and where does Mister TUB appear next?"

"He is booked solid every month till Las Vegas in December for the PBR national championship finals. Next month Houston, then Fort Worth, Kansas City, et cetera. Even Wilmington, Delaware, and Manchester, New Hampshire. And Hartford, and Boston, which normally could not care less about rodeos; now they all want Tubby on the list."

"Do you travel with him?"

"No. Not to all of his appearances. I don't have as much time as he does. However, I plan to go to Jackson Hole, Madison Square Garden, and Vegas."

Goldie pauses for a brief moment while the First Lady sips her lemongrass tea. He whispers, "Do you want to go sometime? I will be much honored. I know you will enjoy it."

She puts her cup down and looks at him. He presses on. "I believe we have Chicago in November."

"I'd love to go with you. But my schedule is not mine anymore. Let me think about it. I will let you know as soon as I have some possibility."

"Thank you very much."

"My pleasure."

"Meanwhile, I would very much like you to meet him."

"I would be honored to meet Mister TUB," says the First Lady.

"The honor will be all his. You are the first First Lady he will ever meet. We will visit him after sunset."

"I can't wait. How many people do you have here?"

"Twelve coworkers, including cowboys and cowgirls and household staff. We use almost no motorized equipment; that's why we have more people than the usual ranch this size. Equal number of children."

"Are they all from around here?"

"Yes and no. Four families are from Texas, one from Kansas, one from Louisiana, one from Nebraska, one from Burundi, one from Guinea-Bissau, one from Russia, one from Brazil, one from Colombia, one from China, and one from India."

"It sounds like a mini United Nations."

"It does indeed. Together, they speak twelve languages—twice the number of official languages of the United Nations."

"You speak all of them? I remember you were always very good with languages."

"I speak only six of them. I can get by in four others. I know some basic Chinese and Hindi, and a few words of Arabic."

"Arabic?"

"The Indian family is mixed. The husband was born in India, and the wife was born in Egypt. They both speak Arabic and Hindi."

"How about their faiths?"

"I built a chapel, similar to the Cadet Chapel at the US Air Force Academy—much, much smaller, of course. They all can worship there under the same roof whenever they wish. They are Buddhists, Christians, Jews, Hindus, Muslims, et cetera. Some are mixed couples and mixed faiths. Yet they live in unity."

"They are like your family?"

"Yes, they are indeed my family."

"Where do the children go to school?"

"I have a kindergarten here at the ranch. The others go to school in Esperanza."

"How did you come to choose this place?"

Goldie has been waiting for this question.

"I had never traveled across America by car and decided to do it when I returned from Asia. I drove from Seattle to San Diego, then from there to Jacksonville on Interstate 10. Somewhere between El Paso and Sierra Blanca, I was caught in a rare sandstorm. Couldn't see anything. I stopped in San Antonio to visit a friend who is a real estate agent. She showed me one house in a wooded area. I bought it as an investment." Goldie adds some hot water from a thermos to the teapot. "A few years later, I decided to move to San Antonio and use it as my primary residence while doing other things around the country and around the world on my own. It had been my dream to have a little ranch, grow my own food, and live off the land, so to speak. One day I drove on I-10 from the Alamo City to Long Beach to attend an AOPA convention, and on to San Diego to go fishing off the coast of Baja California. I saw the For Sale sign and called the agent. I looked at the land on the return trip, got the right price. Et voila."

"It seems to me that you wanted to be as far away as possible from everybody else, at least physically," Rosalee says.

"Yes and no. I go to San Antonio, New York, and LA as often as I can, and when there is something to do. I still have the apartment in Manhattan. And with modern communications, you can be in touch with anybody around the world, visually or otherwise."

"You did create your own kingdom from this little ranch. Tell me about your water management. How about the wells?"

"I have a dozen wells. Each two-hundred-foot deep well normally quenches twenty-four drinkers. Each drinker consumes about twenty gallons a day. I only have Angus here. They are usually one hundred pounds heavier than Herefords."

"How about the hay?"

"I keep about two hundred bales of hay in the barn and they can last for a few years. Each round bale is the equivalent of about twenty-five square ones." Goldie stops and smiles. "I am not sure if you came here for me to tell you about ranching."

"I have felt very guilty for having hurt you. I want to see you again, and I also want to get some advice from you."

"I am all ears," Goldie says, ready to oblige.

"You know a lot about planes and Asia, especially China. There could be a major confrontation in the South China Sea about a plane. Tell me about the Boeing 787."

"Eight is a lucky number for many Asians, especially the Chinese. They hosted their first Olympics on August eighth, 2008 at eight p.m. (eight eight eight eight). Boeing rolled out its Boeing 787 on July eighth, 2007; hence, 787. The eight hundred eighty-eighth 787 is what they want. It will symbolize the EE, or eternal emperor, status."

"I can understand why the Taiwanese and the Beijing leaders want that plane to maintain their eternal emperor status. But why the Russians?" asks the First Lady.

"I think they want to exercise their prowess as well, and they do it to antagonize the Chinese, whose rapprochement with India they see as a threat to their security."

"They are ready to fight a war over a plane? This is quite crazy."

"Well, in the sixteenth century, the Khmers and the Siamese fought for one year over a white elephant. Both believed white elephants to be the prerogatives of kings, just as the Chinese considered dragons to be symbols of the emperors."

Juanita brings a fresh pot of tea and removes the old one from the table, keeping her eyes on the floor without looking at the two old friends.

"So who won?" Rosalee asks after Juanita has disappeared.

"The white elephant lived in Cambodia and wandered off to Siam. The Siamese wanted to catch it to offer it to their king. They began to chase the elephant, which returned to Cambodia. There were no clear border demarcations in the sixteenth century, and the two armies clashed. After a few thousand deaths, they decided to stop."

"What happened to the elephant?"

"It disappeared into the Cambodian jungle. There was also a theory that floated afterward that the white elephant really did not exist but was the hallucination of some hunters who spread the word. And the rumors and the misinformation resulted in a war."

"It is funny that each time we see each other, we talk about elephants."

Goldie pours some tea for the First Lady, making sure he does not spill it this time. "By the way, what happened to the Cambodian elephant?"

"The king told me at the state dinner that night that the elephant recognized me from the beginning. She felt that she was responsible for my fall some decades earlier; that is why she cried and tried to push me away from the edge of the elephant terrace. She was afraid that I might fall again."

"She has known you longer than your husband and the rest of the country. And the rest of the world." Goldie offers some pastries to Rosalee.

"That's what the king said. He decided to give her to me as a gift. The briefing book said we could expect silk and silver as state gifts. We never thought that it could be an elephant. We were caught off guard. Initially I wanted to decline, but our people told me that such gesture could offend the host."

"What is her name?"

"Her name is translated into English as Diamond Girl."

"Srey Pich?" Goldie says.

"That's correct. When she was fourteen, our age when we were in Cambodia, they walked her with a few other elephants from the Mountain of Diamonds to Angkor. It took them about three months to make the trip. Imagine us walking for three months."

"Well. Elephants are very strong, and they never forget. How did you get Srey Pich to the United States?" Goldie asks the First Lady this question although he knows all the answers.

"She was transported in a C5 with her mahout and a team of veterinarians. We have been very careful not to have her suffer the fate of Harry, who was given to Truman by King Sihanouk, one of the king's ancestors."

"He died off the coast of Cape Town," Goldie says.

"That's right."

"I should tell you that I have been on the C5 used to transport Srey Pich."

"Really? Tell me more."

"I serve as honorary commander of the Four Hundred Thirty-Third Airlift Wing at Lackland. They once took me for a ride from Lackland to Rawalpindi over the Atlantic, then to Yokota and back via the Pacific."

"Wow, that was quite a ride."

"It was indeed. Where is Diamond Girl at the moment?"

"She is now on a tour across America. The children are all excited to meet someone who has known their First Lady longer than most Americans. She is leaving the San Diego Zoo today, I believe, for San Antonio."

"You met her when she arrived?"

"Yes, I welcomed her officially at Andrews with a group of children from the Washington metropolitan area."

"Your approval rating skyrocketed after that ceremony."

"We have been flooded by thousands of e-mails and letters asking for an autographed photo of SP and me. The Republicans are not happy that I am using their mascot to stay on top."

"From the elephant back to the plane: ask Boeing to build eight of the eight hundred eighty-eighth Boeing 787."

"I am not sure if we have any influence on an American corporation."

"You can influence anybody, anything."

"You think so?"

"I know so."

"You are too kind. How do I do it?"

"Next time you have a state dinner, seat the Boeing chairman next to you."

"And charm him to death?" Rosalee asks.

"That's right. They can help defuse global tension and make even more money by building eight of the eight hundred eighty-eighth Boeing 787s instead of one."

"Why eight?"

"One for each member of the G8: Canada, France, Germany, Italy,

Japan, Russia, the United Kingdom, and the United States. The Europeans will not take the plane, because they are trying to take the commercial airplane market back from Boeing. They will not want their leaders to fly in an American aircraft. So there will be four of the eight hundred eighty-eighth Boeing 787s to be split between the Chinese, Russian, and Taiwanese. Actually, the Chinese can have two. That will make everyone happy, and there will be no nuclear war."

"You are so smart. You have my private number. Please call me to refresh my memory before the dinner."

"It will be my pleasure. I do read or watch the news regularly. Please let me know when you have a state dinner."

"I will."

The sun begins to set, brushing the western skies with incredible red. They admire the setting sun for a magic moment together. She puts her left arm around his waist. He responds with his right arm around hers. When the sun is completely down, they look at each other and close their eyes.

CAMBODIA

Charles and Laura Hawkins check into the Golden Parasol Resort and Spa, a boutique resort at Kep-By-The Sea, about three hours on a smooth road from Phnom Penh.

According to their best friend Goldie, Kep used to be a beautiful resort city in the sixties. They went to Cambodia with him only once when he was living in Tokyo. At that time, they attended a Cambodian wedding in Siem Reap and drove from there to the capital city of Phnom Penh. Their vivid memory was eating tarantulas at Skoun, once featured in *Ripley's Believe It or Not!*

Goldie has so many connections in the kingdom that he arranged for Charles to deliver a commencement address at the Royal University of Cambodia and receive an honorary doctorate. That is why they were a little nervous when they missed their connection in Shanghai.

They spent a week in Siem Reap seeing all the big temples: Angkor Wat, Bayon, Ta Prohm, Preah Khan. They went all the way to Phnom

Kulen, where the Angkor civilization was founded in AD 802. They were pampered every day with massages and spas. They rode bicycles, motorcycle, oxcarts, water buffalo, and elephants. They particularly enjoyed riding the *Sok Sok*, a horse-drawn carriage, as opposed to the motorcycle-driven *Tuk Tuk*. They really had a blast in what they considered their last visit in Asia while still living in Africa.

They flew from Siem Reap to Sihanoukville, stayed at the Jacqueline Kennedy Suite of the Independence Hotel for a few nights, and drove to Kep. This is where they are really winding down before heading back to Cape Town.

They get up every morning before sunrise, watching fishing boats with their flashing red and green lights converging at the market on the seashore. Kep is well known for its crabs. Many of the boats carry their freshly caught products to the awaiting and hungry customers.

They swim in the calm sea for one hour; the water comes only to their chests a few hundred yards from the jetty. They finish their morning fitness regime with a few laps in the saltwater pool, return to their suite, wash, and change for breakfast.

They have had three-hour spa treatments each day since they arrived in Cambodia.

The rest of their time is spent reading and listening to music.

After five days of complete relaxation, rejuvenation, and reinvigoration, they fly from Ream to Mumbai and to the cape.

SIXTEEN

The Kingdom

JAIPUR, INDIA

S RICHANDRA SHIVARAM, THE Indian prime minister, presses the green button, and his intelligence chief appears on the screen. He receives daily briefings from her in person everywhere in India, except when he is in Jaipur. It is a weekend, and he is on a short reprieve at his favorite country home, not too far from the Rambagh Palace, where he occasionally uses the Maharaja Suite to organize his thoughts.

The intelligence chief is a woman of stunning beauty, matched only by her intelligence. She wears a red sari and an attractive smile. She immediately starts the briefing: "The new and possibly the most important player in Radha Suwanna is actually a cowboy in Texas. He was seated next to the duchess of Edinburgh at the state dinner hosted by Marie de Bourbon. He is a close friend of hers."

"How close?"

"Closer than you and I would have thought."

"Let's not get too much into people's personal lives."

"The French protocol dictates that the spouse of the guest of honor be seated next to the spouse of the host. MDB is not married. So she put the Cowboy next to the duchess."

"Doesn't she have a daughter? She normally uses her daughter as a cohost or cohostess. At least that was when she gave me a state dinner last July."

"The daughter was away, in Colombia. This is what we heard at the dinner."

The intelligence chief begins to play a tape recording for the prime minister.

The prime minister listens intently for forty-five minutes while the photographs of the state dinner flash on the screen, from the receiving line to the dances.

"My goodness!" the prime minister says at the end. "Have you ever come across his path?"

"Yes, sir. I met him when I was stationed in Tokyo as a commercial attaché."

"Do you know him well?"

"Well enough to go on a trip with him to Cambodia."

"Just the two of you?"

"No, sir. There was another couple; some friends of his from Alabama."

"What did you do there?"

"We primarily went to see Angkor. We also went to a Cambodian wedding of one of his oldest friends."

"Well, I will go from here to Thimphu next week. Can you come to brief me more about him?"

"With pleasure, sir. Good day, sir."

"Thanks. Good day."

TEXAS

The phone rings with the tune of "Fly Me to the Moon." Goldie picks it up very quickly.

"Morning, Marty. How are you doing, buddy?"

"I am fine," says Marty Goodson. "I have some good news and bad news for you. Which one do you want to hear first?"

"Bad news."

"The bad news is that our pal José is in the hospital."

"What happened? Is he okay?" Goldie seems surprised by the news.

"He is okay for now. He went to the Northeast Baptist Hospital for an inguinal hernia repair. I took him there this morning. He and I had a conversation with the surgeon in the waiting room before the procedure."

"Iris wasn't there?"

"She's been in Zimbabwe building a hospital with her church group. She is on the way back."

"I should call him." Goldie says, concerned, as always, about the well-being of his friends, especially his flying buddies.

"No, not right now. He is in the recovery room. They will call me when he wakes up. The procedure took about an hour, and it went well."

"When can I talk to him?"

"Probably not until late this afternoon. The nurses told me he should be back to himself noonish. I plan to have him home around two p.m. I will call you when he is ready to talk."

"Thanks for doing all of this, Marty. You are a good friend."

"You're welcome."

"So what's the good news?"

"The good news is that José is okay."

"I should have guessed."

BHUTAN, THE KINGDOM OF THE THUNDER DRAGON

The prime minister of India, Srichandra Shivaram, takes the ninety-minute ride from Paro, which is still listed as the world's most terrifying airport because of its mountainous approach. The road to Thimphu, Bhutan's capital, is very winding, with breathtaking scenery. With him sits the striking intelligence chief, in an exquisite yellow sari.

"What do I need to know about your cowboy?"

"First, I want to make it clear that I did not have any romantic relationship with him. We were very good friends." The chief pauses for a moment, waiting for the premier's reaction.

"I am not interested in personal feelings," he says. "I am not asking any questions until the end. Carry on."

"We met at a conference in Kyoto and became good friends because of our common interests in anthropology, archaeology, architecture, and Hinduism. We both like fish and once went to the Tsukiji fish market, where a six-hundred-pound bluefin tuna was auctioned off for one million dollars. I was in my late twenties and single at the time, and Japan was my first overseas assignment. I was initially attracted to him—"

"Please spare me the personal details," says the prime minister.

"Sorry, sir. I was trying to put everything together for you."

"I'll ask when I need clarification." He turns away and waves to a group of children in school uniforms. The intelligence chief continues.

"The daughter of the Bhutanese ambassador to India, who is also the dean of the diplomatic corps, is under his mentorship at the University of Texas in El Paso. He is quite close to the royal family here. He usually comes to Bhutan every few years, either in May or October, on his regular 'three Buddhist kingdoms' trip, which includes Bhutan, Cambodia, and Thailand. These are the only three left in the world. While here, he usually drives to the Bumthang Valley to visit a friend who runs a cheese factory there. He normally stops in Punakha and Thongsa to visit the dzongs. These two, along with the Tashichodzong, are on your itinerary after your call on the king and the prime minister.

"According to our sources in London, Paris, and Washington, he is closer to the French president, Marie de Bourbon, and the American First Lady, Rosalee Kartona, than many in the intel business could know. The British quickly put together a brief for the duchess, and they briefed her again verbally one hour before the royal couple departed for the Palais."

The intelligence chief turns the page in the leather brief on her lap and continues. "What the Cowboy told the duchess at the state dinner was all facts. But it was the tip of the iceberg. That is, about fifteen percent of the whole thing. I know him well enough to make this conclusion. That's why I wanted to preface my briefing with something personal."

"Wait a minute," says the prime minister. "Tell the motorcade to stop. I want to get out and greet those famers."

"Sorry, sir, you can't just get out like that. We don't know who these people are. Remember Mahatma Gandhi and Rajiv Gandhi."

"I have been here before."

"You were here when you were an anthropology student riding a bicycle across the country. You are now the prime minister of the world's largest democracy."

"I am the prime minister?"

"Yes, sir."

"Then do as I tell you."

"Yes, sir."

The motorcade suddenly comes to a complete stop. Bhutanese and Indian security people jump out of their trucks and vans and establish an invisible cordon as far away as possible from the farmers, who are drying their chili peppers in the sun. The prime minister puts his hands together in front of his chest and smiles. The famers return the *Namaste* with their hands on their foreheads and bow at the same time. The Indian visitor brings his hands higher, to his forehead, and keeps walking straight to the farmers.

TEXAS

The phone rings with the tune of "Fly Me to the Moon." It is Marty Goodson.

"Hey, Cowboy. The chief wants to talk to you."

"Hello, chief," Goldie responds with a smile on his face. "How are you doing?"

"Better already. Great to be home."

"What's next, pal?"

"I am under some sort of quarantine for ten days."

"What do you mean by quarantine?" Goldie asks.

"It is a restriction on my movement. I should lie low for ten long days. No sudden movements and no heavy lifting. Nothing more than ten pounds or a gallon of water. If I cannot urinate in the next three days, I may have to see an urologist."

"A few days go very fast, pal," Goldie says to reassure his flying buddy. "How about eating?"

"I can only eat nonspicy food and light stuff. The doc doesn't want me to have anything that could upset my stomach."

"And the bowel movement?"

"Yeah, I have to keep track of that also. Can you believe I used to control them? Now I have to try to pee and shit as soon and as often as I can."

"You will be okay. You have survived Washington; you can do anything."

"I sure hope so. In DC, I had to kiss a lot of asses. Some asses are attractive and clean. Not only did I want to kiss them, but I also wanted to lick them. Other asses are dirty and ugly. These are the asses that I had to kiss the most of, unfortunately. I almost puke just thinking of them. Now I have to kiss my own ass so that I can shit."

"You will shit soon enough."

"I will give you a shit report when I have one."

"You do that. I have some good news for you."

"What is it? I am ready for good news."

"I am coming to see you next week, and I have something you like."

"Wow. I think I know what it is."

"I'm sure you do. Meanwhile, do me a favor."

"What is it?"

"Don't be too anxious to get around. Take it easy."

"Yeah, yeah. And I'll try to pee and shit for you too."

"Good boy!"

SEVENTEEN

The Landing

THE EIGHT POWERFUL leaders of China are about to raise their glasses for the thirteenth toast of the evening when the president's principal aide comes running in, almost completely out of breath. He puts his right hand over his mouth and whispers into the president's right ear.

"What the hell are you talking about? General Hu, do you know this?" the president shouts in anger.

"Yes, sir?" the head of the People's Liberation Army responds with a soft voice.

"The American president is in Taiwan!"

"No, sir."

"No, sir what? Kartona is not in Taiwan? Or you don't know that he is in Taiwan? Or you don't know that he is not in Taiwan?"

"No, sir. I do not know that he is in Taiwan. Is it a joke?"

"Do I look like I am joking?"

"No, sir."

"Turn the fucking *television* on!"

The screen shows a dozen men in Speedo swimsuits trying to climb a greasy pole to reach the ultimate prize on the top: a beautiful woman in bikini.

"It's a goddamned Taiwanese game show. Who is so stupid to have the channel set on a Taiwanese game show? Get me an American news program!"

The trembling butler drops the remote on the marble floor, the back cover breaks open, and the batteries rush to every corner of the dining hall. Six waiters run after all of them and bring them to the mayor of Shanghai, who puts them back into the remote. He is brave enough to ask his almighty boss.

"Sir, yu won see in in or yu won fuks?"

"What the hell do I care? Just get me an American news channel."

Finally, Fox News comes on the screen, showing a picture of *Air Force One* surrounded in the distance by fire trucks and ambulances. "For those of you who have just joined us," says the newscaster, "President Kartona has become the first sitting president of the United States to be in Taiwan. We are waiting for reactions from Beijing."

VIRGINIA

The phone rings in the senate majority leader's home. He is having a cup of coffee and reading the Sunday cartoons. David Cardey, the chairman of the Foreign Relations Committee, is on the line.

"Bob, turn the television on if you are not watching it."

He does as instructed.

"*Air Force One* has been at Chiang Kai-shek airport for eight minutes already, and we have not heard a word from Beijing yet," says the newscaster.

"What the fuck is going on, Dave?"

"I think he is trying to cut the conservative base away from us, Bob. This is a master coup. And we are totally caught off guard."

"Why don't you round up the usual suspects and meet me in my office in one hour."

"Done."

"Wait a minute. Why don't you all come here? I'll barbeque."

"Fantastic idea. What can we bring?"

"Hold on a second; let me check the fridge. How about some Coors and Shiner?"

"You've got it. Any ice cream?"

"Blue Bell."

"Yes, sir."

Moscow, Russia

Beebee is overjoyed that the Chinese were stung by the US president's surprise visit to Taiwan. He agrees with his pals in the Kremlin. Nobody really believes that *Air Force One* developed mechanical problems on its way to Australia, as the White House publicly stated. The second presidential plane landed immediately after the first one to pick up its precious passengers. The Americans were in and out in thirteen minutes. The Chinese did not even have time to digest the development, much less to react.

By the time they lodged their protest, Kartona was forty-one thousand feet over the South Pacific. By the time they called the American ambassador to the foreign ministry to hand over the protest, the president was on his way from Canberra to Jakarta.

By the time the United Nations Security Council met at China's request, he was already in Warsaw for a NATO meeting.

Beebee is so pleased with the turn of events that he keeps playing Glenn Campbell's "By the Time I Get to Phoenix" over and over. He and his buddy Vladimir Chevsin, the prime minister, air dance with each other through the secure video hookup. And they sing together in unison: "By the time I get to Warsaw, she'll be rising ..."

EIGHTEEN

The Return

WEST AFRICA

B Y THIS TIME, Goldie is back in Letador. This is his fourth visit already since his first return to Africa after a long absence. At that time, he was escorted from the plane to the royal palace at two o'clock in the morning. The highlight of that return trip was that love found him again. He was reconnected to a paradise lost after some thirty years. He was able to solidify fast the lost-but-not-forgotten relationship, with a family Christmas *chez elle*, the president of France.

Another former girlfriend of his has become First Lady of the United States.

But this time, things have changed drastically in Letador, the birthplace of his true love. A violent coup resulted in death and destruction. Hundreds of thousands of refugees fled the war-torn countryside to take shelter in towns and cities. Letador burst into a violent fire.

Corruption, crime, impunity, injustice, and prostitution now reign supreme. A nation that holds great promise for prosperity due to newfound natural resources has plunged itself into one of the worst calamities of fratricidal rivalry.

Goldie's Golden Gate mission is taking on a life of its own. He came to Letador first on a fact-finding mission for a private equity firm. He now has the support of both the American and French governments. Yet nobody gives him any instructions on how to carry out his mission. If anything, they give him carte blanche. Goldie knows that his success depends largely on this ability to adapt to be adopted—*s'adapter et se faire adopté.*

This time he starts his visit on the golden side of the Golden State, the so-called Golden Jungle.

After a long and bumpy ride from the border, he arrives at the huge complex, with a sore butt. This has been a hill station, popular among the upper class of the country. From the French arrival in the nineteenth century until independence—for a hundred years, and afterward—the area has attracted Europeans seeking reprieve from the summer heat and the winter cold. Its elevation is about six thousand feet. It is lush and green and full of wildlife.

"*Suivez-moi, s'il vous plait*" (Please follow me), says the slender and pretty young woman who greets him at the massive and heavily carved wooden door. They walk through the interior courtyard of a well-preserved French colonial building with a fountain at the center. They enter a room that smells like lemongrass incense. There he is asked to take off his shoes. They walk next into a *salon d'attente*, where he sits down and waits for a drink.

A few minutes later, another attractive aide brings him a bottle of water. The door opens, and out comes a burly man with a big grin. "Goldie! My hero, my savior, my brother; great to see you again!"

"Same here, Lionel."

They give each other a bear hug.

"It has been a long while since we went fly fishing in South Dakota."

"Indeed."

"How was your trip?"

"It took me longer to come here from the Angolan border than to fly from Paris."

"The road is very bad two-thirds of the way. But once you enter our zone, it's like a farm-to-market road in Texas. How long can you stay?"

"Two, may be three days max."

"Spend three nights with me. I have a lot to tell you and to show you."

"Okay. I can't wait to hear everything and see everything."

"That's wonderful. Alice will take you to your bungalow and will take good care of you. I'll see you at six o'clock for cocktails."

ABOARD *AIR FORCE ONE*, OVER THE NORTH ATLANTIC

President Bill Kartona is relishing his latest move to outmaneuver the Republican leadership with very little diplomatic cost. His approval rating is up by eleven points. Conservatives applaud his thirteen-minute stay in Taiwan as brave and historic—a feat no president before him dared to contemplate. His visit to Australia, an old ally, and Indonesia, the world's largest Muslim nation and America's new best friend, was a complete success. The NATO meeting in Warsaw reinforced the US position as the undisputed leader of the world.

In the presidential suite, he has his feet on the table as he drinks bourbon and listens to dirty jokes by his senior staff. He calls this HHH, or happy humor hour. He wrote a paper on Hubert H. Humphrey when he was in tenth grade, and the initials stuck with him. Each HHH participant must bring one joke—a new, fresh one that has never been heard before.

By seniority, the chief of staff is called upon first.

"An Australian academic contacted a hotel in Hanoi to find out if she could get a special rate if she stayed a long time. Here is the conversation recorded by Chinese intelligence."

"Hao long yu satay?"

"How long do I stay? One month, maybe two"

"No proh blim; eye sapeisyan for yu on lee"

"You have a special for me only?"

"For yu on lee: voan bed, wit toy let in showa, voan ko fi mah shin—"

"Let me write it down: one bed with toilet and shower, one coffee machine ..."

"fuks mah shin ..."

"Excuse me?"

"fuks mah shin!"

"Sorry. I don't want it in my room."

"No, yu voan fuks mah shin; wen yur fren fuks yu, yu get fuks in rum, yu don cam to me to get fuks."

"Huh?"

"Yu get fuks in room; yu don cam, fuks cam."

"Oh, I get it. You mean fax machine."

"Yeh, fuks mah shin."

"Thanks. Yes. I want fucks in my room."

"Vat?"

"I mean fuks mah shin."

The president cracks up at the chief of staff's joke. As he laughs, his national security adviser tells him that the Colombian president is on the phone. She invites him to attend the Summit of the Americas, which she will be chairing next in Bogotá, after the one he recently hosted in El Paso. He says yes on the spot.

Kartona is about to call on the next joke teller, the counselor to the president, when another phone is handed to him. The French president congratulates him on the successful meeting in Poland and wants to discuss the situation in Letador at the appropriate time. France is going to chair the UN Security Council soon. She plans to call a meeting in order to settle the problem once and for all, and would very much like it if he could fly to New York for the meeting. She wants all council members to be represented by heads of government—at least the permanent five. He says yes on the spot.

The president gets back to his HHH before the bourbon puts him to sleep.

"You seem to have a hard time saying no to women," Sandi Bryce, the national security adviser, says to the president after everyone has left the room.

Still in a good mood, President Kartona beams. "One of the things I enjoy the most about this job is that my words are mantra. They become policy, and I don't have to explain to anybody. I love it. So tell me about Letador." Kartona is finally ready for the briefing.

"You have had a few briefings and meetings on it in the past six months. The first one was on inauguration eve, when I went to report a coup that was taking place in Paridor. I could not finish the briefing." A brief smile appears on Bryce's oval face before she continues.

"Here's to refresh your memory: The Dutch got to Letador first. The Portuguese arrived in the sixteenth century after the Dutch left. They stayed there for a few hundred years. The French chased the Portuguese out in the nineteenth century and have remained there since. They believed in an old legend that the kingdom was full of gold since ancient times." Bryce turns a page of her briefing book. "So they renamed the country L'Etat d'Or, meaning Golden State. The indigenous people transformed the French name to Letador. The population is almost half Muslim, half Catholic. It is now the most important French-speaking country in the world, besides France. Last summer during the conventions, oil and gas were found in enormous quantities. So were diamonds and gold. The Chinese and Russians moved in quickly to establish their presence."

Kartona waves for Bryce to stop while he removes his shoes and puts his feet back on the desk. He then says, "Go on."

"About three months before the election, our sources, corroborated by the French, reported that the prime minister with the support of the army and police would seize absolute power and immediately abolish the monarchy. Ironically enough, the king has provided some sort of stability to the country for decades. Something went wrong …"

"What do you mean something went wrong?" Kartona asks.

"We are still trying to find out the details," says Bryce. "The king was killed in the palace. The queens and some members of the royal family went to seek protection at the French embassy, which is a huge compound on the Enies River. The coup plotters blocked the road in time. Half of the family ended up at the Chinese embassy, and the other half at the Russian embassy. They were airlifted out to Beijing and Moscow. A few months later, the royal brothers reappeared in Letador. Three of them, the ABC brothers, went to Paridor. The oldest one, Jean-Albert, was put on the throne by the so-called crown council, which includes the prime minister. The other three, the KLM brothers, went to the east, where all the natural resources are. Jean-Lionel, the number five brother, is in charge."

"How many siblings are there?" Kartona asks.

"Twenty-four."

"Jesus Christ! How many wives did the king have?"

"Five!"

"He saved the weekend to rest or what?" The president lowers his voice and says under his breath, "What a fucker."

"I beg your pardon?" asks the adviser.

"Never mind. Continue."

"Since Portuguese times, the king was required to have five wives. He must marry a daughter of the chiefs of the five major tribes. It's a way to maintain unity. Each queen should give him at least one son. Only the second and fourth queens have sons. Hence, we have Jean-Albert, Jean-Bedel, and Jean-Claude (ABC) from the second queen, and Jean-Kit, Jean-Lionel, and Jean-Marc (KLM) from the fourth queen."

"So the rest are daughters."

"Yes. But two of them died in a plane crash, two in a car accident, and one in an avalanche while skiing in Switzerland."

"Are they all safe?"

"Yes. Most of them, except the two oldest ones, were living in Europe and Canada with their families when the coup took place. One is in Washington. You met her: Marie-Catherine Samas, the diplomatic dean"

"Oh shit! Fucking shit." Kartona's past is suddenly brought back to his memory.

"Sorry?"

"Never mind. What happened to the rest of the family?"

"Those who were airlifted by the Chinese and the Russians with the brothers were the cousins. Many of them went to France. Some to Senegal. A few returned with the brothers."

"What else?" Kartona is in a hurry to end the briefing.

"The UN did not recognize the new government. Its seat has been kept vacant. The donor community ceased its assistance."

"How much do we give them?"

"About three hundred million dollars a year, mostly in health and education and for women and children. CDC has a research center there. The overall aid program has been in place since the time of George W. Bush, when he provided fifteen billion to Africa's poorest. We are actually the third-largest bilateral aid donor after France and Canada."

"Who comes after us?"

"China, Russia, and Indonesia. About two hundred million each."

"The Chinese and Russians spend the same amount on UTMs."

"UTMs?"

"Under-the-table monies: bribes, corruption, graft, et cetera, which resulted in the January coup. One group went for the Chinese money; the other for the Russian."

"Fucking sons of bitches!" The president immediately ends the briefing.

NINETEEN

The Scandal

THE DIRECTOR OF national intelligence swims every morning for one hour at the University Club on Sixteenth Street. She is always the only one doing laps at four in the morning. She could swim naked and nobody would notice, because nobody is ever there that early. Besides, the swimming pool is closed to other members whenever she is using it.

Today she wears a purple bikini. Her body is as firm as a twenty-four-year-old girl's. She is halfway through her laps when an aide goes down on his knees at the other end of the pool to wait for his boss. She stops and holds her gorgeous body afloat by clinging to the edge of the pool. The breathless aide dares not look at her for fear of catching her extravagant cleavage instead. He manages to tell her that the president is calling a national security council meeting at 0900 at Camp David and that she can give him the intelligence briefing there before the meeting.

"Thank you." She returns to finish her daily swim.

Camp David, Maryland

President Kartona stays behind by himself for fifteen minutes after a lengthy national security meeting. He walks over to the next lodge to meet his guest.

Marie-Catherine Samas, the dean of the diplomatic corps, shows up a few minutes early. The president gives her his right hand. She does not take it. When she realizes they are all alone behind closed doors, she hugs him and begins to sob. The president returns the embrace, which becomes tighter and tighter.

"I think of you all the time. I've followed your career since you became the youngest state attorney general in the country, then the youngest governor in history. I've voted for you; I've cheered for you; I've traveled with you. I've prayed every night that I'd live to see you again."

"I am so sorry. Where are the children?"

"I've named them after you. Bill and Billie. The boy is a doctor in Chad. He moves from one village to another, providing free medical care. And the girl is an architect, an archaeologist, and an anthropologist living in France but working around the world. She occasionally travels with a group of people to very exotic destinations on a private jet."

"They are doing very well. You have been a good mother." Kartona and Samas still hold each other very firmly.

"It is hard to be a single mother, even with family support."

"You did a good job. I am proud of you."

"Thank you. Thinking of you has given me strength."

"Weren't you eighteen or nineteen when we met?"

"No. I was fourteen."

"Oh my God!"

"I look older than my age. Our teenagers usually look older than their age."

"Oh my God!" Kartona closes his eyes while he and Samas are still locked in a tight embrace.

"You were the first to touch me, and I became pregnant and carried your children. You know the rest of the story."

"Oh my God!"

The president of the United States has slept with an underage girl and is the father of her two children, whom he has never met.

TWENTY

The Jungle

GOLDIE JOINS LIONEL in the library, where a big map of the area is spread over a mahogany table.

"Here's your favorite drink to start." Lionel hands a mint julep to Goldie and points to Paridor on the map. "The Parisian crowd refers to us as rebels. I resent that. We are not rebels. If anything, we are freedom fighters. This country is big. From east to west, it is like traveling from Lisbon to Moscow. There are more people living in the western one-third of the country than the eastern two-thirds. But all the oil and gas and minerals and gold are on this side. I'll give you a complete tour tomorrow. Have you ever seen the 2009 James Cameron movie *Avatar*?"

"Yes, I have," Goldie says.

"There are one hundred times more resources here than they have under that sacred tree," Lionel says with great confidence.

"Wow!"

"Goldie, we don't want a divided country. But we are ready to fight for our independence. The Chinese and the Russians can supply us with all kinds of weapons. We can march to Paridor and capture it in three days."

"Lionel, if the Russians and Chinese support you, why do they recognize the government in Paridor? They are the only two in the world."

"They claim they do not interfere in the internal affairs of other states."

"Bullshit!" says Goldie.

"I think they are having their cake and eat it too. They are permanent members of the UN Security Council. They are going to veto any fucking resolutions you propose. Yet they secretly support us through Angola and Namibia." Lionel is getting less diplomatic.

"They are playing both sides."

"They are very clever. You can keep the goddamned seat empty as long as you want. You can stop your aid. You can freeze the accounts. You can impose the trade embargo. You can do whatever you want to make yourselves feel good. But the bear and the dragon are coming here *en masse*. They are going to eat your breakfast, your lunch, and your dinner, and drink your wine and your champagne. They are dancing the tango until the dawn's early light." Lionel walks around the table.

"They cannot do it forever."

"They can outlast you until eternity." Lionel pauses and then says, "Goldie, listen to me."

"I am listening."

"You saved my life, and I'll never forget that. Now you can save my people. Here's what I'd suggest you do ..."

MONROVIA, LIBERIA

The week after Goldie's visit to the Golden Jungle, he is together with Charles again, this time at SONO (Stars of New Orleans) in Monrovia.

"Laura and I are so delighted that you are making peace with your past and coming to Africa regularly. Thank you for stopping by and staying longer this time. I reserved a table right away after I got your message."

"It's so good to see you. You both have been my link to Africa for the past twelve years."

"And you ours to America."

"Where is Laura?" Goldie immediately asks after the two of them have been seated.

"Burkina Faso. Her foundation supports a few orphanages in Ouagadougou and Bobo Dioulasso."

"Do I get to see her this time?"

"Of course," Charles says, reassuring his guest.

"What's new since my last visit?"

"I have some good news for you." Charles speaks slowly, sporting a wide grin.

"What is it?"

"We are going back."

"That is so wonderful. I was going to ask when you plan to return. You've been here for twelve years already. I think you came here at the same time I moved to Texas. Let's drink to that." Charles and Goldie raise their glasses.

"That's right. It's a life cycle, isn't it? That's what you always say: Reinvent yourself every cycle, or every third of it."

"That's great news, Charles. So, where? New York or Alabama?"

"What do you think?"

"Alabama, Huntsville!" Goldie replies.

"Bingo. Laura is the only child. Her parents are getting older. So she wants to spend more time with them."

"And you are the only child too."

"My parents got married late. All my cousins are much older than I am. None of them are in New York anymore. They are all in Florida, Arizona, and California. One in North Dakota. We no longer have any connections there, except that little apartment in Manhattan. We've kept it all these years because of sentimental value. Not too far from yours."

Charles takes another sip of his gin. Goldie does the same with his.

"The two of you met there. I've stayed there a few times when mine was going through renovation. It's so convenient."

"We plan to go there on a regular basis after we return," Charles says. "So you can rendezvous with us again, and we will paint the town red, just like when we were at Columbia."

"We will make it happen. You may have to learn how to fish when you get to Bama," Goldie says.

"I know. I have been a hunter all my life."

"And you've gotten to be quite an excellent game hunter since you got here."

"That's one thing I'll miss, but I can always come back."

"You've got the big five: cape buffalo, elephant, leopard, lion, and rhino. Don't you have enough trophies already?"

"Never. I hate to say this, but it somehow energizes me when I am out in the wilderness tracking, stalking, aiming, and pulling the trigger." Charles waves to a waitress.

"Laura does not mind that you have become such a gun enthusiast. I wouldn't say fanatic."

"In fact, I am more a fanatic than an enthusiast. Ironically, she gave me my first gun as a birthday present."

"What a change of heart! She wouldn't let you own a slingshot when you were dating."

The two friends stop their conversation to order some appetizers, including spiders and tarantulas. Charles resumes their exchange with a philosophical approach.

"Well, you know women. If you put pressure on them, it can backfire—slowly, but surely. Patience and perseverance are what counts. Right?"

"Right. What else did she surprise you with?" Goldie asks.

"On my forty-fourth birthday, she came home from Kampala and asked me to pick her up at the airport. She had never asked me to do this before. We were living in Cape Town at the time. She had already started traveling a lot. If we had provided each other airport transfers, we'd have turned ourselves into a limo service. I did not suspect anything. She'd been away for two weeks. I missed her, and it was my birthday. I thought that we would go straight to a restaurant from the airport. But she told me to drive us home. And when we got there, guess what I saw?"

"A sailboat?"

"No. I've already got one."

"Another gun?"

"No. I've got plenty of them."

"A 1967 Plymouth convertible?"

"No."

"A mo-tor-cy-cle?" Goldie says very slowly.

"Yes!"

"No."

"Yes. A Yamaha V-Twin."

"I can't believe it. That is incredible. She wouldn't even let you have a scooter before."

"I know."

"Did she ever ride with you?"

"No. I once rode from the Cape to Durban. And she drove behind me."

"I am just curious what made her change her mind," Goldie says, fascinated with the latest Hawkins news.

"Well, she is always on an errand of mercy. I think she felt sorry for leaving me alone most of the time with two dogs, two cats, fish, turtles, birds, and a chimpanzee. And there I am staring at a computer all day long. However, she is always very good with letting me know her whereabouts: airports, takeoffs, landings, what she eats, how the meetings or programs go, et cetera. There is always a 'Somebody loves you in (fill the blank)' message. And she calls at least once a day."

"To find out how you are doing?"

"No. To find out if I've watered the plants and fed the dogs, the cats, the fish, the turtles, and the birds."

"I don't believe you. You're joking."

"I am not. She asks quickly how I am doing and spends the rest of the conversation asking about the pets and the plants. How is this one, how is that one doing? She loves Bow Wow, the cocker spaniel."

"She is so caring about others."

"She's never met a plant store that she doesn't like. When I see one in the distance, I try to distract her and speed up. When she realizes that we've passed a plant store and I didn't tell her about it—or, better yet, stop for her—she gets upset, and most of the time she asks me to turn around."

"Now I know why you've always owned a station wagon."

"It's easy for her to carry the plants!"

"What are you going to do with them when you move to Huntsville?" Goldie asks, very intrigued about his friends' return.

"The pets we will take with us. The plants—I think we are going to donate them to friends and neighbors. It will be a sad separation. I trust it will be a short one. Ironically, I've started to like them all, because I am the one who plants most of them and keeps them beautiful. I feel something is missing if I have not held a water hose in my hand for forty-five minutes on a given day."

"I am certain there are plenty of plants and trees to start your greenhouse in Alabama."

"I sure hope so."

"Oh shit. What time is it?"

"Seven p.m. or two p.m. Central, if that's what you want."

"Shit. I need to make a call."

"Here's the key. It's quiet, sitting in the car." Charles takes the keys out of his safari jacket and hands them to Goldie. "It's space oh nine to the right. Turn the ignition halfway; the screen will light up. Dial the number, and the other person's face will appear when the call is answered. Of course, you can use your own cell phone."

"Thanks, Charles. Why don't you order?"

"What do you want to eat?"

"Anything that is edible. I'll be right back."

Goldie presses one of his speed-dial buttons, and the friendly face of José Nochebuena appears on his phone screen.

"How are you doing, chief?"

"I am bored stiff, Goldie; otherwise, I am okay."

"Take it easy, man. Tell me what happened after I saw you," Goldie asks, referring to the convalescence of his flying buddy.

"Well, as you know, I started to pee on the second day after the surgery, and I began shitting on the third day; two problems less to worry about." José says.

"How's your eating and sleeping?"

"I've slept very well. And I am hungrier and hungrier. I'll have my first steak tonight."

"How about the pain level?"

"I think that I am now at a transition between pain and soreness. I've felt less and less pain. I've been using a lot of ice."

"How was the ten-day checkup?" Goldie asks while trying to lower the car air conditioning.

"Yes, we just got back when you called. The doc said everything looks good. He was impressed that I didn't use any painkillers. I told you I removed the gauze on the fourth day and had my first bubble bath. Oh, it felt so great, man."

"You feel better every day?" Goldie asks, pressing for more good news.

"Better and better every day, although doing nothing is killing me, man. I am now under a thirty-day limited activity period."

"What is it?"

"I can do things as my body allows: eat as I please, drink—in moderation, of course. Still no heavy lifting. By the way, thanks for the jerky. Where do you find all those flavors?"

"In Roswell."

"Alien Land?" José asks, wanting to be sure.

"Yes, Roswell, New Mexico."

"How did you land there?"

"I was driving back to San Antonio from Santa Fe and stopped there for gas, and I found this big guy's Jerky; he makes everything himself."

"I love all the thirteen flavors, especially the Cajun, the two chili (green and red), the habañero, jalapeño, salt and pepper, and the sweet and spicy."

"You like hot stuff."

"Yeah. Iris even more. She carries a baby bottle of Tabasco with her all the time. You got the jerky last Christmas, right?"

"Yes, I told you about that road trip."

"Yes, I remember that Christmas trip you told me about. It was below freezing for one week, wasn't it?"

"You have a good memory. There was ice in Santa Fe and snow everywhere all the way to the Texas border, some three hundred miles away. The heaviest was at Vaughn and Roswell."

"Whew, that's too cold for me. How about you? What flavor do you like?"

"I like all of those you mentioned, plus Smoky Cowboy and Chipotle Caliente. I'd better let you get some rest. I'll check in with you in a few days. Take care of yourself."

"Thanks, Goldie. You are a great friend. Safe travels, wherever you are."

"Thanks, José. Ciao."

"You call her every day. How is she doing?" Charles asks Goldie the minute he sits down at the dining table.

"It's not the one you're thinking about. It's a he. A friend of mine had a hernia repair."

"What kind of hernia?"

"Inguinal. On the left side. He didn't use painkillers after the procedure."

"What is he trying to prove?"

Goldie laughs. "Probably how to cope with pain."

"He is one of your flying buddies?"

"Yes. He is."

"How is he doing?"

"He is doing very well, but he is very bored. He is a very active guy, an outdoorsman, and doing nothing is killing him."

"How long is he under activity restriction?"

"One month."

"That's a long time for an active person."

"I've sent him a lot of things to keep him busy: music, books, magazines, and even jerky. He is a jerky man, like you. He has never met jerky that he doesn't like. He is also a hunter, like you. I'll introduce the two of you when you get back. I'm sure he will invite you to his ranch."

"Have you hunted with him?"

"Yes, I have."

"When was the last time?"

"This past winter."

"Tell me more about it."

"His grandfather started this little ranch called Red, White, and Blue in Bandera County, Texas. It's very small—one thousand acres plus, but only ninety minutes from San Antonio. He goes there every weekend during the hunting season, most of the time by himself with a few friends. I wrote a little hunting report on our last outing. Let me see if I can find it."

The waitresses bring the food as Goldie fumbles with his cell phone.

"Here it is. I'll show it to you after the dinner."

"How long is the report?" Charles anxiously asks.

"It's just over a thousand words."

"Let me read now. I can't wait."

"Okay. Here, it is."

Hunting Report: Red, White (Ghost), and Blue God's Country, This February

Day 1: Mateo picks me up at home, and we take off for another men's weekend. We go past Hondo with its welcome sign ("This is God's Country. Please don't drive through it like hell"). Bill and Rosa's Steakhouse and Saloon in D'Hanis, Texas, is a honky tonk kind of a place with lots of Western decor on the wall and hanging from the ceiling. A plaque reads: "WANTED: Good woman; must be able to cook, clean, sew, shovel horse stalls; must have a horse and saddle. Please send photo of saddle and horse." A guitarist performs country and western music from a little stage by the main door. M orders the house special—pepper steak. I have liver. Half a block east stand the country lodge, the post office, and another steakhouse.

We go to the D'Hanis Walmart, a true 24-7 institution. This is what cowpokes do on Saturday nights. We used to spend weekends with spouses, with children, with neighbors, at churches, etc. We get to the ranch around 2200 and go out looking for hogs. I get the AR15 ready while M operates the spotlight. We see deer and no hogs.

Day 2: We go to Devine, Texas, to have a classic Mexican breakfast at Los Arcos and return to the ranch. Roger, whose wife was an executive chef at an oil company, arrives with food and wine from the hill country. After shooting a 1905 Colt pistol right in the ranch backyard, we open a bottle of Oak Leaf Pinot Grigio and watch *Kelly's Heroes*, a classic WWII movie: Clint Eastwood, Telly Savalas, Don Rickles, Carroll O'Connor, Donald Sutherland. M and R take regular smoke breaks outside. The cozy fire renders us weak.

Late afternoon, we take our positions by a mesquite tree. M has the AK-47 and I have the AR15. R is in charge of the spotlight. I climb to the blind but do not fall asleep. After two hours in the cold and windy weather—I am never dressed warmly enough—we call it quits and return to the ranch. We now move to petite syrah and have an incredibly yummy mole. While the city folks go wild with the Super Bowl, we have our own bowls—of chili—and watch John Wayne's *Hondo*. We have no TV reception.

R outdoes M in talking our ears off. His oft-repeated "Anyway, as I was telling you …" is the equivalent of M's "It's to die for." Our last entertainment is another WWII film, *Enemy at the Gates* with Jude Law, Rachel Weisz, and Ed Harris. It's about two snipers trying to kill each other; quite topical. We hit the sack at midnight. I go to sleep fully clothed and completely covered up from head to toe, with a tuque and gloves; the only opening is one near my nose that I breathe through. It's so cold that you could hang meat in my room!

Day 3: Roger goes to Devine (pop. 4,000), a huge metropolis compared to Biry, to get coffee for us. It's a long twelve-mile round trip on Route 173. M cooks on the fire pit, and we have our "to die for" breakfast of brisket, farm eggs, and pork sausages around the outdoor fire. We look for arrowheads and find hog footprints everywhere, laughing at us. We go to the shooting range to get any final aggravation out of our systems.

Day 4: We are in the blind by 3:30 p.m., and we stay there for three hours. I read *Outdoor Life* and *Field & Stream* magazines and take a nap. One deer shows up, but he is too far away. No luck. We return to the ranch around 7:00 p.m., build a fire in the barbeque pit, drink beer, and munch on jerky. We cook deer sausages, rib eye steaks, tortillas, and beans on the pit. After our cowboy dinner, we go to visit Tony, a man in his forties who has spent his adult life restoring old tractors—some that date back to the 1930s. He is the winner of last year's championship with a 1969 Case 530.

As a courtesy, our host calls the sheriff's department to inform them that we are going to hunt feral hogs using spotlights. We don't want them to come out looking for gunshot noise in the middle of the night. We see a lot of deer but no hogs. In the Texas hunting season, we can shoot deer only during the day, from sunup to sundown. We can hunt hogs all year round, 24-7. However, they do not taste that good in the summer. It's all part of wildlife management.

We go to the older red ranch, even farther away, drink more beer, turn all the lights off, and look at the stars and the moon. Not a sound. I fall while coming down a few steps from the patio, my beer bottle still in my right hand. No injury. I should have held on to the handrail, though. We feel that Ignacio, the ghost, may have pushed me. He has never seen me before, and I did not say hello when we arrived. Both of the other hunting guests have been there. Joe practically grew up on the ranch. He killed his first deer, a seven-pointer when he was ten, sitting on his father's lap, with a Weatherby 300 Magnum.

We drive back from the red ranch without our headlights, as we had done on the way there, until we hit the county road. Upon arrival at the blue ranch, I turn in. Joe gives me the Golden Rancher's Suite, meaning I have my own private bathroom. What a treat! I fall asleep around midnight and suddenly awake at 2:00 a.m. to some stomping noises. I see Joe in the kitchen. He and Frankie are just going to bed. It is raining and we call our morning hunt off.

Day 5: I get up at 5:00 a.m. but stay in bed to read till 7:00. I come out and see Joe on the leather sofa with the fire still going in the fireplace. It is such a cozy scene. By noon, the sky clears up. We visit Ignacio's tombstone for me to pay respects. He was born in Mexico one hundred years after the thirteenth president, Millard Fillmore, and died in the area at forty-three. We go to Joe's range and shoot the hell out of every single gun in his arsenal: AK-47 ("This baby will get any frustrations out of your system"), M16, 1903 Colt, Walther PPK, etc.

By 4:00 p.m., we are in the blind again. I set up my telephoto lens and read a few more magazines. It is getting

windier and colder. They are not coming out. The weather
is not supposed to get any better the following day. We
return to the blue ranch, pack up, and depart. No kill, no
problem. Being outdoors is more than hunting. It is truly
reenergizing, rejuvenating, and relaxing. I'll be back!

"Very nice!" Charles exclaims. "When you go back, I'll be with you."
"I'll change it to 'We'll be back!'" says Goldie.
"That's better," says Charles.
"Bon appétit."
"You too," says Charles. "By the way, refresh my memory as to how
you got into hunting. I always thought you were more of a fisherman
than a hunter."
"I was not much of an outdoorsman until I got to Asia. I went
camping everywhere, including Bhutan, Mongolia, Papua New Guinea,
et cetera. When I moved to Texas, so many people asked me if I wanted
to go hunting. I would have had nearly nobody to speak to if I had not
been a hunter. First I thought I could just go bow hunting, since I already
knew something about archery. But bow hunting was much harder than
just shooting arrows. So I went all the way. I learned how to shoot both
handguns and rifles. I trained to get my concealed handgun license.
Since then, I've never missed a hunting opportunity. Now, you know I am
both a fisherman and a hunter. However, I am very far from your level of
hunting." Goldie puts a piece of Cajun antelope meat in his mouth.
"Well, you will get there soon enough. In fact, it would be great if you
could join me on my hunting trip next year."
"Where are you planning to go?"
"I haven't decided yet. I think it's either Botswana or Tanzania."
"How long do you normally go?"
"Seven to ten days."
"Please let me know when you have some potential dates."
"I will."
"Here's to our next safari."
"Hear, hear."

TWENTY-ONE

The Other Plane

LACKLAND AIR FORCE BASE, TEXAS

ONE WEEK AFTER his return from Africa, Goldie is on the way to his orientation. He thinks he has plenty of time to get to the base, where he reports for another familiarization tour in his role as an honorary commander of the 433rd Airlift Wing. The wing commander is a new best friend of his. They met at a motorcycle dealership in El Paso. True to form, he followed up with the contact. They became fast friends because of their common interests in aviation, biking, and horsemanship.

He reflects on how small the world has become. He just arrived from the jungle of Africa the previous week. He is now going to be introduced to the world's largest military aircraft.

He suddenly notices that buildings on both sides of the street have the names of aerospace and defense companies on their facades. He waves to a woman in battle dress uniform coming from the opposite direction in a low yellow convertible Mustang. She stops next to him.

"Could you please tell me how I get to the Growdon Gate?" Goldie asks.

"Which gate?"

"Growdon."

"I think you came the wrong way."

"This is not Lackland?"

"No. It's Kelly."

"Oh! How do I get to Growdon?"

"Go back to where you came from until Route 90. After going under the 90 overpass, turn left and left again at Acme, and turn right on Growdon, follow the winding road; it will take you to the gate."

"Thank you very much."

"You're welcome."

Goldie turns around and calls his liaison officer.

"Are you on base?" his contact asks.

"I am, but at the wrong base. I am so sorry to be late."

"It's okay. It happens all the time. I will ask them to wait for you."

Goldie knows that the military is very punctual, and he walks into the briefing room quite embarrassed. Fortunately, two other people are even later.

He takes an empty seat in the front row and gets ready to absorb the information.

After the usual welcome greetings, the briefing officer speaks loudly and clearly with a baritone voice as the slide animation moves every five seconds.

"The C-5M Super Galaxy is the largest aircraft in our inventory. It was built to carry outsize and oversize cargo worldwide on short notice, over intercontinental ranges. It can take off and land in relatively short distances, on six-thousand-foot-long (one-thousand-eight-hundred-twenty-nine-meter) runways. The C-5M can be loaded and offloaded simultaneously through the front and rear cargo doors, tremendously reducing transfer times.

"Each C-5M has five landing gear totaling twenty-eight wheels to distribute the weight. The nose and aft doors open the full width and height of the cargo compartment to permit faster and easier loading. It has a 'kneeling' landing gear system that permits lowering the parked aircraft to facilitate drive-on and drive-off vehicle loading and adjusts the cargo floor to standard truck bed height.

"It has thirty-six pallet positions. It has full-width drive-on ramps at each end for loading double rows of vehicles. Its system can record, analyze information, and detect malfunctions in more than eight hundred locations.

"It has twelve internal wing tanks with a total capacity of fifty-one thousand one hundred fifty gallons (one hundred ninety-four thousand three hundred seventy liters) of fuel—enough to fill six and a half regular-size railroad tank cars. A full fuel load weighs three hundred thirty-two thousand five hundred pounds (one hundred fifty thousand eight hundred twenty kilograms). It has a maximum cargo capacity of two hundred seventy thousand pounds (one hundred twenty-two thousand four hundred seventy-two kilograms).

"Its maximum takeoff weight is eight hundred forty thousand pounds (three hundred eighty-one thousand twenty-four kilograms). It has a cruising speed of five hundred eighteen miles per hour and a maximum range of six thousand three hundred twenty nautical miles without air refueling. With aerial refueling, the aircraft's range is limited only by crew endurance. Its crew consists of seven members: pilot, copilot, two flight engineers, and three loadmasters. Unit cost is two hundred million dollars …"

Half an hour later, and after dozens of slides, comes question-and-answer time. Goldie raises his hand first.

"Yes, sir?"

"Who are some of your distinguished alumni?" asks Goldie.

"The current chairman of the joint chiefs trained here; so did the air force chief of staff. We also had the governors of Massachusetts and South Dakota, and the senators from New York and West Virginia."

"Very distinguished group of men."

"Women! They are all women."

"I'll be damned," somebody says in the back of the room.

"How about foreign countries?" asks Goldie. "Allies?"

"I would have to say the president of Colombia."

"Is he still flying?" somebody asks.

"It's a she," says the briefing officer, who is herself a woman.

"I'll be damned," says the same voice in the back.

"Excuse me," says Goldie. "Who did you say is also a woman?"

"The president of Colombia, sir."

"I'll be damned," Goldie says to himself.

TWENTY-TWO

The Crash

T HE UNITED NATIONS is holding its General Assembly session in September. This year some one hundred fifty heads of state and government will descend on Turtle Bay, the eastside midtown part of Manhattan. Security will be a nightmare. New Yorkers will experience another limo lock for two weeks during the general debate. They dread those September weeks.

The president of the United States, Bill Kartona, plans to host a reception in honor of delegation chairs next Tuesday. He spends the weekend at Camp David reviewing his schedule with his national security adviser. It is filled with back-to-back thirty-minute bilateral meetings.

As he flips through the briefing book, his adviser holds a photo album with pictures of all his interlocutors, ready to show him when asked.

The first meeting is with United Nations Secretary General Luoes Gnaygnoyp.

"How the hell do I pronounce this name?"

"Louise Nee-ya-yee-yo-ip," says National Security Adviser Sandi Bryce.

The president slowly repeats after the adviser.

"I know you like to be on a first-name basis, especially with women," says the adviser. "For this one, it's easier to call her Madam Secretary General."

"How about Louise?"

"Actually, she is known to friends and colleagues as Louise. Do you want to go that fast? This will be the first time you meet her."

"I'll see how it goes. Where is she from?"

"Zimbabwe."

"Next?" Kartona can't wait for another profile.

"After the SG, you will have a courtesy call on the president of the General Assembly: Alex Orodara."

"That's easy. And where is he from?"

"It's a she: Alexandrine, but known as Alex. She is from Ouagadougou, Burkina Faso."

"Where the hell is that, and what the hell is it?"

"West Africa."

"Two Africans back to back. Background?"

"Sorbonne. Ambassador to Belgium, France, Canada, UN Geneva; education minister; and, finally, foreign minister. Little English. Fluent French."

"So am I supposed to speak French to her? '*Bonjour Madame! Voulez vous coucher avec moi ce soir?*'"

The adviser ignores the president's joking around and continues with her briefing.

"You'll deliver your address to the General Assembly."

"Where's the speech? And how long?"

"It's in its fourth draft and is not ready for you yet. The final draft should be in your hands tomorrow. It's about twenty minutes. They limit each speech to fifteen, but nobody is going to stop you if you go over. You are the host."

"What's next?"

"You go to the US mission across the street to meet with the president of Vietnam."

"What is his name?"

"It's a woman. Here it is, in the subject line of the memo."

"Another woman?"

"Yes, sir."

"What the hell kind of a name is this? I Phuc Yu? 'Nice to meet you, President I Fuck You.' Is that what I am supposed to say to her?"

"It is actually pronounced Ee Fook Yuy. You may call her President Ee"

"Madam President, maybe. Does she have a nickname?"

"Evelyn. The Vietnamese have turned over Cam Ranh Bay to our navy and Danang to our air force. And the United States is now the largest investor in Vietnam."

"How do you say 'thank you' in Vietnamese?"

"I knew you would ask: 'cam on.' And please don't tell her the Aussie phone call joke, please."

"I won't; don't worry. What is it again? 'Come on?'"

"Cam on."

The president repeats the phrase and asks, "Why don't I give her a luncheon?"

"You are having lunch with the SG and other delegation heads at the UN."

"I mean sometime later."

"We will work on that."

"Who's next?"

"The Russian president."

"Oh, I love her."

"Really?"

"Less than you; much less, of course."

"Of course. She is very attracted to you. Be careful."

"Background?" Kartona asks with a somewhat eager curiosity.

"Exchange student in Boise, Idaho, and Kumamoto, Japan. Speaks English and Japanese fluently. Engineering degrees from Moscow State. Manager and then regional VP of the Trans-Siberian Railway.

Visited a number of countries on railroad-related businesses, including Canada, where she traveled on the trans-Canadian line from Montreal to Vancouver, and on the *Sunset Limited* from Chicago to LA. She had a six-hour stop in San Antonio, where she toured the Alamo, the river walk, and the missions. She traveled on France's SNCF and on the Indian railroad from Delhi to Madras. Then she was mayor of Vladivostok for two terms, and became president with fifty-one percent of the vote."

"She got more than I did. What was her campaign slogan?"

"'Seven time zones and a quarter of the earth's circumference in my pocket.'"

"What does that refer to? The length of Russia?"

"The length of the Trans-Siberian express."

"Personal life?"

"Single mother with two children. Are you ready for this?"

"Anything."

"One daughter with your buddy, the distinguished senator from Idaho."

"I read about this the other day. Son of a bitch! He still has a hold on Michelle's nomination as ambassador to Japan. Let me see the photos." Kartona can no longer hold back his insatiable interest in the women.

Dr. Sandi Bryce, the adviser, takes the portraits out of the ring binder and displays them side by side in front of the president. She points to each of them: "Louise, Alexandrine, Evelyn, Marina."

"Jesus Christ. Four women: two Africans, one Asian, one European."

"It could be two Africans, two Asians. Marina was born on the Pacific coast, and her mother is half Korean, half Japanese."

"They are all gorgeous."

"You like women, don't you?"

"I don't know what to say." Kartona shows his sheepish eyes to Bryce and pulls her closer to him.

SRINAGAR, INDIA

Prime Minister Srichandra Shivaram spends the afternoon watching a friendly cricket match between the Indian and Pakistani army teams with the prime ministers of Afghanistan, Bangladesh, Bhutan, Maldives, Nepal, Pakistan, and Sri Lanka. All are members of the South Asian Regional Cooperation Council. They have just finished successfully their annual meeting, and he is hosting a lavish dinner for his guests in the evening.

He stands up to make the final toast. Except for the prime minister of Bangladesh—the only female of the group who does not even shake hands—the men embrace each other and wish every summit participant a good journey.

The prime minister of Pakistan has offered everyone a ride to New York to attend the UN General Assembly. The host declines; he has to go to New Delhi for a parliamentary meeting. He bids a warm *Namaste* farewell to all his guests in the long motorcade on the way to the nearby air base.

It is almost midnight when Shivaram makes it to Srinagar Air Base. He stops at the VIP lounge to wash his hands. As soon as he closes his fly, an aide hands him a note.

"Good Lord!" says the prime minister.

CAPETOWN, SOUTH AFRICIA

Goldie has been on the road again in Africa. He stops in Cape Town to see Laura and Charles Hawkins for the last time before his friends move to Huntsville, Alabama.

While relaxing by the swimming pool, he suddenly realizes that he needs to call home. Home for him includes the ranch, the state trooper, and the Bhutanese princess.

"Juanita?"

"No, sir. This is Juliana."

"Hi, Juliana. Where is Juanita?" Goldie asks eagerly.

"She and Guillermo went to San Antonio yesterday."

"What are they doing in San Antonio?"

"They are getting the house ready for next Saturday."

"What's happening next Saturday?"

"They said you are having a reception for the governor."

"Shit!"

"Excuse me, sir?"

"Never mind. I totally forgot about it. Anything else I should know?"

"Carmelita came by this morning with Miguel, looking for you first, and then for Juanita and Guillermo," Juliana says.

"Why didn't she call?"

"She did call you, but she couldn't get through. It is Miguel's sixth birthday, and he got top grades at school in everything."

Goldie can't help cursing. "God damn it."

"Excuse me, sir?"

"Sorry. Tell Guillermo that I am coming back on Friday and I am flying directly to San Antonio. I should arrive around four p.m. He can pick me up at the upper level. I'll call him when I land."

"Are you going directly to Randolph from the airport?"

"What's happening at Randolph?"

"The annual air show begins Friday night with a concert. And you have a scholarship fund for the top air force children in the country who have lost a parent. They usually announce the winners in the middle of the concert. And they have asked you to be present."

"What time is the concert?"

"Six p.m."

"Okay. I may have time to go home, take a shower, and change."

"You may not, sir. It's the weekend rush hour, and there will be thousands of people going to the concert and the night show. The traffic on Pat Booker will be like a parking lot."

"How do you know all of this?"

"My family used to live in Universal City. Remember, my father retired from the air force at Randolph?"

"Yes, of course. Can you send me something about the scholarship winners?"

"Guillermo has the list with him in San Antonio."

"Thanks. You think of everything."

"One more thing, sir."

"What is it?"

"Miguel looked very sad that he did not find you here. I told him that you left something for him. So I went into your gift closet and found a wooden giraffe you brought from your last trip to Africa. I wrapped it up in your favorite Japanese golden paper and gave it to him, with your compliments, along with a card and birthday wishes. I hope you don't mind."

"Au contraire. You did an excellent job. Thank you so much."

"You're welcome, sir."

Goldie immediately dials another number.

Goldie calls his state trooper friend. "Carmelita?"

"Hold on a second." She recognizes his number on her caller ID and his voice, and she wants to surprise both him and her son. She hands the phone to Miguel. "It's for you."

"Hello?" Miguel says in a quiet voice.

"Happy birthday to you! Happy birthday to you! Happy birthday dear Miguel! Happy birthday to you!"

Carmelita notices a big grin on Miguel's face. He says slowly, "Thank you for the giraffe."

"You're welcome. Do you know how to put a giraffe in a refrigerator?"

"It's too big; you can't put it in," Miguel says quickly. He adds, "Mom wants to speak with you."

"Hi, Goldie. Thanks for thinking of us. Would you mind if I put you on the screen? We want to see you."

"Of course not. Give me a minute. Let me rearrange myself." A minute later, Goldie appears on the screen. "We were talking about how to put a giraffe in a refrigerator."

"How do you put it in?" ask both mother and son.

"You open the door, put it in, and close the door," says Goldie in a laughing voice.

"I see."

"How do you put an elephant in a refrigerator?"

"You open the door, put it in, and close the door," say the mother and son.

Sichan Siv

"Uh uh! You open the door, take the giraffe out, put the elephant in, and close the door."

"I see."

"The lion calls a summit of all animals in the kingdom. One is missing. Who is it?"

"There are all kinds of animals in the animal kingdom," says Carmelita. "We don't know."

"The elephant. He is still in the refrigerator."

"Ha ha!"

"You now must cross a river that is usually full of crocodiles. There is no bridge. How do you do it?"

"We can't. We give up."

"You swim across the river."

"And the crocodiles will eat you," shouts Miguel.

"No. The crocodiles are at the summit meeting chaired by the lion. I got you, didn't I?"

"Very clever," Carmelita says, complimenting her son's godfather.

Goldie asks to speak to her privately.

"I am sorry to have missed you and Miguel when you came to the ranch," he says.

"I should have tried to reach you first. When are you coming back?"

"Next Friday, but to San Antonio. Do you want to meet me there? Bring Miguel along. I don't think he has been there yet, has he?"

"No. He has not."

"There are plenty of rooms at the house. We can go to the air show together. He likes planes. It would be a good birthday present for him."

"He would like that very much. Let me ask the chief first. It's such short notice."

"Why don't you fly instead of driving? Juanita or Miguel will pick you up. I hope to see you next weekend."

"So do I," she says.

He can hear the genuine longing in her voice.

Goldie makes his last call home to the Bhutanese princess.

"Hello, Kunzang?"

"Goldie! So nice to hear your voice. How are you? And where are you?"

"I am doing well, in Africa."

"When are you coming back?"

"Next weekend. San Antonio first, and then at the ranch. Do you want to come out for a barbeque?"

"Thank you for the invitation, but I can't. My uncle, the prime minister, is coming to New York for the UN. He asked me if I could fly there to see him. I have not seen him for two years. So I may have to take a rain check and go to New York."

"Please extend to him my invitation to visit UTEP. He is welcome to stay with me. I'll take care of everything. We can also have a friendly archery competition. I'll send him an official invitation soon."

"I'll be pleased to let him know."

"Thanks. Have a good trip. *Tashi delek.*"

"*Tashi delek.*"

A police car pulls Goldie over in Cape Town while Goldie is on the way to the airport. He is escorted to the French consulate, where the consul general takes him to a secure room. On the screen is his true love, also known as the president of the French republic. They rarely call each other on the secure line, using it only if there is something important and urgent.

"Hi there," she says. "I know you are coming here tomorrow. But I won't be at LFD. I am flying back to Paris in a few minutes. A Pakistani plane carrying the prime ministers of Afghanistan, Bangladesh, Bhutan, Maldives, Nepal, Pakistan, and Sri Lanka may have collided with a Chinese jet fighter over the Siachen Glacier a moment ago. We don't know yet how the near miss or the collision occurred or if the plane has crashed or made an emergency landing somewhere. I am a little distracted and won't be able to give you undivided attention even if you came to Paris. Can you meet me in New York instead?"

"Of course. I can meet you anywhere."

"Thanks. And thanks for the reports from Letador. I like your ideas. We can discuss them in more detail when we are together."

"Absolutely."

"As you know, France is chairing the UN security council this month. And I am hoping to find a lasting peace for Letador. Being with you would give me a lot of strength and determination to see it through."

"You are so kind."

"Bises!"

"Bises!"

Outside the secure room, the consul general tells Goldie that she has found a first-class suite for him on a nonstop flight to San Antonio. It leaves in three hours, and she would like to take him to dinner.

Initially, Goldie does not want to accept the invitation, fearing he is imposing on her. He would love to stay with Charles and Laura at their beautiful house in the vineyard. But they returned to Monrovia in the afternoon. Besides, it might be a Marie de Bourbon instruction that he be given the ultimate French hospitality.

He says, "*Oui, avec plaisir.*" But before they go to dinner, he tells the consul general he needs to make a phone call.

"Do you need to make a secure call?" asks the consul general.

"No. A regular call is fine."

"*Suivez-moi, s'il vous plaît.*" The consul general takes Goldie to her office and points to a credenza behind her desk.

"The black one is nonsecure. Dial one first if you call America. The white one is for France. You can dial the number directly without the country code. I will wait for you in the next room."

"Thank you."

"You're welcome." With that, she departs.

Goldie thinks a moment about what to say, takes a deep breath, and dials. "Kunzang?"

"Hi, Goldie!" the Bhutanese princess says. "So nice to hear from you again so soon. Are you still in Africa?"

"Yes. But I am heading for the airport in a few hours."

"You sound so close. Where are you? Can you tell me?"

"In Cape Town."

"I heard it's a beautiful city."

"It is. Are you by yourself?"

"Yes. I am at the apartment you found for me near the campus."

"What did you do this morning?"

"I've just finished my paper on presidential decision making."

"Who is the lucky one?"

"Your hero, George H. W. Bush."

"Anything in particular?"

"His decision to liberate Kuwait from the Iraqi occupation and not to go all the way to Baghdad to get rid of Saddam Hussein."

"Did you talk about the Security Council resolutions?"

"Yes, I did."

"Perfect."

"You know my uncle is going to be the next president of the general assembly. It's Asia's turn, following Africa's. And he is a consensus candidate. So he is coming to New York to thank everyone for unanimously electing him one year in advance."

"That's great."

Goldie cannot get himself to tell her about her uncle, the prime minister of Bhutan, who was on the Pakistani airplane that crashed in China. He is silent.

"Goldie? Are you still there?"

"Yes, I am here."

"Why are you calling from Africa to ask me about my studies? You never do that on the phone. You always ask me about them only when we are together. Is everything okay with you?"

"Kunzang, I want you to go to the ranch and spend the night there and wait till I arrive."

"What's going on? Why do you want me to go there if you are not there?"

"Juliana will pick you up in about an hour. Stay in your apartment until she arrives."

"Please tell me what's happening?"

"A plane carrying your uncle may have collided with another one a moment ago."

"Where?"

"Over the Siachen Glacier ... Siachen Glacier is where Indian and Pakistani forces clashed in the past. We don't know how it happened. We don't know if the plane has crashed or managed to make an emergency landing somewhere—"

Goldie hears a long "Nooooooo!" and the phone goes dead. He listens for a few more seconds, looks at the receiver, and puts it down. He puts his head between his hands and thinks briefly about what to do next. He calls Juliana and Carmelita back and asks them to go to El Paso and bring Kunzang to the ranch. Goldie then calls the First Lady of the United States on her private number. She answers on the first ring.

"What a nice surprise! Are you hunting somewhere?"

"Yes, I am hunting big game."

"Good for you."

"Do you remember the great migrations we talked about when we were young?"

"Yes. I do."

"Seven of them broke away from the flock, and a hunter shot at them. How many of them were killed?"

"I don't know yet, but I will find out the answer for you soon enough."

"Thanks."

"You are so welcome."

Goldie's last call is to his flying buddy and Fire Chief José Nochebuena.

"Hello, chief. How is it going?"

"Couldn't be better."

"Really?"

"Well since we talked last, I went for my thirty-day checkup. The doc examined me very thoroughly and told me that I had passed the SSI stage. He said that the chance of surgical site infection is slim to none. I should be able to resume my normal activities slowly; not too much and not too fast. I should build up my endurance little by little. It should take from two to four weeks for me to get back to things such as riding my bike. There are three sensory nerves that go through the groin. They are the cause of some sharp pain on rare occasions. His parting words were nothing to worry about. The swelling and that little weenie-like lump will take a few more months to completely disappear."

"What is the weenie?"

"It looks like a little sausage in the surgical site. It will disappear by itself in a few months."

"How about that other activity?"

"What other activity? You mean sex?"

"Yeah."

"The doc said no problem. Just like the other activities, slowly but surely."

"What does it mean?"

"I think he meant no rough sex."

"Can you manage it?"

"Of course, I can. I am not like Marty, whose Ugly Barbarian is always alert."

"Good boy. I will be back next weekend. Let's go hunting."

"Yeah, now you are talking. I want to go to a range first. I've been out of practice for a few months."

"Not to worry. We are going to Joe's ranch; Joe is one of my hunting buddies. He has a shooting range, and he has quite an arsenal. Have you ever shot a Kalashnikov before?"

"No, I have not."

"Well, you are in for a big treat, buddy."

"There are a lot of them around the world. Somehow, I've never pulled a trigger on one of them."

"Neither have I until this year. Yes, there are some one hundred million of them, about twenty percent of small arms in the world."

"Call me when you get in, Cowboy."

"Will do. Get your gear ready!"

Goldie ends the call and walks out of the office. The French consul general asks if Goldie wants to be alone until departure.

"No. Let's go and have a nice dinner."

"How about the Butcher's Knife? I understand you love a good steak."

"Oui, Madam!"

"I am not married."

"Oui, Mademoiselle."

They both laugh.

"I've asked for a private room with a telephone, in case you need to make any other calls," says the consul general.

"Thanks."

After they sit down, she says to him, "We have alerted your private pilot to meet you at SAT upon arrival."

"Thanks."

He studies her while she orders wine and appetizers. She is a slender brunette with a striking figure and is very elegantly dressed. She wears a gentle smile, and her perfume is killing him. He assumes she must be in her late thirties. A complete woman in his book.

As they raise their glasses of red wine, only one person comes to his mind who can think of everything: MDB. Marie de Bourbon. He cannot resist quenching his curious thirst.

"I presume you know the president."

"Yes, I do."

"May I ask how long have you known her?"

"I've known her since I was an intern one summer in her office at the French embassy in Phnom Penh."

"Were you a university student?"

"Sort of. I was first year at the Sorbonne at the time."

"You've stayed in touch with her?"

"Yes, I have. I've learned so much from her. She is the one who told me to get into ENA. She gave me a good recommendation. That's how I got in. My grades were not stellar."

"She is a very caring person."

"She is indeed."

"Here's to her, and to you!" Goldie offers a toast to the president of France and his dinner companion.

"Here's to her, and to you!" The French consul repeats the toast to the president of France and her dinner companion.

They are silent for a moment as they look at each other and smile. She can't resist his glare and looks away through the window.

"What do you like to do on weekends?" he asks his hostess, finally breaking the silence.

"I practice piano."

"What do you play?"

"Mozart, Chopin, Schumann, Tchaikovsky."

"Anybody more recent?"

"Ravel, Saint Saëns, Villa-Lobos."

"Wow. What else do you do?"

"I go out with friends to a play or a concert, or for a drive to the vineyards. And I like catching up with some reading and listening to music."

"What kind of music? I presume classical."

"Classical, of course. And you? What do you like to do on weekends?"

"Well, I don't actually have weekends. Ranchers work every day. And I am having fun every day. If I want to clear my head, I go for a ride on one of my beloved bikes or one of my beloved horses in late afternoon, before sunset."

"How many horses do you have?"

"I have four that I ride regularly."

"That doesn't seem to be a lot for a rancher."

"We have another dozen that the ranch hands ride. Some of the cowboys and cowgirls prefer to ride their own horses. These are work horses, ranch horses, trained to herd cattle and do all sorts of things."

Goldie is eager to move away from the horse topic when his hostess smiles and asks, "How about race horses?"

"Only two. I am actually a partial owner of two, but they do not live on the ranch."

"Where are they living?"

"One in Massachusetts and one in Virginia."

"No Matter What Happens, Never Give Up Hope," says the consul general. "And the other is You Didn't Think I Could Do It, Did You?."

"You know everything." Goldie offers a gentle smile.

"I have my sources. Why such long names?"

"Well, I actually wanted to name the first one Esperanza and the second one I Can Do It. But I was outvoted by my partners. They knew I had been a big fan of *Golden Bones* which pretty much told the story of the author's mother's love and sacrifice."

"And the second horse?"

"My partners also knew that I am a big fan of Ronald Reagan's plaque that read, 'It CAN Be Done.' So they recommended the name You Didn't Think I Could Do It, Did You?."

"Nobody can ever forget those names."

"That's right. A few decades ago, the winners' names were The Sun Rises Soon Enough, I'll Have Another, Daddy Nose Best, et cetera."

"And both of your horses were the first to win the Triple Crown two years in a row."

"They are very good horses."

"And Hollywood is making a movie about No Matter What Happens Never Give Up Hope and You Didn't Think I Could Do It, Did You?. Is the movie's title going to be that long?"

"I think it's called *Do It With Hope* or *Hope Does It.*"

"And who is playing you?"

"I am not in the movie. During our negotiation, I managed to convince everyone that it would be best for the story to have only one owner of the two horses instead of four. So our female partner will have a principal role. Besides, she spends more time with the two horses than the three of us combined. She loves horses more than anybody I've ever met."

"Will you have any credit in the movie?"

"I may be listed as an executive producer."

"When is it due for release?"

"Christmas holidays."

"My goodness. I can't wait to see it."

"I hope you will enjoy it."

"I will give you a review afterward."

"Thanks."

The two diners raise their glasses and sip their wine at the same time. The consul steers the conversation to another of her guest's favorite subjects.

"So, how many bikes do you have?"

"Thirteen."

"Wow. Do you have a favorite one?"

"Not really. I like all of them equally. Depending on where I go and how long the ride is, I choose the bike accordingly."

"What's the longest ride you've been on?"

"San Antonio to Washington. Then from DC to Sturgis, and Sturgis back to San Antonio."

"Are you an Iron Derrière?" she asks with a chuckle.

"You mean Iron Butt?"

"Whatever you say."

"Yes, I am. I am also a Bun Burner," Goldie replies while laughing.

"How does one qualify to be an Iron Burner?"

"Iron Butt? In the past, you had to ride a thousand miles—"

"Sixteen hundred kilometers?"

"Right. Sixteen hundred kilometers within twenty-four hours."

"My Lord. Where did you do it?"

"From Glendale, Arizona to San Antonio, Texas!"

"How long did it take you to do it?"

"About eighteen hours. I had to stop every three hours to get fuel and stretch my legs. I started at four in the morning, saw the sun rise in front of me, and later saw the sun set in my rearview mirrors. When I got off the bike in San Antonio, I walked like a cowboy who had been on a cattle drive for a few days."

The consul general burst into attractive laughter. "Did you want to do that trip, or was there a schedule you had to meet?"

"I had to pick up a new bike in El Paso. So I flew there to get my bike and rode it to Luke Air Force Base, where I attended the change of command of a friend of mine. Then I had to return to San Antonio the following day with the new bike. Ironically, I did that route on a C-5M. It took us less than three hours. During the ride, I was dreaming that if had a cargo plane like a C-130 or C-17, I would put my bike on it. But then I would have never become an IB or a BB."

"What's BB?"

"Bun Burner. Fifteen hundred miles in thirty-six hours."

"Everything in your life seems to have happened for a reason."

"Indeed."

The steak is truly one of the best he has ever had. And the red wine is also something to write about. He compliments his host for the choices. He concludes that it is actually one of the best meals he has ever had in Africa. It is a great combination of food, wine, company, and conversation. He makes sure his host—the French consul general—knows it. And she is very pleased with all the compliments.

In the American United flight from Cape Town to San Antonio over the South Atlantic, Goldie turns on the "do not disturb" light on the door of his first-class suite the minute he gets in. He wants to have all the time to think. There are plenty of drinks in the baby refrigerator.

He has been thinking hard about his next move. There are a lot of what-ifs. He is able to put some pieces together over the South Atlantic two hours after takeoff. He needs a drink. He gets up and notices an envelope being slipped under the door. He opens it and sees a smiling flight attendant. She has pulled the envelope back and gives it to him.

"It's from the captain. I am sorry; I was trying to be as quiet as I could."

"No. Not to worry. I was going to take a walk anyway. I usually try to stretch my legs every few hours."

"That's a good regime. May I get anything for you?"

"No, thanks. I have everything in there."

"Please call me—I am Nancy—if you need anything. Anything at all!"

"Many thanks, Nancy."

Goldie goes back inside and opens the envelope. A message inside reads, "Gun jammed. Birds safe to rejoin flock."

He smiles and says to himself, "Thanks, romeo alpha whiskey." That's Rosalee Ann Whitney. Her maiden name.

DOUBLE E RANCH

Goldie is truly in hog heaven when he is at his ranch. He is usually in the Golden Pavilion one hour before sunrise. He meditates until the rays of the sun hit his face strongly enough to make him open his eyes.

After a breakfast of fruit and yogurt or cereal, he inspects his amazing collection of samurai armor. Each has a complete set of defenses that cover every part of the warrior's body from shins (covered by greaves), lower and upper thighs, body (covered by a cuirass), arms, shoulders, hands, face, and head (covered by a *kabuto* [helmet]). His favorite one is the *suigyu-no-wakidate*, or water buffalo horn. The beautiful armor is made of numerous plates of lacquered metal tied together with beautiful silk.

Neatly displayed against the four walls and between the mannequins are *daishos* (pairs of swords) with the *wakizashi* (short sword) mounted on top of the stand above the *katana* (long sword).

The Golden Pavilion, named after Kyoto's Kinkaku-ji, is Goldie's own version of a war-and-peace room, a contrast of peaceful meditation in a room full of weapons. They are constructed of the softness of silk and the strength of metal. This is where he spends at least one hour a day, either at sunrise or sunset, to organize his thoughts.

He admires his new acquisition. He thought that it would go well here along with all his Japanese collections and close to the butsudan, or shrine. He is barefoot and steps back gingerly on the tatami floor all the way to the opposite wall. He closes his eyes and takes thirty-six deep breaths and opens his eyes little by little to savor the new masterpiece. He moves his eyes very slowly from top to bottom, and left to right, and in the opposite directions. Finally, he whispers to himself, "This is it." He brings his two palms together in front of his chest and bows his head until his upper body is almost perpendicular to the wall.

The phone rings in his study with the tune of "You Are the Sunshine of My Life." Goldie picks the phone up with a smile. He actually always smiles each time he picks up the phone. It is his way to cheer himself up to make the other person feel a pick-me-up mood. Kunzang, the Bhutanese princess, is on the line. Her soft voice energizes him immediately.

"How are you doing, sweetie?" Goldie asks.

"I am better. Thanks for asking."

"What happened?"

"I had an accident," Kunzang says in a quiet voice.

"Are you hurt?"

"No. I am okay."

"What kind of accident?"

"I ran a red light and hit another driver."

"Did you wear your seat belt?"

"Yes, I did."

"Did the airbag go off?"

"No. It did not."

"Did you have any passengers, or were you by yourself?"

"I was by myself."

"Was it a business or pleasure ride?"

"I was on my way to school."

"In your words, describe to me how it happened?"

"I didn't see the light, went through it, and hit the other car."

"I presume you called the insurance company and the police?"

"Yes, I did. And they asked me the same questions you have just asked."

"So they said it was an at-fault accident?"

"Yes, they did. It was a front-end collision. My policy, the one you helped me get, has a few-hundred-dollar deductible."

"And it also covers car rental for fifty dollars a day up to a thousand dollars?" Goldie asks.

"Yes. How do you know so much about all this?"

"I had a similar accident in Houston some years ago. I was daydreaming and did not see the red light, went through it, and hit the car of a pregnant Eritrean woman with a toddler in the backseat."

"Oh my God. Were they hurt?"

"Thank God, they were not. I forgot to ask you about the other car."

"He was not hurt."

"Who is he?"

"He is a veteran of the Second Korean War with a Purple Heart, a double amputee."

"Oh my God."

"I ran to him, and he asked me first if I was okay. I said, 'Yes. And how about you?' He looked at me and saw a pale face and a very shaken girl. He reached out to hold my hand and said, 'The good Lord is looking after us. And I am thankful that you are not hurt and that we are both okay.'"

"Quite a human being!"

"While we were waiting for the police, he asked me if I was from Asia. I said I was born in Bhutan. He thought I was from Korea, because he said, 'I lost parts of my body there.'"

"Did he tell you his story?" Goldie asks.

"Yes, he did. Shortly after the North invaded the South, his unit was the first to push back the invasion and go all the way to Pyongyang. They were the first to occupy the presidential palace. He was walking in the garden, inspecting the flowers, when a land mine exploded and wounded a few of his soldiers. He rushed to rescue all of them and was wounded himself."

"No one would imagine that the North Koreans would plant mines in the presidential garden before they surrendered," Goldie says.

"That's right. Flowers are what he called 'my strongest weakness.' He has quite a collection of orchids in his greenhouse in Ruidoso."

"What service and what rank was he?"

"Colonel Alain Lamenace, United States Marines Corps."

"Sounds like a French name."

"Yes, it is. His ancestors came to America with Lafayette to fight in the Revolutionary War. One went back to France on the same boat with Ben Franklin. One returned to the United States in 1826 with Lafayette and later resettled in Texas."

"Quite a history! You love history?"

"I learned it from you."

"Please go on with the colonel."

"He was operated on in a C-5M on the way to the US military hospital in Koh Kong."

"In Cambodia?"

"Yes, in Cambodia. He lost one leg over Ulan Bator and another one over Danang."

"Amazing. I would very much like to meet him."

"I took the liberty of inviting him to your ranch to see your orchid collection and your gardens. He wanted to see your bikes also. He is a rider like you."

"Both horses and bikes? Or trikes?"

"Horses and bikes and trikes."

"I'll be damned."

"How old is he? He must be at least in his late seventies or early eighties."

"Are you ready? He is ninety-six years young. It was his ninety-sixth birthday when I hit him."

"Oh my God! You hit a ninety-six-year-old veteran, a double amputee, on his birthday? I hate to ask you this, but what were you thinking?"

"You are not going to believe this," Kunzang says to Goldie.

"Try me."

"I was reading a book!"

"You were reading a book while driving? I can't believe this."

"As I said, you are not going to believe it."

"May I ask you why? Don't you spend enough time reading books? Why can't you wait for thirteen minutes to get to the campus?"

"I love Carmelita and admire her strength and her beauty. I love her even more after she came to pick me up and took me to the ranch. I checked out a state trooper examination book and marked the section I wanted to read when I got to the library. At a traffic light, a female state trooper stopped in the next lane. I smiled at her, and she smiled at me and saluted me when she left to get on I-10. I opened the examination book at the marker and switched my eyes between the pages and the traffic on the road. I read, 'The state trooper must be intelligent, healthy, physically strong and agile, emotionally stable and honest.' I looked at the road ahead; it was still clear, so I turned my eyes to the book: 'After completing recruit school and being confirmed as a State Trooper, a wide variety of career choices opens up: aviation, canine, investigation (complaint, criminal), emergency support, laboratory, motorcycle, recruit school instructor, recruiting officer, traffic enforcement, underwater recovery, youth services, etc.' My eyes went back on the road. There was nobody in front of me, and I was still on the same lane. Back to reading: 'After five years of satisfactory service, the lucky trooper can be advanced to sergeant shift commander and detective sergeant.' Bang! I hit the marine's car on the right side of his backseat."

"Oh my God. You could be on the front page of the *El Paso Times*."

"We both were: 'Bhutanese Princess Runs Light, Hitting 96-Year-Old Decorated Marines Vet, While Reading State Trooper Exam Book.'"

"Oh my God! It must be one the longest headlines of the newspaper."

"It is, according to Ripley's Believe It or Not!"

"I'll be damned. I haven't talked to you for one week and you made it into Ripley's."

"I am so sorry if I hurt your feelings for not calling you earlier."

"It's okay. The most important thing is that you both are fine."

"He has become my new best friend," Kunzang says, referring to her marine friend.

"Good for you. The irony in this is that there are laws against cell phone use and texting while driving, but there is none on reading while driving. Because nobody ever thought that somebody would be reading while driving. I bet the Texas legislature is going to have a law against reading while driving soon." Goldie says.

"It is being debated. It was introduced by one of your friends, State Senator Hope Grace."

"Why didn't you call me after the accident?"

"I was so absorbed by the marine's story, and the insurance agent and the police officer were so nice that I totally felt that it would be okay to tell you later. I did call Carmelita, as I thought you were still on the road. She told me that you had just arrived at the ranch, but that you must be exhausted. And since everything was okay, she suggested that I should give you some time to decompress. And suddenly, it has been a week. The other amazing anecdote is that the female trooper who saluted me was actually going to relieve Carmelita on the highway patrol beat."

"I am becoming speechless."

"I think you'll love him. The two of you have a lot of things in common. Like you, he is a history buff and has been to all presidential birthplaces, museums, and libraries in the country."

"Amazing."

"He just returned from Massachusetts, where he visited, for the second time, the JFK Library, and the birthplaces of John Adams, John Quincy Adams, John F. Kennedy, and George H. W. Bush."

"How about Calvin Coolidge?"

"You are pulling my leg. Although he was governor of Massachusetts before becoming president, Coolidge was not born there. He was born in Vermont, although he did live in Massachusetts most of his life. My marine friend told me that it was quite a challenge for him to go from Brookline to the JFK library."

"I bet you know exactly where and when JFK was born," Goldie says.

"Eighty-three Beals Street, on May 29, 1917, three years after his parents married and moved there. They later moved two blocks away, to Abbotsford Road, and lived there till 1927, when they moved to New York."

"How about Bush?"

"Shortly after he was born, his family moved to Connecticut, where he went to Yale, fought in World War II, got married to Barbara, and became the father of his oldest son, the forty-third president." Kunzang replies.

"I am very impressed."

"I tried to keep up to your expectations."

"You have exceeded them, though they are high. When can I meet my—our—new best friend?"

"This weekend, if your schedule permits."

"We will make it happen. I also have something to show you."

"What is it? Please tell me."

"It's a new Japanese painting from the Edo period."

"1608–1868?"

"Yes. You are amazing."

"What kind of painting?"

"It's a thirteen-panel screen, about thirteen feet tall, of an elephant and an eagle."

"Very beautiful. Where did you put it?"

"In the Golden Pavilion."

"I can't wait to see you."

"Neither can I."

TWENTY-THREE

The Twins

CUBA

Henry Goldman lies down in a hammock at his beach house in Cabo San Antonio de Bolondron on the westernmost tip of Cuba, overlooking the Caribbean Sea. He usually brings a few friends with him from New York or somewhere, but this weekend he wants to be alone. He enjoys watching the sunset over Mexico's Isla Mujeres. This is where he relaxes.

The household staff never knows when he is coming, so a bottle of Cristal is chilled every evening. With an eight-thousand-foot runway on his property, Casa de las Esperanzas, he can jet in and out any time without any problem.

He always wanted to own a country—ruling it without running it or ruining it. So when the Cuban people said "Hasta la vista, baby" to the last Castro relics, he was the first to get in. Actually, he left his footprints in Cuba even before the so-called Cigar Revolution took root. In a sense, he planted the roots. He gave a lot of money to nongovernmental organizations, especially those that promote democracy and freedom, such as the International Republican Institute, its Democratic counterpart, and the National Endowment for Democracy, to support pro-democracy movements on the island.

When the US government officially lifted the trade embargo and allowed US citizens to travel to Cuba, only ninety miles from Key West, he was already there. His company has been buying everything: maternity clinics, hospitals, supermarkets, department stores, mortuaries, cemeteries. People say that from the cradle to the coffin, your life is intertwined with King Henry.

Cuba is just the latest country to become the private property of an invisible company. Goldman is, however, very careful not to have his name or his company's name show up anywhere on the island. But the leaders know to whom they owe their positions, powers and pockets, from the president, to the parliament, all the way down to the mayors and the police chiefs—to *El Rey* Enrique!

Along the way, the king makes tons of money for himself. It is a win-win situation, as he often says.

The next country he wants to *own* is Letador, the Golden State. A part of his name is already there. It is more complex and more challenging. And that is what he needs. He has become a little bored and restless with having so much money and getting everything he wants.

He has the following carved on a teak plaque and hung in his study here: "'Restlessness is discontent, and discontent is the first necessity of progress. Show me a thoroughly satisfied man, and I will show you a failure.' Thomas Jefferson."

He needs to do something to keep himself alive and competitive, so to speak. This new endeavor keeps him moving. The thrill of defeating his competitors—business, financial, political, and otherwise—is what he seeks. So far, he has made all the right moves.

For starters, Goldie has been a gold mine.

BARRANQUILLA, COLOMBIA

El Bosque Encantado is an elegant Spanish colonial compound with high ceilings and beautiful blue, green, and golden tiles. The garden is handsomely groomed, with colorful flowers and plants everywhere. The trees include tall palms, with branches flapping in the wind along with the flags of Colombia and France. There are attractive fountains in various sizes.

South of the main house, the two swimming pools are in the shape of Colombia and France. They are connected by an island with waterfalls producing very soothing sounds. A small red, white, and blue pedestrian bridge links Sainte-Mère-Église on the Normandy coast of the French pool to Santa Marta on the Caribbean side of the Colombian pool.

The property sits on top of the highest hill in the area. It is surrounded by an eight-foot fence topped with red tiles. The eastern view stretches all the way to the blue Caribbean Sea. It must be at least six acres and worth millions of dollars. *This is truly a classy place,* Goldie thinks. *It is quite rejuvenating and refreshing just to look around. And it is pure heaven to be with someone I love.*

He flew directly from San Antonio after the reception for the governor of Texas on Saturday night. He did not arrive till four o'clock this morning. He slept till nine and had breakfast by himself on the Brazilian terrace in a gazebo, southwest of the pool.

It is only after his *casse-croute* that he is able to survey the grounds. He now agrees with her that the two best places to recharge are LFD and EBE. He is anxious for her to arrive in order for him to tell her how thankful he is to share this part of her life.

A few minutes later, he holds on to his cowboy hat as the presidential helicopter lands about fifty yards away on the green lawn, the only clearance, not far from the swimming pool. He runs toward the Fuerza *Aérea Colombiana* (FAC) helicopter the minute the propellers stop moving. An officer opens the door, and the presidents exit.

They are two almost identical twins. Both are tall, attractive, and elegant. They wear handsome leather boots, black skirts, and red turtlenecks. One is a blonde, the other is a brunette.

Goldie kisses the blonde on both cheeks and turns to the brunette.

"My twin sister, María. This is Goldie, the person I've been telling you about."

"I am delighted to meet you. It seems that I have known you for a long time. *Encantada!*"

"The delight is all mine. I feel very much the same way. *Encantado!*" He brings her hand to his lips first and then kisses her on both cheeks.

Goldie is beside himself to be with Marie de Bourbon again in such an idyllic place. And the bonus is that he gets to meet her twin sister, with whom he did not get to spend Christmas at La Forêt d'or. He is very intrigued to learn more about how the two sisters ended up running two different countries across two oceans. This kind of rule existed mostly in Europe in the middle ages. In addition, they were born at the same time. How was it possible?

He knows this is going to be another memorable moment that he will cherish forever. The only bad news is that he will be spending the nights alone.

"María is very strict," Marie says to him. "We can spend all the time together, but we cannot spend the night in the same bed, the same room, unless we are married. This is her house, and she makes the rules. I hope you understand."

"I do," Goldie says with total confidence, feeling as though he is at the altar.

"I know you. I knew you would," she says with total confidence. She rewards him with a beautiful smile and a kiss on the lips. "My father was a surgeon. He volunteered every summer to help restore smiles to children in poor villages around the world. My mother was a professor of archaeology at Aix-en-Provence. She took additional training as a nurse so that she could assist my father in his work. And she was able to travel with him every summer. She got pregnant with me when they were here in Barranquilla." Marie de Bourbon closes her eyes as she tells Goldie the story of her family.

"My parents went to a different place, a different continent every year. I was in Mali when I was one year old and in Cambodia when I was two. We returned to Colombia when I was three. This time we went to the Pacific side, near the Ecuadorian border, in a remote village called Santa María. My parents worked in an orphanage for a few weeks. There was a toddler who would cling to my mother's skirt every day she was there with my dad. Suddenly, my parents developed an urge to have another child for me to play with. Somehow, they were attracted to that girl and decided that she would be the one. They were shocked and awed when they learned that the girl's name was María and that she and I were born on the same day at the same time, ten thousand miles apart."

"Incredible. Did you ever find out who her real parents were?" Goldie asks.

"Her father was a deep-sea fisherman. He died in a storm in the Pacific a few months before she was born. Her mother could not afford to keep her, as she already had three other children older than María. She decided to give her to an orphanage after María was born."

"Where did they go?"

"They went first to Bogotá, and then to Barranquilla. María's mother wanted to be as far away as possible from the Pacific, which she considered as having brought a tragedy to her family. She ended up in Soledad, where she got a job at Ernesto Cortissoz airport. She started there by cleaning toilets, and became a supervisor and the head of their sanitation department. She was able to save enough money to buy a little house here. At that time, she was transferred to El Dorado International Airport. An aviation police volunteer recommended her to his friend in Bogotá. The children literally grew up at an airport, where they played and did their homework in various terminals."

"How did you find them?"

"On our side, María and I went to school together. We developed the same interests in music; we both played accordion. In sports, we were in soccer, horseback riding, and swimming. She took Spanish and Portuguese; I took English and Spanish.

"Our parents mentioned that I was conceived in Colombia, and that sparked María's interest to visit Barranquilla. So we told her that she was adopted in Santa María. And her original birth certificate gave Bogotá as her place of birth. When we were sixteen, she went on a mission to find her roots. We gave her all the support. It took her two years to find her natural mother."

"Where did she find her? At an airport?"

"Yes!"

"I can't believe it."

"María was helping an American banker filling out a lost luggage form. The poor guy came from New York on his first visit to South America, and the luggage did not come with him. He spoke very little Spanish."

"Why would they send someone who did not speak Spanish to a Spanish-speaking country?"

"Good question. Apparently, he was their Africa man who was called on at the last minute to take the place of the head of their South American division, who had been killed while rock climbing at El Capitan in California the week before."

"So María and her natural mother met at a lost luggage counter, thanks to a lost soul from New York?"

"Yes, it was at that moment that her biological mother recognized María's small birthmark on her left shoulder. She asked María if she was Colombian and where she was born."

"Oh my goodness!"

"María said she was French but had been born Colombian, in Bogotá, and that she had actually been adopted by a French couple when she was three in Santa María."

"Oh my goodness!"

"At that moment, María's mother broke down. María followed. And so did the banker, who did not understand a word of their conversation. Voila!"

"Amazing. What came next?"

"María and I started going to Colombia every summer, doing charity work. She stayed in touch with the New York banker, who introduced her to a Colombian friend of his. They fell in love and got married. I got married a few years after she did. María's biological brother became a pilot with Avianca, and her sisters became flight attendants."

"And you both became pilots too."

"We did. María had shown an interest in planes since we were little.

One of the first words that came out of her mouth was *"avion."* So, on our sixteenth birthday, each of us received a blank check for flight training. She got her private in one month. It took me one year.

"María joined *Fuerza Aérea Colombiana,* the Colombian Air Force, and became a cargo and transport pilot. She always wanted to fly big planes. She was sent to the United States a few times, including once to Randolph and twice to Lackland. After she left the Colombian Air Force, she went into banking, like her husband, but never got the aviation blood out of her. She later joined Embraer and became their rep in France."

"Where was she when we met?"

"I think she was the Colombian rep for Banco do Brasil. And she came to visit me once in Paridor."

"Did you tell her about us?"

"No, I did not. By pure coincidence, she arrived on a Monday and left on a Friday. That's why you and I never missed a weekend together."

"I guess she went to see you everywhere."

"Yes: Bhutan, Mongolia, Cambodia. She went twice to Cambodia."

"Would you like something to drink?" Goldie asks, knowing his lover Marie de Bourbon must be thirsty after telling such a long story.

"Yes, please. A bottle of water is fine. Let's go for a walk. I'll meet you at the Brazilian gazebo."

Goldie brings two bottles of water and gives one to Marie de Bourbon. They start walking down the hill.

"We were in Cambodia ..." he says, signaling her to resume the story.

"After Paris, my sister went back to Bogotá to be the Embraer rep for the entire non-Brazil market in South America and the Caribbean. She flew directly from Bogotá to Phnom Penh with just one stop in Paris. She looked so fresh and so happy with just her purse and a laptop."

"She did not have any luggage, not even a carry-on?"

"No. When we visit each other, that's all we have. We are the same size."

"I should have guessed."

"We both grew up dreaming about seeing Angkor. The Cambodians say that after having seen Angkor, you go to heaven when you die. And there I was, standing at the end of the Jetway as the French ambassador, waiting for my twin sister with a group of protocol officers, holding a bouquet of orchids and a garland of jasmine at Pochentong Airport.

"María arrived only one month after I presented my credentials to the king. We were in Phnom Penh for a few days. I took her to the royal palace, the silver pagoda, the national museum, the markets, et cetera. Then we went to Angkor. There she was blown away. She could utter only two words: 'amazing' and 'unbelievable.' She said she would be back. She wanted to see a rice field and a real village."

"So when did María go back to Cambodia?"

"She was very busy with her job, but I bugged her to tell me when. Finally, she said that she would go back at the end of my assignment, because she wanted us to fly out of Cambodia together."

Marie de Bourbon takes the bottle from Goldie, drinks some water, and returns the bottle.

"I thought it was sweet that she came to help me unpack at the beginning of my tour and pack up at the end. She was with me for two weeks, and we went to the mountains in the northeast, the beaches in the southwest. We drove around the great lake. We rode motorcycles, elephants, water buffaloes, and oxen. We flew my old Golden Eagle. We attended a lot of farewell receptions and had an audience with the king and the queen. And finally we were off for Siem Reap."

"You saw all your favorite temples."

"We did."

"On our last night, we drove by Angkor Wat, Bayon, and the Elephant Terrace, all lit up, and we both said together, 'Incroyable.'"

"Unbelievable indeed."

"At the airport, instead of boarding one of the airliners, we were taken to a latest model of the Embraer Phenom. María turned to me and said, 'This is our plane.'"

"I can't imagine the look on your face!" Goldie says.

"And I said, 'You rented a jet to take us to see our parents?'"

"What did she say?"

"She said, 'No. We are going to fly it.'"

"Oh my goodness!" says Goldie.

"I was speechless."

"Fortunately you both have kept up with flying and remained current."

"Fortunately, we have," Marie says.

"Were you the only two?"

"No. There was a crew of three, including two pilots. But we were the only two who flew the plane. And María did most of the flying."

"That must be one of the longest flights you've been on."

"The longest as a pilot. Thirteen hours. I still remember by heart those control centers with which we were in contact."

"Tell me."

"Phnom Penh, Bangkok, Yangon, Kolkata, Guwahati, Urumqi, Chengdu, Varanasi, Kokand, Shymkent, Kyzylorda, Aktyubinsk, Atyrau, Volgograd, Minsk, Warsaw, Prague, Munich, Reims, Paris."

"Wow!"

"I still remember that Atyrau gave us seven seven seven seven for the squawk code."

"Great number."

"Let's go inside. I am a little chilly. We have six hours until dinner."

Marie de Bourbon lies on the long leather couch, resting her head on Goldie's lap. He cannot wait to hear the rest of the story.

"You arrived at Le Bourget and your parents were waiting for you."

"They had tears in their eyes. So did María and I. We became overnight sensations. Headlines read, "The Twins Did It!" "From the 12th to the 21st Centuries!" et cetera. We became big celebrities. We were on all kinds of shows and met all kinds of people. And something dawned on us—why not use this capital to do more good?"

"You ran for office?"

"Right."

"María and I ran for mayor about the same time. She for Bogotá, I for Marseille. And on to the presidencies. As they say, the rest is history."

Goldie caresses her hair and bends down to kiss her lips. "I was thinking of you all the time. I got my pilot's license after I returned to

America from Letador. I joined the Civil Air Patrol as a volunteer and have been more active since I built the ranch. I got a simulator at home, and I flew your route from Siem Reap to Paris. It is indeed a long flight, especially when you are flying the plane."

"Longer when you are flying by yourself."

"But never too long when I am thinking of you."

"Likewise. I had your stone with me in my pocket during that flight. Thinking of you kept me going until now."

VLADIVOSTOK, RUSSIA

The prime minister of Russia, Vladimir Chevsin gets an unexpected call from his Chinese counterpart, Shi Won Yu. She says simply she would like to see him in New York.

"Anytime, Anywhere," is his response.

"Only the two of us. No interpreter. No notetaker," says the Chinese prime minister.

"Your wish is my command," Chevsin says to his caller. "*Xie, xie.*"

"*Ber ka shi*" (you're welcome), Shi replies.

Chevsin presses the green button on the control panel. Beebee appears on the screen with a huge Cuban cigar in his mouth.

"What's up?" Beebee asks.

"Shi wants to see me alone."

"You lucky son of a bitch. She wants to take a shower with you?"

"Don't make me crazy. It could be a trap. Remember the French diplomat in China in the 1960s?"

"Yes, but this is almost the end of the twenty-first century, man."

"I've got to go. Let's talk again soon."

"Make sure your fly is zipped."

"Smart ass."

TWENTY-FOUR

The Assistant

BROOKLYN HEIGHTS, NEW YORK

THE VISITOR RINGS the door for a second time.

"Connie? Good morning."

"Hi Elizabeth. Welcome. Sorry, I was in the backyard. Please come in."

"Thanks. You have a beautiful place."

"Thank you. Would you like something to drink?"

"Yes, please. I brought you a box of chocolates." Elizabeth presents the gifts to Connie once they are both inside the nineteenth-century brick townhouse.

"Thanks. You are very nice. How about some tea to go with the chocolates?"

"Perfect."

The two women sit down to have their morning tea in the terrace garden. They are a generation apart. Elizabeth, the younger of the two, listens as Connie begins to speak.

"I normally do not do this. But your cousin Kristen and I were college roommates, and we have been the best of friends. She begged me to tell you about Henry Goldman after she learned you have been recruited by GPS."

"Thank you very much." Elizabeth is eager to learn from Goldman's assistant about the man she is going to work for and with.

"What you see is not what you get. Henry is a very complex person. I've known him for a long time—longer than anybody else, including his wives, his children. I was his first hire." Connie unwraps the chocolate box as she tells the story. "Sometimes I think he may feel insecure. Insecure about losing his place under the sun. First, remember that you must never be on his wrong side. He will destroy you. However, if you are on his right side, he will love you to death."

Connie stops to pour the tea and offers chocolate to her visitor. And she continues. "Do not argue with him once he makes a decision. If he asks questions, it is not because he does not know the answers. It is because he wants you to explain the options. Do not give him only one. Always two or three. But never more than that.

"You are paid a lot of money, and you have to live up to his standards. Not just professional excellence, but also style, etiquette, et cetera. One girl got fired for speaking with her mouth full. He hates it. Another got fired for starting to eat before everybody else had been served. A guy got fired for picking his nose at the dining table, and another one for using his tie to clean his eyeglasses. Always sit up straight. Little things like that. Chewing gum is a kiss of death, even if you are doing it off work. One got fired for arriving at a meeting one minute late. Once the meeting starts, the doors are guarded by security officers. Somehow, this one convinced the security guard to let him in after he said he was the principal presenter."

"Was he?" Elizabeth asks.

"He was, which made it even worse."

"Did he have any excuse?"

"He had to take his wife to the hospital to deliver a baby."

"I can't believe this. Henry fired a successful deal maker for taking his wife to the hospital to deliver a baby?"

"You'd better believe it, honey. For him there is simply no excuse. You don't play by his book, you are out."

"Even if you bring in a lot of money to the company?"

"Yes. Everybody is supposed to make money for the company, as well as for himself or herself. People who work for him and with him sort of know that for him, cash and crash go together. The first one is what you must aim for; otherwise, the second one will be in your face."

"Does he have any heart?" Elizabeth asks, trying to gently challenge her host.

"Yes, he does. In fact, he has a great heart. He is actually one of the top philanthropists in the country, if not in the world."

"I've read about it."

"Did you know about the Met fiasco?"

"The opera or the museum?"

"He has given monies to both, but I am talking about the museum."

"No, I have not heard about it. Please tell me."

"Over the years, he has given a lot of money to the Met, the museum. They named a wing after him. It was the one that held ancient Greek artifacts; most of them belonged to his collections. The new director wanted to make some changes and moved the collections to a smaller gallery without telling him. She was gone in no time, and forever. And she was never again hired by any museum anywhere in the world."

"My goodness."

"Tell me about your interview with him. The first time we met, I knew you were going to be hired when he asked to see you. He rarely asks anybody to have breakfast with him at the penthouse unless the person is truly outstanding."

"You know how we met, right?"

"Yes, but tell me your version."

"Well, we met briefly at a concert at the Southampton Arts Festival. We congratulated the pianist at the same time. She was a stunning young woman who is the new winner of the Chopin competition and had just returned from performing at Zelazowa Wola—"

"Chopin's birthplace near Sochaczew on the banks of the Utrata River."

"That's right. You've been there?"

"Yes, some years ago with Henry and a few of his friends. I remember it's a beautiful place in a natural park of some twenty acres. We actually had a private concert by some of the Chopin competition finalists."

"He is a big fan of Chopin."

"So are you."

"We started with a common interest in music. We met again at Tanglewood, at another reception." Elizabeth sips some tea. "And then I got an invitation to have lunch with one of the partners. I was not looking for a job—"

"But you have the right stuff, something they were looking for."

"After a few more meetings, I was made an offer I couldn't refuse. Then the breakfast."

"That's the most interesting part of the whole process," says Connie. "So what did you talk about?"

"Music, for starters. Chopin, of course. We both play piano. But I am into jazz more than classical. Then arts, museums, travels, sports, et cetera. Not once did he bring up any business-related subject."

"Did you have your cell phone with you?"

"Yes, I did. I turned it off before I went in, even though I always silence it."

"Never bring your cell phone when you meet with him. One got fired for having her phone on vibrate at a meeting."

"He has fired a lot of people."

"Indeed. The *New York Post* calls him the Fire Man! He has fired more people than Donald Trump. Performance, perfection, profits. That's what counts for him." Connie smiles briefly.

"More substance than style?"

"It is actually both. After one year and having put some good deals together, you will be invited to have lunch with him. The next level will be dinner. The highest one will be a weekend at his house in Cuba. People get fired at these levels."

"Why? Sorry to interrupt."

"His expectations are very high. Just because you have put some great deals together does not mean you are safe for life. Nobody is indispensable in his book. Most people think they have made it and begin to let their guard down. Never be too close to him physically. Do not touch any part of his body, except when shaking hands. And most of the time, he will not even shake hands with you." Connie pours some tea into Elizabeth's cup, then her own.

"How does he greet people?"

"'How are you? Good to meet you.' And when he says that, do not reach for his hand. Don't get chummy with him, doing things such as patting his back, his shoulder, et cetera. I know of three people who were fired for tapping him on his shoulder."

"Just like that."

"Just like that, and more. One made a cardinal sin." Connie excuses herself to bring in some more hot water. When she returns, she continues. "One woman was very excited to have closed a multibillion-dollar deal, and she should have been. He invited her to spend a weekend in Cuba. She thought that she had his balls in her hands after that weekend in Cuba. Big mistake. She walked into a reception in Buenos Aires and gave him a hug. She did not notice that Henry was carrying a glass of red wine, which spilled over his white pants. She was sent to Nigeria, where she was fired."

"It's unbelievable."

"You'd better believe it. On the other hand, if he develops some affection for you, do not turn away unless you resign and move to Papua New Guinea. He is irresistible once he sets his eyes on you. You know what I mean?"

"I think I do. How about his marriages and other romantic endeavors?"

"Publicly, he has been married three times: once to a German supermodel, once to an Italian opera singer, and once to a Japanese television personality. All ended in bitter divorces. In between, he has had a number of relationships."

"I've read about these in the press. Is there anything that I do not know?"

"You remember how he met his third wife, the Japanese newscaster?"

"She interviewed him in Nagoya after GPS took the controlling interest of Toyota."

"That's what in the public domain."

"Did she give him her personal contact?"

"Sort of. She gave him an origami crane and said to him, 'You have to kill her to get to her heart.'"

"What did he say?"

"He hesitated a moment and said, 'How do I do it? I don't want to kill such a beautiful creature.'"

"He must be quite smitten by her."

"Completely. He had never fallen for an Asian woman before, but this one was exceptional among all the women who came through his doors, not just among Asians."

"What did she tell him?"

"She said to him, 'I am not worrying about that. This will not be the first time for you. You have done it before. Pull the head and the tail; you'll find her heart. Push the head and the tail together afterward, and the crane will survive.'"

"And what was inside? Her personal phone number?"

"Yes, in Japanese characters."

"What happened to the crane?"

"He keeps it in a golden cage in Cuba."

"Does he see anybody now?"

"I think he has a romantic link to a French architect whom he met in Cambodia. This one may be serious. It does not mean you are totally safe. Be prepared, and enjoy the ride."

"I will keep that in mind."

"Do me a favor, will you?"

"Yes?"

"We never had this conversation."

"Of course not. Thank you very much for making this exception for me."

TWENTY-FIVE

The Colonel

DOUBLE E RANCH

ALAIN LAMENACE, THE colonel, arrives on time in his red pickup truck. Goldie and his Bhutanese friend Kunzang wait for him at the ranch gate next to the US Marines Corps flag mounted on a wooden mast at a 130-degree angle on the right side of the gate. An enormous US flag is flown on a 60 foot pole 120 feet from the fence and 72 feet to the left of the main drive in a little garden of hibiscus, lantanas, oleanders, and rosemary. It is there every day from sunrise to sunset and at night on a full moon. The red truck pulls a trailer that carries a trike.

Goldie walks to the left side of the truck as his guest rolls down the window and salutes him with a wide grin. He returns the salute. "Welcome to my humble abode, Colonel Lamenace. I am very honored by your visit." Goldie can't believe that he is looking at a ninety-six-year-old man. He looks as though he is in his seventies.

"Thank you for the invitation, sir. I am equally honored to be with you." The decorated veteran turns to his new best friend. "Good morning, Your Highness. How are you doing?"

"Good morning, Colonel. I am doing very well. How are you doing this morning?"

"I am too blessed to be stressed."

"Please stop calling me Your Highness. Call me Kunzang. That's an order." She smiles and gives him a big hug the minute he gets on the ground on his artificial legs.

"Yes, ma'am."

"Colonel, if you wish, you may leave your vehicle here and we will continue by horse carriage to the main house. Our horses are Peter and Julia. They are actually cousins. I told them about you. They are thrilled to carry a decorated veteran. I am your driver. You will sit in front with me. Kunzang will be in the back with your service dog, Troy. I believe they have met before, at the accident."

"Yes, they have, on that fateful day."

As the carriage passes by the flagpole, the colonel turns toward the US flag and salutes.

"Please tell me about Troy," Goldie asks his guest.

"Some years ago, I was in San Antonio for an Army All-American Bowl awards dinner. I believe it was in January, and it was unusually cold, and I did not get to see anything. Somebody mentioned that I should return in April for the famous Fiesta San Antonio. I got an invitation to a reunion of US Army War College alumni in the Alamo City in April and decided to stay on for one of the city's most famous and popular festivities. I got invited to the Fiesta kickoff at Fort Sam Houston and then to the Fiesta Military Parade at Lackland. It was there that I saw a canine unit marching in the parade. I inquired more about it and learned that I could actually adopt one of the dogs after it had been discharged and retired. They are trained to detect all kinds of things, from drugs to explosives—including mines. It takes about one hundred fifty thousand dollars to train one of them. The military, police, and emergency and search-and-rescue responders all use them. One of them went on the Navy SEAL operation that killed Osama bin Laden in Abbottabad."

"Yes, I remember that. I was in college at the time," says Goldie. "How old is Troy?"

"He is fourteen, almost my age."

"I visited that dog school once. I think it is officially called the Department of Defense Working Dog School," says Goldie.

"That's correct. It's the Three Hundred Forty-First Training Squadron."

"How many dogs have you adopted?"

"Troy is my seventh."

"Were they all in the military? And all German shepherds?"

"Yes, and no. They were all trained at Lackland, but they served in different services and different areas. My first dog, Bekka, was actually a golden retriever." Lamenace shows a picture of his first dog in a pocket photo album. "She spent her professional life with the Connecticut State Police at New Haven and Hartford airports. The second one was Tar Baby. He was a German shepherd and worked for the Boston Aviation Police. Jacqueline was my third, a Dutch shepherd, and served in the navy. My fourth was a Labrador retriever, Cora. She was a DEA agent's darling and a CBP star working along the Mexican border. She is the only one who can respond to commands in Spanish. The second half of her career was with TSA. Alexandra was my fifth, a German shepherd. She was a veteran of earthquakes, hurricanes, and tsunamis. She was the most traveled dog that I've ever owned; she had been to Africa, the South Pacific, and Antarctica, among other places. The sixth one was a Belgian Malinois, Jeanne d'Arc. She was in the army and spent most of her time at the Pentagon until she was transferred to the Secret Service and worked at the White House. She was my only dog who had traveled on *Air Force One*. She has a flight certificate to prove it."

"Wow. And Troy?"

"Troy is also a Belgian Malinois. He is an air force dog. He has seen action in every continent. He has guarded more air force bases that you and I will ever know."

"Wow. You could write a book about your dogs."

"I did."

"I'd love to read it. What is it called?"

"*Golden Shepherds: What My Dogs Told Me at Bedtime*. You'll get to read it soon enough."

"Thank you. I can't wait."

Goldie suddenly realizes that he has failed to do some research—his homework, as he would call it—on his guest. He normally needs to know a lot about his interlocutor, guest, or visitor, if not everything. He let his preparation slip on this one. So he quickly tries to make amends.

"You seem to like the German shepherds and Belgian Malinois. You have two of each."

"They have the best sense of smell, endurance, speed, strength, courage, and intelligence. And they have an amazing ability to adapt to the most severe weather conditions."

"Did you have some of the dogs at the same time or one after the other?"

"One after the other. Only Troy overlapped with Jeanne d'Arc for a few years. Since Jeanne passed away, he has been by himself. He doesn't seem to mind, but I sense that he is feeling lonely."

"Will you get another one?"

"Yes, I may adopt another one to keep him company. And you? I understand you have some doggies as well."

"Yes, I have three: Tommy, the golden retriever, Michael, the Labrador retriever, and Lisa, the Belgian Malinois."

"Are they Lackland graduates also?"

"I wish they were. I got them when they were puppies."

"I understand you are quite involved with Lackland."

"Yes, a little bit. I am an honorary commander of the Four Hundred Thirty-Third Airlift Wing, which is also known as the Alamo Wing."

"The C-5M unit?"

"That's correct."

"I am also a big fan of Lackland. Each time I am in San Antonio, I have my eighty-second haircut in honor of the thirty-six thousand air force recruits who have their eight-and-a-half-week basic training there every year."

"That's very fast. I would like to try it sometime."

"It would be fun. Then you can have your favorite bowl of noodles around the corner from the BX at the Golden Bowls, which has all kinds of noodles from every country in Asia, including spinach, mandarin, lo mein, thin Cantonese / angel hair, wide Cantonese, mee fun, chow fun, Korean, Japanese, Khmer, Lao, Thai, Vietnamese, you name it. They also have Bhutanese and Tibetan noodles."

"I am hungry already. When we get to the ranch house, we are going to have nice barbeque, served with rice and noodles—two of your favorite staples. Then you tell us your riding experience."

"It will be my pleasure."

Goldie, Kunzang, and Colonel Lamenace sit on a terrace overlooking the pastures. They sip drinks and enjoy the warm breeze.

Goldie can't wait to bring up one of his favorite subjects with his visitor.

"I've heard you set some records in endurance riding, especially the Golden MPS. How did you get inspired in doing all this? And you seem to have fun all the time."

"It was actually George Bush, the father who inspired me. I was a young man when he jumped off the plane at seventy-five in Yuma, Arizona. And as you know he did it again at eighty-five, eighty-eight, and ninety years old. He made the jump from over ten thousand feet with the army's Golden Knights. He had such an active life: jogging, speed golfing, fishing, tennis. I always remember him saying, 'Just because you're an old guy, you don't have to sit around drooling in the corner. Get out and do something. Get out and enjoy life.' In my book, he was the most complete man and one of my favorite presidents."

"He is also one of my favorite presidents, and I think Kunzang even wrote a paper on him."

"I did it because you spoke about him all the time," says the Bhutanese princess. "I am sorry that I focused only on his foreign policy. I should pay attention to his quality as a human being."

"Maybe another paper is in order," Goldie says to encourage his young friend.

"Maybe so," the marine colonel says, adding his support.

"So, inspiration from forty-one," the host says, trying to return his guest of honor to the subject of his interest.

"Yes, you will probably remember that his first parachute jump was after he was shot down over the Pacific in 1944 during World War II. He bailed out at fifteen hundred feet after a bombing mission. Bush promised himself that he would one day jump from a plane for fun, and he did it in Yuma. He jumped again on his seventy-fifth birthday at his library in College Station, Texas. I was there, visiting his library on my trike, when I suddenly got the urge to do something to support presidential libraries."

"And you started the presidential library rally, which is considered the greatest and most fun endurance run in the world. But how did you come up with such a unique rule?"

"I did the Iron Butt and Bun Burner runs when I was sixty."

"Excuse me, but I don't think Kunzang knows these terms," says Goldie.

"I am sorry. The Iron Butt is a one-thousand-mile bike ride completed in twenty-four hours, and the Bun Burner is fifteen hundred miles in thirty-six hours. And then there is also the 50CC—a coast-to-coast ride in fifty hours. I wanted to start something different. Hence the MPS. I thought of it as Marine Presidential Solo, and then it turned into Military Presidential Solo. The first few years were reserved for veterans who are sixty and older. Then it was for anybody sixty and above. Finally, it was opened to everyone of all ages—I mean eighteen and above. But you have to be at a presidential library on either July 4 or January 20 and ride to all the presidential libraries, except Obama's in Honolulu, and have your picture taken in front of each of them, which you submit with copies of all your gas receipts for validation."

"When did you start, and where?"

"I was seventy-two when I did my first MPS. I began mine at the Kennedy Library in Boston. Then I went to FDR in Hyde Park, New York; Ford in Ann Arbor; Hoover in West Branch, Iowa; Truman in Independence, Missouri; Eisenhower in Abilene, Kansas; Reagan in Simi Valley; and Nixon in Yorba Linda. Both of the last two are in California. Then I came back east from Nixon to Johnson in Austin, Bush forty-one in College Station, Bush forty-three in Dallas, Clinton in Little Rock, and Carter in Atlanta. I did not make the Obama library in Honolulu."

"My goodness. How long was it?"

"It's six thousand miles all together, and it took me thirteen days. Since I was the first one to do the run just to raise awareness, there was no time constraint. It is now over two decades old. And people turn this into their favorite charity, raising money not for just presidential libraries, but for all general public libraries and other education-related activities. How about you? What is your riding interest?"

"Well, I did my second Iron Butt and Bun Burner recently."

"What was the route?"

"I went from San Antonio to Fort Worth and Oklahoma City, then to Wichita, Salina, and Topeka in Kansas; next to Saint Joseph in Missouri, and Nebraska City and Lincoln in Nebraska. There I reached my first thousand miles and earned my Iron Butt pin and patch after some twenty hours. I rested for four hours in Lincoln and continued to Grand Island and O'Neill, still in Nebraska, and Gregory, Presho, and finally Sturgis, all in South Dakota, for my fifteen hundred plus miles. I made the last five hundred miles from Lincoln to Sturgis in eight hours. So all together I covered the Bun Burner mileage requirement in thirty-two hours."

"You made very good time. How many of you were in the flight?"

"Only eight riders, plus a chase truck pulling a trailer that could carry three bikes, just in case. The driver had her bike on the trailer already, because she wanted to ride her bike in Sturgis. So there was room for two bikes, if needed. But we did not."

"Did you encounter any problems?"

"None. We were very lucky."

"Well, you were also very safe riders."

"Thank you. You inspire me so much that I might consider doing the MPS next year."

"I guarantee you will feel exhilarated by the views from one coast to another and the cause you are helping. I feel that the older you get, the more satisfied you will be, just like President Bush said: 'Get out and enjoy life.'"

"Both you and President Bush inspire me enormously to challenge myself. I can't tell you how honored I am to meet you. I trust this is just the beginning."

"It is just the beginning. I don't know how much longer I will be on this earth. As long as the good Lord wants me to stay here, I just keep on doing things."

"Let's do it together. Let's go riding."

"Let's do it."

Alain Lamenace is one of the most complete persons, according to the *New Mexican*—and in Goldie's book. He saved more people in the second Korean War than Forrest Gump in Forrest Gump's Vietnam. He lost both natural legs on the way to Koh Kong, where he received new ones. After the operation, he had a choice of recuperating anywhere in the world, and he chose Bangladesh. Why? Because he had heard that the country was the poster child for natural disasters, and he wanted to interact with its people. He was awarded the Congressional Medal of Honor immediately after he returned to the United States. The Pentagon let him transfer from one service to another until his retirement at the full colonel rank. He became a motivational speaker and an early advocate for volunteerism.

He is an avid fisherman and hunter. "I eat what I can get, what I kill," he has been known to say. He writes outdoor columns regularly and is always in great demand for public speaking about survival, service, and sacrifice. He possesses one of the largest collections of pocketknives—1,300 at last count. He carries one with him all the time, except when going through public airports. "I feel completely naked without one," he has stated more than once.

He has also owned about 360 guns and has shot some seven hundred thousand rounds in his lifetime. Loss of hearing? Nah. Only 30 percent. He once said, "I always wear earplugs and other ear protection devices. Like sunscreen, I put it on all the time, never knowing when I am going to need it." He spends more time helping other people than taking care of his own things. He thinks he can have the best of both worlds: serving and serving more.

US Senate Hearing Room, Washington, DC

The senator from Massachusetts is quite upset when the nominee seems to brush off her questions. Lowell, where she was born, is home to the second-largest Cambodian community in the United States and the world, outside of Cambodia. A group of Lowell residents reported to her that they could not find Kennedy Avenue at Sihanoukville, so she is using the nomination hearing to unleash her constituents' anger.

"You were the *chargé* of the embassy in Cambodia for nine months. You never raised a finger with the Cambodian government as to why John F. Kennedy Avenue, which was dedicated by Mrs. Jacqueline Kennedy and Prince Sihanouk in 1967, simply disappeared from the maps and is nowhere to be seen. Did it ever occur to you that Mao Ze Dong, responsible for some sixty million Chinese deaths, and Kim Il Sung, responsible for the starvation of millions of North Koreans—all these communists and dictators have their streets named in Cambodia? And we had one named after one of our presidents, and it never bothered you enough to find out why it just disappeared. Do you know how many streets in Brazil are named after our presidents?"

The White House and State Department legislative officers that monitor the confirmation hearing live shake their heads. "I can't believe this," exclaims one of them. "We are still having a problem with our nominee to Japan because she couldn't answer some questions about our embassy answering calls in local languages. Now this one wants to know the locations of all streets named after our presidents."

"Why don't they ask questions about our bilateral relations or something related to foreign policy? What the fuck are they trying to do?"

"Setting a new record for being obstructionist?"

"No wonder the NONO people say no to them!"

TWENTY-SIX

The Architect

GUADALAHARA, MEXICO

BEEBEE THINKS IT is the right time for him to move; to hit his enemy where it hurts most and destroy him once and for all. He feels that Henry Goldman is a strong competitor to control the mines in Letador. He instructs his people to put the operation into full implementation. He directs them from his yacht in the South Pacific.

His people gather in the basement of their safe house.

"Listen to me very clearly. I want it to be clean, and absolutely no damage to the property."

"Yes, sir," says his hit team of six men and two women.

"Jim, you are in charge of this exercise. You have all the tools. You know how to push and when to pull. Go and do it. Don't call me until you have some good news."

"Yes, sir." Jim, the muscular leader of Beebee's hit team gets up and salutes the shape of his almighty boss on the flat television.

The minute Beebee disappears from the screen, Jim turns to his people.

"You heard the man."

"Yes, sir."

"Have you memorized her face?"

"Yes, sir."

"This is what I have: She will be here for two days to attend a conference. She arrives this morning, rents a car, drives to the hotel, and checks in. At noon, she will come out and drive to Tlaquepaque to have lunch with the members of her panel. The name of the restaurant is Sin Nombre."

"No name!" says Jimmy.

"Right."

"How the fuck are we going to find a restaurant that has no name?" asks Linda, his right-hand person.

"The fucking restaurant has a name. And the fucking name of the fucking restaurant is Sin Nombre. 'No name' in English. Don't you fucking understand?"

There is silence in the room.

"Must I hear anything?"

"Yes, sir."

"By the time they all sit down for lunch, it will be about two o'clock."

"How many of them, sir?" Julio asks.

"Can't you wait till I've finished?"

"Yes, sir."

"Next time, do not ever interrupt my briefing."

"Yes, sir."

"Do not ask questions until I say 'questions.'"

"Yes, sir."

"It will take them about three hours to finish their lunch. There will be an Asian woman, a Caucasian man, and a black man in addition to her. Four of them altogether. When they get out of Sin Nombre, they are going to walk to the market. She loves all those handicrafts and jewelry, especially those made by village women. About seven, they will go separate ways. She will drive back to Guadalajara by herself. Jimmy and Linda, you will have followed her from the airport. Our team bravo should be in place at the airport, the hotel, along the road, at Sin Nombre, and at the market. The pickup should be midway between Tlaquepaque and Guadalajara. Questions?"

"Yes, sir." Jane raises her right fist. "What if something goes wrong?"

"You wait for my signals: 'Push' to move forward, and 'Pull' to drop it. Is that clear?"

"Yes, sir."

"All right. Let's have some fun."

The hit team responds in unison. "Yes, sir."

CHANGSHA, CHINA

The leaders of China are in Changsha for their regular "meet the minds" session. But this one everybody knows is going to be hot and spicy. It has become known as the Taiwan Fiasco. Ever since the president of the United States put his feet on the renegade island, the emperor has been in a bad mood, even if it is all smiles in public. The pictures seen on CCTV show him most sympathetic while visiting people in flooded areas.

The exclusive club members are bracing themselves for a hell of a ride. At least temporarily.

"Let's start with Siachen." The president opens the meeting. He picks up a duck foot with a pair of gold chopsticks, puts it in his mouth, and looks at the giant screen.

General Hu stands up with a laser pointer. He walks back and forth between the screen and the dining table. The first slide shows a satellite photo of Srinagar Air Base in India. The slides change as he carries on his briefing. After a deep breath, the general begins.

"After the leaders finished their banquet, they bade farewell to Prime Minister Srichandra Shivaram and came to this hangar to board the Pakistani plane. It's a modified Boeing 777 that has twelve suites. Only seven were used. As we know, Shivaram had to return to Delhi for a parliamentary meeting.

"About the time the seven leaders were settled in, we launched two Su-36s from Western Xizang. It has been our practice to escort VIP planes through our airspace. Five minutes after the rendezvous, something happened."

"Something?" the president shouts with his mouth full. "Can you be more specific?"

"Our search team is trying to get to the crash site. The progress has been very slow because of the snow."

"So what is that something?"

"It could have been a wind shear that would have pushed the alpha plane to hit the rear fuselage of the Boeing. The bravo crew briefed us after they returned to base that they and the alpha crew were joking about getting close enough to the Pakistani plane to see if its passengers were still awake or snoring with their mouths open."

"I can't believe this. Is that what you trained our fighter pilots to do?"

General Hu remains silent with his eyes on the floor. The room has been silent as well.

"Continue!"

"As we know—"

"Stop saying, 'As we know.'"

"Yes, sir. The Pakistani plane made it all the way to Turkmenistan and had an emergency landing at an American base near the triborder area with Uzbekistan and Afghanistan. The passengers were transferred to a US Air Force plane after a brief medical examination and flown to McGuire Air Force Base in New Jersey."

"Where is the Pakistani plane?"

"It is still in Turkmenistan, being inspected by a team of the NTSB and—"

"What the hell is NTSB?"

"National Transportation Safety Board," says General Hu.

"Don't you ever give me all this crap again."

"Yes, sir."

"Shi is on the way to New York." The president tells the group about the prime minister. "She is going to host a dinner for the South Asian leaders and offer an explanation. I've told her that she can say we are sorry but she cannot apologize. She will also meet with the Russians and the Americans." The president gets up and walks to the restroom.

The leaders reconvene after he returns from the restroom. They dare not laugh upon seeing his fly open.

"The Russians have had a ball since the Taiwan Fiasco," the president says. "We gave them more music to dance to when our fighters hit the plane of one of our best friends. We need to stop the music and end the ball."

General Hu rises slowly when the president turns to him. He knows he has a slam dunk on the next subject. "One of our fishing boats intercepted a transmission from Boris Brandrokochev."

"Beebee?" the president asks.

"Yes, sir. He told his hit team in Mexico to kidnap an architect."

"An architect? What the hell does he want to do with an architect? How much does he think he can get for a ransom? Besides, doesn't he have enough money to buy all the architects in the world?"

"She is not—"

"A woman?"

"Yes, sir."

"She must be very beautiful, like … Miss Universe?"

"Yes, sir."

The president pauses for a moment. The leadership feels a slight sense of relief that the current subject may have slowly diluted the president's anger. After a few minutes of silence while his eyes are still fixed on the screen, he says, "Interesting. Why could he not get her the traditional way? Lou, wouldn't you?" The president turns to his financial adviser, Lewis Li, who immediately puts his gold chopsticks down and pushes the chair away. "Remain seated."

"She is not just an architect, sir. She is also an anthropologist specializing in twelfth-century civilizations. But, most importantly, she is the new love of Henry Goldman, our other competitor in Letador. He is prepared to put in about sixty billion dollars to control the eastern part of the country, where our people are already in place building and maintaining microwave towers." Li seizes the opportunity to take over the briefing from General Hu.

"Beebee does not know that we are his second competitor: we do not have a single Chinese in the country, not even at the Emperor's Golden Dragon. Beebee wanted to hit Goldman where it hurts most and annihilate him. Once Goldman is out of the picture, he thinks he will have Letador to himself. And he is prepared for an all-out battle. He already has tons of weapons in Angola and Namibia, enough to fight a few wars."

"What happened to that operation? The kidnapping of the architect? Does it have a name?" The president turns to Hu.

"Broken Arrow. Ironically, it is the same name as our operation with the Pakistani plane."

"You named the Pakistan escort mission Broken Arrow?" says the president. "That's why we were broken. We lost a multimillion-dollar jet and two crew members. And a lot of face. Don't ever name anything with the word 'broken'!"

"Yes, sir."

"Did Beebee get the architect?" The president turns to Li.

"No, sir. Her rental car had some problems in Tlaquepaque."

"Where?"

"Tlaquepaque, where she had lunch with her colleagues," Hu says. He is not ready to cede the briefing to Li. "She left the car there and got a ride back with the members of her conference panel. The head of the hit team, known as Jim, decided to call the operation off. He reported to his boss, who told him that they should meet at the usual bar in two weeks."

"Do you have a photo of the architect?"

"Yes, sir." She appears on the screen wearing a T-shirt, a pair of jeans, sneakers, and sunglasses.

"By Confucius! She is more beautiful than Miss Universe. She has the lips of Angela Jolie—"

"Angelina Jolie, sir."

"Don't ever interrupt my thoughts."

"Yes, sir." Hu repeats the same answer.

"The lips of Ange Lina Jolie."

"Yes, sir."

"The breasts of Demi Moore."

"Yes, sir."

"The butt of Jennifer Aniston."

"Yes, sir."

"The legs of … the legs of … I know they are all dead. I am talking about when they were in their prime years, in their late thirties, early forties."

"Yes, sir."

"The legs of Jennifer Lopez."

"Yes, sir."

"The eyes of Scarlett Johansson."

"Yes, sir."

"By the way, Scarlett said at the 2012 democratic convention that she attended a public school. I wondered why it was so bad to attend a public school in New York." The president stands up and ends the meeting. "All right, please keep me posted about the architect."

"Yes, sir," the leaders say in unison, drowning out Hu's voice.

TWENTY-SEVEN

The Encounter

NEW YORK

THE RUSSIANS OWN an enormous compound on Long Island. The place has been swept by a joint Sino-Russian security team. Russia's prime minister, Vladimir Chevsin, has been in the residence since his arrival in New York. He places a video call to his buddy, who has by now returned to St. Petersburg.

"Are you hard and ready?" Beebee asks.

"I have been hard and ready since I met her."

"You horny fucking son of a bitch! So what are you going to do? Jump on her the minute she arrives?"

"I may be crazy, but I am not that stupid. I think she wants to talk to me about LPT: Letador, Pakistan, and Taiwan, in their order of importance. Anything you want to tell me?"

"You remember I told you about GPS, right?"

"I do. Vaguely, though"

"Goldman, Plat, Silverstein! Henry Goldman's company?"

"Yes, I do. Very clearly now that you mention his name. He owns Cuba. Now he wants to own Letador. And we must stop him."

"Yes, you have been telling me about him."

"I tried to pick up his girlfriend."

"You what? Where? Why? You can have anybody you want. Why did you do it?"

"Actually, I planned to kidnap her in Mexico, in Guadalajara, to hurt him badly."

"You fucking son of a bitch. Why didn't you consult with me first? The governor of Jalisco is a hunting buddy of Goldman. You must have been followed already. Did you leave any footprints?"

"No. I did not get her. The team left the country immediately."

"Don't ever do anything that stupid again before asking me."

"All right. Let's talk about Shi. I agree with you that it could be a trap. Don't go beyond the subjects that she brings up. And keep your pants up. Tell her '*Ya tebya lublu.*'"

"She does not speak Russian."

"Then say it in Chinese: '*Wo ai ni.*'"

"How many languages can you say 'I love you' in?"

"Not enough,"

"Smart ass."

Shi Won Yu, the first female prime minister of the People's Republic of China, arrives at the Russian compound by herself at the main villa. She wears an elegant red-and-white knee-length dress and a pair of red high heels. She carries a smart red leather purse.

Chevsin takes her right hand, kisses it, and greets her in perfect Mandarin.

"Ni hao."

"Ni hao."

"I am so honored to receive you," says Chevsin. "I don't know if I can thank you enough for this visit."

"I came here to thank you personally for all your kind attention. Especially all the beautiful flowers you sent my way for every ceremony, festival, holiday, and occasion that exists in the Chinese calendar; all your nice handwritten notes, wonderful poetry—"

"I am so happy that you have accepted all of them."

"I enjoy having them with me all the time. I am a human being, and I have emotions too. I can read between the lines."

Chevsin's heartbeat switches gear to a faster pace. He cannot believe his ears.

"I have been thinking a lot about us," she adds. She takes his right hand and squeezes it.

It's coming, he thinks. Then she drops the bomb.

"I am sorry; I can't. It's not going to work." She drops another bomb: "I'm so sorry to disappoint you."

Chevsin has been courting her for two years, and he is not going to give up very easily. He holds her hand between his and tries to defuse the two bombs.

"Please do not say anything yet. If you need more time, I'll be more than happy to wait. I'll be patient. But please do not close the doors. If you need to close them for political reasons, I beg you not to lock them. This is historic. It has never happened before that the leaders of two major powers could relate to each other through their hearts. I beg you to give it a little more time, to give peace a chance."

Shi does not react. She continues to look at a carved wooden sculpture of a two-headed eagle. Chevsin brings her hand up to kiss it. She turns her face to see him, and her lips touch his.

Barranquilla, Colombia

Two hours to dinnertime, Goldie and Marie have finally closed all the loops. They have returned to the present.

"I very much like your ideas about bringing the brothers together in a different family setting. I know that Bedel and Lionel have a lot of respect for you. You have done so much for them and their families. They all value your friendship dearly. They know you have no vested interest in their country, except to bring peace and stability back."

"I can say the same thing about the high regard and deep friendship they have for you."

"In all fairness, I have a strong interest in keeping Letador francophone and francophile."

"This is fair indeed."

"When we go back to New York next week—by the way, thank you for coming here instead of meeting me there. It is more private, and you got to meet my sister."

"I love her already, but I don't like her house rules."

"Be patient. Is patience not one of your virtues? So back to New York. I will meet with Chevsin and encourage Russia not to veto the resolution. I will see Shi separately and will do the same. At the very least, both Russia and China should abstain. Our people have been working with the British, Americans and the ten nonpermanent members of the Security Council on very acceptable language. It is the only way to prevent more bloodshed and bring peace and stability to Letador and to Africa."

"I'll take care of the brothers. If the resolution gets adopted, it will strengthen my hand enormously."

"I will be with you all the way."

"So will I."

"Thank you for continuing to play a key role behind the scenes. I trust you have been keeping Kartona informed."

"I have."

"My hope is to go back to Notneh with you and have a candlelight dinner on a full moon under the tamarind tree by the Enies River."

"It would be a dream come true for me as well."

"Never give up hope," Goldie and Marie say together.

TWENTY-EIGHT

The Aviators

CHANGSA, CHINA

THE LEADERS ARE ready to close their lengthy session. The president is anxious to hear about the results of the meeting between his prime minister and her Russian counterpart.

"She's been there for nearly three hours, and she has not broken his legs yet," the president says. Li cannot resist chuckling, and the others follow suit.

"What the hell is so funny?" the president asks.

"You asked if she has *broken his legs* yet," Li says with a quiet voice.

"You all have dirty minds. I am going to bed. Let me know in the morning."

Everyone gets up at the same time and bows deeply. The president walks to his suite, which occupies the entire eighth floor. He moves across the living room directly toward his bedroom. He smells a very attractive scent.

Two beautiful hands help him take off his jacket. He turns around and offers a hesitant but warm smile.

"What is your name?"

"Wei, sir."

"What are you supposed to do, Wei?" He already knows the answer, but he still wants to hear it.

"Anything you wish, sir."

It is music to his ears.

Esperanza, Texas

Goldie is in double hog heaven whenever he is at his ranch with the military. Especially when he is involved in his favorite activities with them, such as archery, biking, cooking, hiking, riding, and swimming.

He and Colonel Lamenace have many common interests. The conversation around the dining table moves back and forth between biking, flying, and sailing.

Kunzang finally interrupts them when the motorcycle subject comes up again.

"Do you know that the risk of death in a collision for a motorcycle is thirty-five times higher than for a car going at fifty miles an hour?"

The two men turn to the princess and laugh.

"Where did you get this information?"

"At my recent DDC."

"You took a defensive driving course?"

"Yes."

"Why? Because you hit the colonel?" Goldie asks.

"Yes."

"What else can you tell us about the DDC?"

"Well, for starters, the three steps to prevent a collision are what they call RUA: recognize the hazard, understand the defense, and act correctly in a timely manner. There are some thirty-five thousand people killed every year in motor vehicle collisions—almost one hundred a day. If we all drive defensively, we will save lives, time, and money regardless of what happens around us. The simple rule is to exercise courtesy and common sense. On the average, each of us is involved in a collision once every ten years, or six times in a lifetime."

She turns to the colonel and continues. "I know you never had an accident in your life until I hit you."

"Let put it this way. Everything happens for a reason. If we hadn't been in that collision, we would not have become friends, right?"

"Right. You always look at the bright side. I seem to do everything wrong according to the DDC. This is what they call distracted driving. I was multitasking, in a way, by reading and driving at the same time. That is a big no-no. No texting, no reading, no phoning, no, no, no. I feel very sorry for the accident, but I am thankful to have met you and gained your friendship." Kunzang smiles.

"I have been riding a motorcycle since I was thirteen. And thank the Lord, I have never been in an accident. I always think that when it's time to go, it is time to go. There are actually more people who die in bed than in car crashes." Lamenace says to his friends.

"I have been also very lucky," says Goldie. "Never had an accident so far. Knock on wood."

"How about the one in Houston—didn't you hit someone?" Kunzang says, challenging her host, with some affection in her attractive smile.

"I did hit a woman. I was driving a car and not riding a motorcycle."

"You hit a woman? Oh my Lord!" The colonel crosses his chest.

"I didn't tell you everything, Kunzang, because I didn't want you to worry about me," Goldie says.

"I am sorry to bring it up. I was trying to be conversational," Kunzang says.

"I am glad you did. Let me tell you both the whole story. I was driving on a Friday afternoon on Bellaire during rush hour, and I went through a red light—"

"Oh my Lord!" says Colonel Lamenace.

"And I hit a pregnant woman—"

"Oh my Lord!"

"... from Eritrea—"

"Oh my Lord!"

"...who was driving herself on the way to the hospital to deliver a baby."

"Oh my Lord!"

"The baby was born in the car under the Route 59 overpass."

"Oh my Lord!"

"I delivered the baby before the police and EMS arrived. And I became the godfather and a close friend of hers."

"Oh my Lord! Where was the husband?"

"He is a NASA astrophysicist working in the space base on the moon. He was due to return to earth the following month but got delayed for another week because the experiment he was conducting needed more time to complete."

"Oh my Lord!"

Both Kunzang and Lamenace look at each other and at Goldie, completely stunned. For a few minutes, they all are in complete silence. Then the colonel breaks it.

"I hate to ask you this, but I am wondering what was going through your mind that kept you from seeing the light?"

"That's a good question. I've been asking that same question myself. For a split second, my mind was not with me, and then *bang*."

"Everything happens for a reason. Now you have a goddaughter and a grateful family."

"Thanks. Let's change the subject," Goldie says.

"How about aviation?"

"I was trying to get to that subject. I understand that you hold every FAA rating that has ever existed and you have never failed a medical examination. And the FAA has no reason not to let you fly. They must have come up with a new slogan: The sky is not the limit!"

"That's very kind of you. But you ain't seen nothing yet." Lamenace winks at Goldie.

"You mean there is more than what meets the eye?"

"I mean there is someone who has done all of this at half of my age!"

The weekend Goldie spends with Colonel Lamenace is probably one of the best he has experienced in many years. But this is just the beginning. The colonel wants him to meet another of his friends; he thinks Goldie would enjoy the company and friendship as well. Goldie immediately extends the invitation to Golf Romeo. The visitor shows up on Sunday at the Double E Ranch in style. She arrives in her own helicopter, which she has flown from Candelaria.

Georgia Ragan was born in Grenada. Her father is a farmer and her mother a retired US Coast Guard commander. They met while her mother was on a tour of duty on the island. Ragan's father had just returned from his doctoral studies in agricultural economics at Ohio State University in Columbus. He helped his future wife change a flat tire on her rental car by a dirt road. And the rest, as they say, is history. They returned a few years later to visit the village where they met, and Georgia was born there. Georgia's great-grandfather was so overjoyed with the US liberation of Grenada in the early eighties that he named his first son George Reagan in honor of Ronald Reagan and George Bush. The clerk forgot the *e*, and nobody noticed until Georgia's father was born, when he was going to be named George Reagan, Jr.

Goldie thinks that Colonel Alain Lamenace has done more things than a human being can possibly do, but he now realizes that he has not seen anything yet.

Ragan graduated first in her class from the Air Force Academy, where she was the cadet commander four years in a row. She got her first choice—to be trained as a fighter pilot, F-35 Joint Striker, at Luke Air Force Base in Glendale, Arizona, for starters. Then she jumped over to F-48 MPS (multipurpose stealth). She moved from fighters to bombers, transport, and helicopters, and she has not met an aircraft that she cannot fly. She remains the only officer who has served in every single command of the US military. In Africa, she flew helicopter rescue missions that saved thousands of lives in the aftermath of the Indian Ocean tsunami that devastated the east coast. She has received more awards and commendations than anybody of her rank and age.

In one flight from Kabul to Tripoli, she summarized the flight plan to the air crew without reading any piece of paper.

"It should be a simple mission—so simple that you'll have to try hard to stay awake. We take off from here, fly over Turkmenistan and the Caspian

Sea, and should be in Baku in less than two hours. We should be on the ground for about thirty minutes to pick up some packages there, and then we head for Damascus. Same thing in Damascus, and we will head for Tripoli. We should be there for dinner. Alpha, you fly from here to Baku; Bravo from Baku to Damascus. I fly the last leg from Damascus to Tripoli. Do you have any questions? If you don't, let's go and have some fun!"

After thirteen years in the air force, she retired from the military and joined American United, where she reached the rank of chief instructor pilot for the 747-8. She was only thirty-six years old.

In between, she spent one year in Washington as a White House Fellow in the Department of Homeland Security.

Before dinner by candlelight, Colonel Lamenace offers the prayer: "Heavenly Father, we thank you for all the blessings you've bestowed on us, especially the food that nourishes our bodies, the friendship that sustains our minds, and the love that expands our worlds. Amen."

Goldie invites his newest weekend guest, Georgia Ragan, to regale them with her war stories. "I can't wait to hear more details about your interest in aviation and all your achievements."

"It's very kind of you to invite me to join. I have been looking forward to being with you since we got off the phone. Aviation is in my genes from my mother's side. One of my mother's forebears was on the first passenger plane from Key West to Havana in 1927. She was also on the first flight to the Caribbean from Miami, to Havana, Kingston, and Barranquilla. Another one was on the first transpacific flight from Honolulu to Midway, Wake, Guam, Manila, Hong Kong, Pago Pago, and Auckland. This was in 1930 in an M130, and it was preceded by the seven-hour flight from San Francisco to Honolulu.

"Another one was on the first Pan Am transatlantic flight on a Boeing 707 in 1958 from New York to Paris, and on separate flights later to London, Dublin, and Rome.

"The same year my great-grandfather went on the first Pan Am around-the-world flight, which lasted some forty-six hours with stops in Honolulu, Hong Kong, Bangkok, Delhi, Beirut, Frankfurt, and London.

"In 1989, my grandmother was flying from London to Sydney, and on and on. Finally, my mother joined the coast guard and became a search-and-rescue helicopter pilot."

"My goodness. What a history!"

CHINA

The leaders meet for breakfast at 0888. That is how it is listed on the sensitive schedule. It is actually 9:28 a.m., and it is on the eighth floor in the octagonal ballroom of the Golden Dragon Palace.

The president seems to be in a better mood.

His colleagues know that he has had a good night.

"The prime minister of India is visiting us next month. What's the latest on his itinerary?" the president asks the leadership.

General Hu sees the opportunity to redeem himself and tries to stand up with the help of an attendant who rushes to pull out the chair for him.

"Remain seated," the president orders. The general sits down without the chair, which the attendant forgets to push in for him, and ends up on the floor. Everybody is laughing. He tries to make light of it but soon enough finds out the name of the waiter. The poor guy, a disguised army sergeant, is sent the following day to a remote border protection unit working along the borders of Mongolia, Russia, and Kazakhstan.

General Hu resumes his presentation after straightening his uniform. "Sir, as you know, Srichandra Shivaram is the first Buddhist prime minister of India. He spent many years in his youth in Bhutan and Sri Lanka. While an anthropology student, he rode a bicycle across Bhutan from Paro all the way to Tashigang. In Sri Lanka, he did a trip on a motorcycle from Jaffna to Galle. In addition to Hindi and English, he speaks Dzongkha and Sinhalese fluently. He is also conversant in Nepali and Urdu.

"One of his papers was on Henry Steel Olcott, an American Civil War colonel who later became a lawyer and journalist who brought Buddhism to the Western world. He is still revered by Sri Lankans, who credit him with the revival of the study of Buddhism and consider him as one of their heroes."

"He should visit Lingsha," the president says, referring to the tallest copper Buddha, near Wuxi, which was built by the family of one of the closest associates on his leadership team.

"It is on his itinerary, sir," says Hu. "So are the other key Buddhist monuments."

"What is his position on the South China Sea?"

"He came out in support of Vietnam, Malaysia, Brunei, Philippines, and also Taiwan. But he did say that the Spratly and Paracel Islands, as well as the Scarborough Shoal, could be placed under a kind of international control commission, similar to the one set up by the Geneva Conference in the midfifties with Canada, India, and Poland."

"Is he still living in the fifties, or is he doing it just to annoy us?"

The room remains quiet.

"Please keep me posted on his other interests when we get back to Beijing. By the way, Shi is hosting a dinner for the female heads of government or foreign ministers, their first meeting, in Kunming. Does anybody know who are coming?"

"All of them, sir," replies Li. "Mexico, Guyana, Barbados, San Marino, Bangladesh, USA, Lichenstein, South Africa, Colombia, Pakistan, Cyprus, Croatia, Afghanistan, Azerbaijan, Syria, and Libya."

Not to be outdone by Li, Hu quickly says, "The Americans have recently sent a plane to pick up their precious cargo in Kabul, Baku, and Damascus. By the time they got to Tripoli, they will have all sorted out who will do what at the summit. It was an all-female crew commanded by one of the top officers in the air force."

"You make sure that Shi knows about this. Let's change the subject."

The waiters bring the president his favorite dishes: caramelized wild hog and so-called thousand-year-old eggs.

"In next year's Olympics in Guangzhou, I want us to present the ultimate Chinese hospitality. The families and friends of all athletes will be provided with accommodation, transported from door to door, and given food and entertainment with our compliments. I want it to be the new standard that no one can follow, especially the Chicago games that come after ours."

"It shall be done, sir."

"Good. Anything about the architect?"

"The good news is that she is coming to China," says Hu.

"When? What? Where?"

"Next month, sir. She is here to attend a UNESCO conference on monument conservation in Lhasa."

"The bad news is that you are not going to be here."

"Damn!"

"Is she coming to Beijing?"

"No, sir. She is going to drive from Kathmandu to Lhasa."

"What? Is the Golden Man coming?"

"No, sir. Goldman does not like to do that kind of thing. It's a waste of his time, he thinks."

"What *does* he do, if he doesn't want to be with his girlfriend?"

"Well, he wants to be with his girlfriend, but not with a few other people in such rough conditions. She wants to travel in her research with friends and colleagues. The last time Goldman did anything fun was when he attended Oshkosh."

"Os Kos?" the president asks.

"It's the largest annual gathering of aviation enthusiasts in Wisconsin. He is interested in buying some smaller aircraft manufacturing companies and merging them into one, to build single-pilot jets and turn them into a kind of limousine service in the air."

"We need something like that here. Li, you keep close tabs on his pet project."

"Yes, sir."

"What's next?"

"He then flew from Oshkosh, Wisconsin, to Oshkosh, Nebraska, which is about fifteen hundred kilometers to the west."

"He likes Os Kos?"

"Yes, sir. He had one of his motorcycles delivered there, and he rode the remaining four hundred kilometers in just over four hours to Sturgis, South Dakota."

"By himself?"

"No, with six of his riding buddies."

"What is there in South Dakota?"

"It's the largest gathering of motorcycle enthusiasts."

"Does he want to buy motorcycle companies?"

"As a matter of fact, he does. He wants to buy Indian, Harley-Davidson, and Victory and merge them into one."

"He wants to buy an Indian company? Keep another close eye on this one. Does he have any political ambitions?"

"No. He doesn't. But he usually helps a number of candidates at every election cycle. One of his candidates at the last election was totally unknown to the public, much less to the nation. She spent ten million dollars in the primary, beating six competitors, and only one million in the general election. He bankrolled all of her campaign. She became the first black Hispanic senator from Massachusetts."

"Is she leaving any signature in the Senate?"

"She is a rising star of the Republican party. She has no foreign policy experience besides spending two years in Botswana as a Peace Corps volunteer and speaking Spanish fluently. Her first committee assignment was in Foreign Relations."

"They sent a Spanish speaker to an English-speaking country?"

"Well, she actually has a nursing degree. And they needed somebody to teach the villagers about health issues at the time."

"So what kinds of footprints is she leaving in foreign policy?"

"She is what the Japanese call one of the beach people, a state that has a coastline."

"As opposed to what?"

"As opposed to the mountain people, those from the mountain states."

The president puts a piece of wild hog meat in his mouth and says, in slightly garbled speech, "Go on."

"She does not ask questions on foreign policy, but questions that the average Americans can relate to."

"What are some of the questions?"

"'Who was the first president to travel overseas?' 'Who was the first to travel to Cuba?'"

"She asked these questions to anybody?"

"To the nominee to be the assistant secretary in charge of Latin America and the Caribbean, who did not know the answers."

Li now takes over the Q&A session from Hu. "Do you know the answers?"

"Yes, sir. Teddy Roosevelt to Panama and Calvin Coolidge to Cuba."

"Then you should be their man for South America. You still have American citizenship, right?"

Li offers a hesitant smile. Everybody laughs, knowing that the president is just joking. "What other questions?"

"'Who was the first secretary of state to travel overseas?'"

"Who?"

"William Henry Seward, in the Lincoln administration, to the Virgin Islands under Denmark's rule, the Dominican Republic, Haiti, and Cuba, which was under Spain, all in January 1866." Financial adviser Lewis Li pauses for a moment. Hearing no interruptions from the president, he continues. "She and the committee chairman—"

"Is she a beach person also?"

"It is a man, a mountain person, the senator from Idaho."

"What are they conspiring on?"

"They are the authors of a bill requiring American diplomats to know more about America than the countries they are assigned to."

"Why don't we invite them to China?"

"They are coming during the next recess. Both are also on the Asia–Pacific subcommittee."

"Do you have a picture of her?"

"It is on the screen, sir."

"By Confucius! She is stunning. She looks like … What's her name? The Bond girl."

"There are many Bond girls, sir."

"The one who went to Cuba. You just talked about Cuba … Hai Lee Ba Ree?"

"Halle Berry?"

"That's the one. Make sure I am in town to receive her."

"Yes, sir"

"Back to the architect."

"Yes, sir. She is coming with some friends. And they plan to make a few overnight stops, camping along the way."

"Make sure she will be well treated without being too conspicuous."

"Yes, sir. They all will fly to Beijing, and Shi will be hosting the banquet in the Great Hall of the People."

DOUBLE E RANCH

Monday morning after breakfast, Colonel Lamenace leaves Goldie's ranch with Kunzang. He is giving her a ride back to UTEP and continuing on to Ruidoso.

Georgia and Goldie ride their horses back from the gate to the main ranch house. They find out that they have more things in common. "What was the most memorable assignment you had in your air force career?" Goldie asks, starting to draw her background out a little bit more.

"Every assignment had its special memories. But the one that is still stuck with me in my mind's eye is Letador."

"Letador? How did that come about?"

"I was on TDY in Moron, Spain, flying C-5MXs ferrying emergency supplies to Antananarivo in the aftermath of the tsunami. I met a Canadian woman from Montreal who was a Red Cross volunteer. We struck up a friendship, and she asked me to visit her in Paridor when able. I was contemplating leaving the air force when I completed ten years of service. I had already served in all the geographic commands, except for Africa." Georgia steers her horse away from a ditch and continues.

"The commanding general asked if I would be interested in going to Africom to handle its air training component, and I said yes. So Africom was my last assignment in the military. A week after I arrived at the command, I was asked to fly to Paridor from Dijon Air Base carrying some one hundred twenty thousand pounds of supplies for the French military mission. I got reconnected with my Canadian friend. On subsequent trips, she took me to the royal palace to meet with some members of the royal family."

"What's your friend's name?" Goldie asks.

"Rose."

"I'll be damned!"

Goldie listens intently to his guest and cannot wait to tell her his personal connection to the Golden State. He is patient enough to let her finish her story.

"After I left the air force, I got recruited by American United. They sent me to their training centers in Denver and San Antonio. Rose and I see each other every year, mostly in Paris, Montreal, New Orleans, and, of course, Paridor. In fact, I've been there more often than she has been out. I got involved in many of her charitable projects all over the country and in all of Africa."

"How did a Canadian woman end up in Letador?"

"Her father was a Canadian civil engineer building a road for a French company. The road went near her mother's village. That's how they met."

"I'll be damned!"

"So she is half African. But when you see her for the first time, you will think she is completely European or Caucasian. Her skin is very light."

"You were there during the turmoil?" Goldie asks, seemingly becoming more and more intrigued.

"I was there a few months before it took place. I told her that if something bad happened, she could come and stay with me in Santa Fe or Tampa."

"Did she come to stay with you after the coup?"

"No. She was airlifted out by the Chinese and then went to Paris, where I met her. I tried to convince her to go to Canada and even to come to America. But she said that her heart was in Letador, where her mother at one point took care of the royal children. After a few weeks in Paris, Rose went back to Letador with the brothers."

"The brothers? You mean the royal brothers?"

"Yes. I know them well. I know the sisters too. I am very sad about the whole situation. I hope we can help them work out some kind of comprehensive settlement that would be more lasting. I feel sorry for the people. They are some of the gentlest people I've ever met."

"You've become quite an expert on Letador."

"I spend a lot of time studying and learning in the country and elsewhere. The more I know about their culture and civilization, the more I feel attached to the people, the land, and Africa."

"You've been speaking quite a bit about the issue."

"I have, whenever time permits. I spoke twice at the Air Force Academy and twice at the Air War College."

"The one in Montgomery?"

"Yes, Maxwell Air Force Base. And Carlyle, Newport—"

"What were their reactions?"

"At USAFA, they were younger, so they were quite intrigued by the royalty, especially the prophecy that predicts the end of the dynasty with the death of the late king father, otherwise known as the ninth king. Those at the colleges are older, so they are more interested in the current situation of the brothers and the sisters."

"Over lunch, perhaps you would share with me some observations about the brothers."

"The brothers? I know them well. With pleasure."

TWENTY-NINE

The Brothers

DOUBLE E RANCH

THE PROGRAM FOR today includes a barbeque and a bonfire at six, followed by stargazing after dinner. Horses have been saddled up. Wranglers are standing by to guide anyone for a short or long ride.

Kunzang, Carmelita, and Miguel are in the swimming pool.

Sylvie is taking instruction from Juliana on how to shoot arrows. They are joined by Alice, Lionel's aide, and Rose, Bedel's protocol officer who took Goldie to the palace in Paridor at two o'clock in the morning. Except for Carmelita, all the girls are about the same age, single, and strikingly attractive. One Asian, one American, one European, two Africans.

Goldie is wearing his favorite yellow swimsuit, a straw hat, and a pair of sunglasses. He covers his naked upper half with a *krama*, Cambodia's multipurpose scarf. He has no shoes. He rarely has any footwear. He has made the two-acre grounds of the ranch house completely "barefootable."

The upper floor of the main ranch house, where his master bedroom, office, and study are located, is off limits. Staff can go there only when they are called. He is truly in his element when he does not have anything on.

Goldie is always comfortable when he is in a swimsuit, a western outfit, or pajamas, or when he is naked. By himself, he always swims nude.

A mint julep within reach, he is rereading *Un Amour Incomplet*. This is the nth time he has read the international bestseller. He has also watched the movie version numerous times.

Goldie loved the book even before he knew for sure that it had been written by the love of his life, Marie de Bourbon. He now wants to continue the story and complete it. He wants to turn *An Incomplete Love* into *Un Amour Retrouvé*. (Love Regained). Or maybe *Un Amour Unique* (A Unique Love).

It is not a long book. It is only some forty-five thousand words. It piques the reader's interest from the beginning. It is so smooth and real, so connected and inviting. It moves at a breathtaking pace. It is "unputdownable." It is a steady flow of liquid golden words poured from the author's heart.

All the brilliant details of each place the author describes attract those who have been there. They give those who have not been there an immediate incentive to visit and retrace the story. The sequences are incredible.

It is so hot that he can hardly touch the pages fast enough. He almost needs a chart to keep the plotlines going. Each chapter leaves him almost breathless. He is speechless at the end of each chapter, and he can utter only one word: "wow." He can't wait to turn the pages, yet he wishes that it will never ends. The mind and talent of the writer are truly amazing.

When the book was made into a movie, everybody knew it was going to be the movie of the year, maybe of the decade. Then it went to the top: Cannes, Golden Globes, Oscars. Somehow, most people find the work incomplete. It may remain *Un Amour Incomplet* forever. However, fans continue to pray that the anonymous author will complete the love story.

Kunzang gets out of the pool, picks up a huge towel with a tiger motif and wraps it around her exquisite body. Etienne rushes to her and asks if she would like to drink anything. She decides on a sweet iced tea. She walks toward Goldie, who is sitting by himself under the umbrella. He gets up and pulls out another green metal chair so she can sit beside him. She kisses his right cheek before she sits down.

"What would you like to drink?" That is his usual question for his guest. He never asks, "Would you like to drink something?"

"I've already asked Etienne for an iced tea," she replies.

Goldie puts the book down. He takes the tea from Etienne and gives it to her with both hands. She also receives it with both hands.

"Thanks."

"My pleasure."

The princess draws some tea from the bent plastic straw between her pink lips. When she finishes, he takes the glass from her and puts it down on the green metal table.

"Goldie."

"Yes?"

"I don't know how to thank you for being so kind to me."

"It has been my pleasure."

"I will miss you when I leave."

"So will I. But we shall meet again. Either here or there."

"Either here or there. That's what you always say to me. You have been a true friend. A loyal friend. Anybody is lucky who has you as a friend."

"You are the same to me. I am lucky to have you as a friend."

"I am sorry I hung up on you when you told me about my uncle's plane."

"It's understandable."

"My uncle has a son who is my age. We grew up playing together, going to school together. We are like twins."

"Where is he now?"

"He is taking a semester off from Oxford to do volunteer work in Africa. You have been to Africa a lot since we met."

"Yes, I have. Where is your cousin in Africa?"

"Letador."

"Where in Letador?"

"A small village named Notneh."

"I'll be damned."

"Sorry?"

"Nothing. Incidentally, our visitors this weekend are from Letador. Alice and Rose are from there too, but they are both métisses; Alice is half Belgian, Rose half Canadian. So you will have a chance to find out more about the place where your cousin is."

"That's wonderful."

Jean-Bedel Lemel is the first to arrive that morning at the Eagle and Elephant ranch, by helicopter. His half-brother Jean-Lionel Kadak decided to drive from Sierra Blanca airport.

Goldie greets each of them separately with a brotherly embrace.

Each has two aides, and they occupy opposite wings of the ranch house—Bedel, the northwest wing, and Lionel, the southeast wing.

The brothers come out of their suites at the same time, accompanied by their male assistants, who carry two boxes wrapped in golden paper. They all wear western outfits from head to toe: felt cowboy hats, cowboy shirts with two *E*s (the first *E* is embroidered backward: ƎE), jeans, and boots. Their belt buckles bear an eagle with its wings spread, sitting on top of an elephant with its trunk raised.

The women—Carmelita, Juliana, Kunzang, Alice, and Rose—are dressed the same way.

Everybody is a cowboy or cowgirl. Even Miguel, the youngest guest, is in complete western gear.

The two brothers take turns hugging and kissing Goldie on both cheeks. Bedel goes first. He is older. They turn to each other and shake hands.

"Come on, you can do better than that," Goldie says, offering encouragement.

They embrace each other but do not kiss.

Then they are introduced to the other guests.

"Carmelita Martinez. She is a friend and neighbor. Kunzang Wangdi, another friend and neighbor. My colleague Juliana Onerio."

The two brothers say *"Enchanté"* three times and bend to kiss their new friends' hands three times.

"And you know Alice and Rose." The two women giggle and curtsy to the brothers.

"Don't be silly. We are in Texas." Bedel kisses them on both cheeks. So does Lionel.

Goldie repeats the same introductions for the two royal assistants— Bedel's Paul and Lionel's Richard. He finishes the introductions by presenting his other key staff to his new guests: Juanita, Guillermo, and Etienne.

"Now let's do what we are here for; let's have fun. But first, let us pray together."

They all hold each other's hands around the bonfire, close their eyes, and bow their heads.

"Lord! We thank you for all the blessings you have bestowed upon us. We thank you for the food before us, the friendship between us, and the love among us. Amen!"

PARIS, FRANCE

The French president Marie de Bourbon presses the green button in the middle of the first ring. She has been expecting this call.

A golden voice from a smiling face under a black felt hat comes from the screen. *"Bonsoir, chérie!"* This is a portrait that she always loves to see and hear.

"Bonsoir, mon petit choux!" Marie de Bourbon says to her boyfriend.

"Congratulations on the resolution. I am very proud of you," Goldie replies.

"Congratulations to you too. You made me even prouder."

"You got the news already?" Goldie asks.

"Only the overall sketches. Sylvie has been reporting to me." Marie is hungry for more. "Give me the details."

"Saturday: barbeque, bonfire, stargazing. Then we gave Kunzang a surprise birthday party."

"How old is she?"

"Twenty-four! I alerted the brothers, who brought her very nice presents."

"What did they bring?"

"Almost identical exquisitely carved wooden roosters."

"Roosters?"

"Kunzang is a rooster."

"Like me."

"Yes! You still have the tiny rooster I carved for you in Notneh?"

"Yes. Right here. I put it on my lucky charm bracelet." Marie says. " Sunday?"

"Sunday, yesterday: horseback riding, swimming, archery, bonfire, stargazing."

"Same program?"

"Except that Lionel surprised us by cooking the dinner."

Marie seems surprised. "I didn't know he cooked."

"He was actually trained as a chef. He gave us a delicious six-course meal."

"I am salivating."

"Not to be outdone by his brother, Bedel treated us to postdinner musical entertainment."

"What does he play?"

"Guitar and piano. And he is quite accomplished."

"What did you all play and sing?"

"Bedel played a lot of Sinatra, Beatles, Bee Gees, et cetera. He is a sixties guy."

"So are you and I."

"So we are!" Goldie says. "He is so good that when you hum something, he plays along right away."

"You had a ball."

"We did."

"Today?"

"Today, Monday, full moon, grand finale: Horseback riding, swimming, hunting, bonfire, stargazing, moon gazing. I had a few telescopes. It was so clear that we could see the epsilon peak on the moon's surface."

"Did you see anything else?"

"We all sang 'Fly Me to the Moon,' and we pointed at each other when we said, 'I love you.'"

"Who did you point to?"

"To the moon. I saw you standing there!"

"Thank you."

"My pleasure."

"How did you get them to agree on the resolution?" asks Marie.

"I had Kunzang and Sylvie deliver a copy of the resolution to them the minute we received it from you. In the late afternoon, they asked me to go riding with them. Just the three of us. I showed them the wells, the irrigation system, the solar panels. I told them everybody who lives on the ranch dries their laundry in the sun." Goldie pauses to drink some water. "I told them this used to be hostile territory. Nothing grew. It was brown as far as the eyes could see. Now everything is green. It's my little corner of paradise. We were on horseback for about forty-five minutes before we stopped to rest at a cowboy shelter. I got them some cold bottled water. Then Bedel began. He repeated, almost exactly word for word, what you and I said last week at El Bosque Encantado: 'Goldie! Lionel and I appreciate very much your invitation. We have high regard and deep respect for you and Marie. You have done so much for our families, our people, and our country. We all value your longstanding friendship dearly. We know you have no vested interest in Letador except to bring peace and stability back. We have talked to our brothers in Letador. And we are speaking on their behalf. We are ready to implement the resolution.'"

"Bravo, Goldie," Marie says, congratulating her boyfriend again.

"Without you, I couldn't have done it."

"We have worked together as a team. And we will continue to do so. And the great thing about this is that you didn't put any pressure on them. You waited for them to come forward themselves. What did you say to them?"

"I thanked them on your behalf for putting the interests of their people and nation above everything else. And we hugged and kissed each other."

"Congratulations again, *mon petit choux*. You have helped prevent a war."

"Thanks, and thanks to you too. But I may have helped create another war."

"What are you talking about?"

"I think Bedel and Lionel are vying for Kunzang's affection. Although I was smart to put her between them when we held hands to pray, and I had Juliana and Sylvie on their other sides, I did not expect that the full moon's ambience could accelerate a budding friendship into romance that quickly."

"I think you may have overdone yourself. And all for good reasons. Tomorrow?"

"Tomorrow we'll get up early to again watch the sunrise in the cupola. But this time we will have breakfast there. Then we will ride horses to the ranch gate and take a mini bus to UTEP. There Kunzang will give us a tour of the Bhutanese-style campus. We will have lunch with the university president and a few faculty members, including the heads of their Africa and Asia departments. After that, we will take the brothers and their parties to the airport. Kunzang has invited Sylvie to spend a few days with her before returning to Paris. I think you already agreed to Sylvie's request for additional leave."

"I did. It's more work than pleasure for her. But she seems to enjoy it."

"After the brothers' departure, Carmelita, Miguel, Juliana, and I will return to Esperanza."

"Excellent. Thank you again. Sweet dreams."

"Sweet dreams."

THIRTY

The Lovers

HENRY GOLDMAN IS pacing the tarmac of his runway at Cabo San Antonio de Bolondron. He arrives directly from Teterboro airport after having fired two of his bankers for having said "to be honest" and "to make a long story short" twice in their presentations. The word spread around GPS from the beginning that he dislikes those terms. He views the users of those terms as being dishonest and taking too much time to close the deal. He feels that people must be otherwise, to keep saying things such as "to be honest," "to be frank," "to be direct," and "to be candid," and that they take more time by saying "to make a long story short." That is his reasoning. It is one of his golden rules. Those who have the gold make the rules, and he has the gold. And he also fires people who get into the elevator with him.

Goldman wanted to fly out here with Billie Samas, his current love, picking her up on the way. But she told him to go first for the Columbus Day weekend. She wanted to spend more time with her family in Washington. So he sent his jet to bring her from Manassas, Virginia. And this is the first time she accepted a ride from him.

He has been courting her for one year, and this is also the first time she has accepted his invitation to spend a weekend with him in Cuba. On one condition: she will have her own place, as before.

"I'll do anything to make you happy," he said to her on the videophone when he called her in Guadalajara to reconfirm the weekend.

Goldman ranks thirteen on the *Forbes* list of the richest people. Despite his enormous success in business, he is almost a total failure in love.

The first woman with whom he fell in love left him for a politician in the south. His three wives and all the women who had been through his door had been interested only in his money. For this one—the architect—his fortune, fortunately or unfortunately, has not impressed her. It is his philanthropy that attracts her attention. And more importantly, it is his attention to her. It is so unique that she is almost scared to be with him.

He has flowers sent to her everywhere in the world on her arrival. They are delivered every three or four days to her house in Chartres whenever she is at home. Any charity she has interacted with has its funding enriched by a million dollars after her visit: orphanages, teacher training, abused women, human trafficking victims, mine clearance projects, art schools, handicrafts, monument preservation, archaeological sites, architectural competitions, and anthropology research.

After three months of gift showering, she was completely soaked and decided to accept his invitation to dinner in New York, following a Broadway show. At that time, they agreed to see each other every month. They scheduled the following eight dinners, each combined with a cultural or charitable program: Washington (Kennedy Center Honors), San Antonio (The Alamo and Spanish Missions preservation plus *Madam Butterfly*), Mexico City (Museum of Anthropology), São Paulo (Academy of Art, Culture, and History), Tokyo (Ueno Park Rededication), Paris (Rodin Museum's Les Danseuses Cambodgiennes), London (British Museum's three hundredth anniversary), and Johannesburg (End Poverty

World Summit and photo safari in Botswana). The locations were chosen because one of them had to be there for business. They stayed at the same hotel, but never in the same suite, per her request.

The Gulfstream jet positions itself in such a way that Goldman faces his visitor when she exits. The door opens, and the stairs descend to the ground, almost touching his feet.

Out comes Billie Samas, one of the most stunningly beautiful women in the world. She wears a T-shirt under a leather jacket, blue jeans, sneakers, and sunglasses. She carries an oversize leather purse and an inviting smile.

"Welcome to paradise!"

"Thank you for having me here."

Goldman extends his right hand to help her down.

He kisses her on both cheeks and walks her to the yellow Hummer. He opens the passenger door and helps her to get in. He walks to the driver's side and slides behind the wheel. One of his staff who has been holding the door closes it and disappears.

While starting the car, he receives a kiss on his right cheek. He turns toward her and receives another one on his lips. It is the first time she has ever kissed him on the lips. Despite his numerous conquests of some of the most beautiful women in the world, Goldman feels he is floating in midair.

"What is that for?"

"For being so nice to me."

"It has been my pleasure."

ESPERANZA, TEXAS

Goldie always looks forward to what he calls his own Children's Summit. He tries to hold it once a month when his schedule permits. He invites all the children of his staff and close friends aged six to twelve to have dinner with him. There are usually twelve of them, including Miguel, who has joined the summit after his sixth birthday. This is Miguel's first attendance. As the newest member, he is seated on the host's right.

It is Goldie's way to overcome a sad chapter during which he lost everyone who was dear to him in the first cycle of his life. The summit is free for all discussions. But the children have learned from previous sessions that they have to do their homework or they won't be invited back.

Goldie asks each of the children to take turns saying a prayer.

He calls on Miguel.

"Lord, we thank you for the love before us, the food between us, and the friendship above us."

"Thanks, Miguel. I'm impressed. You heard it just the other day. I'll write it down for all of you to have it handy." Goldie makes a point not to admonish the children unless they make the same mistake twice.

"Who wants to tell us about the most exciting thing he or she has done since our last session? Lila?" He calls on the first girl with her hand up.

"Me and my parents went to visit my grandparents in California."

"My parents and I went," Goldie says, suggesting to Lila that she rephrase her sentence. "Jim? You have a question?"

"Where are your grandparents at?" Jim asks.

"Where are your grandparents?" Goldie says, telling Jim to drop "at." He then says, "San Francisco."

"Did you leave something there?"

"I left my heart in San Francisco."

"What is the other big city in California?"

"Los Angeles."

The conversation takes on a life on its own. Goldie lets the children carry it and jumps in only when there is a striking mistake or when he wants to ask a question. He wants to instill in the children spirit, discipline, purpose, and pride. These are the values he learned from his involvement in City Year, a program in San Antonio that gives young people up to twenty-four the chance to help underperforming children at local schools.

The children take turns in asking each other and answering.

"What is the nickname for California?"

"Golden State!"

St. Petersburg, Russia

It is an angry meeting at the bar. Beebee slaps Jim very hard the minute he sees his face. Jim stands there receiving his boss's blows without protecting or defending himself. He feels lucky that he has not been taken out of action already. The failure of Broken Arrow was not his fault. But for his boss, a failed mission does not exist.

"From now on, no communications between you and me. You get instructions from me only when we are face-to-face. Do you understand?"

"Yes sir!"

It is going to be another angry session, Beebee thinks. He plans to blast his friend for what he has just done to him, to his friendship. "Why didn't you veto the fucking resolution?" he asks the prime minister of Russia the minute he gets into the ornate room.

Vladimir Chevsin responds without lifting his head. "Marina wanted me to return to Moscow before she arrived in New York. We are never together in the same town outside of Russia. She must have changed her mind before she got into the chamber."

"Why couldn't you just abstain?"

"I would have, but I wasn't there."

"Did Kartona charm Marina to death?" Beebee asks, still angry.

"She did not give me any details, except that the meeting went very well."

"Very well? So Kartona got into her skirt?"

Chevsin tries to calm his friend down. "There was no interpreter, no notetaker. Just the two of them. I do not know if he got into her skirt or she pulled his dick out of his pants."

"Just the two of them. Just like you and Shi. So did you screw her, or did she screw you?"

"Watch your fucking mouth!" the prime minister of Russia, Vladimir Chevsin, shouts at the richest man in Russia, Boris Brandrokochev, his closest friend.

His friend does not relent. "'Watch your fucking mouth'? You spent three hours with the Chinese chick, and now you've become holier than the pope."

"Are you done?"

"I am."

"Now it is my turn."

"Go ahead."

"What was going through your sick mind to pull that shit in Mexico? Were you crazy? Stupid? Or both?" Chevsin bangs the table to emphasize his points.

Beebee does not respond and sits on the arm of a leather chair in the corner.

Chevsin points his finger at Beebee. "Put this in your little fucking mind. And listen to me good. The Americans are usually one step ahead of you. Goldman spends millions of dollars on his French chick. He lets her travel like ordinary people all over the world, doing all her charity shit. There are always at least two people traveling with her all the time. She does not know it. The rental car did not have any problem. It was Goldman's people who pulled the plug, literally, when they knew you were going to nab her between that place and her hotel. You are some lucky sons of bitches to get out of there alive. Goldman's people would have pulverized you then and there. But I think they wait for the right moment. If you listened to me or consulted with me, you wouldn't be that foolish. From now on, don't lift your fucking fingers until I say so."

"All right! Are you going to tell me about Shi?"

"No. Not today. Come to my dacha next weekend."

THIRTY-ONE

The Blue and Red

ENGLAND

T HE BRITISH PRIME minister and his Indian counterpart, Shivaram, are alone on the western veranda of the enormous country estate of Lord Chamberlain, the king's closest aide. The lord chamberlain and his families have owned the property for centuries. It is right on the water, a short drive from Gloucestershire airport on A48.

The lord's youngest son, Geoffrey Boyd, who became leader of the British Labor Party and prime minister a year ago, has been using the estate almost every weekend to entertain his closest associates and friends. This Friday he leaves 10 Downing Street with the Indian leader. They take the train to Bristol. He drives his guest, the Indian prime minister, to Severn Beach, where they get on a boat and go north to his father's castle. A very discrete security detail has been with them all along.

The British and Indian leaders have known each other for a long time—since their college years, when they played cricket together.

It is tea time, their favorite moment of the day.

"It's so good to spend the weekend with you again, Sri. Thanks for making time for me."

"Same here, GB. I thank you for your friendship. You have been there for me all the time from the beginning."

"Don't mention it, mate. You have done the same for me. You are full of wisdom, and I always look forward to spending time together and benefiting from it."

The two leaders have been such close friends that they can finish each other's sentences.

The recording devices that are being monitored a few thousand miles away switch between blue light for the British prime minister and red light for his Indian counterpart.

Blue: "I presume you want to talk about the South China Sea and Letador—"

Red: "Where none of us has any horse to play."

Blue: "Right! You and I can both sit on the sideline if we want to."

Red: "But I don't think we should."

Blue: "We are both concerned about the rise of China and Russia."

Red: "Right!"

Blue: "They are getting richer and richer, and more and more powerful."

Red: "They can be dangerous and get out of control if we do not do anything."

Blue: "They can become real bullies."

Red: "And we will suffer the consequences of doing nothing."

Blue: "What's your take on the Chinese and the Russians?"

Red: "I think the Chinese premier is a well-meaning person. I find her sincere and straightforward. She is very easy to deal with, and quite responsive. Unfortunately, she is totally powerless. All powers are in the hands of the president and, to a certain extent, his seven closest associates, who nobody knows about except you and the Americans."

Blue: "I was the first to speak with Kartona during the inauguration in January. At the time, he did not seem to know or care much about Africa. It was in total contrast to one of his predecessors."

Red: "George W. Bush?"

Blue: "He spent billions of dollars fighting HIV/AIDS and caring for women and children in the continent. Nobody gave him credit. He didn't seem to care about credit."

Red: "Just like what Ronald Reagan once said."

Blue: "'There is no limit to what a man can do or where he can go—"

Red: "'If he doesn't mind who gets the credit.' By the way, I am quite fascinated by the fact that Bush got along quite well with one of my predecessors."

Blue: "Manmohan Singh? The first Sikh to be India's prime minister? He got along with one of mine too."

Red: "Tony Blair! Back to Letador. Actually, the person who is most knowledgeable about Letador is not even working for the American government."

Blue: "I know who it is."

Red: "We are talking about the one the Chinese call the Cowboy."

Blue: "Exactly. He has been doing everything by himself, with little support from the government, yet he gets a lot of things done. Our people in Ghana reported that without him the bloodshed would continue unabated."

Red: "That place is so rich that the Chinese and Russians were ready to fight it out for all the bounty. And the Americans are going to stop them by helping the French without appearing to do so. All thanks to the Cowboy."

Blue: "How about the South China Sea? You are going to China shortly, and you made some stunning remarks supporting the Southeast Asians—Brunei, Malaysia, Philippines, Vietnam—and yet calling for the disputed islands to be under a kind of ICC."

Red: "I've met with them on a regular basis. The Vietnamese prime minister came to Delhi last month"

Blue: "You gave her quite a reception. You took her to Varanasi and other Buddhist sites and to quite an exclusive meditation center in the Himalayas."

Red: "We are both Theravada Buddhists, and we drew quite a bit of public attention when we started out."

Blue: "You are the first head of government of a Hindu nation."

Red: "And she is the first female prime minister of Vietnam, one of the fastest-growing economies in the world."

Blue: "She is very smart and quite attractive just like the Chinese premier."

Red: "She is one of the younger leaders who do not care much about ideology, only pragmatic results. The old communists have died out, and the younger ones think about their children and their children's children. Saigon is now competing with Shanghai and Singapore as a world financial center."

Blue: "And the Americans have two of their largest military bases in the world in Danang and Cam Ranh."

Red: "To the east, they have Subic Bay. And their navy is so powerful—more powerful than all the navies in the world combined. Ours have had exercises with them and the Southeast Asians for decades. It would be suicide for the Chinese to provoke the Americans. That is why the South China Sea problem is not going anywhere. It has been like that since ASEAN failed to issue a joint communiqué in Phnom Penh in 2012 for the first time in forty-five years, despite repeated requests from Brunei, Malaysia, Philippines, and Vietnam."

Blue: "It was called the ASEAN miscommuniqué. It seems like a lifetime ago. I guess since you and I were in grade school."

Red: "And now the Russians are making noise about their maritime claims, which antagonize the Japanese and Koreans. Chevsin took it upon himself to move the capital to Vladivostok to project their Pacific presence and power, and to a certain extent to please Marina, who was born there."

Blue: "She is another cutie. I have never seen any woman so beautiful at that age." The British prime minister sighs.

Red: "You forget Marie de Bourbon."

Blue: "She is in a class by herself. At dinner, maybe you and I can compare notes about the most beautiful leaders in the world. Let's change the subject. You are hosting the next nonaligned summit in Kolkata. A lot of people have come to think that it is completely irrelevant. People have been asking what you are aligned against, and if you are being more misaligned than nonaligned."

Red: "The Kolkata Summit may be the last one for the movement. It has been dying of old age, and it is going to die a natural death. Nehru and his contemporaries got it started in the midfifties at the beginning of the Cold War to stay neutral between East and West. In 1979, Tito made his swan song speech in Havana. Reagan came to power two years later and accelerated the defeat of communism and the end of the Cold War, which occurred when George Bush the father was in the White House. You and I were in high school."

Blue: "Another lifetime ago. It was then that the movement began to outlive its usefulness. And you kept on going for a few more decades, because it gave you a platform."

Red: "The time has come that we do not need that kind of forum anymore."

Blue: "You and I should get together to celebrate the end of an era, maybe at the next commonwealth summit at Bandar Seri Begawan."

Red: "I am with you on that. Let's plan on doing it inconspicuously. Tell me more about the Russians."

Blue: "Totally opposite of the Chinese, the Russian president does not have a lot of power, even though she was democratically elected by the entire nation. She does not run the government on a daily basis like Chevsin, whom she appointed to deal with the economy and the dragon."

Red: "He speaks Chinese fluently and has been trying to get close to the Chinese."

Blue: "To the Chinese prime minister especially—closer than the world knows."

Red: "I dread the day I see them together. I don't know whether it would be even possible. They are not ordinary people. They are the heads of government of very powerful countries."

Blue: "If it happens, one of them will have to resign. I can't see how they can be married and still remain in their posts."

Red: "It would be the first time in the history of humanity that such a marriage could take place, much less last."

Blue: "What are they going to do? Commute between Beijing and Vladivostok on weekends? Now it makes me think that Chevsin moved the capital to be physically closer to Shi or that his name is already there. How about Vlad in Vlad? It's a win-win proposal for him. He did it to please Marina so that she doesn't feel he is a threat to her. And at the same time, he can project Russia's global economic and military power, and be closer to Shi."

Red: "GB, I have something very personal to share with you. Remember the bicycle trip you and I took across Bhutan?"

Blue: "I certainly do. It is quite memorable. We met in Phuntsoling and went all the way to Tashigang. I'll never forget the Tongsa Pass. We saw the dzong in front of us, and it took us half a day to get there."

Red: "I may have a Bhutanese daughter whom I've never met."

Blue: "Oh Sri! How could it happen? I was with you the whole trip."

Red: "I went back briefly one more time to complete my research. That's when it happened. She is already twenty-four years old and a student at the University of Texas in El Paso."

SAN ANTONIO, TEXAS

Goldie, José, and Marty are together again to carry out a border patrol mission. They pick up the Cessna 182 with Garmin 1000 at Stinson and fly to Del Rio, where they get briefed at the mission base. They spend the weekend there launching two sorties a day before returning to Stinson.

"I know you both are very healthy, but I have to ask you the 'I'm safe' questions anyway. Do you have any illness?"

Joe and Marty respond in unison. "No, boss."

"Are you taking any medication?"

"No, boss."

"Are you under any stress—physical, physiological, psychological?"

"No, boss."

"Have you drunk any alcohol within eight hours, or within twenty-four hours?"

"No, boss."

"Do you have any fatigue?"

"No, boss."

"Have you been eating well? Are you well nourished?"

"Yes, sir."

"Good boys!" Goldie says to his crew. "The only new thing is that the president is coming to San Antonio for a fund-raiser today and there is a TFR. It does not affect us, but I want to make sure you are aware of the special bulletin in case you miss it." Goldie opens the preflight briefing and proceeds to pass the FAA temporary flight restrictions around to his crew.

FAA TO ESTABLISH TFR OVER SAN ANTONIO, TX THIS FRIDAY

A NOTAM has been issued that will restrict flight in the area during President Kartona's planned visit.

32 NM RADIUS TFR

Location:

On the SAN ANTONIO VORTAC (SAT) 209-degree radial at 7.9 nautical miles

From the surface up to but not including 18,000 feet MSL

Times: 11:00 a.m. local until 4:30 p.m. local

10 NM RADIUS NO-FLY ZONE

Location:

On the SAN ANTONIO VORTAC (SAT) 179-degree radial at 10.2 nautical miles

From the surface up to but not including 18,000 feet MSL

Times:11:00 a.m. local until 4:15 p.m. local and 3:15 p.m. local until 4:30 p.m. local

8 NM RADIUS NO-FLY ZONE

Location:

On the SAN ANTONIO VORTAC (SAT) 267-degree radial at 7.9 nautical miles

From the surface up to but not including 18,000 feet MSL

Times:1:30 p.m. local until 4:00 p.m. local

AFFECTED PUBLIC USE AIRPORTS

KSAT San Antonio Intl.

T94 Twin-Oaks
KSSF Stinson Muni
8T8 San Geronimo Airpark
1T8 Bulverde Airpark
5C1 Boerne Stage Field
74R Horizon
1T7 Kestrel Airpark
53T Cannon Field
KCVB Castroville Muni
KBAZ New Braunfels Muni
E70 Huber Airpark Civic Club LLC
23R Devine Muni

Goldie continues the briefing after passing the FAA report to his aircrew. "We are going to take off from runway one four, sterile cockpit up to one thousand feet, and turn left to go south of Kelly. There are a lot of C-5Ms and F-35s today. Then we fly to Uvalde cruising at ten thousand five hundred feet. There, get your cameras ready. The world glider championship begins today. There will be a lot of gliders in the air and on the ground. It is going to be quite a scene. I was in one last year. It was very exhilarating. From UVA, we will take the Laughlin VOR, then direct to Del Rio International. I have flown this route a few times; I am certain that's what the ATCs will direct us to take. If you don't have any questions, let's drain the main vein and plan to launch at zero nine hundred hours."

England

After the dinner, the two leaders sit in the library having their brandy. The British prime minister, Geoffrey Boyd, is still stunned by the revelation of his close friend Srichandra Shivaram.

"How can you be sure that she is your daughter, Sri?"

"I am not absolutely sure, but I am quite certain that she is the one. My intelligence chief has received regular reports from one of our agents who is on Goldie's staff. He has seen her regularly at the ranch. He has even cooked some curry dishes for her. I feel so terrible about this episode. I am at a loss at the moment."

"It's not your fault that you did not know about it for two decades. The mother chose not to tell you about the accident. When she passed away, your daughter was brought up by one of her uncles."

"I want to meet her and take my responsibility, GB. But I don't know how to proceed."

"Sometimes things seem to work out by themselves. You know that, Sri, don't you? For now, you may want to—"

"Go to my meditation center and search my soul."

"And cross the bridge when we get to it. I very much appreciate your sharing this with me, Sri. I am with you all the way. Whatever you want to do, whatever you will do, you will have my support."

"Thanks, GB. We've been together for a long time. I am thankful that we continue to be together."

THIRTY-TWO

The Test

HENRY GOLDMAN POURS the champagne for Billie Samas and raises his glass to his golden girl. "To you!"

"To us!" she says.

"How was your panel?"

"It went very well."

"Glad to hear that. What was it about?"

"The interactions between architecture, archeology, and anthropology."

"Your three favorite subjects."

"Yours too, especially since we met."

"I've learned quite a bit about these subjects from you since Angkor."

"It has been my pleasure to share them with you." She looks at him with a glowing love in her eyes and continues. "Henry, I came here to thank you personally for your attention and affection."

"It has been my pleasure."

"You've said recently you know me more and more each time we are together. You put it at ninety-six percent. That's a lot. I'd say sixty-nine percent."

"That's it?" Goldman arches his eyebrows.

"We are almost there. And you have been very patient. I think it's one of your virtues. I thank you for that. I want to clarify one more thing."

"I am here to listen to you, and I will do everything to make you happy."

"I trust your words. You have done a lot of good things with your fortune. I've been very impressed. But sometimes, although very rarely, you use it to get even."

"I don't remember doing that."

"There was one person who stole your first love from you. It happened a long time ago, when you were much younger. You must have spent at least half a billion dollars trying to destroy him and his people. You know whom I am talking about?"

Goldman is not usually out of words. He thinks for a moment and says, "Kartona?"

"Yes. William Alexander Kartona, president of the United States!"

"What does he have to do with us?"

"A lot. He is my father."

Goldman is stung, stunned, and completely dumbfounded. He feels like he has been run over by a thirty-four-wheeled truck. Never in his life has he been in such a position. Is this another battle in which he will have to accept a loss in order to live for another day to fight another fight?

It takes him a few seconds to say, "Thank you for sharing this with me. We will work something out. I will do anything to make you happy."

"I knew you would."

"Who else knows about this?"

"About what?"

"That Kartona is your father."

"Besides him, my mother, and me, I think there are only my great-grandmother—the Queen Mother, who called Marie de Bourbon, who called her cousin in Canada to take us in. That's why my brother and I were born there. And now, you. Even my brother does not know that the president is our natural father. My mother told me only last year, after you and I started seeing each other regularly."

She takes his hand and pulls him out of the dining chair.

"Let's go for a walk under this beautiful moon."

She puts her left hand in his back left pocket. He wraps his right hand around her waist. The lovers leave the dining room and walk through a tall glass corridor with exquisite orchids on both sides of the enclosed narrow foot passage. They exit the main house and move to the rose garden on the western side of the property and sit down by an Italian fountain. She holds his hand and looks at the beautiful sky. Henry follows her.

"This is truly heavenly, Henry, to be alone with you on such a wonderful night. November is a transition month for sky watchers like me. I have a romantic appreciation that you have planned this very well."

Henry smiles, acknowledging that his visionary strategy has been working better in the personal arena than in the professional field. For a moment he loses track of the fact that he has been seeing the daughter of his nemesis. He has spent tons of money defeating the current occupant of the White House, the father of the woman to whom he is eager to propose and with whom he is eager to have children. He knows that it is the time to make the final move—now or never. His thoughts are interrupted when she squeezes his hand.

"You see, the fall says au revoir to the summer constellations and encourages the winter constellations to feel welcome. The three most important star families in November are Andromeda, Cassiopeia, and Pisces. Here, we are still in the northern hemisphere, about twenty-one degrees north, and this is the best time to see the Andromeda constellation high up in the sky. Tonight the full moon is covering our earth with exhilarating soft light, but it hides the other important constellations from the naked eye. In the southern part of the heavens, you usually have Aquila, Sagittarius, Capricorn, Pegasus, Aquarius, Pisces, and Taurus. When I look at the sky, I look for you, the Pisces. Its constellation is in the shape of two fish that are joined at their tails by a common star."

He begins to gently wrap his arms around her. She wraps her hands around his in return and continues her admiration of the sky.

"Cygnus and Aries should be at the midway. In the north side, we have Hercules, Cassiopeia in the shape of a giant *W*, and other constellations. My favorite is Ursa Minor, which is mentioned in *Golden Bones* as one of the star families that guided the author out of the Cambodian jungle to safety in Thailand in the spring of 1976."

She stops to kiss him briefly on the lips.

"I like Andromeda, also known as Messier 31, a lot because it is a spiral galaxy, similar to our own Milky Way, but it is some two and a half million light years away from us. That reminds me of the bas relief depicting the churning of the Sea of Milk at Angkor Wat."

"I remember you told us that it was quite uncanny that these people— like other ancient civilizations, such as the Mayans—used astronomy and astrology to build their capitals. It is truly mind-boggling."

"You have a good memory, Henry."

"Only for very important things."

"We will always have Angkor." She puts her head on his chest and says, in a soft and gentle voice, "Oh, Henry, this is so magical. I am so happy to be with you." She whispers into his ear, "I don't want to be alone tonight."

HUNTSVILLE, ALABAMA

The whole country is in a festive mood between Thanksgiving and Christmas: lights, decorations, shopping. It is truly a holiday spirit that fills the air. It is also a time to forgive and forget.

Charles and Laura Hawkins are so happy that the first visitor to their new home is their best friend from Texas. He has come to spend the Thanksgiving holidays with them. It is the first Thanksgiving he is away from his ranch and his family. They have a lot to catch up on.

They are out this morning to get a twelve-pound turkey. That should be enough for the three of them. Charles drives; Goldie is the front-seat passenger. Laura spreads out her things in the back. She has fully recovered from the accident in Ghana.

At the time of the accident, they were living in Cape Town. Laura started her HII (for Hope Is It) foundation. One day they were in Accra to visit one of her school projects. They went to a gas station to fill up the car. A few minutes later on the road, they were hit by a truck in a head-on collision. They were on the left side of the highway. After living in South Africa for a few years, Charles forgot that the traffic in Ghana is right-hand. Both were hurt, but Laura more severely than Charles. She spent several months in a hospital and in rehabilitation. For a while, she was walking with a cane. She got rid of it six months before they returned to the United States.

Driving in Alabama is less dangerous than in Africa, Charles thinks. He is happy to see Laura happy to be home. They have been away for twelve years. A life cycle, per Goldie's rule. Everything that they started in Africa is on automatic pilot. They were able to leave the continent they came to love in good conscience. Now it is time to be thankful. A turkey will help bring everything together.

The two friends in the front seats are chatting away, and Laura continues organizing her things.

"Charles, it looks like a plant store about fifty yards ahead on the right," Goldie says loudly enough to be heard by everyone in the car.

"Okay, we will make a stop," Laura says from the backseat.

"It's not open yet, Laura," Charles says to his wife. "We can come back after we get the turkey."

"No. Let me take a look through the window to see what they have there."

She puts her right hand over her forehead and moves from one store window to another. She bumps into Goldie, who hands her a key.

"Why don't you open the store? It has your name on it."

She looks a little confused.

"You see: 'Laura's Pets and Plants.' It's yours. Congratulations!"

That is Goldie's present to welcome his friends back to the first state in alphabetical order.

CAMP DAVID, MARYLAND

President Bill Kartona is alone with the director of national intelligence for the first time since he took office. He is interested in the meeting between the prime ministers of China and Russia that has never taken place.

"Here are the transcripts of the conversation." The director hands over a leather binder. At forty-eight, she appears to be half of her age. The president tries not to look at her incredible legs. As much as he is attracted to beautiful women, he has a rule not to mess around with his staff. Not yet, anyhow.

"Three double-spaced pages? They were together for three hours and we have only three pages?" He normally does not read anything longer than one page. But he is disappointed not to find something longer on a subject that could create the scandal of the year.

"After they kissed, it went blank for ninety minutes. The next thing we heard was all about painting, poetry, and shooting—three of their common hobbies."

"I can't believe this. So after three hours they gave each other paintings and exchanged poetry or what?"

"Yes sir. Actually they did. He gave her a sketch of two birds perched on a cherry tree. And she gave him a landscape of mountains in western China. They produced the artwork themselves."

"The poetry?"

"He wrote 'Night is darkest for those who wait.'"

"And she?"

"'The sun will rise soon enough for those who are patient.'"

"In which language?"

"In Chinese."

"I can't believe this. I was preparing for a war, and here I am listening to Chinese poetry."

BEIJING, CHINA

The president of China calls in the usual suspects. He is still upset with the series of recent events: Taiwan, Pakistan, New York, and Li-Ta-Do.

He has been in such a bad mood that he is in a bad mood even when he is in a good mood.

He has a perplexed expression on his face. The usual suspects speculate that they are in for another wild ride.

"The Central Intelligence Agency and the Federal Bureau of Investigation? I told you to cut the fucking crap. Do I look that stupid? I know what the CIA and the FBI are."

"Yes sir." General Hu responds with a quiet voice that is almost inaudible. He has had a bad hair day each time China's exclusive club has met. He knows that he is still around thanks to his wife's close friendship with the president's wife. They do everything together, including playing mah-jongg every other night. The president trusts him because they have been together for a long time. "The CIA and the FBI's FCI—"

"The FBI's FCI? What kind of crap is that?"

"It's the foreign counterintelligence branch of the FBI."

"Why didn't you spell it out? How the hell would I know about a branch of the Fucking Bureau of Intimidation?"

Nobody dares to correct the president about his misspeach of the FBI. They all have their eyes down.

Hu continues his briefing slowly: "They have been tracking our tracking of the Russians. The Americans, British, and French are sleeping together. And the Russians changed heart after the Long Island meeting with our premier."

"I'll get to the New York vote later. Tell me about Li-Ta-Do. Tell me about the brothers. I thought we had them in our pockets already."

"The two brothers who went to see the Cowboy in Texas have been closer to each other than the rest of the family. They were born on the same day. On a full moon. They have different mothers. Bedel's mother is the second queen, and Lionel's mother is the fourth queen. Bedel is older by a few minutes, which gives him seniority in the palace. They usually sit next to each other at royal ceremonies due to their rank. Bedel went to Moscow, and Lionel came here after they were airlifted out of Paridor during the coup. A few months later, they all left for Paris and returned to Paridor."

"Training?"

"Bedel was a classmate of the Cowboy at Columbia. They were very close friends. They stayed in touch with each other and went on vacation together occasionally. Bedel practiced law for a while in Paris before returning to Paridor for good until the coup. When the Cowboy returned to Letador after nearly thirty years, Bedel had him brought to the palace at two o'clock in the morning and discussed the future of the country."

"The other one?"

"Lionel was also a classmate of the Cowboy."

"At Columbia?"

"No sir. At Choate-Rosemary in Connecticut, the school Kennedy attended."

The president shouts and bangs the table. "Which one?"

"President John F. Kennedy, sir."

"Why didn't you say so? There are a hundred of them."

"Throughout the years, the Cowboy has been a mentor to Lionel, who owes his life to him."

"The Cowboy was his lost father or what?"

"He rescued Lionel after he fell through the ice of a frozen pond while skating in New Hampshire."

"Go on."

"Lionel was trained by the CIA and went to South America. After he finished his training, his first job was in a restaurant called A Carne de Vaca Dourada (or the Golden Beef) in Indaiatuba, a beautiful city about ninety minutes north of São Paulo, where many Brazilian members of the upper class have their principal homes."

"The CIA has agents everywhere. Don't they? What did he do at the restaurant? Was he a waiter, listening to customers' conversations to pick up useful information?"

"No sir. He worked in the kitchen as the first sous-chef."

The president frowns.

Hu suddenly realizes that he may have confused the president with the acronym.

"Sir, Lionel was actually trained at the Culinary Institute of America, the CIA, to be a chef. There are three of them in America: Hyde Park in New York; Napa Valley, near San Francisco, California; and San Antonio, Texas. Lionel was trained in the last one, which specializes in Latin American cuisine."

The president, feeling his intelligence has been insulted, throws the napkin on the table and leaves the room.

"I have had enough of this fucking crap."

SHANGHAI, CHINA

The president asks his prime minister to meet him at the country home of the mayor of Shanghai, who has vacated the place for his boss. There will be only the two of them.

China's exclusive club members tremble at the thought of the face-to-face meeting. She will have her head chopped off for disregarding the instructions on the UN Security Council vote. They think. They are bracing for another wild ride.

He gives the opening salvo the minute she sits down. "I have worked very hard to maintain our country's status as a superpower. I have worked very hard to project the image of China as a modern state. I have worked very hard to convince the other central committee members to put you at the top. A single woman who is beautiful and smart is prime minister of the world's largest nation. You have done a good job during the past few years. And we are all very proud of you. But I am puzzled by your decision to press the green button at the UN. You could have at least abstained. What was going through your mind? How am I going to explain to the central committee members about your vote, our vote?"

Prime Minister Shi Won Yu sits up straight with both hands on her lap and her eyes on the ground. She speaks with a voice so soft that the president complains, saying, "I can't hear you."

"I said I wanted to come to see you right away after I got back from New York. I wanted to come to personally thank you for letting me be a member of your team. We have put China on the top of many of the world's lists, thanks to your vision and leadership." Shi looks at the president briefly and continues slowly. "The past two years, I have been a little distracted."

"Vladimir Chevsin?" asks the president.

"Yes, sir."

"I should have realized."

"You knew about it?"

"I did. But I did not expect that it would go that far and that fast."

"I am thirty-eight years old, and I have never been with a man before."

"Stop it," the president says.

Tears appear in Shi's eyes.

"Please let me finish my thoughts. All I have done so far is study hard, work hard, and be on the top of every single list. The most beautiful of all the world's leaders, the most this, the most that … I've made the cover of every magazine ever published. I've done all of this for you, to make you proud of me. But something seems to be missing." She pauses, takes a deep breath and a sip of water, and continues. "What I need now is love. Vlad makes me feel good. For the past two years, I have been everything to him. And he is prepared to leave everything for me. Now I am prepared to do everything for him."

"Stop it!" The president shouts.

Crying, the premier stands up. "No, you stop it. Here is my resignation. Thank you, Father!"

THIRTY-THREE

The Turkey

WASHINGTON, DC

THE SENATE APPROVES all the nominations that have been pending for the past few months and prepares to leave town for the holiday. The senators and their colleagues in the house have been energized by the landslide victory of their party during the midterm elections and subsequent ones.

The leadership has asked for an intelligence briefing before they all head for Ronald Reagan airport to be home for dinner. The leadership members meet in the office of the majority leader; the chairman of the senate foreign relations committee sits to his right.

Three briefers pass leather binders labeled "Eyes Only" to all the leadership members. There is no pen, pencil, or paper on the long wooden table or anywhere in the room. After a few minutes, two of the briefers go around the room to collect the briefing books.

"I'll be happy to answer any questions," says the chief briefer. "Otherwise, happy Thanksgiving!"

"Happy Thanksgiving!"

The leadership members almost step on each other exiting through the door to go to the airport. The chairman of the foreign relations committee stays behind. He normally gets a ride from the majority leader. They are from the neighboring states of Idaho and Montana and have been friends for a long time. They usually manage to fly home thirty minutes apart.

"Bob, what's been bugging me is that the Indian prime minister turned down the invitation from his Pakistani counterpart to fly to New York together. There was no meeting in the parliament that he was going to attend the following day. It was cancelled while they were watching the cricket game."

"I don't know, Dave. Maybe Shivaram didn't want to fly with all the others for security reasons. Maybe he knew that they all could be a target by the Chinese. Let's not lose sleep over this. I want to get home as soon as possible and have a nice dinner with my family."

"Yes, let's get home and be with our families. If I have any other thoughts, I'll call you."

"Do that. Call me also if you want to go hunting. I am in the mood for a moose. I believe you hunt the traditional way. Am I right or am I not wrong?" the senate majority leader says, teasing his friend.

"I have been bow hunting all my life, but I haven't gotten a moose yet."

"There is a first for everything."

"Yes, I like that."

ALABAMA

The phone rings in the middle of Thanksgiving dinner. Laura Hawkins answers it and says, "Please hold a minute." She turns to Goldie and suggests he takes the call in the guest room.

Goldie knows who the caller is before closing the door of his bedroom behind him.

"*Bonsoir, chérie!*"

"*Bonsoir, mon petit choux!*" says Marie de Bourbon. "Happy Thanksgiving!"

"Thank you."

"I have some good news for you."

"Tell me."

"I have accepted Kartona's invitation for a state visit to Washington next year. He is going to host a state dinner for me. I would like it very much to have you as a guest."

"Thank you."

"And also please give me some names of people you want the White House to invite to the state dinner."

"That's very generous of you. Can you tell me when?"

"It's going to be late August. Probably after the conventions and before Labor Day. I'll give you more details when you are here for Christmas."

"Thanks. Good night. And sweet dreams."

"Good night. Sweet dreams."

Goldie returns to the dining table with a smile on his face.

"You look like you won a jackpot," says Laura.

"Charles, Laura, how would you like to go to the White House for a state dinner?"

"Wow. Is that what the call was about?" Charles says. "I've not set foot at the White House since you and I were interns."

MONTANA

The phone rings in the middle of Thanksgiving dinner in Bozeman, Montana. The majority leader, Bob Kaufman, answers it.

"Bob? This is Dave. Happy Thanksgiving to you and your family."

"Thanks, Dave. Happy Thanksgiving to you and your family too."

"Hey, Bob, I am also in the mood for a moose. I'll join you next week."

"All right. Stand by. I'll give you the details soon."

IDAHO

The phone rings in the middle of Thanksgiving dinner in Boise, Idaho. Senator David Cardey, foreign relations committee chairman, assumes it is the majority leader, ready to tell him when and where to meet for bow hunting.

"So when and where do I meet you?" Cardey says after he picks up the phone.

There is silence on the other end.

"Where and when do I meet you?" the senator says again.

"Dave? This is Marina!" It is Russian president Marina Shakarova, his former girlfriend.

"Marina? What a nice surprise!"

"How can you still read my mind after all these years?"

"Of course. I think of you all the time. How have you been?"

"Very busy. I think of you too. Thank you for all your kind attention."

"My pleasure."

"Dave?"

"Yes?"

"Is it possible for you to come to Vladivostok for Christmas?"

Cardey is surprised at her invitation. Although they have not seen each other for a long while, they have stayed in touch.

"Well, I haven't thought about it. But thank you for thinking of me."

"It's very hard for me to travel outside Russia. She wants to meet you very badly. I think it's time for her to meet her father in person. You'll make me very happy if you can do that for me, for us."

"I'll do anything to make you happy, Marina."

"I know you would."

VIRGINIA

The phone rings in the middle of Thanksgiving dinner in Strasburg, Virginia. The butler answers it. "Ambassador Samas's residence."

"May I speak to Billie, please?"

"May I tell her who is calling, please?"

"Henry Goldman!"

"Please hold on a minute, Mr. Goldman."

Billie runs to the foyer after the butler tells her that her boyfriend is on the phone.

"Happy Thanksgiving, Henry."

"Happy Thanksgiving, Billie. Sorry to interrupt your dinner."

"Not to worry. It's so nice to hear your voice."

"Same for me. I am wondering if you want to go skiing."

"When?"

"This weekend?"

"Let me check. Can you hold on a second?"

"Certainly."

Billie asks her mother if she has planned anything for her and returns to the phone quickly.

"Yes, I'd love to."

"Wonderful. A helicopter will pick you up at ten in the morning and take you to Manassas for you to fly to Angel Fire, New Mexico. I'll wait for you at the airport. We will go to lunch before hitting the slopes."

"I can't wait."

"Same here. Sweet dreams."

"Sweet dreams."

MARYLAND

The phone rings in the middle of Thanksgiving dinner at Camp David. The officer on duty walks to the dining room and whispers into President Kartona's right ear. The First Lady looks at the president, but he tries to avoid her eyes. He then walks to the next room to take the call. "Marie-Catherine? Thanks for the turkey. Happy Thanksgiving to you and your family."

"Happy Thanksgiving to you and your family, Mr. President."

THIRTY-FOUR

The Conversation

T HE LARGEST ARMY in the world is the hunters of America, if counted by hunting license sales. This season there are some 700,000 hunters in Wisconsin alone. This puts it in the top ten largest armies in the world. This makes it more than the number of people who serve in armed forces in Iran and Venezuela combined. These hunters are deployed to the woods of the 20th largest state of some seven million people. The 6th-, 7th-, 8th-, and 9th-largest states of Pennsylvania, Ohio, Michigan, and Georgia deploy another two million people who hunt with their firearms. No one is killed in the process, and they all return home safely.

Vladimir Chevsin puts the magazine down when his phone rings with the tune of "By the Time I Get to Phoenix." He is not happy that he is being interrupted during one of his favorite pastimes, reading everything about firearms and hunting. In one of his previous incarnations, he was trained to defeat his competitor in the most furious and fastest way. Like the mayor of Chicago, whom no one dares to cross, he always moves first to deny, delay, disrupt, denigrate, dismantle, demolish, and destroy his enemy.

He is even less happy that the caller, regardless of how close he is to him, is still in the doghouse. He looks at the phone and lets it ring until it stops. He picks up the magazine to continue his reading, but the phone rings again, this time with the tune of "My Way."

He presses the green button on the remote, and Beebee appears on the screen.

"What's the matter with you?" Beebee shouts at the Russian prime minister. "Why didn't you answer my call?"

The Russian leader shoots back. "I am not in the mood to have a conversation with anybody, especially you. Why did you call me again at this number? I told you to use it only in case of emergency. Are you getting killed or something?"

"The one who can kill me has not been born yet. And he will never be born. It is you who will be getting killed, if you don't listen to me."

"What's the fuck are you talking about?"

"I am in Shanghai. So are the president and prime minister of China."

"You are with them? And you didn't tell me about it?"

"I am not with them. We are only in the same town. I have some urgent meetings with my Chinese comrades. And my sources told me that your chick is going to be fired." Beebee is referring to Chinese prime minister Shi Won Yu.

"Bullshit. I just talked to her this evening. She told me she was going to visit her father, as she has not seen him for a few weeks since she went to New York."

"All right. You can wait and see, or you can do something. Where are you now?"

"Only a few time zones away."

"I thought you were in St. Petersburg."

"I was there, but now I am here."

"It's impossible to keep track of you."

"You'll never get used it, even after all these years."

"You are in Vladivostok to be closer to your Chinese chick. I should have guessed. Shi got into trouble with the leadership when she did not veto the UN resolution. So her boss is taking her to the doghouse. You should also know that the Chinese are aware of our weapons in Angola and Namibia. You should know there is a heavy Chinese presence in Letador, even though there are hardly any Chinese living or working there."

The video conversation between the Russian tycoon Beebee Brandrokochev in Shanghai and the country's most powerful man, Vladimir Chevsin, in Vladivostok has been encrypted from the beginning. They feel at ease talking and cursing in their most natural way, without knowing that their conversation is being monitored in the nearby city of Suzhou and on the Korean island of Jeju.

Shanghai/Beebe: "It seems the Cowboy has a new partner; somebody named Ragan likes the former American president. This Ragan is as ruthless as the former president. Do you know anything about him?"

Vladivostok/Vladimir: "It's a woman who could be your worst nightmare. She is beautiful and she is even more dangerous."

Shanghai/Beebe: "I have never met a woman who can be a nightmare to me. They all are my dreams."

Vladivostok/Vladimir: "You'd better be careful. Among many things, she was a member of the air force pistol team, and she was once their champion for two years in a row."

Shanghai/Beebe: "How do you know about an American air force chick?"

Vladivostok/Vladimir: "Don't ever say 'how do you know' to me again. Ever. You seem to forget I was a professional intelligence officer and that I am the leader of a superpower."

Shanghai/Beebe: "Excuse me. I am sorry, sir."

Vladivostok/Vladimir: "I have followed her closely since I read that she became the winner of the World Gliding Championships in Uvalde."

Shanghai/Beebe: "Where the hell is Youvaldee?"

Vladivostok/Vladimir: "Uvalde, Texas. It's about ninety minutes west of San Antonio. You know where that is, right?"

Shanghai/Beebe: "Yes, I do. I have been there once on the way to Venezuela. It seemed at the time that all flights to and from Central and South America changed planes or crews in San Antonio. And some of my colleagues changed planes there once on the way to Mexico."

Vladivostok/Vladimir: "That was when you pulled that stupid sting. Don't get me started on that. I flew to San Antonio to go to Uvalde when I went for the gliding championship competition"

Shanghai/Beebe: "I almost forgot you were also a glider pilot. That was the year a Lithuanian doctor and a Ukrainian engineer beat you. But you had a good time, didn't you?"

Vladivostok/Vladimir: "I had a swell time. The people of Uvalde were so hospitable that a local banker gave me the key to his house, where my teammates and I stayed for three weeks. The weather there is usually perfect for gliding in July and August. There was only one clear blue day when there was not enough moisture in the air to form cumulus clouds at the top of thermals, where the lift is located. These thermals can keep the gliders in the air five or six hours; that's why they returned to Uvalde for the fifth time. The only two other American cities to host the event once each were Hobbs in New Mexico and Marfa in Texas."

Shanghai/Beebe: "Martha, Texas?"

Vladivostok/Vladimir: "No, Marfa: mike, alpha, romeo, foxtrot, alpha. The town is also known for some mysterious lights that are seen every night."

Shanghai/Beebe: "Where the hell is Marfa?"

Vladivostok/Vladimir: "It's about a five-hour drive west of Uvalde."

Shanghai/Beebe: "What are the gliders made of?"

Vladivostok/Vladimir: "They are made of carbon fiber except the tail, which is made of fiberglass. They have all kinds of instruments, can soar over one hundred miles per hour, and can cover five hundred to six hundred miles. Each pilot also carries a parachute, just in case."

Shanghai/Beebe: "So how do you compete in a gliding championship?"

Vladivostok/Vladimir: "The competitors are given a zigzag route to fly. It is usually about four hundred to five hundred miles long. The gliders are monitored through electronic devices. The winner is the one who returns to base in the shortest amount of time."

Shanghai/Beebe: "What was your best time in Uvalde?"

Vladivostok/Vladimir: "I covered a five-hundred-mile route in four hours and thirty minutes. Do you know anything else about Uvalde?"

Shanghai/Beebe: "Isn't it the home of a former movie star?"

Vladivostok/Vladimir: "Matthew McConaughey! And it is also the birthplace of John Garner."

Shanghai/Beebe: "The other movie star?"

Vladivostok/Vladimir: "No, you are thinking about James Garner. Not that one. This is John Nance Garner."

Shanghai/Beebe: "What's so special about John Nance Garner?"

Vladivostok/Vladimir: "He was the thirty-second vice president of the United States, serving under—you know who?"

Shanghai/Beebe: "Hillary Clinton?"

Vladivostok/Vladimir: "No, she was never president. She was First Lady and secretary of state. You only remember women."

Shanghai/Beebe: "I thought she was cute when she was First Lady with that headband and thirty-six different hairstyles, but still not as attractive as Michelle with her extravagant dresses. And her legs. Oh my God! I love that picture of her descending *Air Force One* in shorts."

Vladivostok/Vladimir: "Both Hillary and Michelle were cute. Garner was a vice president under Roosevelt. FDR! You know what he was famous for?"

Shanghai/Beebe: "What is this? An American history lesson? How the hell do I know what the thirty-second vice president was famous for? He probably hated his job and said in an open mike, just like Michelle's husband told Medvedev, that he would be more flexible after the election; that he'd rather be president instead of being number two because his job was not worth shit. Am I right or am I not wrong?"

Vladivostok/Vladimir: "I hate to say this, but you are quite good on this one. I am impressed. He said that the job of vice president was not worth a bucket of warm spit. He turned ninety-five years old on November 22, 1963, and JFK called him to wish him a happy birthday. A few hours later, Kennedy was dead."

Shanghai/Beebe: "Did Garner feel bad about Kennedy's death? If JFK hadn't called him to wish him a happy birthday, he would have missed the assassin's bullets. I hate to ask you this, but why do you know so much about this guy Garner?"

Vladivostok/Vladimir: "When I was in Uvalde, my host family asked me what my interest was besides competing in glider flying. I said history, so they gave me one of their trucks and showed me on the map where the Garner museum was. I spent a few hours there. I even went to Garner State Park, just thirty minutes north of Uvalde."

Shanghai/Beebe: "That's why you lost to the Lithuanian and Ukrainian guys—because you spent more time in museums and parks than you spent resting."

Vladivostok/Vladimir: "That was not the case. They were actually in different classes—the fifteen-meter class and the eighteen-meter class. I was in the open class. But they did get more points than I did, over seven thousand each. And the press made such a big deal because they were from our former Soviet republics. Back to Garner. He was also the forty-fourth speaker of the American House of Representatives before he became veep. And he lived to be almost one hundred. He died in 1967, two weeks short of his ninety-ninth birthday. He was the longest living vice president of the United States."

Shanghai/Beebe: "It's normal now that people live to be one hundred and over, but that was not the case in the twentieth century. Do you want to live to be a century old?"

Vladivostok/Vladimir: "Only if Shi is with me!"

Shanghai/Beebe: "You are incorrigible. What is going to happen to you if it doesn't work out?"

Vladivostok/Vladimir: "I'll cross the bridge when I get to it."

Shanghai/Beebe: "Didn't you go to Argentina and Spain after Texas?"

Vladivostok/Vladimir: "I did, but not to compete. I was already in the spying business, so I went there as a journalist."

Shanghai/Beebe: "That's where you learned how to tango, in Buenos Aires and Madrid. And you impressed the whole world when you invited the First Lady of Argentina to dance with you in New York."

Vladivostok/Vladimir: "Remember, I danced with Shi first."

Shanghai/Beebe: "It was not tango. It was bossa nova when you danced with Shi. And you tried to bring her closer to you. And she tried to keep some distance between your dick and the lower part of her incredible body."

Vladivostok/Vladimir: "You were looking at us that closely?"

Shanghai/Beebe: "I know you better than the rest of the world; that's why I keep an eye on you all the time. Back to this Ragan woman you mentioned earlier—what about her?"

Vladivostok/Vladimir: "She has become a partner of what the Chinese call the Cowboy."

Shanghai/Beebe: "His girlfriend?"

Vladivostok/Vladimir: "No. They have met through a ninety-six-year-old veteran of all the latest wars. They have teamed up to work on Letador. They can be our formidable foes, in addition to the Golden Man. And that's just the Americans alone."

Shanghai/Beebe: "And we also have the invisible Chinese as well."

Vladivostok/Vladimir: "So be very careful. Don't do anything stupid without checking with me first. Things can get very ugly. I don't want to leave any footprints in this."

Shanghai/Beebe: "Are you saying we should back out, slow down, or come to a full stop?"

Vladivostok/Vladimir: "I am saying we should slow down and take another look at our strategy. The Cowboy and the Ragan woman are the only two people the brothers listen to. They have spent more time in Letador than you and I have spent at home."

Shanghai/Beebe: "I need more information about the Ragan woman."

Vladivostok/Vladimir: "I'll give it to you in person. Get your smelly ass out of Shanghai and China altogether as soon as you can, before your Chinese comrades screw you."

THIRTY-FIVE

The Resolution

C HARLES HAWKINS GETS up at six o'clock, which is as dark as midnight in the winter, and finds his copy of the *Wall Street Journal* on the front steps. His neighbor has beaten him five days in a row by delivering his paper to the front door before he is able to do a similar courtesy. He also beat him on returning the trash container to the side of his garage two weeks in a row.

His morning ritual includes watering the flowers, the plants, and the big trees, which include live oaks and Spanish oaks. He does not use sprinklers and soakers. They deprive him the pleasure of hearing the sound of the water hitting the bottom of his green company.

Their fauna and flora inventory is quite impressive: aloe bed at the entrance, baby's breath, boxwood, Japanese yew, lantana, nandinas, oleanders, pomegranate, big purple sage, salvia, sword palms, trumpet vines, and a beautiful old stand of wisteria. The house is surrounded by hardy rosemary beds, and the two-acre property is protected by fully grown primrose jasmine all around the perimeter. They have also planted asparagus ferns, bougainvillea, and different kinds of citrus (guava, key lime, kumquat, Meyer lemon, and tangerine). In the swimming pool area, they have geraniums, ginger, many colorful hibiscus, jasmine, lemongrass, moonflower bush, night blooming cereus of Laura's family, sago palm, shrimp plants, and succulents. In the backyard in the north also stand numerous pecans and loquats, in addition to some one hundred oaks, both Spanish and live. Some of them are sixty feet tall. Charles and his yard man have kept the root flares clean and visible.

It usually takes him about forty-five minutes to finish his morning chores. He waters the big trees only every three days. He has been a little frustrated that the six crape myrtles he planted after they bought the property have not bloomed. He decides that the best time to transplant into full sun is while they are dormant in the winter.

Laura is still asleep, as she goes to bed later than he does. He goes for a quick morning swim naked and takes an outdoor shower in an area completely surrounded by tall bamboo. After dressing casually, he gets ready for one of his favorite moments of the day: consuming a breakfast of baguettes and caffe latte while watching the sun slowly rise behind the live oaks.

He usually starts the paper from the right side of the front page. Then he switches to the left side, where a short clip catches his eye:

The United Nations is implementing the latest Security Council resolution by establishing a UN advance mission in Letador (UNAMIL). Plans are under way to deploy 20,000 UN peacekeeping personnel to stabilize the country and organize an election within one year. This is the second-largest peacekeeping operation, after Cambodia in the early 1990s. Thirty-six political parties have registered to participate in the polls under the supervision of the United Nations.

Charles Hawkins picks up the phone and calls his best friend, never knowing which time zone he is going to be in. The phone rings thirteen times before he hears his friend's voice.

"Thanks for calling and leaving me a golden message. May you always be blessed!"

"Goldie! Congratulations. You did it! I love you, man!"

THIRTY-SIX

The Golden State

EACH TIME HE is in the Golden State, Goldie says to himself, "I'll be back," borrowing a famous line by Arnold Schwarzenegger. He feels energized the minute he gets off the plane, even though he does not care much about the traffic on its freeways.

This time he flies to San Francisco and rides a rented Harley-Davidson to Concord, about forty minutes east of the city. It has become his annual ritual.

He fell in love with the Golden Gate Bridge after he once flew a single-engine Cessna 182 at only one thousand feet above the bridge. He does not ever forget the view on that June day. The sky was perfect blue, as blue as the one over Mongolia, otherwise known as the Blue Sky Country.

This morning he took off from Concord in a rental plane and flew directly to the bridge. On the way, he saw Richmond on the right and Berkeley on the left. He wonders if the people are still having their *grasse matinée*, a French expression he learned in Letador that refers to sleeping late, especially on Sunday. Near the bridge, he slows down to ninety knots. He has become an expert on slow flights in his search-and-rescue training. Pilots must fly low and slow if they want to look for and find something.

After the bridge, he salutes Redwood National Park in Humboldt County, home of the tallest trees on earth.

Back on the ground, he rides a motorcycle to the park and gets his lifetime membership of the national park system on the spot. On his mental bucket list, he adds "Visit all the national parks in the country, including walking the Appalachian Trail."

Back at his ranch, he decides to paint the verandah of his ranch house red in honor of the redwoods.

Goldie was so overwhelmed by the view he had from the air during his low flight that he promised himself that one day he would walk across the Golden Gate Bridge. At 4,200 feet, it was the longest bridge in the world between 1937 and 1964. It has slipped to number ten since then, surpassed by the Verrazano Narrows, which, at 4,260 feet, held the record between 1964 and 1981 and still remains the longest in North America.

He added to his bucket list walking the ten longest bridges in the world so that he could keep the Golden Gate as a benchmark. He began to compile his list and check it off one by one as he completed each walk: Akashi Kaikyo (6,532 feet) in Japan, Xihoumen (4,414) in China, Great Belt (5,328) in Denmark, Yi Sun-sin (5,069) in Korea, Runyang (4,888) in China, Humber (4,626) in England, Jiangyin (4,543) in China, and Tsing Ma (4,548) in Hong Kong.

The first bridge he walked across was not even on the top ten list, but he felt he had to start somewhere. It was the Brooklyn Bridge, which he crossed one beautiful Saturday in May some years ago.

That day he also walked the entire length of the High Line on the West Side of Manhattan, which has become a popular spot among tourists and New Yorkers. He was even more delighted to know that it was designed by someone from his hometown of San Antonio.

After the Brooklyn, he walked across all the bridges in New York (Manhattan, Williamsburg, Queensborough, Triboro, George Washington, and Verrazano Narrows). This was the year before he reached the Golden Gate.

Goldie normally crosses the GG, as he affectionately calls it, around its anniversary at the end of May, when he also goes hiking in Redwood. He missed it this year, because he was in the other Golden State, Letador.

Texas

Georgia Ragan was also in Letador that May. She did not cross paths with Goldie, but she was carrying out a mission on her own to save the country and people she came to love during her last assignment in the air force. She was doing the same thing as Goldie—anything she could do to help stabilize the country in order to find a lasting, peaceful solution to looming conflict between China and Russia that could prove deadly for the people of Letador.

She took time off from her airline job, flying on the average one thousand hours a year and spreading the word.

At a lecture at the National Defense University at Fort McNair in Washington, DC, she kept the standing-room-only audience captivated by her presentation with slides of unusual photographs. She displayed an incredible knowledge of the key players, the average people, and the country with a very personal touch.

Shortly after, she met Goldie through her mentor, USMC Colonel Lamenace.

She and Goldie immediately joined hands to fight for a common cause: freedom and democracy—for Letador in particular, and Africa and the rest of the world in general.

As the superstar of the US Air Force of her generation, she truly moved at lightning speed—faster than Eisenhower, who went from lieutenant colonel to five stars in fifty-five months.

After the Air Force Academy, she spent fifty-three weeks at Laughlin Air Force Base, which produces a group of freshly minted pilots every three weeks. She graduated at the top of the thirteenth class of her basic pilot training. The twenty-four members of her class went on to train further in initial type ratings, including bombers, fighters, tankers, and transports. They spanned out to various air force bases all over the United States, from Alaska (Elmendorf) Air Force Base to Florida (Tyndall), and everything in between: California (Beale, Travis), Arkansas (Little Rock), Arizona (Davis-Monthan, Luke), Kansas (McConnell), Louisiana (Barksdale), Oklahoma (Tinker), and South Carolina (Charleston).

Four of them went to Air National Guard bases: Sioux City in Iowa, Rosecrans in Missouri, Hancock Field in New York, and Rickenbacker in Ohio. Two went to Kadena in Japan, and two to Ramstein in Germany. Most of them stayed on in their field and would become the best of the best officers in the US military, not simply in the air force.

Ragan was first among equals. Had she remained in the service, she could have been the first female chief of staff of the air force less than the average thirty-six years after graduation from the Air Force Academy. However, after only thirteen years, she ran out of challenges and decided to leave her beloved air force. She did not go far from aviation and from the air force, though; she stayed connected to the air force by immediately joining the US Air Force Reserve. Since then, she has had the best of both worlds: serving and serving more.

The airlines were engaged in a bidding war to have her join their pilot corps. After going on board, soon enough she became its chief pilot for the 747-8.

According to a cover profile published by *Ladies First,* the magazine that specializes in the most successful women in the world, she is one of the 10 percent of the American population who are left-handed. "She is the first woman to have won the World Gliding Championships in the open class that took place in August last year in Uvalde, Texas. Her glider, built in Poland, has a thirty-two-meter wing span, one of the widest in her class."

She never forgets where she came from. After the awards ceremony, she drives seventy miles west to Del Rio to visit Laughlin. On the way, she passes Brackettville and regrets not ever having a chance to see the location where John Wayne shot *The Alamo* in 1960.

The commander of Laughlin Air Force Base, who was trained there a few years after Ragan's graduation, gives her a huge welcome-home party. August can be a brutal month in South Texas; it was 102° F in Uvalde and 104° F in Del Rio. The event was held in the stadium of the base, which is only five miles west from downtown. It was packed by air force members and their families, and many of the thirty-five thousand citizens of Del Rio, who brought their children to meet their future role model.

She decides to drive to town the following morning to visit some of her favorite hangouts under a drizzling rain. At the Greasy Table, the place is packed with families and children who recognize her from the previous night. The far corner table to the right is full of tattooed men and women in leather outfits. They are having the Tall Texan breakfast with piles of pancakes, bacon, sausages, and eggs on each plate.

Ragan drives to Main Street to have a look at her favorite seafood restaurant, Las Playas de Mis Sueños. It is still there with the same hours of operation: 10:00 a.m. to 10:00 p.m., seven days a week. She smiles and goes to Chick-fil-A to order a number-one meal.

CALIFORNIA

Goldie usually builds in enough time to visit at least one of the presidential libraries whenever he is in the Golden State. After San Francisco, he flies to Santa Ana, rents a car from John Wayne Airport, and drives north to Yorba Linda. He has not been to the Nixon Library for a few years and wants to take a look at any new exhibits. Nixon is the only presidential library that is also the presidential namesake's birthplace.

He was attracted to Richard Nixon first because the president was born in a year ending in thirteen, like Gerald Ford. Somehow, he can also associate himself with Nixon, who once said, "Only when you've been in the deepest valley can you ever know how magnificent it is on top of the highest mountain."

After a few hours at the Nixon Library, he returns to John Wayne and flies to Bob Hope Airport in Burbank. There he picks up another rental car and drives to Simi Valley. He wants to spend a few hours in the afternoon at the Reagan Library before his other favorite time of the day: sunset.

The Ronald Reagan Presidential Library has the largest collection of all the presidential libraries and commands exquisite views all the way to the Pacific, especially at sunset.

Goldie takes a deep breath of fresh air in the rose garden, closes his eyes, and dreams that he is flying all the way to Angkor, where he has collected so many fond memories. Then he continues to Paris, just as the love of his life did a few decades before with her twin sister. If he were to leave LAX this evening, he would get to Siem Reap in twelve hours and to Paris from there in another twelve hours. Paris and Marseille have been the highest peaks of all mountains that he has climbed. His is the last plane to land in Paris. All aircraft over the western part of Europe have been grounded. An ash cloud from a volcanic eruption in Iceland has slowly begun to blanket England and France.

All trains and buses are fully booked. But nothing can stop Goldie from seeing his lover. From Paris, he takes a motorcycle for the 777-kilometer ride to be with MDB at the Golden Forest. She is just beside herself to see her lover at the front door.

"Sir, sir." The security guard of the Reagan Presidential Library wakes Goldie up from his dreams. "The library is closed."

JAIPUR, INDIA

The British and Indian prime ministers return from hunting on the backs of elephants. They are alone on the terrace of the enormous hunting lodge, which was built by a seventeenth-century maharaja. Some lodge. The waiters immediately disappear after serving the VIP hunters their favorite beverages: gin and tonic for the British prime minister and freshly squeezed lime juice for the Indian host. They toast each other for a successful hunt. Both have their feet on ottomans. They admire the last rays of sun on the horizon.

"GB, I want to thank you very much for stopping by here on your way back to London from Melbourne. When we were last together in England, we agreed to meet at every opportunity to share thoughts and compare notes. You have just visited France before going to Germany and Australia. And I just returned from China. So I thought it would be good timing for us to be together again."

"I thought the same way, Sri. Perfect timing. Thank you for the invitation. You go first."

"The Chinese are going through a soul-searching period. I did not learn all about it when I was there, but several of our sources corroborated after we learned that the president and the prime minister had a heated one-on-one meeting the week before I arrived. It seems that this year has been an annus horribilis for the Chinese: the Taiwan fiasco, the Pakistani plane, and the UN vote. Now they have no choice but to go with the resolution."

"You made me think of our own annus horribilis in 1992, when Queen Elizabeth II gave a speech on November 24."

"To mark the fortieth anniversary of her accession as queen of England. Unlike Frank Sinatra's, it was not a very good year."

"It was not. In March, her second son, Andrew, the Duke of York, separated from his wife, Sarah, and in April, her daughter Ann divorced her husband. And throughout the year, her daughter-in-law Diana was the subject of tabloid rumors regarding an affair. Finally, four days before her speech, Windsor Castle caught on fire, which destroyed some of its historic buildings."

"And now the Chinese have their annus horribilis."

"Everyone was so surprised that the Chinese voted yes on that resolution. We suspected that the best we could get would be an abstention from both China and Russia. This is one of the few times since the early 1990s when Singh, Thatcher, Bush, and Mitterrand were in power that we got a unanimous vote at the Security Council."

"I have to admit that Marie worked very hard on this one. You could see that it came from her heart, a truly passionate endeavor to prevent the bloodshed from continuing and returning peace and stability to one of the countries where she spent an early part of her life. She also has had some good help from her ex-husband, the restaurateur, who started out in Suzhou and now owns the largest and best restaurant chains in the Chinese-speaking world."

"And he has a very strong and solid connection to the leadership."

"That's right. His wife is related to one of the members of the leaders' council."

"A daughter of the governor of Jiangsu Province."

"And she managed to get sensitive information to her husband, who passed it on to his ex-wife. The world is sometimes upside down. In the sixties, the Chinese spied on the French, and now it is the French who spy on the Chinese and get the better part of the deal; they can have their cake and eat it too."

"The French are interesting people. Remember Hollande?"

"I do. I was laughing when he beat Sarkozy in 2012; he got some fifty-one percent of the vote. A man named Hollande was elected president of France. He fathered four children with the previous presidential candidate of his party, and they remained friends. Just like Marie and her ex-husband. It is very French."

"But we should not forget the Cowboy. He and his new partner have probably done more behind the scenes than anybody else. And they also did it out of the goodness of their hearts. It is interesting that Kartona has tried to stay away from Africa and let his people handle it more directly."

"Poor guy, I feel sorry for him. His administration has been embroiled in scandal after scandal. His party has lost more seats of any incumbent president than Carter and Clinton combined during the midterm elections. His chances of getting reelected seem to get slimmer and slimmer by the day. He can easily die of a thousand cuts."

"He was quite arrogant when he got to the White House, throwing his 'I won the election' around, antagonizing the opposition. He did not realize that Washington, more than any other place, is really an automatic revolving door."

"You go in and you come out, and if you don't time yourself well, you can get crushed by the door itself."

"I am not sure if he has any chance at being reelected."

THE WHITE HOUSE

It has been another tough week for President Kartona. He has developed a stronger distaste for Washington day by day. He cannot wait to get out of town. He buzzes his personal secretary to round up the usual suspects for his HHH moment before he heads out for Camp David. The First Lady and her family have already been there for the past few days. She has been under heavy criticism for spending nearly a million dollars of taxpayer money on a lavish trip to Milan to attend a fashion show.

The president calls on the political affairs director for the latest joke.

"During a naturalization examination, the officer asks the usual questions to ensure that the potential citizen can carry on a simple conversation in English.

'Do you speak English?'

'Yes, ma'am.'

'What is your name?'

'Kalunee.'

'Clooney? That's your new American name.'

'Yes, ma'am.'

'Sex?'

'Yes, ma'am. Three or four times a week.'

'No, I mean male or female.'

'Yes, ma'am, male, female—sometimes camel.'

'Holy cow!'

'Yes, ma'am, cow, sheep, animal in general.'

'But isn't it hostile?'

'Yes, ma'am. Horse style, doggy style, whatever style!'

'Oh dear!'

'No, ma'am. Deer runs too fast.'

The president cracks up. He declares at the end before leaving the Oval Office for the helicopter that there is a tie between the chief of staff and the political director for the best dirty joke contest.

TEXAS

Goldie reads the instructions one more time before he heads for the airport. This is the first time he has had the new engines overhauled on his Golden Eagle 421S. According to the recommended procedure, he should perform the ground run four times to check for any leaks. For the first flight after the overhaul, he should perform normal start and run up, and taxi to takeoff immediately to minimize the time on the ground.

He should reduce the power to 75 percent as soon as feasible and try to maintain cylinder heat and oil temperature within the green indicator until the oil consumption has been stabilized. During this initial period, he should avoid steep climbs and touch-and-go landings. He plans to carry no passengers during the first ten hours.

He scans his e-mail to find anything urgent. There is none.

He lies back on the leather chair and puts his hands behind his head and his feet on the mahogany desk. The phone rings at the sounds of aircraft jet engines.

"Goldie, how are you doing, buddy?" Marty Goodson is on the phone.

"I am fine. Thanks. How about you? What's up, buddy?"

"We missed you here, pal. I am sorry you couldn't make it to the McAllen mission."

"Tell me what happened."

"He was the owner of one of the FBOs. Took off Thursday afternoon and was not heard from again. No flight plan. No nothing."

"Where was the mission base? And where did you go?" asks Goldie.

"We had the mission base set up at Kingsville, the high bird orbiting over El Coyote. My crew and I headed west from McAllen along the Rio Grande all the way to Garcena, and Marty and his crew flew east along the river all the way Los Indios."

"Did you find the poor guy?"

"We picked up his ELT on the Mexican side, just north of San Miguel de Camargo."

"Were you allowed to cross over?"

"No. Normally we would be, but it was getting dark and a rainstorm was heading that way. We were able to pass the coordinates to the Mexican side."

"Did they find him?"

"They sent a ground team to the area; found the pilot slightly wounded. His wife and two children had some scratches. They were huddled about two hundred feet from the wreckage."

"Thank God. You did a good job, Joe. You saved four lives. I am proud of you."

"Are you coming to San Antonio next weekend?"

"As a matter of fact I am. Do you want to get together?"

"Are you flying or driving?"

"Are you kidding? I am going to ride. My bike is due for the twelve-thousand-mile service."

"That's perfect. I was thinking maybe we can do the Three Twisted Sisters again."

"That sounds like a good plan. We can meet at either Junction or, better yet, at Leaky and do the TTS with the usual suspects. Can you round them up?"

"Wilco!"

"Roger and out!"

Goldie smiles at his Golden Butt Award. It was presented to him by the Texas Motorcyclist Association for having ridden the most often between two points, El Paso and San Antonio.

On one of the long rides, he was dreaming that if he ever wanted to be in politics, he could run for the US House of Representatives in Texas Congressional District 23, which stretches between the two cities. It is among the largest districts in the country in geographical size. Fortunately, he has no interest in elected office.

He turns to the window and sees a hawk perching on the westernmost pole of the ranch house. He goes to get his fauna list and smiles when he sees that the bird is already there. Visitors to the Eagle and Elephant Ranch include butterflies, blue jays, cardinals, hummingbirds, hawks, squirrels, and deer. At least a few of them were born on the ranch.

THIRTY-SEVEN

The Family

CHRISTMAS EVE IS rather casual for a family that is this distinguished. Marie de Bourbon, the president of France, is reading *All The Best* by George Bush, the forty-first president of the United States. Her daughter, Camille Isabelle Antonietta, is playing chess with her boyfriend—the president's, not the daughter's. Only the three of them are in the enormous mansion.

Everything is beautifully decorated in red and green. Even the candles.

"Checkmate!" Isabelle says with joy.

"Congratulations. You are so good." Goldie says, complimenting his chess partner.

"I think I am lucky. Thank you, though. You are a strong competitor. Congratulations to you too." She stands up, stretches a little, and turns to her mother. "*Maman*, do you want another gin and tonic?"

"No, thanks, *chérie*. I am fine. How about you?"

"I think I am going to have a Bloody Mary. Goldie?"

"I'll have a Bloody Mary too. I'll make two for us."

"Thanks, Goldie. I think I am going to play the piano."

"Please give us a concert, *chérie*," the president says to her daughter.

"With pleasure."

Goldie brings Isabelle the Bloody Mary. He kisses Marie's head and sits down by her.

"She is so amazing, so beautiful, so charming, so darling, and just like you," Goldie says to his girlfriend. In the background, Isabelle switches between Beethoven, Chopin, and Schubert.

"She bikes, rides, flies, and sails, just like you." Marie takes a moment to reaffirm her daughter's skills, as she has just finished a song. "Incredible. You did an excellent job. Congratulations. I am very proud of you." She then turns back to Goldie. "Talking about bikes, we are going to ride across America next year."

"You are kidding. It will take you four or five days at least. You'll be exposed six, seven, eight hours a day, depending on how long you want to ride every day. The Secret Service will go crazy."

"It is for a good cause."

"What is it?"

"When we were young, my sister María and I joined the Golden Riders."

"Golden Riders? I've seen them somewhere. Are they an all-female club?"

"They are. And it's not for everyone. You can join only when you are between twenty-four and thirty-six years old. And you will remain a member for life. In order to be eligible, the candidate must be a bicyclist, a horseback rider, a pilot, and a sailor. She must have been involved in some charity work for at least two years. She has to be recommended by two members and interviewed by two more members who are living in different towns that are at least two hundred miles apart. And she must ride her bike to the interviews. Voila!"

"I presume Isabelle is also a member. And the three of you will ride together?"

"Four. My niece Isabela will also be there."

"My goodness. I would hate to be the special agent in charge of your security. Two foreign heads of state and their daughters. I would hate to be the guy—"

"Or gal," Marie says, correcting her boyfriend.

"The guy or gal in charge of logistics. You have to stop every two hours to get gas. Imagine filling a few hundred motorcycles at once."

"A thousand as of this week. The number has doubled from five hundred, when they decided who the lead rider would be. The deadline is New Year's Day. They may get a few hundred more. The total may reach twelve or thirteen hundred. They originally planned to raise ten million dollars for various charities. Each participant pays a five-thousand-dollar fee to join the ride. It covers food, fuel, and accommodation. They may net more than ten million in the end."

"Who is the lead rider?"

"Actually, there are two. One is a ninety-six-year-old woman named Goldia Strong from New Jersey. She is the oldest member of the Motor Maids, an all-female riding club like ours, but not so restrictive. She will be riding with her seventy-year-old daughter and her sixty-eight-year-old son."

"My goodness. And who is the other leader?"

"The other leader is also ninety-six years old. He is a veteran, the only one who has served in all US armed service branches: army, navy, marines, air force, coast guard. And he will be riding with his eighty-four-year-old baby brother."

"What is his name?"

"He is not French but does have some French ancestry, rather famous though."

"Did he start out in the marines?"

"He did."

"Did he lose both legs in the Second Korean War?"

"He did."

"Oh my God!"

"Do you know him?"

"Yes, I do. Alain Lamenace."

"That's the one."

"Amazing. What is the ride called?"

"From Long Beach to Long Beach. It starts in Long Beach, New York, and ends in Long Beach, California. Do you want to join us?"

"Of course. I'd love to. I was going to ask if I could join. Maybe I should register this weekend."

"You have been registered. I did it for you."

"You think of everything. Thank you."

"My pleasure. I knew you would enjoy it."

In the background, Isabelle has moved from classics to more modern tunes. She has just finished "Put Your Head on My Shoulder." She is now playing "Strangers in the Night."

Goldie pulls Marie from her reading chair and wraps his arms around her. They sing and dance toward the grand piano. They put their index fingers on each other's chests when the lyrics come to "I must have you."

Isabelle next plays "Fly Me to the Moon." The trio sing together and point at each other when they say "I love you."

New Year's Day

Goldie, Marie, and Camille have stayed up late at La Forêt d'Or after the dinner to watch the fireworks and celebrations around the world. Their trans-Atlantic family joins them on video from El Bosque Encantado. They have been oohing and aahing all evening since they caught the firework displays in Melbourne. They follow the fireworks westward: Tokyo, Shanghai, Angkor, New Delhi, Baku, Tehran, Moscow, Cape Town, Budapest, Frankfurt, Paris, London, São Paulo, Bogotá, New York, San Antonio, Los Angeles, Anchorage, and Honolulu.

They all stand up and cheer loudest at Paris, Bogotá, and San Antonio.

After each visit, it is always very hard for Goldie to leave La Forêt d'Or. He has spent four Christmas holidays with Marie. It has gotten harder and harder each time. This one is even more special. Blue moon and quality time with Isabelle. She is almost a duplicate of her mother.

Sometimes Goldie feels that he is in love with two women of the same personality. *Partir c'est mourir un peu.* (To leave is to die a little bit.)

Goldie and Marie are locked in a very tight embrace for a long time. Finally the magic words come out: "I will love you forever," Goldie whispers into Marie's ear.

"So will I," replies Marie.

They then say together, "And forever is not long enough."

The embrace becomes stronger when their lips touch one another's.

THIRTY-EIGHT

The Dinner

I T IS ANOTHER presidential election year. Four years have flown by quickly. The primaries have come and gone. The conventions have come and gone. The rest of August should be quiet, except for one event.

The *New York Times,* the *Washington Post,* and the *Washington Times* social pages analyze the previous night's state dinner. They show photos of diners. Gentlemen look like they are all in uniform, in tuxedos. On the other hand, ladies are all glamorous and glittering.

All papers list the names of the two hundred privileged people at the gala, with the guest of honor at the top, followed by others in alphabetical order:

> Her Excellency Madame Marie de Bourbon, President of the French Republic
>
> and Mademoiselle Camille Isabelle Antonietta de Bourbon
>
> ...

Mr. Goldin Baume and Ms. Georgia Ragan, Esperanza,
Texas

Mr. and Mrs. Charles Hawkins, Huntsville, Alabama

The Honorable David Cardey, United States Senate, and
Ms. Marina Shakarova

...

His Royal Highness Prince Jean-Lionel Kadak and Ms.
Juliana Onerio

Her Royal Highness Princess Kunzang Wangdi and His
Royal Highness Prince Jean-Bedel Lemel

Her Excellency Mrs. Marie-Catherine Samas, Dean of
the Diplomatic Corps,

and Monsieur Bill Samas

Mademoiselle Billie Samas and Mr. Henry Goldman

The press first alerts their readers that Marina Shakarova is obviously
not the Russian president but rather her daughter; there might be a
budding romance between the handsome and single senator from Idaho
and the First Daughter of Russia. They point out that Kadak, Lemel, and
Samas are from Letador, where people's names can be spelled backward
and still read the same way.

They describe the disdain that the president and Henry Goldman
have had for each other, and they credit the First Lady for bringing them
together to make peace. Some of her initiatives have received strong
financial support from Goldman. No one ventures into the grudge that
Goldman has for the president for stealing his first love away from him.

Under the heading, "The Conqueror Is Finally Conquered!" the
Wall Street Journal devotes one full page to Goldman and Samas (as in
Billie). It describes in every detail the places and times they have met
around the world, and the amount of money Goldman has spent to
court her: a staggering $1 billion. The *Journal* article is accompanied by
three photos: the two lovers holding hands upon arrival at the North

Portico, Henry shaking hands with the president, and Henry dancing with the First Lady.

All newspapers dedicate a good deal of coverage to Goldman's new lady and France's First Daughter. They report on the colors and styles of their shoes, dresses, purses, jewelry, makeup, and hairdos. They have a perfect combination of everything. The only thing they do not tell is the color of their underwear. *People* magazine has photos of both of them side by side on the cover under the heading "CIA vs. AAA," a reference to France's First Daughter, Camille Isabelle Antonietta, and the architect/archaeologist/anthropologist Billie Samas. *Town & Country, Vogue, Newsweek* and *Time* use more ink on the two than on the substance of the Franco-American summit. The *New York Post* carries a photo of France's First Daughter on the front page: "The CIA you will love forever."

Goldie is very thankful that, besides the guest list, his name is not mentioned anywhere in the media coverage.

LETADOR

In Notneh, Kunzang Wangdi's cousin Jigme is fishing under a tamarind tree when he hears the explosive sound of a blown tire. The driver loses control of the car. It swerves toward him, ready to plunge into the Enies River. It hits the tamarind tree and activates the airbags and the alarm.

Jigme runs up the riverbank and gently pulls the unconscious driver out. She is wounded on her head, and blood is coming down her cheeks. Jigme carries her into his house and puts her down gently on the wooden platform bed on the verandah.

THIRTY-NINE

The Daughter

TEXAS

AFTER THE LONG Beach–to–Long Beach ride, Goldie says good-bye to Marie, María, Isabelle, and Isabela at El Toro Marine Corps Air Station. They are flying to Barranquilla to spend the rest of the week at El Bosque Encantado to rejuvenate and refresh after an exhausting but fulfilling ride.

Goldie flies back to Esperanza. Guillermo picks him up at Sierra Blanca.

He spends the afternoon putting newspaper headlines in frames on the wall:

"The Twins Did It Again!"
"From the Atlantic to the Pacific: The Twins, the
Grandmother, the Veteran Did It Together"
"The Twins Did It Again: From the Empire State to the Golden State"

He inspects them one more time before closing the toolbox.

Thirty minutes before sunset is Goldie's favorite time of the day. He grabs a bottle of red wine, a baccarat glass, and some saucisson and climbs up to the cupola.

The fading sun is below the horizon.

The full moon appears slowly in the east. The stars begin to twinkle in the cloudless skies. It has been a memorable week: Washington, New York, a coast-to-coast bike ride, Los Angeles. All with his two beloved women—maybe four. And now Goldie is home in time for the sunset.

Letador is on the way to peace and stability. Goldie is pleased with what he has done to contribute to the process. He thinks of everybody who has crossed his path. He thinks of his faith, family, friends, and freedom. He is sorry about the lives that have been lost, and he is grateful that he was able to save many more lives. He is thankful that he has been able to serve.

He opens the wine bottle, pours his glass half full, and cuts the saucisson into small slices. He bows his head and whispers, "Lord, we thank you for the food before us, the friendship between us, and the love among us."

The phone rings with the tune of "Fly Me to the Moon." Goldie smiles. "*Bonsoir, chérie!*"

"*Bonsoir, Mon Petit Chou!*"

"How was your return trip?"

"Uneventful. How was yours?"

"Same. How's Isabelle doing?"

"She is doing very well. Thanks. She is quite taken with you. The two of you hit it off from the beginning. I am so happy."

"I am quite taken with her too. Thank you so much for another golden memory. I can't wait to see you both again."

"You may see Isabelle first."

"Really?"

"She wants to see you again before going to Letador to work on the election. Will you have some time for her?"

"Of course. I have all the time in the world for her. It will be like having you here," Goldie says, sending some positive energy to his lover.

"You are so sweet. She and I will look at the full moon together tonight."

"So will I. I will see you both standing there. This is so wonderful."

"See you tonight. Please take good care of Isabelle."

"I will forever."

"I know you will. She is *our* daughter!"

"She is indeed. And I love you."

"I love you so much."

GOLDEN BONES Excerpt For *GOLDEN STATE*

I WAS A LITTLE bit confused at what was going on around me. As the youngest son, I was the official mourner of the family. My head and eyebrows were shaved and I was draped in white cotton cloth, the color of mourning. My father's body was bathed clean and dressed in new clothing. His hands were joined together on top of his chest to hold three unburned sticks of incense and candles. A silver coin was put in his mouth before he was covered with a white sheet. He was later placed into a specially built coffin. At 6 feet 3, he was extremely tall, probably one of the tallest Cambodians of his time. I remember seeing some of his group pictures: his French colleagues came up to his chest. His important social rank at Pochentong required an elaborate funeral service.

The funeral procession, however, had to go to the market and circle the main square before entering the temple. The longer route was taken in order to let people bid a final farewell to my father.

I was told to sit in front of my father's coffin on the well decorated funeral truck. I held some flowers, three unburned candles and incense in both hands which I kept in front of my chest. Between me and the coffin was hung my father's uniform with all his decorations and medals.

My brother and other male cousins dressed in white were honorary pall bearers and stood around the coffin. There were two funeral bands that preceded an open truck carrying Buddhist monks who kept chanting and saying prayers. The funeral vehicle was surrounded by police officers forming a symbolic protective cordon with their rifles pointing to the ground.

My family members, dressed in white, walked right behind the funeral vehicle. They were followed by former colleagues of my father and friends of the family, including hundreds of villagers. Everyone had a small bouquet of flowers with candles and incense sticks. When we passed in front of the district headquarters, the sentry in his ceremonial uniform stood at attention and saluted my father. Other people gave a *sampeah*. This is the traditional Cambodian greeting with the two hands joined in front of the chest, the lips or the forehead. The level of the hands indicates the degree of respect.

At the monastery, the coffin was carried around the crematorium clockwise three times before it was put on the pyre. After many Buddhist chants, the abbot ignited the pyre to burn the coffin and my father's body. The funeral band of percussion instruments, including two big drums, performed the last heartbreaking music while my mother, Sarin and other female relatives cried and wept. Their voices and tears tore my little heart apart. I did not cry because to do so would show my weakness which should not be part of male emotions. But inside, I was uncontrollably sad. After more Buddhist blessings, the funeral ceremony was over. We later collected my father's ashes which we cleaned by pouring coconut juice over them and put them in a silver urn.

At nine years old, I became fatherless. But as a Khmer saying goes, "It's better to lose a father than a mother; it's better to have a shipwreck than a fire." Our lifestyle changed completely. We went from a well-to-do family to surviving at a subsistence level.

...Although I hated to be away from my mother, my year at Kampong Cham taught me some new values in life: mainly how to adjust to a new environment and make the most of it. It was this adaptability that would keep me alive 15 years later when I was trying to survive under the Khmer Rouge. Without saying a word to me, my mother had begun to train my mind and soul to cope with unusual and hostile circumstances, to stay alive and to always have hope.

In 1960 I returned to Pochentong after developing some skills in cooking, swimming and writing. I began to read more about what was happening overseas. The first political news I learned was the race between Democratic candidate John F. Kennedy and Republican Richard M. Nixon for the American presidency.

After Sichhun left home, I had to double up on my work to help my mother. First, she sold lotus leaves at the Pochentong market. In the afternoon, she went on a small boat to cut the leaves from a pond behind the village Buddhist temple. After I got out of school, I went to help her wash the leaves and put them together in sets of five. I folded them only once and put them together in bundles of five sets each. I got up early in the morning and went to the market to distribute them to my mother's customers. Lotus leaves were used as the basic wrapping material for all kinds of fresh produce.

Later, my mother sold some kinds of Khmer breakfast called *bawbaw trey kaw*, porridge served with small fish and vegetables. I got up every morning at four with my mother and helped her make the fire for cooking. Sometimes I fell asleep again until everything was cooked. I put all the pots, pans, plates and spoons in a cart and pushed it to the market. I set up the selling stand for my mother and returned home to get ready to go to school.

...The United States Information Service (USIS) Library was the most convenient. I developed an insatiable appetite for knowledge about America. To me, it was a big and powerful land where people seemed to have unlimited freedom and resources to create—from automobile to airplane, aspirin, light bulb, and telephone—in order to improve the quality of human life.

I learned more about the United States through the library's Khmer, French and English materials and its enormous selection of books, magazines, and newspapers. I read Robert Frost, Ernest Hemingway, and Mark Twain—in French. I was excited when Frost was chosen to read one of his poems at President Kennedy's inauguration. I studied with great interest the geography and history of the United States. I knew the names of all 50 states and capitals, the largest lakes, the longest rivers, and the highest mountains by heart. I knew that Missouri was the same size as Cambodia. And that the Statue of Liberty was a gift of France. I saw many pictures of it along with the Empire State Building, Chrysler Building and other Manhattan skyscrapers.

America's history seemed much shorter than that of Cambodia. Before I immersed myself in the USIS Library, I had heard only of Eisenhower, Kennedy and Nixon (during the 1960 campaign), and Johnson. Then I was hooked by the 18th century and read everything I could find on the Founding Fathers. I was later able to recite in precise chronological order all presidents from Washington to Johnson.

I followed the U.S. space programs religiously: Mercury, Gemini, and later Apollo. I knew all the astronauts' names. Mercury 7: Scott Carpenter, Gordon Cooper, John Glenn (first in orbit), Virgil Grissom, Walter Schirra, Alan Shepard (first in space), Donald Slayton.

One day, I heard over the radio that President Kennedy had been assassinated. I walked into the USIS Library and saw his picture in a black frame with a black ribbon. I sat down, prayed, and signed the condolence book. I was sad and even sadder when diplomatic relations between Cambodia and the United States were severed. The USIS Library was closed and I lost a major source of information and knowledge.

...On the way back, the sergeant's voice stayed with me. "Be careful. Do not leave the road."

Stay on the road! Do not leave the road!

But which road were we on? The road to war or the road to peace?

...We traveled around in a four wheel drive to inspect our projects anywhere that was accessible. We went through and to some of the most dangerous places, where we could be easily ambushed or shot at any time of the day. We discussed ways of finding solutions to crises and problems on constant deadlines as lives were always at stake. We shared ideas and opinions. We listened to each other's argument, especially when we disagreed. With June's broader perspective and my indigenous knowledge, we were comfortably complementary. We had quick meals together with our driver at street food stalls and got back on the road right away. At the office, we usually exchanged notes and poetry to maintain our sanity. Her favorite poet was William Carlos Williams; mine was Robert Frost. I occasionally added a few poems which I translated from Khmer or French. I admired June tremendously for her down-to-earth character, her commitment to help the needy, her humanitarian vocation of caring and sharing, and her austerity (she used every space available on a piece of paper to write). She seemed to be born to provide relief, rehabilitation, and hope to those in need. She was the perfect savior. I had never worked with Americans before and June gave me a great impression of what the United States and its people stood for.

The emergency relief efforts were intense and dangerous. Despite numerous interruptions, we managed to keep the program moving. The staff, especially those in the field, were extraordinarily dedicated and constantly exposed to life threatening situations. I counted our blessings: during the final months of the war, we did not lose any of them.

In the meantime, I learned how to keep my head low, survive in hostile environments, and carry out my duty without questioning the morality of the war.

...We witnessed more depressing scenes. Charred cars and trucks were everywhere. More and more people died along the roads that seemed to lead to nowhere. They died of hardship, exhaustion, and summary executions by the Khmer Rouge. We saw decomposing bodies with arms tied behind their backs. One had the throat slit open. One had a big black mark at the back of the neck. A woman had her baby still at her breast.

...In the dark of the night, I went to Mother and asked for her blessings. It was a heart wrenching moment.

"You should have left with the Americans," she reminded me of my

30 minute tardiness. She knew that I could not decide to leave without her. Before I could say anything, she added, "You should not worry about me. I am old. I can die any time. You are young and you have a full life in front of you. Remember what I have been telling you since you were a child: 'No matter what happens, never give up hope.'

Yes, Mother, I whispered back to her. I held her hand very tightly. I felt a tear on my hand. Next to me on my right side, Sarin sobbed silently. She reached for my right hand and put some money in it.

"May all the merits I have made in my life protect you," *Mae* continued. Then she gave me her wedding ring and a gold necklace that had belonged to her father, Sok Chea, the governor.

The day of the departure, I strapped a yellow bag of rice and some dry fish to the rack of my bicycle behind me. I wrapped Mother's red and white checkered *krama* around my neck. I said goodbye to Mother, Sarin, Sichhun, Peou, my nieces, and nephew without saying a word. Our eyes said it all.

I "saw" *Mae* saying, "May you be protected by the merits I have earned in my life." She added, "Never give up hope" without moving her lips. I knew that Sarin was weeping, but there were no tears. I felt she was saying to me, "I have always loved you. I always will." I "told" her, "I know. So do I." Sichhun and Peou transmitted these words, "Be strong, be well, and be successful" without producing a sound.

It was the most heart breaking moment.

I turned around quickly before anybody could shed a tear.

...I was the loneliest person on earth. Not knowing what had happened to *Mae*, sister, and brother was torturing me. But I had to move onward. I woke up with the fisherman before dawn. He floated the boat down the river and started to throw his net into the Mekong. He caught a lot of fish and I helped him empty his net. A few hours later, he let me off the boat at Piamcheekawng. I gave him some rice and he offered me some fish. I gave him a *sampeah* and said *Awkun!*

As I was steadying my bike on the bank, the fisherman came to me and whispered, "I hope you will find your family." He knew that I had lied to him about my background. I was not supposed to salute him and thank him. There was to be no courtesy in the new and pure society. But he added slowly, "Be very careful! *Stay on the road!*"

…Blinking slowly, almost unable to believe my eyes, I saw how fortune was continuing to smile on me. The armed guard, still alone, was climbing into the cab of the logger. Already, the engine was chugging, and the Khmer Rouge soldier was settling onto the front seat beside the driver, being careful to place the butt end of the automatic rifle between his feet.

I studied the layout with microscopic intensity. The driver of the logging truck, another prisoner, would be no threat. And since the truck mechanic who also usually joined us on these runs was off visiting a relative in nearby Tamaw Puak, I knew that the only real danger would come from the young man with the AK-47. There was no question that he would shoot to kill, if he saw me fleeing.

He would also be quick to sound the alarm, by screaming and laying on the horn. And if I were unlucky, that might alert some of the nearby labor crews and their heavily armed *Angka* masters to join the pursuit… so that I would be hunted down quickly, and then executed without mercy (the Organization penalty for "desertion" was always death).

We were rolling now.

Pulling out of the timber camp, the mud smeared logger rattled onto Route 69.

Somewhere off to the West—somewhere behind that golden, sinking sun—lay the border of Thailand, and the road that might eventually take me to freedom.

Did I really have a choice?

Dear Lord Buddha, let my mother's prayer-merits help me now!

Perched alone atop the teak logs, I watched the rifle-carrying guard turn in his seat, then glare back at me. I held my breath…then got a violent shock, as I saw him bending to the floor to retrieve something—his still wet *krama*!

I watched, amazed, as he lifted the dripping, bright red and white checked scarf and began to hang it over the truck's rearview mirror.

Yes…the guards at the timber-works had gotten a chance to take one of their rare baths, earlier in the day, and our gun carrying guard had gone into the water wearing only his *krama,* which was still soaked. And now, with the bulky truck able to clatter along at no more than 15 miles an hour (so that the garment wouldn't blow away), he was hanging his laundry out to dry, and using the mirror as his clothesline!

The reflecting glass was covered now. It was a gift. The guard would be able to see me only by twisting awkwardly in his seat to look through the back window. And I was alone at the back of the truck.

Unsteadily, I crawled to my knees on the topmost teak log.

I felt a wave of icy dread roll over me, as the truck swung through a long curve, then leveled off on what looked like a mile long straightaway.

The moment had arrived.

Crouching as low as possible, I began to slither along the stack of logs.

Inch by inch, I crept along the slippery teak. My heart was hammering inside my ribs, and I kept gasping for air. A few more feet, and I would reach the back end of the stack.

Am I really doing this?

Am I really about to put my life on the line for a dream of freedom?

Close to panic now, I took one last look back over one shoulder: The shotgun rider was still chatting aimlessly away with the driver.

The logging truck was putt-putting along the flat road, throwing up clouds of orange dust…dust that would help to camouflage my next move, if only I could find the courage to make it.

Clutching my water bottle, I patted my belt: the bayonet-knife was still anchored securely.

I paused for one last instant. And I knew it was a moment I would never forget. On both sides of the dirt road, the teak forest stretched away to the horizon—a vast sea of rolling greens, broken here and there by jagged-looking sawgrass stands, wind-bent thorn trees, and snake-like vines that clung to the tree trunks as if intent on strangling them.

My Cambodia.

I tensed my body for the leap…and heard my mother's voice somewhere deep in my soul. She was calling out to me with the same loving words that she had used so many times before, during the first agonizing days of the "revolution": "Kanee, whatever you do—never give up hope!"

I jumped. It was about 12 feet, from the top of the teak logs to the dirt road—and as I tumbled through space, eyes closed, I could feel my legs already beginning their mad scramble into the jungle cover that I hoped would shield me from the deadly snout of the AK-47.

I tumbled… and tumbled… and suddenly was grabbed in mid-air! I was stunned. I felt some huge powerful force take hold of my heavy fatigue jacket. And then, a moment later, I was being dragged along behind the truck. In a flash, I understood the worst: the jacket had gotten hung up in a row of "crocodile teeth." These were heavy metal clamps, like two grinning jaws, that were used to keep the logs from sliding out of position on the truck.

Unable to raise my arms because of the ferocious pull of gravity, and unable to keep my feet on the ground because of the truck's speed, I floundered desperately, with my shoulders slamming into the back end of the teak logs again and again.

Ten seconds…twenty seconds…with my vision blurring and shooting pains through my chest, I knew that my chances were growing slimmer by the moment. I needed another miracle—and fast.

Was it my mother's prayer-merits with Lord Buddha that caused the truck to hit a jumbo-sized pothole? A moment later, freeing the jacket from the vicious-looking saw-toothed clamps and flinging me high into the air, I plunged to earth butt-first, and rolled like a sack all the way to the edge of Route 69.

Clambering to my feet, I shuddered with relief, as I saw the logging truck continuing to rumble placidly down the road, throwing up a boiling cloud of orange dust behind it.

So far, it seemed, they had not noticed my departure.

And I had no intention of sticking around while they did. Within a few seconds, I reached the edge of the tree line, and dove head first into the deep gloom of the jungle canopy.

A moment after that, I was tearing along in full-fledged panic.

Ignoring the thorns and vines that lashed my every step, I groaned with terror as I heard the dry leaves crackle beneath my feet…it sounded as if a giant were stomping his way through this noisy foliage!

I ran on and on, thorns ripping at my hands. More than once, I stumbled into jarring, head first collisions with tree trunks, producing numbing blows that knocked the wind from me and left me sprawled and panting in the deep undergrowth. At last, having covered at least 500-600 yards, I paused to gather what was left of my wits. With my right hand, I patted the wet spot on my cheek…and felt the blood that had been raised by the whipping thorns. I could hear my own breath whistling in and out of my mouth: I sounded like an overworked horse struggling to remain on his exhausted legs.

But I was still alive.

I had a chance to achieve the unthinkable: To escape from the hellish firestorm of the *Angka* genocide. Once again, my mother's milk/merits had plucked me from the flames!

Quickly now, I took stock of my situation. Bayonet-knife: okay. Water bottle: okay. No broken bones…I could feel my strength returning little by little.

Frowning with effort, and breathing a bit easier now, I tried to remember my geography. According to the maps I had studied earlier, the Thai border lay almost directly to the west. It was late afternoon—which made my direction clear: I must walk directly toward the sun.

When darkness fell, of course, I would be able to orient myself by studying the moon—so that I could continue moving throughout most of the night. And then in the morning, if I *survived* until morning, I must "put the sun behind me," at least until noon, if I wanted to remain accurately on course.

I was ready now.

I was going to try to walk out of Cambodia—through numerous border patrols and Khmer Rouge encampments, and past hundreds of lethal land mines that had been placed all along the border, precisely in order to stop runaways like me.

I took a single step. Then another. Soon, full of determination, I was following the dim shafts of sunlight that filtered through the jungle canopy.

And with every step, I could feel the guiding, loving presence of *Mae*, my mother:

Kanee, Sichan, my Beautiful Moon . . . No matter what happens, never give up hope!

I followed the last beam of the setting sun and tried not to deviate from my course. "Be careful, do not leave the road," the voices of the sergeant, the fisherman, and Chim Chun resounded in my ears.

When the jungle became completely dark, I rested until the moon came up. It should be behind me for a few hours. I stopped when it hovered above my head as I could not tell which direction it was moving. At about 3 o'clock in the morning, I saw a bright light projected on the top of the trees. It came from a few hundred yards away. It must be a forest fire. I could not see very clearly without my glasses so I kept on crawling inch by inch toward the source. I got close enough to find two soldiers sitting around a camp fire with guns, while the other two were deeply asleep on the ground.

I quickly crawled back into the darkness. Never play with fire. About 30 minutes later, I could no longer see the light on the big tall trees. I lay down on my back and fell asleep. I woke up when I felt something heavy moving over my stomach. I opened my eyes little by little and saw the scales of something big reflecting under the moon light. The scales were moving very slowly to the right. I held my breath until the shape of a tail appeared at the corner of my eyes. It got smaller and disappeared. It had to be a big snake. It could have been a boa constrictor. I waited for a few minutes to make sure that the snake had moved far enough away. I jumped up and ran in a different direction.

The next morning, the sun rose behind me.

I am still on course, I thought to myself.

I have been walking for one night. Where is Thailand? And how will I know I have arrived?

I moved on slowly but steadily. I avoided the jungle paths. Those were where the land mines were laid. Staying on the road meant I should stay on course, not necessarily on the well-trod path. Cutting across the forest was slower, but certainly much safer.

Although the jungle was thick, the day still got hot very quickly. It was also humid. I sweated a lot. I stopped for a few hours when I could not tell where the sun was going, probably between 11 a.m. and 1 p.m. Occasionally, I put a short stick on the ground and tried to determine the directions by following its shadow. The books I found at the Sisophon school yard told me that I could tell the directions by touching the trunk of the trees. The warm side is usually the side of the sun. But the forest in northwest Cambodia was a dense tropical jungle where the sun light could hardly reach the tree trunk.

I ran out of water by mi-afternoon although I had consumed it moderately. As the sun was setting, I came upon a pond in the middle of an open field. I crawled toward it. I put my face down to the level of the water. On the other side, my eyes caught the sight of two bloated bodies being devoured by ugly looking vultures and giant flies. I crawled back without being able to quench my thirst.

It has been 24 hours now: one night and one day. And Thailand is nowhere to be seen. I cannot go on without water for three days.

Either I get to Thailand within the next 24 hours or I would die of exhaustion, if not be killed by land mines or KR patrols.

I pondered on what to do next. The moon rose behind me. It was a full moon. It was so pretty. "Kanee, Sichan, My Beautiful Moon! Never Give Up Hope, No Matter What Happens!" I searched for *Mae*'s face on the moon.

…At the central courtyard of the Kabinburi jail, I was lined up with other new prisoners. We were ordered to take off our clothes. We stood naked while the other prisoners looked at and made fun of us. Thirty minutes later the guards returned with our clothes and threw them at our faces. I touched my torn trousers at the waistband and felt that my family heirloom was gone. Since May 1975 when I left Hanuman, I managed to hide my grandfather's necklace and Mother's wedding ring in that secret safe and some $60 my sister Sarin had given me. The Thai prison guards succeeded in finding them. They also took my U.S. army boots which were instrumental in helping me getting through the jungle.

Not all was gone. Mother's red and white checkered krama and a tiny yellow cotton bag I had been using to store my meager food supply were still with me.

And of course, my heart full of hope was going to be always with me.

I pondered briefly on what was lying ahead. I would probably never know what had happened to my family. Ironically, I was separated from them by the end of a war, by peace. The world's most brutal tyranny under Pol Pot and his Khmer Rouge goons had enslaved an entire populace and violated every standard of human dignity, where slave labor was the only means of production, backward agrarian output was the only support of the economy, and death the only correctional remedy for mistakes.

…I had survived a brutal year of starvation, exhaustion, fear, horror and terror. But my future was full of promise and innumerable opportunities for a successful life. I looked forward to the challenges of a great society which guaranteed freedom and peace to all people of good will. As I dreamed of a beautiful future ahead, I dozed off and fell asleep.

Within a short period of time, I had been exposed to two extremes of modern civilization: the killing fields of Cambodia, and the world's most advanced society of the United States. My mantra became: "Forget the painful past and focus on the brighter future. Adapt and be adopted." The curse and sorrow of losing my country, of not knowing what had happened to *Mae*, Sarin, Sichhun and my family remained a burning grief inside me. But, like what I had told my fellow refugees in Aranyaprathet, there was no use to continue feeling sorry about the past and worrying about the future. The best means to cope with this would be to keep busy. So I did.

…There was a series of questions, mainly about directions. One asked: "How do you get from the Waldorf-Astoria to the UN?" I had no idea where these places were, much less how to get from one to another. This was the most difficult test I had ever taken. At the end, I handed the piece of paper to the examiner and kept my fingers crossed. He glanced at the test sheet. He looked at me from head to toe, again, and again. My heart was palpitating. He looked at me one more time. My legs were trembling when I saw him shaking his head and sighing. He finally said, "You passed!"

…After being sworn in, I sat down in the high back leather chair with four wheels and took a few deep breaths.

"Is this really happening to me or am I dreaming?"

"Am I really at the White House working for the President of the United States?"

"Could it be possible that 13 years ago I was fleeing hell on earth and now I am a presidential aide?"

"Only in America!"

…As I rode the White House car from Andrews AFB back to the office, I was grateful that not only had I survived, but that I had so far prevailed because of *Mae*'s message of hope. And because I managed to make my way to a country where such hope—along with lots of hard work—can make the most improbable dreams come true.

Only in America!

CPSIA information can be obtained at www.ICGtesting.com
Printed in the USA
BVOW07s1653260614

357471BV00002B/8/P